Praise for Empty Sky

"…an incredibly engaging, truly unique read. … a mix of sci-fi and urban fantasy with strong mystery and thriller elements and even a touch of horror. It's got some very technical scientific elements too (and I learned several new terms), and wonderful philosophical questions and considerations with timely messages about despair and hope and dreams. There's some heartbreak in the story, and plenty of wonder. The descriptions that set the scenes are often full of beautiful imagery, approaching the poetic. … I was definitely rooting for the 'good guys' and didn't want to put the book down until I knew how the story would turn out."

"If you like inspiring, fantastic, elaborate stories, this is your novel. Rich in detail, beautifully written, whether it is from the point of view of a dog or the moon, the reader can identify with all of them. A real mind movie treat."

"Empty Sky moved me in ways I hadn't expected. It combines the thrills of a great spy novel, the excitement and adventure of science fiction, and the fascination of ancient wisdom, all wrapped around a truly moving story that actually managed to bring me to tears. I can't recall reading any other book that so deftly caused me to feel so many emotions. I would call it a rollercoaster ride of a read, but that wouldn't be doing it proper justice. I highly recommend it."

"Let go of expectations because this book is trippy and multi-dimensional. The plot works well as a murder mystery or a detective story, or a fantasy/mythology/SF fusion. As well as insightful psychology, it entangles computer science, AI, and quantum physics. So, it has no boundaries but does have lots of suspense, a truly psychopathic villain, and what I felt was a satisfying conclusion. Carrabis books are not for the faint of heart or lazy readers."

Joseph Carrabis

Empty Sky

Northern Lights Publishing

Nashua, NH

Paperback ISBN 979-8-9878048-3-4
ebook ISBN

Library of Congress Control Number

Editing by Jennifer Day, Susan Carrabis
Front cover image by John Bernard Scullin http://skolenimation.com/
Book design by Jennifer Day

Printed and bound in the United States of America
First printing May 2023

Published by Northern Lights Publishing
www.northernlightspublishing.com

For Susan
(because everything should be)
And AJ
(who said I could)

To Maschaak, Fenris Ulf, and Boo:
I've only had a few dogs,
and I've always had the best dogs

Thanks to
Rick Lent, Jennifer Day, Joseph Della Rosa,
Tina O'Hailey, Susan Boucher, Rox Burkey,
Clarabette Fields Miray, Editor, and Dr. Micheal Schultz, PhD,
for reading and reading and reading until I got it right.

Thanks to
Michael Nalen and Susan Strickland at
Aquatic Escapes Dive Center, Londonderry, NH
and
Kyle Vandemoer, PE,
Appledore Marine Engineering
for technical information

Thanks to
Claudiu Murariu and Randy Roberson
for their help with Romanian geography

Also by Joseph Carrabis

Fiction

Empty Sky
Tales Told 'Round Celestial Campfires
The Augmented Man

Non-Fiction

Reading Virtual Minds Volume I: Science and History
Reading Virtual Minds Volume II: Experience and Expectation
Reading Virtual Minds Volume III: Fair-Exchange and Social Networks
That Th!nk You Do: 60 Ways to Be Healthy, Happy & Hold Off Harm

Empty Sky

Chapters

Hope lies in dreams, in imagination and in the courage of those who dare to make dreams into reality.

- Schiller, The Piccolomini, III, 4.

There are infinite worlds both like and unlike this world of ours.

- Epicurus

When we dream we speak a language which is also employed in the most significant documents of culture: in myths, in fairy tales and art, recently in novels like Franz Kafka's. This language is the only universal language common to all races and all times. It is the same language in the oldest myths as in the dreams every one of us has today. Moreover, it is a language which often expresses inner experiences, wishes, fears, judgments and insights with much greater precision and fullness than our ordinary language is capable of.

- Erich Fromm

In the Beginning there was only Sky and Earth: dwelling in the earth was Ungud, in the form of a great snake; and in the sky, Wallanganda, the Milky Way. Wallanganda threw water on the earth; Ungud made it deep. And in the night, as Ungud and Wallanganda dreamed, life arose from the watered earth in the forms of their dreams.

- Unumbal Great Serpent Lore, northern Kimberly, Australia

...it is so important how you educate the child to think for himself/
herself and how to know his/her value without external factors 'spoil-
ing' him/her.

And that's important exactly because the parents won't be forever
by his side. And the most valuable lesson a parent should teach his child
is that the way he behaves, thinks and reacts in order to value his life,
himself and also remain grounded and humble, but never forgetting
his worth and strength.

In my vision, a constructive long-term long-lasting love is translated
in the way you project this love in a deeper level to the other human
being (in this case, the child) as in giving him the structure of living an
enthusiastic life.

- *Amalia Alexandru*

The sun sees your body, the moon sees your soul.

Chapter 1

The Cabin

Jamie woke to Shem's tail thumping his legs. The big golden retriever sat at the edge of their bed and stared out the cabin window.

Jamie reached over the quilt and grabbed his tail. "What, Shem?"

Outside, peepers and crickets chirped. Raccoons chittered. Opossum and skunk hissed. Owls hooted and loons called. A wolf howled in the distance.

Shem looked back at Jamie and whined softly.

Jamie's tiny hand ran through his ginger hair and looked past Shem to the oak, elm, and pine of Michigan's Upper Peninsula forest. The moon, full and bright, illuminated the trees and the small, one-room vacation cabin at their center.

"Shem go pee?"

Shem jumped off the bed and scratched at the door.

Jamie glanced at his parents, Ellie and Tom, asleep in their own bed on the other side of the cabin and put his finger to his lips. "Shh. Mom and Dad sleeping." He crawled out from under the quilt and tip-toed in his stars-and-moon print Doctor Denton's to the door. Standing on a chair, he drew back the bolt and lifted the latch.

Cool winds changed rustling treetops into brooms sweeping low-hung clouds from late September skies. Dust devils spun mists where night air met day-warmed rocks. Trees bowed to the rising moon as its face changed from meteor-impacted gray to a beautiful, white-skinned woman's.

Shem walked into the night. Jamie followed.

The Moon continued her ascent.

The woods fell silent.

Silent.

Ellie sat up in bed. Her hands clenched the blanket and held it tight against her. A cold, dank wind swirled through the cabin, lifted things slightly as if inspecting them then putting them down, and drew a musk of old earths in its wake.

Moonlight entered the cabin's single room.

Ellie's eyes fixed on Jamie's empty bed.

"Jamie! Shem!"

Tom's eyes bolted open. He followed her gaze then rose and put his boots on in one motion. "Where are they?"

She hurried with her own boots. "The door's open."

Tom threw Ellie her coat. "They must be together. Shem won't let Jamie out of his sight."

"Something's got them. Some wild animal."

"There's no blood anywhere, Ellie. Shem'd raise hell if something got in the cabin or near Jamie." He grabbed an iron poker from the woodstove.

Ellie stopped at the door, a silhouette in the moonlight. "Shh."

Tom came up beside her. "What the...?"

"Shh!"

"What are they doing?"

"It looks like they're playing."

"With whom?"

Jamie and Shem romped in a grassy clearing twenty feet from the cabin. Moonlight cast long shadows everywhere as they danced about, the sole performers under a celestial spotlight.

Tom looked to the rutted dirt road that served as the camp's driveway. No cars but theirs. He scanned the shadows.

Ellie whispered, "Can you hear that?"

Tom pulled back. "He's laughing?"

Jamie danced in circles and laughed as if being tickled, his arms up as if waiting to be lifted, little hands grasping, little fingers curling.

"Shem's bowing."

"Isn't that dog for 'Let's play', bowing? He's not facing Jamie. Who's he playing with?"

Shem jumped and bowed and ran around as if playing catch with someone throwing his Frisbee.

The Moon rose above the trees and lit the clearing from above. Jamie's and Shem's shadows crept underneath them. The wind stilled.

Ellie grabbed Tom's arm. "Do you see that?"

Other shadows entered the clearing, some Jamie's size, some slightly larger. Shadows with nothing to cast them. Shadows where there shouldn't be shadows. Shadows standing upright, not cast on the ground.

Jamie danced with them and they danced around Jamie. Shem ran among them, played tag with them. Jamie laughed. Shem barked.

Not a warning, not an alarm.

Recognition.

Something twinkled in the shadows, prisms breaking the intense moonlight into hundreds of bright, tiny rainbows.

On the edge of the clearing, in the dark where the trees stood in ancient vigil, eyes gathered in the moonlight.

Ellie woke, the covers clenched in her hands.

She looked across the cabin and saw Jamie and Shem, sleeping together as always, in their bed.

She let out a breath and shook her head. It was a dream. The full moon's light came in through a cabin window. It must have disturbed her, woken her, worried her in her sleep.

She rolled over, away from Tom to give him a little more room.

Dew-laden, toddler-sized footprints and paw prints made a path across the floor from the cabin's door to Jamie and Shem's bed.

She sat up as the cabin door closed.

Chapter 2

A Bizarre Crystal

Jamie looked at his dad's reflection in the car's passenger window. "I miss Mom."

"I know, Jamie. I miss her, too."

"She liked the cabin, dad."

"I know that, too, Jamie. Is it alright us coming up here?"

"I guess."

"'Cause we can turn around and go home, if you like."

"No. Shem'll like it."

Shem woofed from the backseat. Jamie took off his seatbelt and turned around to pet his aging dog, his muzzle whitened with the years.

"You have a beard, Mr. Shem."

"He's getting old, Jamie."

"I know, Dad."

"Just want you to be prepared, Jamie."

Jamie's eyes watered. "I know, Dad."

"But it won't be for a while. He has plenty of time. We all do."

Jamie returned to his father's reflection in the window. "You just saying that, Dad?"

"No, Jamie, I'm not just saying it."

"You think they'll ever find mom?"

"That's my hope, Jamie. That's my hope."

"Me, too."

"Mine, too."

Jamie echoed his father. "Mine, too."

"Put your seatbelt back on, please, and I have a question for you: how come you always look at people's reflections when we're driving? Doesn't matter if it's me, Uncle Jack, Bobby … the only one you'll look at directly is Shem. Why is that?"

"I can see people better that way."

Tom shrugged, not understanding and not wanting to push things, only wanting them to have a good time.

JAMIE AND SHEM SLEPT SIDE BY SIDE, RESTING QUIET-ly between dreams.

The Moon, her light walking through the forest on white-slippered feet, lifted her arm to better see.

Tom slept opposite Jamie and Shem, on the far side of the cabin in the bed once shared with Ellie. He'd twitch, kick off his covers, grow chill and pull them up, repeating the pattern while The Moon watched.

Her children, the Oneiroi, little black silhouettes, shadows in the darkness of night, hovered over the sleeping Tom. They came and went, opening and closing their multicolored, multifaceted, crystalline eyes: kaleidoscopic Gates, little rainbow bridges allowing humans passage from one dream reality to the next.

Above Tom's bed, a dot, smaller than a piece of dust, winked into existence. It floated down, riding the heat eddies of the woodstove, as if wanting to rest in his ear.

Once beside him, it grew horizontally, becoming a slit, then vertical-ly as something stretched it open, spreading it wide. A deeper blackness, not one of the shadows, more an emptiness, a hole in the night, difficult to see and unheard, formed legs, pulled itself free, walked through and stood beside Tom.

The Moon held herself motionless in the sky, her light growing from crescent to full.

"Wake up, Jamie!" beamed The Moon. "Wake up, Shem!"

Shem raised his head, sniffed the air, saw the creature and bared his fangs. He looked at Jamie, looked back at the deep blackness standing beside Tom, and slowly rose as if his hackles lifted him to his feet.

The creature formed amoeba-like pseudopods ending in reaching hands and grabbed the Oneiroi hovering over Tom. Its silhouette crumpled like wadded paper, its life drained from it.

Tom moaned in his sleep. "Ellie."

Shem growled at the creature.

Jamie woke wide-eyed, his face cold with the damp night air. The smell of heavy, dying earth surrounded him like an unwelcome blanket. The Moon's bright light screamed full upon his face from the cabin's window.

"Dad?"

Tom's twitching stilled. The Oneiroi rose like mists from the cabin floor, fleeing, escaping the searching emptiness.

One Oneiroi remained to ensure Tom's safe return from his dream.

The creature grabbed it.

Tom kicked off his covers.

Jamie sat up.

Shem stood over him, not letting him off the bed.

"Shem, get off me! Dad's having one of his dreams."

The trapped Oneiroi's eyes grew dull then dark, its supple shape becoming hard and angular like struck flint. An eye burst from its skull, a bizarre crystal erupting from its little human-shape as its body shattered into black flakes.

Tom hadn't returned from his dream. He let out a quiet sob. "Ellie."

The opening in the night winked itself shut, closing horizontally then vertically, space folding like a napkin until only a pinpoint remained, then it, too, disappeared.

Dark night filled the cabin.

Shem leapt to the floor, sniffing the air and whining.

Jamie stood over his dad, curling his feet against the cold wooden floor tendrilling through his thick wool socks. He shivered, the cold October night reaching through his long johns as he listened to his father whimper. He wiped a tear from his own eye and tucked the covers around his dad.

Shem put a paw on Tom's bed and looked at Jamie.

"It's okay, Shem. He's dreaming about Mom again. He'll be okay in a minute."

Shem went to the door and whined.

"You're a pee-bucket, Mr. Shem. Come on, you old dog."

Shem and Jamie went out into the cold in the clearing near the cabin. Jamie's shadow stretched out long and full in the full moon's light, his shadow given sharp edges by the moon's intensity. He'd never seen his shadow like that, not even in the noonday sun.

He stood silent for a moment and watched it echo his movements, waving its arm when he did, walking when he did. The moonlight even shadowed the mist from Jamie's breath as if his shadow breathed when he breathed.

The Moon's face changed as he watched. Mom told him about Rabbit and Mouse, about The Old Man in the Moon, all sorts of stories people believed about the moon. This was the first time he clearly saw a woman's face, though. Mom told him about Selene and Artemis and Luna. Maybe this was one of them?

The Moon looked down at him and shed a tear, turned her face away and waned from full to crescent.

"Have you ever seen anything like that, Shem? We'll have to tell Dad."

He looked around. Night frightened most of his friends, even Bobby Games, but it didn't frighten Jamie. Not even full mooned nights. Uncle Jack told stories about werewolves, shapeshifting people who howled on bright moon nights. Bobby hated those stories but Jamie just sat and listened. Bobby asked, "Aren't you scared?" and Jamie shook his head, no.

He'd always been more comfortable at night. He didn't know why.

Maybe because with the moon so bright everything could be seen, clearly revealed in black and white.

THE WOODSTOVE STOOD COLD AND SILENT AT THE side of the cabin. Dad always got up early and added more wood to the stove so the cabin would be toasty warm, its fire crackling, when they got up.

But Jamie heard no crackling fire, smelled no burning wood, felt no warmth. Nor were his legs stiff from Shem pushing up tight against him all night. He reached down to scratch Shem's ears but the big dog wasn't there.

Shem whined from the other bed. He lay on Tom's legs.

"Shem, you come over here right now. You know Dad doesn't like you sleeping with him."

Shem whined but wouldn't get up.

Jamie threw back the covers and tiptoed towards his father.

"Dad?" he whispered. "Dad?" Then louder, "Wake up, Dad."

Tom MacPherson didn't move. It seemed he didn't breathe.

Shem woofed.

Jamie shook his dad. First softly, then harder and finally as hard as he could. "Wake up, Dad."

Tom didn't move.

Jamie saw his dad's mobile on the nightstand. Dad always told him, "Push 5 if there's trouble, Jamie. Push 5 and it'll find Uncle Jack no matter where he is, okay?"

The phone beeped and clicked and a woman came on the line. "Dr. Games's office."

The woman listened. She spoke calmly, slowly, making sure Jamie understood. "Are you okay, Jamie?"

"Yes, ma'am."

"How's Shem?"

Jamie went over to his dad's bed. Shem hadn't moved. "He's okay."

"Do you know if your dad is injured? Do you know if he fell during the night? Do you know what blood looks like, Jamie? I need you to walk around the inside of the cabin and let me know if there's any blood anywhere. It's okay if you don't know what blood is. Look for wet, sticky puddles."

"He seems fine, ma'am. I can't find any puddles anywhere."

"You're doing great Jamie, help's on the way. Did you hear anything strange? Did you hear gunshots?"

"Dad doesn't have any guns, ma'am."

She said she knew. Tom MacPherson lost his father to a hunting accident when he was Jamie's age and refused to touch handguns and rifles ever since.

She stayed on the phone, speaking calmly, carefully, listening and asking simple questions, and kept him talking until he heard the MedFlight helicopter overhead.

CHAPTER 3

Al Carsons

AL CARSONS' LEATHERY, CALLOUSED PALMS PUSHED down on the white, threadbare vinyl of his '77 Ford F-150 pickup's bench seat. It crackled as he slid out into the knee-deep, Hallock, Minnesota snow. He liked the crackling, the cold.

He reached back in for his lunchbox and blew a kiss to the empty seat. His lunchbox whacked the gearshift as he lifted it over the front seat rifle mount. He tapped the shift, making sure his old rig was still in gear and wouldn't slip.

He kept his pickup all these years because of that bench seat; he and Effie would sit side by side and not have to reach over an armrest to give each other a little pat or sneak a little kiss. He brought it home to show her, a long time ago, half a century ago in fact, when he and Effie were just starting out, all shiny new, red with white trim, a five-speed half-ton long bed and they went for a drive, my god did they go for a drive, he with one hand on the wheel and one around her, holding her close, only letting go when he had to shift.

He could drive forever like that. She even joked about it, calling him her "Forever Man."

He patted the seat where Effie'd sit. She told him they made Charlie that day they went for their first drive in their new pickup. He taught Charlie and Ben how to drive and hunt in that same pickup.

Now, like him, the hinges squeaked a bit.

He closed the door and patted the windshield. "Just you and me now, huh, old girl?"

His green wool pants swished between his thighs as he waded through low drifts, sounding almost like breaths against the *shhsing* whispers of the falling snow. His black workboots cut a path towards his plow and he thought of explorers in the Arctic. He slowed passing under the maintenance depot's one streetlight to watch his shadow shift from tracing back to his truck to stretching out towards his plow, all in one step.

Except a little piece of his shadow moved off to the left and stayed as Al moved on.

He liked being called for double-overtime during storms. Storms were great. Especially late fall, early winter storms. A mess of whirling winds, little specks of light bouncing back as his headlights fought the darkness, black night sky slowly gaining color as if slowly gaining sight.

And the cold. Cold that made vinyl crack. Even with the big plow's defrosters on full he could still see his breath misting at the end of his shift.

And the solitude. Quiet. Nobody to listen to him go on when he talked to the wind, telling Effie what he'd been up to, what he'd done, asking how the boys were and all.

Effie'd gone to that drunk driver five summers back and the two boys, Charlie and Ben also gone, one to a holdup and the other in Afghanistan.

He knew something was wrong when the Death Notification Officer showed up in his Class A's. He'd seen Ben in his Class A's once. He and Effie were so proud, their Ben in a parade in his honor, one of our own being deployed to the other side of the world.

Effie kept hugging Ben and messing up his uniform and saying, "If only Charlie were here to see you. He's so proud of you, Ben, you know he's smiling down on you waiting for you to catch the football."

"I know, Ma. I know."

"And you make sure you come back home to us, you hear?"

"I will, Ma. I will."

But that drunk driver took Effie and a week later the Death Notification Officer showed up at Al's door and they talked and shook hands and he explained that the bomb that took Ben out didn't really leave enough to ship home but Ben was going to get a proper military funeral just the same and Al shouldn't worry about anything, Ben was coming home.

When Al couldn't see the Army car anymore, when it had passed through the fields and trees and into the night, he went to his closet and got out his deer rifle and put one shell in the chamber and locked it in the front seat rifle mount and drove a little west because any further north he'd be in Canada and Al didn't want to cause any international incidents.

He parked in the morning light, slung the rifle over his shoulder and marched up into the tree-covered hills until he found a nice rock he could lean against and watch the sunrise, the muzzle tucked under his chin and a finger ready to push the trigger.

And then, wouldn't you know it, a beautiful ten-point buck walks right out of the woods and stares at him.

"Go away. Today you get a bye. Besides, you're out of season. I could get in trouble for shooting you, so get outta here."

The buck stood looking at him.

"Shoo! I only got one shell and it's mine, okay? Now get."

The buck glanced back over its shoulder then looked back at Al and nodded at him.

Nodded at him?

As if saying "Is this the guy you were talking about? He's right over there."

That's when the wolf came out of the woods and stared at him.

The buck walked away, its job done.

A buck and a wolf working together?

"I'm dreaming."

The wolf said something. Maybe. Its mouth moved like it was talking. Not moving like a wolf's mouth moves.

The wolf came closer but Al wasn't afraid. He'd never seen a wolf this close. Not a live one, anyway. There seemed to be something wrong with its eyes. They didn't look right.

"Poor thing. Must be blind. All alone, no pack. That's why the buck's not afraid of him."

A little dark man, a midget shadow, stood next to Al folding something.

A picture. Kind of. Of that place with the rock in the woods. Except things moved in the picture. The buck continued walking up the hill, through the trees. The wolf walked away, too, but in another direction, almost like it walked up into the sky.

Impossible.

The wind whirled through the trees.

The little shadow creature folded the moving picture up and handed it to Al.

"Thank you."

Al felt cushions underneath him. He looked up at his living room ceiling. He'd fallen asleep on his couch, his rifle in his closet and the chamber empty. No smell of being fired.

That was the last dream he'd had. The last one he remembered.

Now, just him and his old Ford pickup to remember. Just him and the wind. To keep his mind engaged, to keep his dreams away.

He continued to the big plow and checked it over, walking around it once, a pilot's visual inspection before takeoff. Inside, he turned the key and ignited the glowplug. It would be about thirty seconds before the glowplug would be hot enough to ignite the diesel fuel. The new engines didn't require much time to fire but he couldn't break the habit.

Something caught his eye outside the cab. He sought it first in the dark, then turned on the lights. In the night-dark and blowing snow it looked like a man, a tiny, little man, but more like a shadow than anything else.

Hadn't he seen one before? In a dream?

It walked on the hood without making a sound or leaving prints. The wind picked up and it stood in the center of the swirling snow, its eyes twinkling and making little rainbows in the night.

But then it was inside the cab and there wasn't any wind to blur the image. It was a child-sized, paper-thin man, a shadow, and its eyes twinkled like tiny Christmas lights.

Al blinked to clear his eyes.

And then the shadow-man didn't matter because Al was with Effie on the porch swing the day he'd finished it. Effie brought out lemonade and they sat and rocked and cuddled and kissed and acted like teenagers like when they were courting and Effie's dad would stand just inside the front door, listening, making sure this big, strapping lad didn't do anything to his little girl. Then Charlie and Ben came up the walk, dirty and tired from football practice, racing each other home, saw their parents and laughed. Charlie gave his mother a kiss and asked for some apple pie.

Ben nudged his father's shoulder. "Hey, Al, wake up."

Albert Carsons smiled. "What'd you say, Ben?"

"Al? Albert? You okay? It's me, Whit."

Al opened his eyes. The snow had stopped. Clouds covered the west but a belt of clear winter-blue sky girdled the east. The sun peeked over the horizon sending red, orange, and purple bands into the clouds. On the dashboard, breakers indicated they'd shut down the glowplug before the batteries drained. The lights were on but dimmed, as if the big plow shared a night's rest with Al, as if shaking off sleep was a challenge.

"You okay, Al? Tony sent me to check on you when you didn't stop for your eight-o'clock coffee and donut."

Al Carsons looked into his friend's face and felt tears slide down his own. "I dreamed, Whit. For the first time in five years, I goddamn dreamed." The tears came big and hard and he reached for his friend. "I dreamed about Effie and Charlie and Ben, Whit. Oh, Jesus Christ goddamn."

Whit, hesitant at first, reached around Al and let the big man cry.

AL SAT IN COUNTY YARD #1's DISPATCHER's OFFICE, Tony's office, hat in hand, coffee steaming in a styrofoam cup at the edge of Tony's desk. County Yard #1's dispatcher's office was the oldest county office not located in city hall and Tony did everything in his power to keep it that way. He was dispatcher, main mechanic, and unofficial Kittson County DPW manager, and had all three titles stitched onto his ever-present overalls to prove it. He once told Al, "Stay away from politics and politicians. Especially small-town politicians. They got to piss on everything just to let you know they can."

The office sat at the front of the big county garage and, unlike the rest of the building, had its own door and windows to the outside. The office's interior walls matched the building's exterior walls - green to about three feet up then white up to the ceiling, also white. Unlike the rest of the building, it had a Kentucky Bluegrass indoor-outdoor carpet so Tony could push his chair away from his desk or over to his filing cabinets without the rollers rocketing him across concrete and into the green and white walls.

Al helped Tony put that carpet in one weekend when both their families had been out of town visiting their respective relatives. Tony wanted a real carpet but had no money in the budget.

"Cap'n Sally's closing shop," Al offered. "Maybe he has something we can use?"

He and Tony drove the orange Kittson County DPW pickup out to Cap'n Sally's Miniature Golf Land/Batting Cages/Arcade. A big hand-painted "For Sale/Going Out of Business" sign hung over the front gate.

A voice called from the Arcade, "We're closed."

Tony called back, "That you, Burt?" He turned to Al. "How long's he been here and he still sounds like he's in Maine lobstering?"

"I heard that."

Burt Sally, sole owner and proprietor of Cap'n Sally's Miniature Golf Land/Batting Cages/Arcade, onetime Maine lobsterman who'd never been further inland than he could drive out and back in half a day, came out and stood on the Arcade's porch.

Rail thin, a white beard full enough birds could build nests in it and bushy white hair coming out in all directions from an authentic yachtsman's captain's hat, Sally nodded, "Tony. Al."

Tony said, "Nice hat."

"Ain't for sale."

"Looks new."

"Twenty-four dollars on eBay."

Years back the bottom fell out of lobstering. Sally sold his boat and all his traps to two UMO dropouts for a hundred-thousand dollars from the bank and a guarantee of either ten percent or ten thousand dollars per year for ten years.

Other lobstermen asked, "Where you heading, Sally?"

"West." He patted his boat, burned the worst of his traps, started driving and didn't stop until his timing belt blew fifty feet from where he stood now.

Except he had a suitcase filled with one-hundred-dollar bills in his hand and people thought that strange. He'd pull out a thick #10 business envelope from a back pocket and wave it at them. "Got all my bona fides in here, you got any questions."

His story checked out and he was a quiet, peaceable neighbor, good with his hands and had his own tools.

Sally'd rolled up the sleeves of his red and black plaid flannel shirt revealing arms still lobster boat sunburnt and covered with a glistening sweat.

"Been working?"

"Packing."

Tony looked around the parking lot. "Good day for it."

Sally passed a hand over his beard, pulling it down as if straightening it. He looked up at the sky, removed his hat and wiped sweat from a face so dour you could squeeze vinegar from it. But Sally's bright blue eyes gave him away. He was laughing about something. All the time.

He looked around the empty lot. "Ayuh."

Sally went back inside and returned with a wooden kitchen chair in one hand and a bottle of *Johnnie Walker Red* in the other. He angled the chair back until it rested like a tripod, its two rear legs on the Arcade's porch and the backrest against the wall, sat and put his feet up on a cooler that'd seen better days.

Tony looked over at the miniature golf course. "What you got in the cooler, Captain?"

"Ice and *Old Milwaukee*s. Might be a *Sam Adams* or two near the bottom."

"Need some help finding those?"

"Gotta get your own chairs."

"Mind getting us a couple of chairs out of the Arcade, Al?"

They sat. Tony reached in the cooler, pulled out an *Old Milwaukee*, shook off some ice, popped it, took a sip, sighed like he was a bee full of honey, put it down on the porch beside his chair then put his hands into the bib of his overalls.

He and Sally kept their eyes on the trafficless road outside the Miniature Golf Land/Batting Cages/Arcade's gate, their mutual respect for each other built immediately on the understanding that neither was going to look at the other.

"Got a proposition for you, Captain."

"Ayuh."

"You got any artificial turf left over from your fairways?"

Sally laughed. "'Fairways', is it? Puttin' Greens, you mean?"

Tony nodded without acknowledging the man's presence. "Puttin' Greens. Yeah."

"Got a few."

"I'd like to buy what you got left."

"Ain't for sale."

Al was about to speak up but Tony's look kept him quiet.

"At no price?"

"Oh, I got a price. Just ain't for sale. You can have 'em for barter."

Tony nodded, reached down, and inspected his beer. "What's the trade?"

"When I'm ready, I'm going to gather what I can and head back home to settle down. Going to find out if them kids either made their way or sunk my boat. You can take all the greens you want. It's not Astroturf, by the way, it's indoor-outdoor carpet. Can-tuck-ee Green, they call it. What I can't sell or barter I'm going to have to haul to the dump." Sally's eyes flicked briefly to the orange Kittson county pickup but other than that he paid it no mind. "What I don't want to haul to the dump might fill the back of a pickup for the trip back east. I'll worry about that when the time comes. But I'll need a dumper right before then."

Tony looked in the general direction Sally was looking in. "I think we could spare you a dumper or two."

"I'll take one dumper and a bucket loader to fill it. Half a day at the most, when the time comes."

Tony considered. "There might be some other things around here I'll want to take. Maybe my friend here might find something he'd like."

Sally's gaze shifted slightly so he wouldn't accidentally look at Al, either. "Ayuh."

"I guess I can live with that."

Captain Sally's chair rocked forward and he stood in one smooth motion. "I guess I can, too." He smiled at Al, his blue eyes still not revealing the joke. "Charlie and Ben your boys?"

"Yes, sir."

"They's pinball junkies, you know that? They got more free games one day than the machines could count. Since then I just give 'em free games to keep 'em around. Good boys, those two."

"Thank you. I'll tell their mom you said that. It'd please her."

"They favor *Terminator*, *Twilight Zone*, *The Shadow*, and *Johnny Mnemonic*. They spend a lot of time staring at *Scared Stiff Elvira* and if I was younger, I would, too. You see something in there you like, you take it. I got the books on most of them so you can bypass the slots. If you're handy you can keep any of them going for years."

Al went in.

Tony said, "Going to be hot today."

Captain Sally said, "Ayuh." A beer can popped and fizzed.

Two hours later Al had the five machines in the back of the Kittson county pickup and Tony had thirty-seven square yards of Kentucky BlueGrass indoor-outdoor carpet, one yard wide and thirty-seven yards long, rolled up beside it.

Two months later Tony and Al came back, Al driving the dumper and Tony in the bucketloader. Captain Sally met them holding the same *Johnnie Walker* bottle and only one or two fewer cans in the cooler.

Tony said, "You'll never kill yourself that way."

"Ayuh."

But that was years ago. Sally never called for the pickup, that part of the barter forgotten, and stayed on. "Living on my 'vestments."

Now Al sat in Tony's office, hat in hand, coffee in a styrofoam cup steaming at the edge of Tony's desk and Tony looking out the window so he wouldn't have to face his friend. "I don't suppose you can explain this to me."

Since the first morning he'd been called for a double-shift, Al found it easier to sleep in the cold of the plow's cab or his pickup than at home. Today's stunt topped it.

"Just so you'll hear it from me first, I looked into getting you retirement with full benefits."

"I don't want to retire, Tony."

"Good, because the town said no. I called the union, too. They said the contract with the town was solid and couldn't do anything, either."

"That's - "

"Unless there was a physical, not psychological, reason for you to retire."

"Tony, I'm as - "

"Then this nice woman says to me, 'Do you know Doctor Edward Martin?' and I said 'Of course I know Doc Martin. Everybody in Hallock knows Doc Martin. He's been the county's medico as far back as anybody can remember.' and she says, 'Did you know Doctor Martin took the union's side in the last two contract negotiations?' and you know what happened then, Al?"

"Uh - "

"I smiled, Al. I smiled, I thanked that nice lady and I called Doc Martin and you're going to go see him."

"Tony?"

"You're going to see him, Al, or I'm going to have to fire your ass, and I don't want that any more than you want it done."

Al stared down at the Kentucky Bluegrass indoor-outdoor carpet. It hadn't faded or worn in all the years since they'd laid it. He nodded without realizing it. "Yeah, sure. Okay. I'll go see Doc Martin."

Tony lowered his voice to a whisper. "I don't give a fuck about the trucks, Al. But I'll be damned if I'm going to see you get hurt."

It was the nicest thing anybody said to him since Effie and the boys died.

"Now get the fuck out of here and go see Doc Martin." He scribbled something on a yellow Post-It and handed it to Al. "That's the time and you know the place. Until I hear from him, you're on medical. You got time coming and the union already said they'd cover your bills. Now get."

CHAPTER 4

Joni Levis

JONI LEVIS ROLLED OVER AND BURIED HER HEAD against Virgil's pillow. Still asleep, she settled herself into the bed and inhaled deeply, pulling in his aromas, his shampoo, his sweat, and smiled.

She felt a trill, a tingling contraction, her body caught between the notes of excitation and sleep, and felt a brief muscle spasm in her vagina. A moment later there was another quiver and she half opened her eyes. Awake, the contractions became more immediate and demanding. She looked at the large, red numerals on her clock: 4:35AM.

She smiled and rolled towards his side of her bed: it was Fucking Time.

Virgil always woke her up within a few minutes of 4:35AM for a little lovemaking. It didn't matter if she was turned away, on her back, on her stomach, curled in the covers, facing him or whatever; always the gentle nudge, the liquid parting, and his lips would be on her, his penis in her. Busy-busy-busy for a few minutes and then asleep once again.

She reached for him and her hand closed on empty sheets. Her eyes opened wide. No Virgil and the bathroom was dark.

"Virgil?"

She turned on the lamp beside her bed. His clothes were gone. The only part of him remaining in her Boston BackBay condo was his scent on her imported cotton sheets and his necklace around her neck.

"Fuck you, Virgil."

Her eyes darted around the bedroom and stopped on her reflection in the mirror. "Ugh." She turned away, pulled her nightshirt down - again! - and crossed her arms over her chest; her body reminded her of a little girl's that had suddenly sprouted too much boob. She stopped wearing t-shirts with sayings on them because the punchlines were always hidden in the shade.

She pulled her knees up under the sheets and held them tight against her, flattening her chest, and checked herself again. "Ugh."

Her hand reached to her nightstand for a cigarette and came up empty.

"Guess today wasn't the day to quit smoking."

She'd replaced the ashtray with a bowl of cherry *Tootsie-Roll Pops*. Rocking slightly, she unwrapped one, crinkled the wrapper, tossed it down on Virgil's side of the bed, and sucked hard on the round head of candy as it entered her mouth.

"What're you going to tell me this time? You had to go feed your dog? Your friend, 'Sarah', couldn't take care of things tonight and you had to get home?"

She took the lollipop out of her mouth and jabbed it like a pointer at the vacant side of the bed. "You know, people have been telling me to hire a private detective to find out about you. I'm thinking about it, you know."

The necklace's cheap stone pendant slithered between her breasts.

"And this fucking necklace."

She laughed. Virgil called it a fucking necklace because "I like you wearing it when we fuck."

She lifted the stone to her lips. "Come in, Virgil. Six-O-Seven-Niner on the old Ten-Four, good buddy."

She snapped it off and threw it across the room. It banged against the wall, shattered, and let out a dying squeal.

"What the?" She retrieved it and held it under a light. A tiny circuit board grew dark. "You bastard. I was kidding. You fucking bastard."

Another twinge. This one deeper, higher. In her womb. "I'm a month late, Virgil. Did you hear that? Is that why you left? You always seem to know these things. If I have it, will it be a lying little bastard like you?"

Outside and several stories below, a tractor-trailer headed east through Boston along Interstate-90. A car horn screamed and the big truck's airhorn drowned it out. The car horn became stationary while the truck's horn continued on. "Yeah, that's right." She nodded, listening to the sounds evaporating in the night. "That's exactly right." She reached again to her nightstand, opened the drawer and lifted out a vibrator. Black letters on its white side read "DaVinci's *Personalé Vibrateur*".

"Fuck you. Just fuck you." She put the wet, sticky lollipop on the nightstand, turned the vibrator on, and shut off the light. "Fuck you."

The vibrator quaked between her legs and her bedroom door opened. She walked through into her parents' house in Denver.

Her mother walked out of the kitchen wearing clothes and a hairdo straight out of the early 1990's. It was like watching a home video. Joni kept looking for her twin sister and brothers to enter the frame.

Her mother held a broom and swept between Joni's legs.

"Scat!"

"Mom?"

Her mother turned into Shakespeare, complete with long hair, ruffled collar, puffy shirt, tights, beard, and everything. Shakespeare pointed out the door Joni had entered. "Out, foul thing."

Joni walked out the door into heavy rain. No, not rain. A shower head hung directly over her in the sky. Water poured down but only wet her groin. She reached down. She was soaked. There was something else, something hard and unyielding.

"What the..." She woke quickly, the dildo still in her hand, her body shaking with the last pulses of orgasm.

Something moved at her window.

She saw it again. A black silhouette, like a small man's shadow. It walked through her window and up into the sky.

Dr. Honey Fitz's wrinkled face watched for reactions. "You say this is the first time you've had this dream, and you think it has something to do with your boyfriend?"

Joni sat in a plush, comfortable, high-backed chair that belonged in a wealthy family's sitting room, not a psychiatrist's office.

But this was McLean Hospital, and this was Belmont, Massachusetts, and Dr. Fitz got four hundred dollars an hour to sit on her skinny, old, Boston Brahmin butt and listen, so the furniture had better be damn nice. For that matter, the whole damn office looked like a wealthy family's sitting room. Everything matched: the chair Dr. Fitz sat in, the dark rosewood desk, the chair beside it, the oriental rug that hushed the steps of anyone entering her office; the painting of her namesake, Boston's own Mayor Honey Fitz, smiling benevolently as his great-granddaughter listened to secrets he would've used to make himself richer. Hell, even the coat rack matched the chairs and desk. How many places did you know did that?

Joni stared out the window to the beautiful lawns and sculpted arborage guarding the hospital's eastern wing from the citizenry beyond. "I don't like calling him my boyfriend. He has a name. Virgil. The Virge."

"You're objectifying him."

"I object to him, period."

Dr. Fitz flipped through some notes. "Before you referenced him as your boyfriend."

"Things change."

"What's changed?"

Joni's thumbs spun the rings on her fingers like a magician practicing coin tricks. She pursed her lips and continued to stare out the window.

"Well?"

Joni ran a slim hand down the green silk of her blouse as if to straighten the pleats. Would her bosom grow larger or shrink to nothing if she had the child, or even if she waited too long before aborting it? Her mother's breasts had shrunk to hanging prunes. But she'd breastfed four children. Her sister's boobs had ballooned to the point she couldn't go anywhere without men and women tripping on curbs or running into store displays when she walked past.

Funny. Her mother had breasts and both she and her sister had boobs.

Boobs. Tits. Knockers. Masougas. Momboes. Hangers. Hooters. Kleevcos.

That last one came from a website Virgil talked about.

"I'm pregnant."

"Okay."

Joni looked up at Dr. Fitz's old wrinkled face. Were Dr. Fitz's tits as wrinkled as her mother's? Did Dr. Fitz ever have children?

She'd drop her jaw if Dr. Fitz had ever had a lover or been in love.

"'Okay'? I pay you how much for 'Okay'? You don't have any suggestions? You don't think I should go out and kill the son-of-a-bitch? You don't think I should wait until he's asleep some night and pull a Lorena Bobbitt on him? Wasn't there some movie with some Swedish actor where the wife did that?"

"*Pele the Conqueror.*"

Joni laughed. "That's right. I'll have to go find it."

It didn't surprise her that Dr. Fitz knew the movie off the top of her head.

"I want to know what you think you should do."

Joni threw her hands up and stared at the ceiling. At least the ceiling looked like it belonged in a hospital setting: two rows of fluorescent lights that Dr. Fitz never turned on. To save electricity? Because it would ruin her rug? Or her great-grandfather's portrait? Maybe she preferred the subdued lighting of her accountant's desk lamp and two floor lamps?

"I don't know what to do. I want to ask you a question for once."

Dr. Fitz said nothing.

"How much of what's in this room is you and how much is about you?"

Dr. Fitz remained silent.

"Ah, that's right. We can't allow transference. Always make sure it's about the patient, not about you. Isn't that what they teach you at shrink school?"

"This is bothering you quite a bit, isn't it, Joni."

"You are pathetic, you know that? You think a simple ploy like that is going to draw me out?"

Dr. Fitz placed her notes in her lap and put her pen down. "I'm open to any suggestions you care to make."

Joni sighed. She closed her eyes until her beautifully sculpted lashes embraced. "Did I ever tell you Virgil's last name?"

"No, I don't think you ever did."

"You know movies so you'll get a kick out of this. Tibbs. Virgil Tibbs."

"The man's a *schwvarze?*"

Joni's eyes popped at the sudden Yiddish. Dr. Fitz's face was a contortionist's mask of laughter suppressed. They caught each other's eyes and guffawed simultaneously. Joni slid off her chair, doubled over with laughter. Dr. Fitz squeezed her legs together and started hacking like a six-pack a day smoker. She got out "Excuse me" and left, her laughter echoing down the hall to the ladies room.

She returned, cleared her throat, and took her seat.

Joni sat wiping tears from her eyes. "God, that was good. I haven't laughed like that in years. And by the way, no. I think his mother just liked the movie."

"Or Sidney Poitier."

"Whatever."

"So what are you going to do?"

"I'm going to have an abortion."

"Okay."

"I'm not going to tell him about it."

"About the child or the abortion?"

"I don't know. Right now, I don't know if I ever want to see him again."

"Okay. What about the dream?"

"That was weird, wasn't it?"

"Do you think there's any meaning to it?"

"You mean do I think I'm fucked or not?"

"Well...something like that."

"I don't know. You're the shrink. You tell me."

"I think you should let me know if it's repeated. It's an interesting dream."

Joni looked at the diplomas on the walls. "Would that be a Jungian or a Freudian perspective?"

"Assagiolian, I suppose."

"Yeah, right, whatever."

Dr. Fitz checked her watch. "Session's over."

Joni gathered her things. "Figures. We start making headway and it's time to go."

"Joni?"

"Yeah, Honey?" Joni chuckled. "I love saying that."

"All your family's in Denver? I mean none of them are close by?"

"No. Yes, I mean. Correct."

"How about close friends. You still work at Halliday & Finch?"

"Best damn digital marketers on the planet."

"Anybody there you can turn to?"

Joni snorted. "You're kidding, right? Ninety-nine percent of the people in digital anything are either in therapy or should be. And I can quote numbers like that because I'm a digital analyst." She snorted a second time. "The money we make? And not a damn one of us knows what we're doing or will admit it. You ever walk through a digital marketing office? The industry's made up of manic depressive bipolars. It's an industry requirement. Talk about imposter syndrome..."

"Have you been self-diagnosing again?"

"What's where I work have to do with anything?"

Honey Fitz came around her desk and leaned back on the edge facing Joni, her hands on either side of her gripping the edge of the desk as if it were the edge of a cliff. "Because if you decide on an abortion and you want somebody there for you and there's nobody you can ask, give me a call."

Joni stared at the petite, tight-assed, prissy schoolmarm of a woman standing before her. "You'd do that?"

Now Dr. Fitz stared out the window. "Yes." Her hand went over her flat stomach.

Joni'd read enough to recognize the unconscious act: Dr. Fitz had no pictures of husband, children, family; only her namesake Honey Fitz on the wall looking down on her. The lack of personal memorabilia had less to do with concern for transference than it did with a lack of anything to remember.

"Thank you, Dr. Fitz. I appreciate that."

CHAPTER 5

Jack Games

JACK GAMES LEANED AGAINST ROOM 343'S WINDOW. 343 was the largest private patient's room in his clinic and the only one with a picture window overlooking the University of Chicago Medical Center's quad. He watched some med students play Hacky sack on the lawn while others sat on benches soaking up the early Fall sun. The quad was surrounded by the Medical Center's white, gray, and tan facades. The university hospital stood just out of sight off to the side.

He pulled back from the window and gazed at Tom's patient monitors, their multicolored lines and blinking numbers a thankfully steady but defeating rhythm in Jack's mind: no change. No change. No change. No change.

"What are we going to do, Tom?"

Tom MacPherson snored, a gentle *hnnh* sound.

Thirty PhDs, MDs, DScis and related specialists worked for Dr. Jackson Arthur Games. He chaired the University of Chicago's Neurosciences Department, co-chaired the Center for Narcolepsy Research at the University of Illinois, Chicago, was on the board of the Defense and Civil Institute of Environmental Medicine in

Toronto, Ontario, Canada, unofficially owned the third floor of the Brain Research Institute, sat on the board of the BRF Center for Molecular Neurobiology, and on Monday afternoons held an online, invitation-only Sleep Disorders Specialty Clinic.

None of which meant shit right now. Jackson Arthur Games had come a long way from DC's Prospero House, the largest orphans' home in the tri-state area, and most of it with the MacPherson family's financial backing.

"Smart investment, eh, Tom? You spent how much money on my education and I can't do a frickin' thing for you now?"

Tom *hnnh*ed. Tom *hnnh*ed in his sleep for as long as Jack knew him.

Jack remembered one day when he and Tom were in Jack's college dorm room. Jack got dressed while Tom sat on the bed, watching Jack's silhouette against a not quite as large window.

"Holy shit, Jack. You're black."

"All the way down and for most of my life, smart ass."

"No, I mean, I've always known you were a 'black man', but I never noticed your skin. It's black. Darker than mine anyway. Wow. That's neat."

Jack held up his hand as if to check Tom's statement then caught himself. Tom's sincerity was both stupefying and contagious. But Tom had always been innocent and naive in ways Jack couldn't quite fathom.

"You are truly color blind, my friend."

The bond cemented in their junior year. Tom was packing his car for Christmas break and Jack blocked his path. "Can I ask you a question?"

"When did Admin put a wall here?"

"No, serious now."

Tom leaned against his car. "You okay?"

"No, I'm not. And you're the reason."

"What did I do?"

"How come you never invite me home for Christmas break? Or Thanksgiving? Or any break?"

"Well, I - "

"Is this where you tell me your family's members in good standing of the local KKK and you broke free?"

"No, I - "

"Do you think I got someplace to go? Do you think somebody's filling a stocking for me? Saving me a drumstick? Hiding Easter Eggs for me to find?"

"Hey, fuckhead."

"What?"

Tom picked up a laundry bag and put it in his trunk. "Sorry, I just never thought to ask."

"You never thought to ask? What the hell? Did you not have any friends growing up? Did you not invite your schoolmates home to play? Watch TV? Listen to music?"

Tom stopped loading. "No, I didn't."

Jack stared at him. Tom's naivete caught him again and Jack fumbled a recovery. "You got a crazy uncle locked in the attic?"

Tom stopped mid way to his trunk with a box of books in his hands. "No. Go get your things. I'd love to have you with me for the holidays."

They drove two-hundred highway miles in silence. They exited the highway and traveled some low mountain roads until they came to an old village built along a river.

Jack said, "Is that a waterpowered mill?"

"Yes. Still operational. Doesn't power anything, just something to look at and remember."

Jack looked at the company store turned country store, the hitching posts, rail guides, and water troughs still prevalent along Main Street. "Wow, what a sense of history."

Tom snorted."You got that right."

They rode another twenty minutes in silence. Tom turned up a gravel drive hidden by trees at the far side of town. The drive stopped at an ivy-covered mansion buried in a copse of oak, ash, and pine.

"Tom, I'm sorry. This was a stupid idea. I'll head back to town and hitch back to school."

"Why?"

"I've been here before, Tom. I've made friends before whose family thought the darker the skin the darker the man. I don't need to be your proof that desegregation doesn't work."

"Come on." They walked through the front doors, their arms full. Tom headed up some stairs. "I'll get you settled. Then you can meet Mama."

"Mama?"

"Yeah, Mama. You've gone this far, you might as well get the whole show."

"Look, Tom, just tell me. Am I going to be the show?"

"What are you talking about?"

"I can imagine it now. The sweet smile, the warm handshake, the genteel and curious questions. Then when you and Mama are alone, 'Get that nigger out of my house.'"

They dropped their packs and books in a room with aircraft models hanging from the ceiling and ship models on the shelves. Superhero and car posters covered the walls.

"No Farrah Fawcett poster?"

"A, she was before my time and 2," he pointed, "it's hanging in my bathroom."

Jack stared, unmoving, unbelieving he was this close to the Grail. "You got a private bathroom?"

"Sure do." Tom headed out the door. "Follow me."

They walked down a thickly carpeted hallway of heavy wood paneling. Every few feet there was a picture of an old white guy. Tom opened a door.

Jack took a deep breath and followed him in.

And stopped.

It was a child's room. An elderly woman rode a rocking horse. An equally elderly nurse sat by the window reading a book. "Hi, Tom. I thought I heard you come in."

"Hi, Mabs. How's Mama?"

"She has her days."

"This is my friend, Jack. I emailed you and Mama about him."

Mabs got up from the window and gave Jack's hand a good, strong shake. Tom went over to the woman on the rocking horse. "Mama? It's me, Tom. You remember me? Tommy?"

She stopped rocking and looked at Jack. "Tommy? You've been out in the sun too long."

"No, Mama. I'm Tom. Right here. Next to you. That's my friend, Jack. You remember I wrote you about my friend, Jack?"

Mama dismounted the rocking horse and dragged it over to Jack. "You like to ride, Jack? Tom used to love to ride when he was younger. Now I couldn't get him on a horse if I had to."

"Mama!"

Jack held his hand up. "No, Tom. It's all right. Sure, Mrs. MacPherson. I love to ride."

She looked from Jack's beefy six-six frame to her rocking horse. "Hmm. I think we'll need a Percheron for you, son."

"It'll be fine." He straddled the rocking horse without dropping his weight onto it. Slowly, watching Mama all the time, he began rocking.

"That-a-way, Jack," Mama said in a strong western accent. "You ride that sum-bitch!"

Mabs went back to the window and her book. Tom looked at Mama, smiled, then looked at Jack.

Jack watched Mama, looking for signs of discomfort with this stranger in her house.

He saw discomfort. But different than he was used to.

Tom's eyes watered and he wiped them.

They had a great weekend. Mama accepted Jack like a second son. He became a regular. Several years, college through grad school. They stayed close even when Jack moved up to Dartmouth then around the globe doing multiple internships, designing his own specialty. Jack always found his way home for Thanksgiving, Christmas, birthdays, Fourth of July, any day ending in a "y", ...

And that was that.

Jack stared at Tom's monitors. "Tom, why can't you wake up?"

MABS CALLED JACK AND ASKED HIM TO COME UP TO the house. "All Tom does is sleep all day. He comes down to eat, he takes a shower and shaves, then he goes back to bed."

"Mama's been gone close to a year now. We all miss her - "

"It's not that, Jack. He's gotten worse."

"Worse since the funeral?"

"Worse. I don't remember when he last saw daylight."

"I'm on my way."

Tom was the last of his line and Mama's condition prevented anything beyond casual friendships with most people. But that Mama-powered boundary no longer existed. Jack guessed Tom suffered some form of Parolee Societal Reintegration Syndrome: the sudden lack of penitentiary structure caused most cons to recidivate. Tom recidivised by isolating himself in the mansion.

Mabs opened the door and Jack took a moment to smile.

"Jack. Thank you for coming. God, I must look a fright. I've been so worried about Tom I haven't taken care of myself right, have I?"

Mabs made Mama her life. Tom gave her the west side of the mansion and a handsome allowance and no real concerns in return, but she'd aged rapidly since Mama passed. When she opened the door she looked like something out of a Faulkner novel. A lesser known, mostly-ignored-and-rightly-so Faulkner novel. Jack imagined her walking through a moonlit graveyard at midnight wearing nothing but a white flannel nightgown and slippers, throwing dead rose petals on an illicit lover's grave and mumbling some incantation hoping he would rise.

Thick, white hair hung in two long pigtails around her neck and down her back, either a scarf or hangman's noose and Jack couldn't tell which, and framed her wrinkled, liver marked face as she spoke.

"How are you doing, Mabs?"

She smiled and his trained eyes fixed on her discolored gums. He caught her breath and hid his reaction.

She caught his eye and smiled. "Oh, you're such a good doctor, Jack Games. Nothing's hid from you, is it?" She laughed. "It's oncogenic nephritis, advanced. There's a real fancy name for it but it's killing me just the same. I have six months. Maybe a year."

"Jesus Christ, Mabs. How come you never told me? Did you tell Tom?"

"My people are long gone and if I told Tom he'd go before I did." She shifted her white robe around her plump little body and took his arm to lead him into the house. "Underneath here I've got more puncture wounds from where they've tried to draw the little boogers from me than Custer had arrow holes. I even have a machine in my room I hook myself up to at night so my kidneys can function for another day."

"I appreciate your letting me know."

She led him upstairs to Tom's room. "Time for this family's next guide dog, I guess."

Tom huddled under the sheets in the middle of his bed, the covers forming a tent over him, a little boy home with a cold. His room hadn't changed since Jack's first visit except Mama's rocking-horse now rested against the common wall.

"Tom?"

No response. Not even a ruffling under the sheets.

"What's going on, Tom."

A voice from inside the tent. "Nothing."

"You think this is normal?"

"Huh?"

"You think it's normal for me to be talking to a pile of laundry?"

"Did Mabs forget to do the laundry?"

"You think it's normal for a grown man to be hiding under his bedcovers?"

"I'm fine. Just thinking."

Jack pulled clothes from Tom's bureaus and closets. He slammed drawers and doors as he did to make as much noise as possible.

Tom called from inside his tent, "What's all the noise?"

Jack threw clothes on Tom's bed, collapsing Tom's tent.

Tom poked his head out from under the covers. "What are you doing, Jack?"

"Me? I'm saving your life. We're going to find you a nice inner city apartment. I don't care which city. You? You're going for walks every day. In a park, downtown, to the library, I don't care where and you'll walk or take a bus or subway, do you understand?"

"Yeah, but - "

"But nothing. If I can manage it, you're getting a job. You're going to meet people, talk with them, I don't care if they don't want to talk to you, you're going to at least say hello to them. Do you understand?"

"Yeah, but - "

"No buts," Jack shouted. He grabbed Tom by the arms and lifted him from the bed. "I'm a big black man from the ghetto. You don't want me pissed off at you. You're going to do what I tell you, understand?"

"Yeah, sure. Of course. But I have to pee first."

Jack's concern lessened as Tom smiled up at him.

"Have Mabs make us some coffee. I'll be downstairs once I clean up."

"TOMMY, IT'S ME, JACK. REMEMBER ME? BLACK JACK? Remember back in college when you discovered I was black? I'm still black. Don't you want to wake up and tell me I'm still black, Tom?"

Tom *hnnh*ed on the bed.

Jack lifted his oversized tablet and flipped through reports, scans, x-rays, tomographs, biopsy results and bulletins on indigenous plant and animal life around Tom's family cabin in Michigan's Upper Peninsula.

He looked up when a research specialist walked in.

The woman shook her head before he spoke. "He's not responding to Provogil or anything else. Nothing's inhibiting the sleep patterns. He goes right through stages one, two, and three in a matter of one or two breaths then into stage four and stays there, except he never dreams a bit."

"Nothing?"

"Alpha goes, he becomes desynchronous so we know he's entering stage two, we get sleep spindles and K-complexes then his delta waves start so we know he's in stage three, then he goes fully delta so we know he's in stage four. But nothing else happens to indicate a dream state, no REMs, no hypno-, narco-, neuro- or hemo-chemistry change complexes. He's asleep, only nothing about him knows it."

"Did research turn up anything?"

"I did get something from MedLine. From your alma mater. Maybe you studied with the guy. Capoçek Lupicen? Ever hear of him?"

"I remember the name, vaguely. Not from MedSci, though. What's his specialty?"

She hesitated. "Same as ours."

"Yes?"

"Same as ours, I think." She pointed to the tablet he held. "It starts on screen five. You should read the whole thing."

He flipped and swiped. "Ok. Neuroscience, neurophysiology, neuropathology. Neurotopology? That's a typo. They meant 'Neurotopography'. Sleep disorders research. Oneirologist? Nice but not special. We have two dream docs here."

"Keep going."

"QuantumNeuroGeoDynamics? Never heard of it." He swiped some screens. "What is it? How come it's not described in this report?"

She tiptoed out the door while he continued swiping screens. "According to what I could find, it's a mix of Quantum Physics, Cultural Anthropology, Psychology, and about a hundred and twenty other fields."

He looked up, realized she was missing, saw her standing in the hall.

"Really?"

"Look at the last four pages."

Games swiped, paused, read, swiped, paused, read. "How come we've never run into him before?"

"Damned if I know, Jack. I called and talked to a Sandy Olafssen, his research assistant. I think she runs his lab for him. Anyway, she said he doesn't spotlight himself much. At this point, what could it hurt? He seems to be just what your friend ordered. Give Lupicen a call."

Tom's ragged voice came from the bed. "Do what she says."

Jack barked orders and demanded personnel in the two steps it took him to stand beside Tom. "Tom, can you hear me?"

Tom MacPherson's eyes opened, fluttered, closed. Words came out labored, quickly in a rush of breath. "Been awake four times since cabin."

Deep breath.

"First time can talk."

Breath.

"More awake each time."

Breath.

"Not long."

Each breath, each rush of words took increasing effort. Tom started to lift his head and Jack put his hand under it. "Easy, Tom."

"Jamie?"

"Jamie's fine. He's with Rita, Bobby, and me."

MacPherson's eyes fluttered open. They rested but didn't focus. "If anything happens...Jamie..." Tom swallowed his son's name as his head sank back onto the pillow.

"Like he's my own, Tom. Like he's my own."

"Ellie said...do what she says." Tom drifted away again.

"Wait! What? Ellie? Tom?"

The team arrived. "He was conscious for less than a minute. Do a full workup. Check everything again. He mentioned his wife, she's been gone for over a year. Did he dream or hallucinate? Check for differentiated and non-differentiated luciferase and any elevated cyano- or chrono-bacterium in his bloodstream. See if there's a depressed expression of cytochrome or BiP. Look for alterations in the monoamine system. Something's got to be doing this. And whatever I forgot to tell you, do that, too."

They wheeled the unconscious MacPherson out.

Jack went back to the window and looked for the Hacky sack players, wanting something normal to balance the chaos. Instead he saw a massive black woman seated on a bench staring up at the room. "Detective Johnson," he whispered cordially. "How are you today?"

Even though she couldn't hear him, Chicago PD Special Investigations Detective Colodnie Johnson stood and waved, dwarfing the Hacky sack players about ten feet behind her. Standing, she was as tall as Jack and a hundred pounds heavier.

"How'd you find out Tom was here? You follow him up north in the hopes he'd dig up Ellie's body? No, wait, I got it. You did this to him."

He waved back. "No, you're not smart enough to do any of that. But you still think he killed Ellie, don't you. And you're never going to let him go until you can prove it, right?"

She waved again and headed towards the clinic doors.

"You stupid, fucking idiot." He sighed. "Ah, but I repeat myself." He picked up the phone beside Tom's bed. "Tell security Detective Johnson is entering the building. Hold her at reception. I'll meet her there. No one sees Tom MacPherson without my prior written authorization. I want two security and two nurses with him, door and bedside, twenty-four-seven."

Dr. Games watched Bobby and Jamie turn the Games' thick gray hallway carpeting into a HotWheels™ raceway and remembered his promise: Like my own, Tom, like my own.

He kneeled two stairs down from the landing where the raceway grew, his elbows resting on the top stair, his hands together and fingers intertwined in front of him as if in prayer. Little, brightly colored cars and trucks came his way and he knocked them back towards the track. Shem, sleeping behind Jamie, only opened his eyes when a car bounced at him.

Jack had to tell Jamie about his dad. But how much could the little fellow take? God knows he wasn't as frail as his old man. Jack was shocked Tom survived Ellie's loss. At least Tom could bury Mama and Mabs. But they never found Ellie's body and Tom never gave up hope. He'd argue, "They found her car but they never found her."

Both true.

There were no signs of a struggle and it wasn't an accident. To be honest, it seemed she just walked away, out of their lives, and more than one person made that point to Tom.

But Jack knew Ellie. Her abandon Tom and Jamie and Shem? Impossible.

The boys had created a jump for their HotWheels™ but one side kept flopping over in the heavy pile carpet. A red Maserati jumped the track and bounced into the bathroom.

"Darn." Bobby crawled after the car. "We need something to hold up that part of the track."

Jamie reached into his pocket. "How about this?"

It looked like a stone. It had black edges but its center seemed to pick up the colors of whatever Jamie held next to it. In Jamie's hand it appeared as a finely cut Caucasian colored quartz with a thin black outline. When Jamie put it on the rug Jack could barely find it in the thick, gray pile.

"Where'd you get that, Jamie?"

Jamie pulled it from under the track just as Bobby sent another car hurtling towards the jump. "Hey!"

"One of the helicopter doctors found it on the cabin floor." He held it up for Jack to see.

Jack held it in his palm and all that remained was a black outline against his flesh. He rested it on the back of his hand and had to look closely to see the outline against the color of his skin. But it had weight. Heft. Substance. It was solid. Colorless throughout but solid. You could throw it and it would travel.

"This was on the cabin floor and your dad never noticed it?"

It measured half as long as his index finger and, at its center, as thick as his pinky. He scratched it with his nail but couldn't leave a mark. Its shape was, for all his experience with such things, like a quartz crystal, but one this large with no visible imperfections - octagonal and the finest of black lines where the faces met - was surely worth a lot of money. He rolled it on the carpet then against the floorboards and wainscotting and finally held it against the blue and gray wallpaper. It disappeared like a chameleon in a forest each time. But this was mineral, not animal or vegetable.

Collision? He remembered something from a required but long forgotten physics survey class, something about optical dark being due to quantum collisions. That would account for the edges, maybe? But on something this size?

"Your dad never noticed this at all?"

"No, Uncle Jack," Jamie said. "One of the helicopter doctors picked it up and gave it to me."

"One of the helicopter doctors?"

"Yeah, there were four of them, two pilots and two doctors. Or nurses maybe. The ones who took care of dad and brought me here."

"Oh. Right. One of them found this in the cabin? Do you remember which one?"

"The Indian one. Graywolf. He had funny eyes."

"There were four of them and one was an Indian named 'Graywolf'? You mean a Native American?"

"Yeah, that's right."

Jack knew the team that flew Tom from Michigan's U P to CCMC and Jack's team transferred Tom from CCMC to UCMC. That U P MedEvac crew transported emergencies into either Chicago or Detroit routinely. "Did they stop to refuel, Jamie, and Graywolf got out?"

"No, we flew straight here."

"But there were only three people in attendance on that flight, Jamie. The pilot and two EMTs, one of whom can fly. None are Native Americans."

Jamie looked down at the HotWheels™ scattered around him then back at Jack. "But there was, Uncle Jack. He was with me on the helicopter. Graywolf. That's when he gave me the Gate. He told me he found it on the cabin floor and that I was to keep it, that it's important to Dad."

Jack hefted the crystal in his palm. "'Gate,' Jamie?"

Jamie's eyes started to water. "Really, Uncle Jack. It's true." His chin tightened and his lips quivered.

Jack ruffled Jamie's thick, red hair then kissed both boys on their heads as he stood up. "I'm sure it is, Jamie. You said there was something funny with his eyes? What was that?"

Jamie's face brightened. "One was brown and the other blue." Jamie had only recently learned his left from his right and waved his hands to show which was which: right blue, left brown.

"Are you sure, Jamie?"

Jamie waved his hands authoritatively. "Yes, Uncle Jack. This eye is blue, this one is brown."

Right blue, left brown.

That would be a sure giveaway to finding the man, but to make the picture more complete, he asked, "Can you tell me what he looked like? Aside from his eyes, I mean?"

"His skin was dark, Uncle Jack. Not like yours or Bobby's or Aunt Rita's, but lots darker than mine or dad's. And he was tall, not as tall as you but taller than dad, and he was skinny, and he had long black hair, a big ponytail, tied down his back."

Not as dark as Jack, Rita, or Bobby, so not black, but darker than Tom or Jamie, so maybe Pakistani-Indian, maybe Central or South American, but then there was the hair Jamie described. "That sure sounds like an Indian, doesn't it?" Jack offered.

Jamie perked right up, convinced Uncle Jack believed his story. "It sure does."

Jack went into his study and called up the flight manifest. The flight and medical crew listed three names: John O'Leary, pilot and navigator; Shuresh Rumaniji, first flight EMT and emergency pilot; and Cassie Bremen, second flight EMT and RN. Cassie he ruled out automatically because Jamie called Graywolf 'he.' Shuresh Rumaniji was a dark skinned southern Indian but not Native American and not even Jamie would make that mistake more than once. That left the pilot, O'Leary, but Jack knew the man and again, a tall, red-headed Irishman did not a Native American make. He even spoke with a brogue. He searched for personnel with heterochromia iridis, the different colored irises Jamie had mentioned. Nothing. That, for sure, would be a giveaway feature. Unless the person was disguised or wearing contacts, but that was being paranoid and made no sense at all.

He swiveled his chair to look out his study window. A bright quarter moon lit up his backyard, casting shadows in silver and gray, its light coming in and splaying across his desk and computer screen.

Something caught Jack's eye. Why didn't he notice this before? An entry for an unnamed flight technician at the bottom of the manifest. Maybe Jamie didn't know the difference between a flight technician and the medical personnel?

Poor little guy.

Jack went back out into the hall. The boys were taking turns looking through the crystal.

"Hey, dad, look through this. Jamie looks like an old man." Bobby winked at his father through the crystal.

"Bobby says I look as old as you, Uncle Jack."

Jack laughed. "Oh, yes, that is old. What does Bobby look like, Jamie?"

"He looks like Bobby."

"Can I try?"

Jamie handed Jack the stone. Sure enough, Bobby looked like Bobby. An old black-and-white photograph but recognizably Bobby.

But Jamie...

Jamie looked like Jamie, still a little boy, but a kaleidoscopic aura emanated from him surrounding him like a cloak. Still Jamie but a different Jamie. Not maturity. Age? Knowledge?

No.

Patience. Wisdom. A sense of time, of age without being tired.

Jack remembered a term from a philosophy of religion elective: an "old soul"?

He could understand Bobby saying Jamie looked like an old man but it was more the energy around him than Jamie himself.

"Jamie, do you have any other stones like this?"

Jamie shook his head while he motioned a tiny dump truck towards a tiny skip loader. "No. Graywolf only gave me the one. How's Dad?"

Jack picked up Jamie and held him. "He's sleeping again, Jamie. But he woke up for a while. He told me to tell you he loves you and not to worry, we'll get him through this."

"I know, Uncle Jack."

"Oh? How's that?"

"Graywolf had me look at Dad through the Gate. He told me to believe whatever I saw through the Gate, that it couldn't lie. That's why everything you see through it is in black and white, like at night. When I looked at Dad he was awake and okay."

Jack looked through the stone again; Bobby, his own son, black and white. Jamie, colors.

Probably emotional exhaustion. That explained it. On both their parts. Nothing strange, just some interesting minerology and emotional exhaustion working as one.

He looked at Jamie again. Still an aura. Still an old soul.

Shem thumped his tail on the carpet.

Jack's mind came back to his original problem: how much to tell Jamie.

Tom came in and out of consciousness but showed no signs of trauma or dissociative disorder. He was awake for several hours at a time now. His wake/sleep cycle followed a sinusoidal rather than circadian rhythm. But when he went out it was immediate and catastrophic.

Jack reached out to Lupicen and Lupicen requested Tom be brought to him.

A plane would be faster but couldn't carry the necessary equipment should Tom's autonomic and sympathetic systems go into cascade failure. A plane big enough to carry the equipment couldn't land anywhere near Dartmouth, so it would be Boston, Manchester, or Burlington and then a three-plus hour ambulance ride and again, no ambulance could carry the necessary equipment. In both cases, emergency landing, if necessary, would be an issue.

No, a plane wouldn't do. A bus would take too long to modify and there would be traffic issues, arranging escorts, possible accidents, and traffic delays.

A train. The trip would take a day, two at the most. "We're going on a trip, Jamie. A train trip to see someone who will help your dad."

Jamie nodded and Shem stood up next to him. "Okay, Uncle Jack. Can I have my stone back now?"

Jack handed it back. Jamie lifted it to his eye and looked at Shem.

Shem sniffed the crystal, licked it and Jamie's face, then wagged his tail. "Good boy, Shem. Good dog."

"Come on, Jamie. Let's help Aunt Rita pack us some traveling bags." Jack held out his hand.

Shem followed close behind.

CHAPTER 6

Al and Doc Martin

AL CARSONS TOOK OFF HIS SHIRT WHILE DOC MARTIN read the official letter Tony sent to explain the situation. He placed the letter on top of Al's folder and placed both on the examining room table. He reached into his pocket and pulled out some Post-It notes, their tops folded over so they wouldn't be sticky.

"What are those, Doc?"

Doc Martin patted the examining room table. "Up."

Al sat on the table. Doc Martin read the Post-It notes, nodding at each as he shuffled them, then put the bunch of them in the sink. "You smoke?"

"You know I don't."

"Wait here."

He went to his office and came back with a small box of wooden matches, lit one and held it to the Post-It notes.

"Doc?"

"You would like to test for a Class 5 HazMat TT license. I am going to examine you to make sure there is nothing to suggest you shouldn't test for that license, but which would not stop you from maintaining your Class 4 Construction Vehicle license. Do you understand what I told you?"

Al smiled. He and the Doc went way back. On his first visit, Al was a strapping, blonde-haired, cowlicked buck fresh out of high school who'd just started working for the county and, in the middle of his union physical, confessed he'd just met a girl and wasn't she pretty? Al remembered the Doc talking to him, confirming and denying things Al had heard about but never experienced, things about being "safe."

Doc had been a tall, lean, man about fifteen years older than Al. Tall and lean and wiser than anybody Al ever knew.

Now Al had a gut and what hair he had he cut close. Still thin but now not as tall, Doc seemed more like a pussywillow bent with the weight of the silvery puff on top. The Doc seemed to be getting thinner and more hunched these days.

"Why, sure, Doc, I understand, but - "

"Good." Doc reached into a drawer and came back with a reflex hammer. He whacked Al square on the forehead hard enough to open the big man's eyes.

"Hey!"

"This test confirms you should not test for the Class 5 HazMat TT license." Doc Martin raised the reflex hammer again.

"Doc!" Al lifted his arms and turned his face away.

"That's what you should have done the first time." He made a note on the letter then put it inside Al's folder. "Now, what's Tony talking about?"

Al kept his eyes on the hammer still in Doc Martin's hand. "You talking about my sleeping in the truck cabs?"

"Are you just a damned fool or do you think there's a sane reason for that?" Al hesitated and the Doc raised the hammer again. "You're too damn old to have the cat get your tongue, so tell me what the hell's going on, Albert Carsons."

Al sat on the examining room table, his shirt off and big belly exposed as Doc Martin tossed the hammer into the drawer and pulled out a stethoscope. The smell of Doc Martin's office hadn't changed in all the years Albert had come to him. The smells of the hospital had changed from the time Charlie and Ben had been born till the time Effie died. But Doc Martin's office smell hadn't changed. It was still mediciny, like alcohol and mercurochrome and iodine and smells Al remembered from being a kid.

But Doc Martin hadn't changed his heavy, mahogany, green cushioned furniture in all those years either. For all Al knew, the smells might come from the furniture and have nothing to do with the medicines Doc Martin kept locked away.

"You going to tell me or do I put the glove on?"

"In the cold of the cab, in the early morning, before the sun's up and you can see the moon and stars and there's nothing between you and them except miles of clear morning sky... In the early light, I dream, Doc. I dream of Effie, before she passed away. Effie and Charlie and Ben."

Doc Martin moved the stethoscope around Al as the big man talked. "Breathe."

"I haven't dreamed anything in years and now I dream every night, but only about Effie and Charlie and Ben."

"Deep breaths."

Al sighed and Doc knew it carried more than the requested deep breaths. He held an ophthalmoscope to Al's eyes. "You know, Albert, we both started working for the union about the same time."

Carsons nodded. "You and me, Doc, we seen some."

Doc Martin nodded right along. "You know I'm retiring this year? Maybe next, but this year, I think. You must be ready to retire, too, aren't you?"

Carsons shrugged. "I figured I'd work a few."

Doc Martin smiled and patted Al on the back. "Yeah, me too." It was late. Doc Martin's nurse and office girl had gone home. The town was dark except for the streetlights and downtown pubs and moon overhead. He handed Carsons his shirt. "Can I buy you a beer, Al?"

"You and me, you mean? Sure, Doc. That'd be great."

"How come you've known me for forty-five years and you never called me by my first name?"

"Well, why, because you're the Doc. That's why."

"Do you even know what my first name is?"

Al glanced at the diplomas on Doc Martin's walls but couldn't figure out the names from the Latin. "Edward? I think I heard someone call you Edward Martin once."

Doc Martin smiled. "That's what the paperwork says now. My real name is Eduardo. Eduardo Ignatius dela Martina, and I never drink with a man who won't call me by my first name." He held his hand out and Al shook it. "Nice to meet you, Al."

"Same here, Doc."

Doc Martin glared at him.

"Well I sure in hell ain't gonna call you Eduardo Ignatius."

They settled into a dark booth in a local pub. Al slid over the cracked red leather cushions and rested his big hands on the polished dark oak tabletop. "Some place, Doc. You come here a lot?"

Doc Martin looked around. He'd come here once or twice since Margerie passed. Regularly before then. They'd meet here when she was in town. He'd never paid attention before because all of his attention was on Margerie, his always bride. Was the music the same now as it had always been? Sinatra crooned from a recognizable jukebox lit against the wall at the end of the bar. Not a CD player. Must cost some to keep that going. "Oh, once or twice."

A woman came up and Doc Martin took a moment to appreciate the waitstaff. No kids, all career waitresses. Full-figured, the woman looked comfortable in her loose-fitting, flower print blouse. He caught the light scent of a subtle, violet perfume. She had a pleasant voice as she put down menus. "Something to drink?"

They each ordered a thick-steined draft. Doc let Al talk and Al talked a lot. It was as if all the time his Effie'd been gone, Al'd talked to no one else and needed her there to be with; just to be in her presence; she was so easy to be with, she just listened and let him talk, and that was something no one else ever did.

But Doc Martin couldn't stop being Doc Martin. Al's words foretold a deepening problem, a worsening trauma, a psychosis starting to flower.

Al let slip the little shadow men he'd seen more than once when he woke up suddenly from his dreams.

"That rings a bell."

"You mean I'm not crazy?"

Doc smiled and patted Al's hand. "Well, not yet, anyway. Give me a minute. Something I heard about, something I read."

He closed his eyes. Al thought he grimaced.

"Got it. Somebody's doing research on what's called Charles Bonnet Syndrome."

"Who's Charles Bonnet?"

"Not important. He was the first to describe it. Hallucinating tiny people when your eyes are closed. And don't worry, it's just getting old and being tired and not getting enough sleep."

"You got it, Doc?"

Doc Martin laughed. "Not yet, anyway. I got that old and tired thing working but I'm still getting my eight for eight. Do you have any vacation time coming?"

"I haven't taken any vacation since Effie passed."

"Let me make a few calls. You need to take some time off."

"But - "

"You take some time off or I'll make sure you lose your benefits."

"Okay, Doc. Okay. No need to get feisty about it."

Doc Martin scratched his side, a long, pressing scratch as he checked his colostomy for fluid and pressure levels. He didn't have much time left. Certainly not the few years he and Al had joked about. His cancer was well along. There wasn't much more to take out and he knew it.

He couldn't do anything for himself but he couldn't stop being Doc Martin, even as his colostomy sac filled and he started to smell the seepage informing him what little gut he had left absorbed the beer too quickly.

"Al, you okay to see yourself home?"

"Yeah, sure. Why?"

"I got to head back to the office for a minute. Something I forgot to do. While I'm there, I'll look into Charles Bonnet some more. See if there's something we can do for you. That all right with you?"

"Well, yeah, sure, Doc. But - "

"But you promise me, you'll do what I tell you to do."

"Always have."

Doc Martin nodded.

"You okay, Doc?"

"Yeah. just tired."

They walked outside and into the clear night sky. The moon was caught between two dark, downtown office buildings like a float bobbing in a well.

Al looked up at it and smiled.

Doc Martin followed his gaze. "Sure is beautiful tonight, the moon."

"I got to tell you something, Doc. And I don't want you to get worried by my saying it."

"Depends on what you got to say, doesn't it?"

"I... I think I'm going to meet Effie again soon. Effie and Charlie and Ben."

Doc Martin's eyes went wide.

"No, not like that. I'm not thinking about doing anything stupid. And I don't think I'm going to die all of a sudden. It's just a good feeling I have. Ever have a feeling just fills you with joy? That's what I got, Doc. Don't tell me it's something's got to go away."

Doc Martin studied Al's face as Al smiled at the moon. "Look," he said. "You get out of here. I got to go back inside and go to the can. When I get back to my office, I'll get something together for you and have it on Tony's desk tomorrow morning."

"Whatever you say, Doc."

"Good, good. Now go on. Git."

Doc went back and slid into their booth. He caught Al watching him through the big picture window and smiled and waved, slowly turning so Al wouldn't see him scratching his side. He knew Al would do as he was told because he always had and nobody was there to tell him to do otherwise.

Back in his office, Doc made some calls and pulled in a few favors, wrote everything up, put it in a packet and dropped it through Tony's office door mail slot on his way home.

"Al?"

"Yeah, Tony."

"You got about two month's vacation time coming what with seniority and comp time and all that shit. You know that?"

"I wasn't keeping track, no, but - "

"Here's a package for you from Doc Martin. I ain't read it. I ain't read it all, anyway. But I read enough to know it says you're going to New Hampshire, to Dartmouth College for a holiday. Maybe you'll learn something, you big ape. Now you take it and you do it and when you're done you get back here and your IH Diesel'll be waiting."

"I don't want any - "

The phone rang and Tony motioned Al to sit down. "Well hello and how are you." He smiled into the phone, glanced at Al and nodded. "It's been a few years. I began to think you'd forgotten and I was off the hook." He grunted a few times. "You don't say." Pause. "No kidding." Pause. "That's great." Pause. "That's just about as goddamn perfect as it can get." Pause. "Yeah, in fact I got your man right here. I'll put him on." Tony handed the phone to Al.

"Hello?"

The accent seemed to precede the words. "I understand you're driving back east."

"Captain Sally?"

"Ayuh. You going back east?"

"Well, I - "

"Had an agreement with your boss and gave you some games to boot, as I remember."

"I guess to New Hampshire. Is that far enough?"

Sally talked slow and measured, as if every word had to be considered and inspected lest a good one get away. "That's a start."

"You wanted to go somewhere in Maine, right? Will somebody be able to come get you and take you the rest of the way?"

"I can find my way from there."

"Oh, okay. We can drive in shifts and get there sooner. Can you drive part of the way?"

"Drove out here well enough."

"Okay. Right. When do you want me to pick you up?"

"You come by, I'll be ready."

$$\text{———}$$

CHAPTER 7

Joni and Honey Fitz

JONI STARED AT THE BROOKLINE ABORTION CLINIC'S red- and gold-lettered sign from across Beacon Street.

She shook her head in disgust. What betesticled marketing moron came up with those colors for an abortion clinic?

Two buses, one with a Boston's Pro-Life Action Network banner and the other unloading Operation Rescue sidewalk counselors, formed a phalanx from the sidewalk to the clinic doors. Ever since John Salvi III opened fire here and at its sister clinic about a mile away, and with most red states sending busloads of safe sex refugees north, this stretch of Beacon Street became one of the safest most dangerous places in the greater Boston area. Police cars patrolled routinely. Male and female undercover cops chatted up anyone and everyone walking anywhere near the clinic.

The Supreme Court repealed Roe V Wade but Massachusetts took up the banner and created a safe zone for people wanting to enter and exit the clinics, and this safe zone included quite a bit of the sidewalk and street surrounding the clinic. People on their way elsewhere learned to stay on the side of the street opposite the clinic, thus the only people nearing it were those having business there.

Such as Joni, today.

Joni held a pencil in her hand as if it were a cigarette. She lifted it to her lips each time she felt her breakfast of barely thawed Brüdermann's frozen pizza and cold Starbucks coffee coming back on her.

She belched. "Ugh. Morning sickness is one thing but you didn't do yourself any favors here, Levis." She checked her palm for escaping pieces of pizza. "I should never have given up smoking."

Sitting in a safe haven of a sidewalk bench across the street from the clinic, Joni watched an obese woman with a video camera and two small children in tow. The children orbited the woman more like satellites than offspring; the woman was large enough to warrant a small planetary system of her own.

All the other people, all the other protesters and contesters, all the police, all the counselors, all the passersby and traffic in between, evaporated until only this one woman, video camera in hand, her greater and lesser moons of Phobos and Deimos orbiting via unseen gravitational umbilicae, spun away from the others, walking and talking her way into a universe of her own.

She held vigil under an ash tree, a cat waiting for a specific bird to arrive. She kept telling her kids to stay there. At least it seemed she was. She might have been saying, "Stay here until I move five feet away. No more. Five feet, do you hear? Then come running after me. Scream for me. Clutch my skirt, climb onto my coat, pull me down into the earth with the weight of you. Make sure you're loud and obscene and obnoxious enough for all others to see. We are here to show them what it means to be a mother."

Joni's hand went to her stomach. She couldn't feel any life there yet. "Small comfort." Instead she felt the pizza and coffee making plans for a violent escape. She wanted to be prepared.

How did the woman pick her targets? Did she only go for women like herself? Like herself in what way?

Joni watched her walk back to her ash tree after each encounter, back to the bulging, plastic shopping bags she dropped there. She seemed confused by them, unsure of all they contained, some kind of alien cornucopia. One held extra video cameras, extra batteries, a voice recorder, extra mobiles, a portable hand-crank phone and USB port charger, and pictures her children waved at those who sought entrance. The next held sandwiches and Cokes, Hostess peanutbutter-cheese crackers, Twinkies and M&Ms, a thermos and extra cups. The last held disposable diapers, clothes, towels, and a Gladlock bag of moistened hand wipes.

She had come prepared. Maybe Joni could bum a plastic shopping bag and a hand wipe when the pizza and coffee made their escape?

"Fuck that. Does she have a cigarette?"

After each encounter the woman's shoulders sagged, whether as victor or vanquished Joni couldn't tell. Her back arched, her gait stiffened and slowed until she shuffled and did not walk. She checked her camera, checked her phones, gave her children some soda or some food. She inventoried the contents of each bag then looked sideways at her children, a look of concern, maybe worry, on her face.

Or suspicion? Exhaustion? Confusion? Joni provided monologue as if watching TV with the sound off. "What? These brats are mine? How did that happen? Who made that decision?"

The woman dressed simply, her clothes made by children overseas for a national chain. Her shoes came from a bin, a twofer from someplace in a strip mall where there was no one to help her, no one to massage and measure her feet and appreciate her nylons and pedicure, a place where she had to help herself, a place where she argued with the cashier: "You're running a twofer sale and these are kids' shoes. They're lots cheaper than mine. They should count as one twofer against mine."

All the while her two children would orbit her in the store, making noise, making a show. The people in line behind her would first smile, then frown, then purse their lips in disgust, then shuffle, and somebody would mumble something and the cashier would catch one person putting down their shoes and would yield and the planetary woman would hide her smile of victory and then only then tell her children to be quiet.

Did she actually think nobody knows her game?

Her hair was done only on special occasions, only when somebody took her out, and then by her sister or mother or the neighbor upstairs or down.

"Down." The neighbors would be downstairs and this woman and her two children lived in a third, fourth, or fifth-floor walkup. That way this woman could leave the heat off in winter, or at least on low, and let the apartments below hers wick their heat up to hers, the palm warmed as it rested over the candle flames.

This woman lived alone with her children. She collected coupons and foodstamps, wrote TripAdvisor reviews for places she'd never been using Groupon as a guide. She either collected boyfriends based on mutual dependencies and needs or had one boyfriend who came and went and didn't tell her much and was as fucked up as she was.

Joni laughed and stopped, frowning. That last one. Wasn't she describing her relationship with Virgil?

Don't think about that. Not here, not now.

This woman learned how to wear makeup from the latest magazines and online tutorials. When she couldn't get the latest magazines, when she'd run out of minutes on her phone, when all the library's computer terminals were in use, the tabloids would do.

And everything Jerry Springer, Fox News, and Dr. Phil said was true.

Joni couldn't figure out how the woman selected her targets; who would she accost as they approached the clinic? It seemed random. Thinner women, broader women, women taller, shorter, blonde, brunette, African, Hispanic, ... The woman herself was black-haired with putty-white features.

The woman's radar would go off and she would tell her children to wait the proper amount of time and space and her shoulders would square and her back would go straight and her steps would become fierce and proud as she walked up to some woman and screamed "DO YOU KNOW THERE'S A LIFE INSIDE YOU?" while her camera recorded and her phone clicked and the redlight on her voice recorder blinked as it swayed from the cord around her neck.

Joni listened. The woman wasn't recording the women coming into the clinic. She played sounds of babies crying and cooing and mewling and puking.

About this time her children would begin their orbit, pictures from the grocery bags in hand, graphic pictures of mutilated fetuses. "SEE WHAT HAPPENS TO THE LIFE INSIDE YOU? BUTCHER! HARLOT! DON'T YOU CARE ABOUT YOUR UNBORN CHILD?"

The woman didn't scream so much as her words hung like clouds over her targets' heads, raining on them as she reined them in.

Her targets. Not her children.

Sometimes her words and cameras and recorder didn't work. She'd fall to her knees, gather her children to her, smother them in cheap perfume and foolishly bouffant hair, then stand, walk like a lost soul to her bags under her tree and set her radar to work again.

If she claimed a success, she waved down a taxi and sent her victims on their way.

None of the other pro-lifers paid any attention to her. They avoided her. The best they could.

Joni checked her watch. It was time. She stood.

The woman's radar went off before she got back to her tree. She spun to her target before her children had time to return to their places.

The younger child, a toddler, spun out into the street, gaining momentum like an asteroid flung from its orbit by a chance encounter with a greater planetary mass.

Right into the path of an oncoming car.

The woman was shrieking "DO YOU KNOW THERE'S A SACRED LIFE WITHIN YOU?" and didn't notice. She paid no attention to the screaming, pointing people around her.

Joni's feet moved. Perhaps all that time in the gym was paying off?

Her hands went under the child. She lifted and moved, the wind of the car raising her skirts as it swerved past. The child was crying. The crowd was cheering.

Joni understood.

It wasn't about having children or not. It was about having wanted children. Having children who knew they were wanted.

The woman grabbed her child. Her eyes drilled into Joni, her radar active, seeking its echo. Instinctively Joni's hand went to her breast, a proclaimant, an act of protection, and closed on the fucking necklace.

It was still sticky where Joni pried out the circuit board and glued the remains back together. "Once I'm out of the stirrups, Virge, you and this necklace are going in the nearest trashcan," she'd told herself, a triumphant farewell to The Virge.

The woman, clutching her child, followed Joni's hands to the necklace.

The sudden exertion caught up with Joni and her stomach heaved. Up, up, out and down, all over this woman's cheap coat and cheap socks and cheap shoes and cheap recorder and cheap cameras.

The woman froze for a second. This wasn't part of the plan. Still holding her child and still looking at Joni and still covered with bile and vomit she screamed into Joni's face, "DO YOU KNOW THERE'S A LIFE WAITING TO BE BORN INSIDE YOU?"

Joni wiped her mouth with her hand and answered calmly. "Yes, I do. I just don't know whose."

"HARLOT!"

"Joni." Dr. Fitz weaved her arm through Joni's and moved her towards the clinic doors.

"Easy. You're breaking my arm."

"All those years as a schoolmarm. Quick as a lick with a hickory stick. You should see me with a rapier or a saber. Sorry I'm late." She eased her grip on Joni's arm. "You okay?"

"Sure, Honey." Joni laughed.

Two hours later they were in the backseat of a cab heading out towards Dr. Fitz's McLean office. Honey held Joni while she cried.

"It's amazing how many tissues you can fit in that purse, Dr. Fitz."

"Practice."

"You do this for all your patients?"

"Hell no. I have to do this for my family. That's enough, believe me."

"Huh?"

"I'm a Fitz, remember? What's the one thing Old Joe couldn't get enough of? Well, he passed the need onto every male child the family ever raised."

"I didn't know you were that involved. I didn't even know you were in touch with that side of the family."

"Ever see Pacino in *Godfather III*? 'Just when I think I'm out, they pull me back in.'"

"Hey, that was pretty good."

"Practice."

In her office, Dr. Fitz sat behind her desk and motioned Joni into one of the two chairs opposite.

"Oh, something's up. These aren't our usual places."

"I know. What I have to say is better said over here than over there." She nodded towards their usual places.

The weight in Dr. Fitz's voice pushed Joni into the chair. "What do you have to say, Honey?"

"I can't see you professionally anymore."

"What?"

Honey held up a hand. "What I did today I shouldn't have done. I could be with you at this place or BaldPate or LakeShore or BrookSide. I could even be with you at one of the psychiatric wards in any of the Boston generals, but I couldn't be with you at an abortion clinic as your psychiatrist and retain my license or my ethics. Professionally."

"Then why did you do it, dammit? I thought we were making some real progress."

"We were. You are. Would you have gone through with the abortion if I didn't go with you?"

"I don't know."

"Guess."

"Probably not."

"How good a life would you have given the child?"

"I don't know."

"Guess."

Joni remembered the woman and her small satellites. "No. I don't have to. It's too late now, anyway."

"Would you have given the child up for adoption?"

"How come you didn't ask me these questions before, goddamn it?" Her eyes welled up.

Dr. Fitz pushed a box of tissues across the desk to her. "Because these are things you can only decide for yourself. Whatever you decided, you have to live with it. Not me. I wasn't about to make the decision for you."

"Oh, like you've had lots of experience with this."

Dr. Fitz spoke quietly, "I have."

"Yeah, right. With who? JFK and Bobby and Ted and all the generations that came after?"

"No."

Joni's eyes cleared. The ornate plainness of the office. The lack of any family memorabilia. Only the family patriarch glowering down on her after all these years.

"You?"

"Me."

Joni's eyes dried and anger filled her. "So this was the ultimate transference? You getting back at the old man?"

Dr. Fitz tilted her head and snorted. "Give me some credit. I neither endorse nor reject your decision. I accept it's your decision. I just wanted you to be able to make it. You did. Congratulate yourself."

"That's it?"

"No. Personally, Joni, I think you made the right decision. You made the right decision for whatever reasons, but the right one just the same. If you had the child, you would have loved it, sure, but I wouldn't want you to find out in thirty years that your son or daughter didn't have the life you wanted them to have and start blaming yourself all over again. Most women with your education and background wouldn't have considered adoption, and I don't think you would have either. But if you did...well, nowadays birth parents and orphaned children have options they didn't have before. Still, you might have wondered. You might have wondered and ached and not been prepared for a meeting, should it have come, or never knowing at all, which is often the case." Dr. Fitz walked over to her windows and gazed into the fading sunlight. "No, I think you made the best choice. There are no 'afterward' questions this way. It's over. It's done. You can have other children if you want. It all comes down to whether or not you're comfortable with that."

"In time. Not just yet."

Dr. Fitz took an envelope out of the drawer and handed it to her. "There's the names of the top ten people within the 128 beltway. I took the liberty of talking to each of them briefly. They're all willing to take you on."

"Thanks. You sure you didn't do this for yourself?"

"Quite sure. Good question, though. I'm proud of you for asking it. That tells me you probably don't need much help anymore. No. I did it for you, Joni. I did it for you."

There was a moment's silence. "Thanks."

Dr. Fitz nodded. "There's one other thing." She laughed. "A plus side to being of a certain lineage, I guess. Before I tell you more, I want you to tell me you accept today is the last time we're going to see each other professionally. I need to have you tell me you don't want to see me as your psychiatrist anymore."

"Okay."

"Say it."

"I don't want you to be my psychiatrist anymore, Dr. Fitz."

"Good. I trust you to mean that and not to come after me with some harebrained malpractice suit in five years. Now that I'm not your psychiatrist anymore, I can share some research I did. Not much more than asking a few questions, but for this I could really lose my license. I gave some of the information you gave me about your boyfriend to some of my friends."

"Oh?"

"You want to hear this?"

"Do I?"

"It may be to your benefit. Being a Fitz means you can get lots of things done in this neck of the woods."

"What don't I want to know?"

"There is no one named Virgil Tibbs in the town you said he lives in."

"I figured that."

"That name is in use by a man who's under suspicion for cybercrimes, cyberstalking being one."

"What?"

"A man using that and several other aliases moves about the country setting up cyberscams. A programmer for hire, a hacker when he needs to be and evidently a damn good one."

"You're shitting me. If what you say is true, this guy's a stone around my neck until I die. No matter what I do he'll find my records on some computer somewhere and that'll be the end of me."

"The good news is he loses interest in his victims when he moves from one place to the next."

"A computer genius with a short-term memory. Something poetic about that."

"I'm afraid, Dave. Dave, my mind is going. I can feel it. I can feel it. My mind is going. There is no question about it. I can feel it. I can feel it. I can feel it."

"What are you talking about?"

"The movie, *2001*. Dave Bowman's pulling out HAL's memory?"

Joni rolled her eyes. "Yeah, sure. Whatever. How long is Virgil going to be around here?"

Dr. Fitz shrugged. "No one could say. That brings us to another thing, my last professional act for you."

"Which is?"

Dr. Fitz took out a notepad out of her top drawer and scribbled down some information. "I researched the types of dreams you've been having. It turns out one of the best dream people is up at Dartmouth and looking for people to work with him right now. I called and they'd love to have you, if you're interested." She tore off the top sheet and pushed it towards Joni. "That's his name on top there, and his address. The name underneath, Sandy Olafssen, she's the one who runs the show." Fitz rose and extended a hand. "That's it, Joni. That's all I can do for you."

CHAPTER 8

Earl Pangiosi

EARL PANGIOSI SAT IN THE *EMPIRE BUILDER*'S Superliner Snack Coach's upper level, a pillow behind his head and a blanket covering his legs, peering through dark, wraparound sunglasses at people's reflections in the round, full-length domed windows. When someone nodded off, he'd dip down his glasses and peer at them briefly, purse his lips then shove the glasses back up his face. Once in a while he'd catch his own red-haired, high-colored reflection as he followed people walking past.

Earl liked being around people so he could practice. He had his own car - disguised as two back-to-back LandSea containers on a flatcar and marked "US Mail" - further back in the train. It brought a brief smile, the change in rail regulations that allowed all trains to transport freight and passengers simultaneously. It made his private car's subterfuge possible.

But people were Earl's focus. He tolerated the miasma of greasy hamburgers and soggy fries, too-strong coffee and unwashed bodies, screaming children and louder screaming parents, and the occasional whiffs of diesel to indulge in a pastime he enjoyed since his childhood:

watching people's reflections in glass.

He first noticed his gift on an early Fall night much like this one.

Dad, suit and tie and freshly shaved and mustache neatly trimmed, drove their new, '59 burgundy Lincoln Continental back to the old neighborhood. Mom sat opposite Dad, wrapped in her furs, wearing her best clothes. Dad told her she wore clothes too tight sometimes but she told him to never mind, didn't he want everybody to know what he had every night?

Mom and Dad left the old neighborhood a year before and never told Earl why. But once a month, maybe twice, he and Mom and Dad would get in the car and go back north to the old neighborhood with presents for everybody. Dad was in the meat business and he'd hand out steaks and chops and roasts and cutlets and hotdogs in summer and hamburger and ground pork if somebody wanted to make meatballs. Everybody was so grateful and Mom would smile and nod as she stood beside Dad, his hands reaching deep into the coolers in the dark of the trunk, coming back into daylight, his hands full of brown paper wrapped meats neatly tied with butcher's twine. They asked questions about the new car and Dad would tell them it was a Lincoln and Mom would correct him with "Lincoln *Continental.*"

They drove home, the coolers empty and tucked in the trunk, heading south on a clear, moonless Sunday night. Earl saw the Rhode Island border sign. Soon Dad would slow for the Providence traffic and take the Federal Hill exit.

An only child, Earl had the entire backseat to himself. He could lie down and take naps if he wanted to. Now he sat behind Mom, his hands folded and face pressed against the rear passenger's window, his knees pulled together and tucked under him because he had to pee but Dad said they weren't going to stop, they only had a little further to go and Earl was a big man and he could hold it, couldn't he?

Sure, Dad.

Except Earl really had to pee. The leather seat sent shivers of cold up through his bare knees and that didn't help. He had bare knees because he wore shorts. Shorts, a winter jacket, and a hat Mom made him wear even though all his cousins wore long pants.

They already laughed at him because he had different color eyes: the right brown, the left blue. Mom didn't say much and his cousins and some aunts and uncles said that made him a freak. She made him wear dark sunglasses and told everyone Earl had sensitive eyes.

His cousins would dance around him. "Earl has *sen-*si-*tive eye*-eyes. Earl has *sen*-si-*tive eye*-eyes."

He caught his reflection in the window as his exhalations frosted the glass. Mom's and Dad's reflections, too.

He'd never noticed them before. Maybe reflections were something you only got in a Lincoln *Continental*? The dashboard gave off so much light.

He watched his father's profile as they drove. Mother said things and Dad occasionally winced on the side Mom couldn't see as if somebody jabbed him with a little knife.

Mom would go *ya ya ya* and Dad's nose would twitch and his mustache would rise a little then go back down. Mom would go *da da da* and Dad's eye would wink shut quick and then back open to watch the cars on the road. Mom would go *sa sa sa* and Dad's lips would move forward and back like he wanted to spit something out.

Earl watched his father and something happened in Earl's head. His father stopped being a person and became a book, a map, a reference, something to be read. He tasted what his father felt. He did not know the word but he understood the emotion: despair.

"You don't like what Mom's saying, do you, Dad."

His dad stared at him in the rearview mirror. He could almost feel his father's thought: are you asking me or telling me, son?

Earl opened his mouth to answer but Mom said, "Where does he get that, I wonder?" and looked out her own window the rest of the way home.

"That's not a nice thing to say, Earl," his father said. "You know that's not true."

Earl's eyes left the reflection and looked at his dad direct.

He knew what his father thought. Maybe not the exact words but he knew the feelings.

He was sure of it.

What he was most sure of, especially sure of, as sure of as he was sure it was cold and night and he had to pee, was that what he said *was* true: Dad didn't like what Mom said.

He also knew that if he questioned Dad about it he would get a spanking when they got home, maybe before.

That's when he saw the Icelin. He'd seen one once before but didn't have a name for it back then, didn't know the Iceli were just his and that no one else could see them. A little wink in the darkness of night.

The dashboard lit his father and mother and didn't light the seat between them. He should've seen his mother's purse pulled up tight against her and his father's gloves on the seat beside him but there was nothing there. No seat, no gloves, no purse, just a child-sized bubbling hole where everything should be.

No face, no eyes, no hands or arms or legs, just a roiling blackness.

Yet he was sure it looked up at him. It knew he was there and it knew he knew it was there.

And it did nothing about it.

That made Earl so happy! Finally a friend who accepted him. Oh, joyous, happy, *happy* day.

"What're you smiling about, son?"

"I like our new Lincoln, Dad."

Mom said, "Lincoln *Continental*."

Dad said, "Good, son."

EARL'S HOUSE WAS THE ONLY SINGLE FAMILY IN THE neighborhood. It had a yard and a flagstone patio out back. He helped Dad put up a high picket fence the first week of summer vacation. The only people who could see into the backyard lived on the second and third floors of the surrounding multi-families.

Earl watched them. The men, especially. Those who worked second and third shift; who woke up in the middle of the day and had a breakfast of eggs and toast and beer; who walked onto their porches wearing tank tops over swelling bellies with suspenders holding up pants too small but still too good to be thrown away.

One day Mom came out wearing shorts and a t-shirt that was almost nothing at all on top. She plugged in a fan and let it blow her hair back and forth over her face. She took an icecube from her lemonade and ran it up and down her legs until it melted completely away.

All the men came out onto their porches and drank their beers and ran their hands over their bellies and balding heads and rough unshaven faces and smiled down into Earl's yard.

Mom sat in her chair, rocking back and forth, her eyes fixed on nothing at all.

She caught him staring. "What're you looking at?"

"You're deciding how you can get something past Dad. You're figuring out how to play the angles, so when you're all done he won't be able to do anything about it."

He had no idea what he was talking about.

She beat the shit out of him.

He peed his pants and soiled himself. She held him up by the back of his collar and kept slapping his face until he stopped shrieking and screamed, "Never hit me again."

She looked at him and laughed. She grabbed the front of his shirt, raised her hand and rocked his head back with the impact.

She made him clean himself and the mess he made on the patio stones while she watched. Laughter echoed down the multi-family canyons.

"How a weird-eyed, red-headed little fuck like you came out of me, I'll never know," she said. "Must have been those two brothers I met at the grocery store. Shaved bald and wouldn't take off their sunglasses, but boy could they fuck."

He would forever thank his mother for the beating she gave him that day.

It was that day he decided to practice. Whatever it was he could do, he would practice it and perfect it and become the best he could at it.

HE CALLED IT THE *KNACK* AND HE LEARNED THE BA-sics quickly.

Starting with Mom.

Who became forgetful.

Who used lye flakes instead of soap flakes in the bathtub.

Who added bleach when she washed her fine, colored clothes.

Who used hemorrhoid cream instead of toothpaste when she brushed her teeth.

Who used DDT instead of hairspray when she got ready to go out.

The day she almost sliced a finger off cutting vegetables, that was the day she left. She must have felt the knife hit the bone. She shook her head and looked up.

Earl stood in the doorway.

She wrapped her hand in a dishtowel, grabbed her purse, and left.

He cleaned up the kitchen, washed the cutting board and knife, washed the vegetables, took out two steaks, and prepared dinner.

His father came home an hour later, loosening his tie as he entered the kitchen. "Where's your mother?"

"I don't know, Dad. She was making dinner then she grabbed her things and left."

SURELY THERE WAS SOME PRECEDENT. SOMEWHERE in history there had to be others who could do what he could do. Master influencers? Propagandists? Manipulators? Salespeople? Spies? Murderers? Saints?

He convinced Miss Turgeon, Head Librarian at the town library, to let him shelve books after school. She took him under her wing, guiding his readings, providing him books far beyond his years: philosophy, anthropology, language, folklore, mythology. "Return each to me when you're done."

It became a pilgrimage of sorts, Earl carrying a heavy tome to her desk at the back of the library, hidden deep in the Stacks, and returning with another. She had a Bleeding Heart of Jesus picture on her desk, facing her. "That's our Lord and Savior," she said.

He nodded, said nothing, took whatever book she had for him and left.

He studied. He read avidly. Quietly.

Once, in the late afternoon quiet of an almost summer day, when all the librarians sat at their desks in the front of the library with the front doors open to invite a breeze, he started his pilgrimage but stopped four stacks away.

His nose twitched. What a rangy, sour smell! What was that?

He walked slowly, following the scent like a rat on a trail, his nose up in the air, breathing deeply, closing his eyes every few steps to focus on the smell.

Then, over the tops of some books and through two rows of stacks, he saw Miss Turgeon sitting at her desk in the back of the Stacks. She had a thick, spiral bound notebook and ran it back and forth between her legs, under her desk. Her breathing grew heavy and her face flushed and her chest heaved until she shook and stopped.

It wasn't the last time. It wasn't always the warm, slow days.

But she'd always stop with a shiver, a little shiver, once or twice, after she'd finished.

The real clue was the Bleeding Heart of Jesus picture on her desk. It lay face down while Earl watched and she'd face Jesus back up when the last shiver finished shaking her body.

His last day in the library, she looked up to see him staring.

"Do you enjoy that, Miss Turgeon?"

She had the same look his mother had.

She grabbed his right ear, twisting it and walking him into a janitor's supply closet, banging him into pails and brooms and mops. "I've been watching you, Mr. Pangiosi," she hissed. "You don't think - "

He tied the memory of her shivering to the Bleeding Heart of Jesus.

"Ooh," she moaned, leaned up against the door, and shook. She let go of his ear. Both hands pressed her groin. She groaned. She slid down the door, shivering, until she sat, her legs tucked under her, rocking forward and back facing Earl as if bowing before him, a supplicant.

Earl smiled back, thrilled to know he could provide her such pleasure.

He heard clacking footsteps hurrying towards him. Ms. Gayle kneeled beside him. "Miss Turgeon! You're Earl, right? What happened?"

"I don't know. Miss Turgeon looked sick and I heard something fall and came to see."

Miss Turgeon reached for him. Earl smiled. Her mind filled with the Bleeding Heart of Jesus lying facedown on her desk. Her eyes glazed. A shiver shook her head violently: right, left, right. She tried to say something. All that came out was *Nn* followed by a choking gasp as Earl made her feel the spiral bound notebook in her hand.

She tucked into a tight little ball and shivered.

"Earl, go to the front desk and tell them to call an ambulance. Hurry."

"Yes, ma'am." But he stood there. He lessened his "grip." Miss Turgeon, her lungs heaving, untucked and looked up at him, her face white, her eyes wide and livid.

Oh, no, that will never do. Her mind filled with the Bleeding Heart of Jesus again. She curled up again. Her mouth foamed. Blood trickled from her nose. Her eyes closed. Her breathing stopped.

"Earl, go!"

He gave himself rules. Guidelines.

Do not look at people when you do these things.

Don't tell people what they think.

Don't let people know you know when they've lied.

And make sure you fuck them as hard as you can so that, should they ever figure out what you can do, they'll know enough not to do a damn thing about it.

He learned to bookmark people, to dog-ear pages of their memory, to make them forget things that happened, remember things that never happened, to accept the unacceptable, to do the unthinkable.

And he watched himself carefully. He understood it was tit-for-tat - by practicing on others he gave others the right to practice on him.

But how else could he learn, develop?

It terrified him: was there someone - no, more than one. Others - out there practicing on him? Had he been bookmarked? Was there someone somewhere, somewhere close by, laughing at him, mocking him? He checked himself for slight forgetfulnesses, for barely noticeable miscalculations, for tiny errors in judgment.

He practiced in slow, precise steps, always listening for silent laughter. He did bigger and bigger things, each day a little more, not too much, always careful, to determine his limits.

Bookmarking everyone who knew he killed Martin Crescengi. That was a bigger thing. That stretched his limits.

Martin Crescengi was Andy Crescengi's older brother by ten years. Andy was a prick but more so an idiot. He copied his big brother the best he could but never acquired Martin's skill at humiliation and Earl was Martin's favorite target. Martin was a coward with his fists but he was a Friday Night fighter with his words. Mr. Crescengi died in Viet Nam. Andy never knew him but Martin did. Everybody spoke well of Mr. Crescengi. Earl wondered, if Mr. C was so cool, how did Martin become such a prick?

One day Earl went over to Andy's house to get some homework. The Crescengi's old, rusted blue Fairlane was parked half-in, half-out of their garage, the front end inside and supported about a foot and a half off the ground by a hand-pumped hydraulic jack. Martin rolled on a creeper underneath it in the cool of the garage. The warm engine smell and steady, syrupy, puddling sound told Earl Martin was changing the oil. He didn't have any safety jacks under the frame or chockblocks under the tires, though.

Stupid.

"Is Andy home?"

"Hey, it's Piss and Shit Pangiosi. How you doing, Piss and Shit?"

"I have to get some homework from Andy. Is he here?"

"I don't know, Piss and Shit. But don't go in our backyard. We don't have any towels back there. You might have to clean something up."

Earl walked out of the garage and looked up and down the street.

Nobody. He came back in and surveyed the garage walls. The Crescengis didn't have a yard so the garage walls held no rakes, no shovels, no hoses, no mowers; nothing that smelled of grass or anything green. Only the smells of cars and engines and oil.

"Maybe I should call you 'Little Dick'. Isn't that what they call you in gym class? The Dobbie twins said you had the littlest dick of anybody in the class. Little Dick Pangiosi."

"You shouldn't talk to me like that."

"Sounds like an Indian name, doesn't it? Little Dick? 'Tonto, take Little Dick and find the sheriff.'"

A big tool chest at the head of the garage caught Earl's attention. Some big wrenches in it. A ball-peen hammer.

"I heard your mother call you a bastard once." He laughed. "She would know. You didn't get that red hair and fucked up eyes from anybody around here. You ain't the milkman's kid."

"Stop it."

Earl looked at Martin's legs sticking out from under the car.

"Your momma must've really stepped out the night she made you, Piss and Shit."

The last of the oil plopped into the drain pan. Earl walked to the front of the car and pulled back the jack's safety pins.

"What are you doing?"

"Good bye, Martin."

He opened the jack's release valve.

The car descended.

Earl got on his hands and knees on the cool, damp concrete garage floor and smiled into Martin's face as the ton-plus of rusted blue car crushed the life out of him. "Don't make a sound, Martin. You talk too much as it is."

Something occulted Earl's view for a moment. Had oil spilled on Martin's face?

"Oh! Hello. How have you been? Where have you been? What are you?"

The air winked. An impenetrable darkness. An Icelin.

It crawled under the car next to Martin. The light went out of Martin's eyes and Earl tasted the same taste he got from long ago driving home with his parents on a near-winter night: despair.

When the blood flowed freely from Martin's nose and ears and mouth and Earl couldn't hear any more ribs or other bones cracking, he ran out of the garage.

"Help! Help!"

Andy and his mom came first. She screamed. Andy pumped the jack. He didn't check the valve. He stood there pumping like he was at a well dying of thirst. Earl could hear the cylinder gasping for air from the street.

People came running. They started talking. They looked at Earl and Earl smiled.

He was precise. He was methodical. He bookmarked them all.

He had a headache for two days afterward.

"Son, you're getting a lot of headaches lately. I'd like us to go see a doctor. Make sure everything's okay."

To be honest, Earl didn't know his father loved him enough to notice. Or cared.

He never bookmarked his dad. Or paid much attention to him. He was always just kind of there. Like a lake or river. You didn't question where they came from or how they got there, they were just there and you used them or not as needs dictated.

But Dad was bigger than a lake or river. More like an ocean. Except his father never had any storms. Always just smooth sailing. Sometimes a light breeze. He appreciated his father's evenness, levelness.

"Could be your heterochromia iridis, Earl," the ophthalmologist said. "Your different color eyes. Doesn't seem likely but let's start with the obvious and work back. I'll prescribe caffeine-ergot for the head-aches and how about some tinted contacts for your eyes."

Earl took the caffeine-ergot once as an experiment. Too groggy. He liked being sharp.

But the contacts were a plus. People stopped noticing him. He could be subtle.

Nice.

"EARL, DO YOU REMEMBER VINCE KOHL? FROM WORK?
We ran into him at the hardware store a while back? He's been attending that new church over in Mount Pleasant. Asked if we'd like to meet him there some Sunday. What'd'you say?"

Earl remembered Miss Turgeon and the Bleeding Heart of Jesus. "Sure, Dad. I'd like that."

Church people interested Earl. He wanted none of them as friends but these people, young and old, talked about the things he could do. In their prayers, their hymns, their books, their meetings, ...

Jesus, the Apostles, the Prophets. These people could do what Earl could do.

But the church people only wanted to talk. Anybody able to actually do these things terrified them. Actually do these things and you were in league with the Devil, a covener of Friendly Angels.

"Friendly Angels"?

Earl loved the terms they used at church.

Angels, friendly or otherwise, fascinated him. Earl's little Angels of Despair - his little Iceli of absolute, impenetrable darkness first seen long, long ago, seen again driving back that late Fall night, last seen when Martin gasped his last breath under the car, ... - seemed twinned to most everyone who attended. Didn't the church give people hope?

They certainly used that word a lot.

EARL AND DAD PUT IN A SMALL GARDEN OUT BACK.
One day, Dad asked, "You think Ms. Forester would like some vegetables?" He had a faraway look in his eyes. It was the first time Earl actually saw a "faraway look". He'd read about it, now he saw it.

Did someone bookmark Dad and Earl didn't know it?

"You can ask her tomorrow at church, Dad."

Dad blushed. A southern Italian, dark skinned, tanned from the sun, and he blushed. "Oh, I...I don't know...I"

"I'll ask her."

"That'd be nice, son. That'd be a nice, friendly thing to do."

Earl wanted Dad to be happy.

More than that, he wanted to make sure Dad hadn't been bookmarked.

That wouldn't be right. Dad was his. If anybody was going to bookmark him, it would be Earl. There were rules to these kinds of things.

Earl desperately wanted there to be rules to these kinds of things.

COLD AND SHY AT FIRST, MS. FORESTER HAD NEVER been married and never known a man. First, she was willing to know Dad. Earl discovered Dad liked it early and often so Ms. Forester liked it early and often, too.

When Earl saw Dad was happy, Ms. Forester - Miriam - was willing to be married.

One night over dinner his dad and new mom Miriam asked, "Have you ever thought about college, Earl?"

"Not really, no." Earl, now a high school junior, didn't say, "I can bookmark people to do and get what I want. I've been bookmarking my teachers for years. You never see me study, do you? What'll college get me that I can't get already?"

Instead he said, "I mean, I'm not sure what I'd get out of it."

"There's a college the church uses to get pastors," Miriam said. "They teach more than Bible, though."

Dad said, "Think of all the new people you'd meet. People from all over the world, probably. It's a great opportunity."

From all over the world?

Earl considered. Time to grow, explore, expand?

"Sure. I'd love to go." He paused. He'd kept his angels away from his parents, out of his house. But kids at school talked about college. It was expensive. When they talked, Earl's angels gathered. He didn't want that here. "What'll it cost?"

"The church can get you a scholarship. Just keep your grades up."

He bookmarked some of the people at church. His angels flocked when he bookmarked someone. At least his angels appreciated his skill, his talent, his constant striving to improve.

AN ADMINISTRATION SECRETARY STOOD IN THE doorway to Earl's Psychology of Social Perception and Cognition class. She cleared her throat and Professor Reid turned from his blackboard.

"Yes, Ms. McCarthy?"

"I need to see Mr. Pangiosi."

It was Earl's dad. Pancreatic cancer, advanced.

Miriam sat at Dad's bedside in the hospital room.

Dad said, "Give us a minute, would you, love?" He took Earl's hand. "You're doing well at college."

"Yes."

"Don't."

"Beg pardon?"

"Don't stand out. Don't draw attention to yourself. Draw attention to yourself and somebody starts paying attention. They start expecting things. You have to start doing things. Just do your twenty-five years, keep your head down, get your gold watch and get out."

This was the philosophy of the man who loved him? Who reared him? Who never questioned his first wife, Earl's mother, walking out one day for no reason at all with nothing but the clothes on her back? She never even touched their bank accounts. She left all their personal papers in the house.

Get your gold watch and get out? Only to learn there's a ticking time bomb in your gut that you didn't know about?

Why make plans?

Earl's angels floated around him, through his father's hospital room, kept watch over new mom Miriam pacing in the hall.

Alarms sounded over dad's bed.

Nurses rushed in. Somebody escorted Earl out.

A week later Dad was in the ground, in his best three-piece suit, new shoes, clutching his gold watch.

Earl unbookmarked new mom Miriam. Her nose started bleeding.

The look in her eyes fascinated him.

"Do you feel like you've woken from a dream?"

She stared at him. Nothing else. Not her surroundings, not her house. Only him.

"Do you know who I am, Miriam?"

An intense stare. Brow furrowed, eyes tight with tension, cheeks aflame, teeth clenched, nostrils flared.

"Would you like a Bleeding Heart of Jesus, Miriam?"

He walked her to a hallway mirror. "Don't you think you look like those people with dementia, the ones who come back, so to speak, for a moment or two before slipping away again? You know, that look in their eyes when they realize they've been gone for a while and might quickly go again. It's that 'what's going on here?', a 'where am I? how did I get here?' look. A 'who are you?' look."

Blood covered the front of her blouse. Blood dripped from her ears to her shoulders.

"Do you wonder where you've been for the past five years, Miriam?"

She fell to the floor, dead. A severe brain hemorrhage, an intraparenchymal bleed.

Earl wrote in his journal, "Holding a bookmark too long or releasing it too quickly can cause problems (Oops!). Find out which.

"PS) Test Dad's hypothesis."

EARL SLOWLY LOWERED HIS GRADES. HE SPENT LESS time bookmarking his professors and more time practicing with dorm and classmates. Dean, for example. Tall, thin, sandy-haired, quick with a smile, bespectacled Dean.

Earl and Dean both lived on Erans 3E: Erans Hall, third floor, East. The dorm had three levels on each side. The dorm was crowned by a Rec Room with knee-high to ceiling windows, one side looking out to the campus, the other to a beautiful copse of trees and the highway beyond. At least once a day, Dean walked down the dorm halls calling out, "Anybody want to play ping-pong? Take a break? Anybody?"

Freshman year lots of people played. Sophomore year Dean walked down the dorm halls calling out, "Oh, come on. Don't be a wuss. Play a game."

Junior year the only people Dean could con into a game were freshman and transfers who hadn't gotten word; Dean didn't play a friendly game.

You could hear the uninitiated calling out their scores. "One-Eighteen, Dean! One-Eighteen!", "One-Seventeen, Dean! I've got you, Dean!", sometimes even "Woa, Deano, One-Twenty! I should'a put money on the game!"

Then Dean scored and scored and scored as unrelenting as the waves on a beach or the moon in its orbit.

And not close-oh-you-almost-got-it shots. Dean was SkyLab to his opponents' Estes Model Rocket.

Two years of watching Dean play and never an unexpected outcome. Those slow to learn played again and again. Dean allowing them closer and closer, his smile broader and quicker with each finishing stroke.

Earl's Iceli feasted on Dean's opponents. Did Dean know what he was doing, destroying hope through a simple game? It was one thing to use guns and bombs to destroy entire villages and cultures at a time, but to use a simple ping-pong paddle? To humiliate someone and call it friendship? To destroy someone's hope while talking about love and peace and brotherhood?

And to do it all one person at a time.

Dean was surgical.

Hitler, Pol Pot, Ceaușescu, they could learn something from him.

Earl dreamed. He never dreamed. For as long as he could remember, no dreams.

But now he dreamed of a black wolf, old, its fur splotchy, mangy, its eyes bloodshot, standing on skinny legs, undernourished. It stared at him and breathed heavily like his dad did in the last moments of his life, each breath an agony, each breath a necessity.

Earl tripped over his own feet and fell to the ground. Gray. Cold on his hands. It was rocking, swaying. Sloshing sounds. Water lapping? A brine smell made him sneeze. He stood, his feet wide to steady himself and still he swayed with the movements of the...iceberg?

Where was he? Where was this? So vivid, so real. An ice sheet, surrounded by water?

Surrounded by the ocean.

His breath misted, the air so cold his lungs ached with each breath. The cold bit through his slippers and sent tendrils crawling like ants up his legs, over his knees, up his thighs.

Winds came from every direction, battling each other. He pulled his bathrobe tighter to no avail.

Is this what all dreams are like? Is this how other people dream?

Not according to his readings. He could see, taste, touch, feel, hear, smell everything.

The sky was clear but black, no moon, no stars, no lights from anything anywhere in the sky. The wind continued howling, battering, out of control, confused.

The wind is confused?

Earl looked for the wolf. Where had it gone?

It never left. It's still there, now huge. The sky is not black, it is the wolf's coat. The winds are not howling, it is the wolf breathing.

The wolf is drooling, its spittle falling like a cold, killing rain. It's panting, hungry.

Earl sees them. His little Iceli, like lupine remora cleaning dead skin from the wolf's drooling lips, hovering, nipping, sucking up the wolf's saliva, gnats on an open wound.

Earl reached up. He touched a hair of the great wolf's fur. Hard, thick, wizened, like a tree trunk. Lifeless. He touched one of the wolf's legs, like a pillar, gaunt. The wolf's drool washed over him like a river and Earl felt himself in the presence of a god.

Somebody was clapping their hands and laughing in the hallway. "You've got to see this! Dean's getting creamed in the Rec Room."

Earl opened his door as a rush of people flowed past.

Dean was playing ping-pong with some kid. Earl didn't know who the kid was. He didn't live on 3E. Dark skinned, long, black braid.

Who wears their hair in a long braid anymore?

Dean's sweat dripped from his nose onto the table. He stood in an athletic stance, on the balls of his feet, his paddle in front of him, one hand white-knuckled to the handle, the other white-knuckled to the blade, his eyes fixed on the ball the kid tossed into the air.

"Come on."

"You sure, Dean? I mean, it's been deuce game for, what, thirty minutes now?"

The kid hadn't broken a sweat. The windows were open and the room was cool.

"Come on come on."

"We can close the windows, if you'd like. Maybe there's a cross breeze coming in, ruining your game?"

"Play."

"You want a towel? Wipe off your side of the table?"

Dean shook his head. "Doesn't matter. Just serve the damn ball."

Dorm Father Jory Parker said, "Watch your language, Dean."

Earl's Friendly Angels. They crowded around Dean. In all prior games they feasted on his opponents. Now they swarmed on Dean like flies on the dead.

Earl sidled over to Jory. "What's going on?"

"This kid's held Dean at Deuce for," he checked his watch and pulled back at what he saw. "Forty minutes now." He showed his watch to people craning their necks.

Earl smiled. "Who is he?"

"Never seen him before."

"What's he doing?"

Al Guerton, another Erans 3Eer, said, "What he's doing is not letting Dean win."

Somebody from Erans 2E called out, "Hey, Dean. Good game, huh?" People laughed.

The kid put the ball down on the table. He covered it with his paddle. "I'm done."

Dean's face flushed. "Come on. Just one more point. You can't quit now."

The kid said, "It's over, Dean."

The voice from 2E echoed, "Yeah, it's over, Dean. He could beat you anytime he wants."

Dean spun at the voice, his paddle head-height, pulled back in a fist. "Shut up!"

Jory Parker said, "Enough, gentlemen. The game's over, Dean. Or do I have to close the Rec Room?"

People left, most stopped to shake the kid's hand or pat his back or give him a word of thanks.

Not congratulations, thanks.

And the kid watched Dean the entire time, just watching, not smiling, not triumphant.

Kind of sad.

Rory said, "Help me close the windows, would you, Earl?"

The Rec Room emptied. Just Dean and the kid. And Earl, in a chair in the back, quiet, wondering.

Dean said, "Everybody's gone. Come on. One more point. Winner take all."

The kid shook his head.

"Why not?"

"Because you don't know how to win."

"What are you talking about? I always win."

"That's the point. You're the best player on campus. You're yards better than anybody here. But you never teach anybody how to play better, how to offer you a really good game. You win and never let anybody else win."

"What's wrong with that?"

Earl wondered the same thing. What's wrong with that?

"Because of the way you win. You give them hope then snatch it away. It's not the winning you enjoy, it's the snatching away of hope, shattering dreams, seeing people despair at something as simple as a game of ping-pong, that gives you pleasure. You don't want a good game, you want to destroy the hope of winning."

Earl leaned forward. Who was this kid? How could he know this? Only Earl could know this.

Dean said, "You're crazy."

The kid laughed. It seemed he came off the floor, as if his laughter gave him wings. "If that's all I am I count myself lucky. But you. You, Dean." The kid shook his head, turning to leave. "I don't know what happened to you as a kid, but it must have twisted you bad."

Dean's athletic stance became more pronounced: tenser, tighter, coiled, a serpent ready to spring. He kept the paddle in front of him, chest height, a shield. His eyes widened at the kid and his voice traveled from deep in his chest to high in his nose. "Shut up."

Dean's paddle smashed into the wall behind the kid's head.

The kid turned. "What is it about shattering dreams...snatching away hope..." The kid's eyes narrowed but his body relaxed, his focus on Dean. "I mean, exactly..." His eyes closed but he moved his head around like a searchlight penetrating the dark.

The dark around Dean.

As if looking at Earl's Angels. Counting them.

Earl's nostrils flared. Blood tinted his face. His teeth clamped together like prison walls. Those are my angels! You keep your damn hands off!

"...because you have no hope so others can't?" The kid's face scrunched up. He kept sweeping his head back and forth, his eyes closed.

Earl sat forward. Nobody ever talked like that, nobody ever said things like that. Earl's angels hovered over Dean and Earl hadn't done a thing.

What's this kid doing? What's he looking for?

"Ah, okay, there it is." The kid's face relaxed. He licked his lips. His nostrils flared and he inhaled deeply. His eyes remained closed but he smiled. "Found it."

Found what?

"You and your brothers...your parents thought the only good hope was Biblical hope? Is that it?"

More searching. "Nope, there's more. A little to the left."

To the left of what?

"You were never allowed to hope for anything outside what the Bible offered so now you can't let anybody else hope, even if it's winning a game of ping-pong?"

The kid's face reddened, tightened. He clenched his hands but not into fists, more like he reached for something without moving his arms, something he wanted to hold in his hands.

Dean's head shook, more like a vibration took hold of it, a vibration he couldn't control. His eyes welled up with tears.

"No. It's that you want their hopes. You...consume them. Like food. The truth is you don't want to beat them, you just don't want them to hope because you don't want them to hurt the way you do. Did. So you consume their hopes thinking the frustration here is better than the crying later."

The kid opened his eyes, his body relaxed, he stared at Dean. He spoke, his voice softer, tender, caring, loving, giving. "Oh, Dean. I'm so sad for you."

Dean consumed hope? Dean was a human Icelin?

The kid picked up Dean's paddle, tossed it to him, then turned to Earl. "Don't you think that's sad, Earl, that Dean can't let anybody hope?"

Earl's Angels...one of them left Dean and floated over to him slowly, lazily, like a dandelion puff blown on a gentle wind.

"No!"

"See, Earl? Even you need hope."

Earl's rage quelled to fear. After all these years, wondering if somebody practiced on him?

Whoever this kid was, whatever he could do, he could do it better than Earl. To see that far into someone that quickly? And not even bookmark them?

The kid had eyes like Earl's, only reversed. Right blue, left brown.

The kid went back to the ping-pong table. He picked up his paddle, looked at the ball underneath, held the paddle, deciding, then put it back down, covering the ball, stilling it on the table. "I give you a gift, Dean. I give you knowledge of yourself. Now it's your decision what you do with it."

Dean didn't move. Dark angels left him. Ones, Twos and now and again in Threes. Coming to Earl. To hover over him. To fall on him. Like drool from some gigantic maw.

Earl must know The Kid. Understand him. Must...

Must bookmark him.

Earl focused on the kid.

The Dark Angels stopped, hovered, winked in and out, back and forth, which way to go? What to do?

Earl used the *knack*.

He hit a wall so hard his nose bled.

Just one drop.

The kid faced Earl and laughed.

Slowly shook his head and laughed.

"Now you'll have to figure out if your greatest fear was that someone else could do it, or that someone else *like you* could do it."

The Kid left.

Dean shook his head violently, as if waking from a too-real dream. His face pulsed red in rhythm to the beating of his heart. White fingers clenched his paddle tight against his chest.

But it was the look in Dean's eyes. Like the look in Earl's new mom Miriam's eyes.

Earl ran after The Kid. "Where'd that fellow go who just left the Rec Room?"

People shook their heads. "Who?"

He turned in the other direction. "Albert, Scott, anybody see the fellow who just left the Rec Room?"

He raced to the foyer. "Did someone just come through here? A kid? Another student? Young. Where did he go?"

Back to the Rec Room. Empty. Nothing. Nobody. Not even the

scent of too many bodies in a too warm room.

The Kid disappeared. Nobody knew who he was or saw him come or go. It seemed, like the lightness of his laughter, he went around some corner, grew wings, and flew away.

Earl went to a window facing the college quad and scanned the students walking between buildings, between classes, between futures and pasts. No dark features, no long braid.

To the other side. Nada. Zip. Zero.

Earl's Dark Angels hovered. His mother - his real mother, not Miriam - looking out a third story window told him, "Make people believe they can get what they want and they'll follow it to their own destruction." Earl was a toddler then, not even three if he remembered correctly. He saw his first Icelin, his first Dark Angel then.

Since then, Earl never dreamed. He could remember his dreams if he had any. He had more than enough discipline for that.

Then the Ragged Wolf dream.

Now The Kid.

Earl wrapped his arms around himself, hugging, rubbing his arms against a chill.

Hide. Make sure they can't find you.

Dad was right: Don't stand out. You'll get noticed. Somebody'll pay attention. The end result isn't always what you counted on.

EARL SPENT THE START OF HIS SENIOR YEAR REPLAY-ing The Kid's "hopes and dreams" conversation with Dean. His grades dropped to mediocre and stayed there. He studied "hopes and dreams" the best he could without drawing attention to himself.

Professor Reid found him alone in the college library stacks one time, going through the psych shelves. "I didn't know you were inter-ested in this stuff, Mr. Pangiosi."

Earl often wondered about Professor Reid. The other professors spoke his name as if it were an ethnic slur, PAN-G-O-C, giving each syllable equal weight and emphasis, always with the hint of "My time is valuable and you're not. What do you want?"

But not Professor Reid. Earl always felt there was a hidden capital-S Sir when Professor Reid spoke his name, a "Mr. Pangiosi, Sir."

Reid pointed at the books crooked in Earl's arm. "May I?"

He glanced at the spines. "Mahdi? Pearson? Thompson, Radziwill, Wierzbicka? Impressive reading list, Mr. Pangiosi."

Sir.

Earl readied to bookmark him.

Reid pulled a 3x5 notecard out of his sport coat's inside pocket along with a pen. "Here." He scribbled down some names. "These are the people you want to read." He drew a line. "And these are the people you want to meet. Most of them are in Cambridge. MIT and Harvard." He made a star next to a name. "She's at Tufts in Medford." Then another. "Brandeis. There's others, of course. These people will know of others."

"Why are you doing this?"

"I wanted to become a doctor, not a psychologist, did you know that? Focused on brain hemorrhages. Couldn't stand the biology, though, the cadavers. I remember one case, this was years ago, about a librarian, a Miss Turgeon."

Earl stiffened.

"Fascinating case. Complete blowout of the subarachnoid space in her brain. Blood and cerebrospinal fluid in places they had no right to be. No medical reason. Healthy as anything and then one day she's working in the stacks," he stopped and glanced around him, "and boom, she drops, goes vegetative and dead all in a few minutes."

Earl's hand went to his glasses.

"Read the report. Your name's in it. Or someone with your name from your home town who'd be the same age as you."

Reid handed Eart the 3x5 card. "I don't believe in coincidences, Mr. Pangiosi."

Sir.

Reid backed away, keeping his eyes on Earl until he rounded a corner.

A pneumatic door hissed shut. Earl, card in hand and books back in the crook of his arm, went to the window. Reid hurried across the soccer field to the faculty parking lot, looking over his shoulder as he ran. Halfway he pulled a handkerchief from a pocket and dabbed his nose. He slowed, dabbing more. He got to the berm and didn't look as he stepped off, didn't hear the car horn.

Earl doubted he felt the impact.

Earl read the card and smiled.

Rarely on campus the rest of that year, Earl borrowed dorm mates' cars and traveled far and wide to read books in special collections, to sit in on lectures and talk to people - "It's obvious social information is processed during desynchronized, dreaming sleep, but I can't find anything in *Science, Nature,* not even in journals like *The British Journal of Medical Psychology.*" "Mr. Pangiosi. Induced narcolepsy, REM Behavior Disorder, status dissociatus, impaired state boundaries, hypnopompic and hypnagogic hallucination? Study something practical for god's sake."

It sounded like "Mr. PAN-G-O-C has *sen*-si-*tive eye*-eyes."

A month to graduation, Earl exhausted Reid's list and Reid's list's lists. Where to find the resources necessary to continue his research?

Some dorm mates held up the cafeteria line looking over a bulletin board. Albert said, "Hey, Earl. Guess who's coming to dinner."

A listing of dates and times of visiting recruiters.

His eyes followed Albert's pointing finger.

He smiled.

THE DARK ROOM DIDN'T INTIMIDATE HIM. THE hushed voices didn't bother him. The quiet susurrations of cool air comforted him. The clicking of keyboards and tapping of screens tickled his fancy; it sounded like a science fiction symphony, an auditory establishing shot, a way of signaling the moviegoer what to expect when the screen lit up, the menacing tubas and cellos of *Jaws,* the sweeping overtures of *Star Wars.*

What bothered him was not knowing how he came to their attention. He'd followed his father's advice: stay low, go slow.

He'd stayed low and gone slow for two years when, sitting in his small, windowless office, he received a TXT from an account he couldn't backtrace. Too many blocks and if he enlisted others, flags would be raised. Three men appeared at his office door at the appointed time. One tall and shaved bald stood on Earl's right. To Earl's left stood a short, flat-faced man. Between them stood another man, average looking compared to the other two if you didn't notice his exquisitely tailored suit.

One too tall, one too short, the other just right?

How did they become aware of him?

The just right man took the lead. "Come with us, please." He turned and started walking, not waiting for a reply. Too-tall and too-short came up slightly behind on either side.

Earl followed through doors he didn't know existed, down corridors curving in bizarre angles. He looked along walls, ceilings, floors for guides, markers, passageway names, indicators, differences in lighting.

How do they know where to go? What route are they following? What are they seeing I'm not seeing?

The just right man started talking. Not to Earl, not to too-tall and not to too-short, just talking. "Be too average and someone will notice you excel at nothing. Everybody has one, perhaps two things they do better than others, a bit better, just enough better so people can label them. Jim's a good golfer. Betty makes one hell of a cheesecake. Tony can't change a light bulb without blowing every fuse in the house."

They paused at a door at the end of a dark hallway. No markings on it, no labels. "People will dismiss you once they give you a label. Put you in a box on a shelf and forget you. But someone with no pluses or minuses? A person that doesn't fit in a box? That person stands out in their mediocrity and intentional mediocrity is difficult to maintain. Sooner or later, someone will notice. Sometimes the right person will notice."

He turned from the door and faced Earl dead on. "You, Mr. Pangiosi, got noticed."

The door opened.

People sat in the shadows on the far side of a crescent shaped table. He saw silhouettes against a darkness.

Who were these people? The living embodiments of his angels?

"Mr. Pangiosi," a woman's voice. At least a feminine voice. Higher pitch, smaller larynx. Confident, though. No false bravado. Someone aware of what they could do.

"Yes?"

"May we call you Earl?"

"Yes."

"You have special skills, Mr. Pangiosi."

Why ask to call me 'Earl' then return to 'Mr. Pangiosi'? Have I been bookmarked?

"No comment, Mr. Pangiosi?"

"Thank you."

"Many people mentioned you."

Many?

A new voice, a male voice. Basso Profundo. But hollow. A thin man, probably tall. Six-foot plus. He could almost hear the soundchamber of the chest shaking as the man spoke. Not a strong man, not a physically powerful man. "Let us play a game, Mr. Pangiosi."

Silence. A screen lit up. Earl caught a reflection: glasses, long hair, aquiline face, no lines or creases.

A she.

Earl couldn't guess an age. Might be due to the screen light. What does she look like in normal light?

Earl stared. The face wasn't where the woman's voice came from. There were two women in here? In authority positions?

What group was this?

Another male voice, left of center of the table. Mellow. But a catch in the breathing. An older man? The *shoosh* of an inhaler. An asthmatic?

"Mr. Pangiosi?"

Earl turned to the voice. "Yes?"

"A game, Mr. Pangiosi."

"Yes."

A chuckle around the table. "You keep yourself to yourself, Mr. Pangiosi."

He waited, not acknowledging with a nod, a wink, not even a breath. Another chuckle.

Earl stood motionless. Was this the game? See who would talk first?

Another voice. New. From the right corner of the room, behind him. "Mr. Pangiosi?"

How large was this room? Was he in an auditorium unawares? Was he center stage, on display and unawares?

One more voice. The final voice. A voice or real power, real authority, from the center of the table. "You research in highly specialized fields, Mr. Pangiosi."

The voice was anatomically neutral. Earl couldn't guess the speaker's size, gender, ethnicity, anything. No hint of an accent. Geographically neutral. Well trained? Or mechanical.

If so, the best Earl ever heard.

Earl allowed himself an internal smile and cleared his throat. "We can weaponize dreams."

Again from the center of the table. "Mr. Jones."

From the right corner, "Do you have a name for this, Mr. Pangiosi?" The right corner had a name. Mr. Jones.

"Sandman."

A chuckle from the center of the table. Others joined in a moment later.

Again from the center, "Find out what he wants. Give it to him."

EARL STOOD UP AND OFFERED HIS SEAT, PILLOW, AND blanket to a young family entering the Snack Car. He stood out in his courtesy to others.

Back in his own car he poured himself a Macallan 1928, neat, from a small but formidable wet bar - he learned to savor good Scotches. There. Two things he excelled at. He was done - removed his sunglasses, folded the temples and placed them neatly in a gutter at the head of a well-appointed table running the length of his car's entrance room. He paced the length of the table, Macallan in hand, and gazed out windows disguised as gray, rusting exterior steel walls on both sides of the car. Earl could look out but none could look in. A single, green-shaded casino light hung on a chain from the ceiling and swayed with the movements of the train, swinging shadows back and forth against the mahogany paneled walls.

The table was made from some indefinite but definitely strong material and resembled a giant autopsy table, its purpose concealed by a tablecloth and some accountant's lamps. Chairs waited snug up against the table, their casters locked, keeping them motionless, allowing individuals to walk by on either side without knocking into those who sat.

Passenger and freight manifests for the second leg of his journey waited for him in two neat piles at the head of the table. He always asked for such manifests. He liked to know with whom and what he travelled.

Ringing the table were equally neat stacks of the Chicago trials' reports. Each subject's report individually shrinkwrapped and sealed with a wax relief of his name, thumbprint and title: NSA SubChief, Research, Neurosciences, Oneirological Studies, Sandman Project.

Each report was flash coded with his NSCID number. Open any package without proper identification and you'd be holding ash before you broke the seal.

Earl let the Macallan's sweet heat burn down his throat and smiled. How many tens if not perhaps hundreds of millions had been spent because he, Earl Pangiosi, said "We can weaponize dreams"?

The Deputy Directorate loved the idea. "Think of it!" she said, her eyes wide with possibilities. "Weaponize dreams! Imagine! Don't want a people to war? Have the entire nation dream that war will be disastrous. Want them to elect this candidate over that one? Have them dream this one's good and that one's bad. Want them to buy a certain car, phone, or coffee? Have them dream the desired product will make them better, stronger, able, and worthy."

Earl wondered if she'd been bookmarked. She never noticed him before. Now she practically offered to have his children.

"I'll start in Chicago."

She smiled and winked as she got out of bed. "Keep me apprised."

He set up his lab and showed his subjects DVDs of games, people playing, sports, at work, copulating; with all manner of body language, views, movements, close ups of body parts. Each subject had micro-electrodes implanted into single cells in select brain regions, each part of a specific neural ensemble: amygdala, cortical, adjacent limbic, all processing emotions wrapped around social interaction information and all to be counter-processed during sleep.

But there were too many failures of too great a degree. The three Chief Directorates asked too many questions for him to continue.

He told his staff, "Shut it down. Total neutralization of all effects. I'll come by later to ensure clean closure."

He circled the table, tapping some folders, letting his empty hand slide over others, recognizing subjects by each report's case number.

Here was the little girl terrified of falling asleep.

"Whatever are you afraid of, child? Everyone sleeps."

She clung to Earl's vest like a spider monkey climbing a tree. "They'll come get me if I fall asleep."

Earl stroked her hair and kissed her forehead. "Who will come get you? Can you tell Uncle Earl what they look like?"

Snappy little shakes of the head, no.

"When was the first time you saw them?"

She didn't know. Time periods were too fluid to her. Nor did her history provide any information. What "they" were, how her psychosis originated, even what "they" looked like or how "they" behaved, no one could ever get from her. But she insisted if she fell asleep again "they" would come and take her away. Forever.

"Give her biogenic amines, a full spread. Use dermal apps."

Whenever her skin temperature or galvanic response indicated her body cascading into sleep behavior, she would get enough norepinephrine, dopamine, and serotonin dumped into her body to create a fight/flight/fright response conducive of convulsive state seizures.

"Make sure you patch her scalp. Weave her hair through the apps if you have to."

A four-year-old blonde bonnet of a child with a patch load of every third inch. The only place she didn't have patches were her mouth, her eyes, her nostrils, her ears, her vagina, and her anus.

"Build her a playground. Improvise something."

Earl played with her, getting her so tired her body avalanched into sleep state. She'd start to fall down then the amines would pass into her dermally. The increased neurotransmitter and neuromodulator levels forced a central nervous system reaction gradient and she'd jump three feet in the air, every muscle in her body visibly vibrating. The convulsions moved through her intramuscularly, like the blue fluid in a desktop wave-motion machine.

"God, this is beautiful to watch, isn't it? It's like an ambulatory rainbow, don't you think?"

But she couldn't last like that and Earl didn't want to give up his toy just yet. "Remove the dermals. Hydrate and salinize it. Give it a week and a half to clean itself out and cycle its blood to remove anything its body isn't producing itself."

He came to her each day to brush her hair and talk to her and bring her games.

"The urine tests are returning pure and the blood is clean. Start monoamine inhibitors and fluoxetine. I received a note about a highly experimental tricyclic antidepressant. I'll forward the info to you. Add that to the cocktail. That little body and precocious mind might have taught themselves never to sleep."

She drifted off with the most adorable little snores before the needle was removed.

But the little bitch continued to drift off. She never came back.

Earl, sitting on her bed all the while, shrugged as his team came in. "I guess she was right. 'They' came for her after all."

"What shall we do, Sir?"

"Get rid of it, naturally."

That nameless little girl was mistake number 1.

He put his empty glass down on mistake number 2's report and fetched the bottle.

Leyden? Leyman? Earl couldn't remember mistake number 2's name. Leyden-Leyman demonstrated a similar psychosis to the little girl except his 'they' took form; black, shadowy beings - creatures he dubbed "Midnight Men" - came and talked to him in his sleep.

Little black shapes? Could someone else see Earl's Iceli, his Dark Angels? His Dark Angels never talked. Was Leyden-Leyman more their intimate than he?

Leyden-Leyman woke in the dark of the night, sweating, rigid, a tightness in his bladder he slept through on other nights. His eyes opened wide and probed each nuance of shadow until he caught a movement across the room, something coming out of the closet, something coming towards him, something shaped like a child-sized man. He screamed for his wife with a voice softer than cats walking on thick carpet.

Ah, not his Dark, Despairing Angels. They didn't have the shape of men, child-sized or otherwise.

Curious, Earl invited Leyden-Leyman to repeat the things being said. Whatever Leyden-Leyman was imagining, he gave his Midnight Men quite a vocabulary. Vocables from all language families but few recognizable words. Language Division postulated languages not spoken in centuries, possibly millennia.

"Could we have him, Earl? For just a little while? The man's created a one-sided idioglossia so rich it's damning. It's as if someone's trying to teach him a new language 'through a glass darkly', as they say."

Leyden-Leyman's somnapsychosis produced paralytic fear, his heart breaking through his ribs and tears filling his eyes as he lay there, unable to move as the Midnight Men approached. They came to him, stood next to him, leaned over him and whispered something that couldn't quite be heard: a social interaction in which the processing was annulled. He sobbed, he wanted to scream to wake his wife and couldn't.

Instead he let his bladder go.

She'd move sharply in her sleep, sit up, shake him even as he let his urine flow. His face and body would remain stiff, his muscles so tight veins and arteries lined his neck, arms, chest, and face. He'd look at her, his eyes like an animal's and his face white.

She'd put her arms around him, cover him with her self, protect him from the bullets, from the swords, from the dragons, the nightmare monsters, offer herself to the attack that never came. He'd quake for a moment then, as she rested on him, he'd catch his breath and let go a child's scream.

In all accounts and in all ways Leyden-Leyman was a healthy individual. Neither psychological nor physical trauma at any point in his life. No military duty. An uneventful childhood followed by an uneventful adolescence followed by an uneventful adulthood - My god! This man could've been my father! - He voted regularly, had a good job, was a good father, a member of the PTA and PTO. Had no physical or neurological problems.

"What causes this seemingly average person to experience such things out of nowhere and for no rational reason? Let's start with an increasing regimen of hypnotics." Earl handed his operations chief a neurotopograph with areas marked off. "Start at normal mental activity but shunt these brain regions."

That brought unsatisfactory results. Leyden-Leyman wasn't able to bring on his somnapsychosis.

"Inhibit some neurotransmitters. One way or another this fellow is going to dream his most frightening dreams."

Nothing.

Earl tested Leyden-Leyman through anxiety relief, disinhibition - which was a riot. Leyden-Leyman may have had a dull life but his fantasies were among the best - to sedation, hypnosis, general anesthesia, coma...Leyden-Leyman clinically died three times before his somnapsychosis demonstrated itself.

But then, like the little girl, it was too late. Leyden-Leyman had ridden the rollercoaster of hypnotics so many times he couldn't describe what caused him to become rigid with fear, so rigid he had to be placed on a respirator because his lungs would not fill with air. Brain activity remained but at such an agitated state nothing could be made of it. The only parts of him left on the table were his terror and his reaction to it.

Failure number two.

"Put him in a home somewhere. Give it some time, then pull the plug. And bring me the RH Emotional-Empathy Test results."

"Yes, sir."

Two days later, Earl emerged from the Chicago facility's private suite, printouts in hand. "In all these cases, failures and otherwise, there's a boundary, a border between hope and despair. Complex but it's there, as if multi-dimensional landscapes exist and dreams serve as the gateway. Social interaction gets you there but dreams allow you passage through, from one to the other."

Earl smiled at his realization, a kid with a new toy.

"That's why dreams are so socio-emotionally active!"

His staff nodded.

"I've developed a questionnaire which may be useful in selecting subjects. Use the involuntary recruitment program."

His staff chorused, "Yes, sir."

That brought in failure number three, Eleanor MacPherson. The involuntary recruitment selection protocols garnered homeless people from the street, clubs and bars via Ibogaine II, Ambien or Rohypnol, faux marketing surveys in local malls and, as was failure number three's case, faux routine traffic stops and police inspections.

They got some of their best subjects via the faux traffic stop protocol. Skilled recruiters could determine a target's fitness for a particular study within seconds.

Earl sipped his Macallan and flipped through her fifty-five page report with his free hand. One page held nothing but a brightly colored micro-SD card.

"All of our work, Ms. MacPherson, recorded for our review."

Earl tossed the card and caught it as if flipping a coin.

"You left us, Ms. MacPherson. You left us and I have no idea how you did it."

Some fool left her for a few minutes and she quite literally disappeared, on camera and while strapped to a dissection table, a stage magician's trick with no magicians to perform it.

"No security violations, no rescue attempts. Bio, thermal, and auditory sweeps reveal no hidden bodies, no wandering life forms."

Earl lifted the glass to his forehead and rested it there.

"How did you leave us, Ms. MacPherson? We never found a body. No stink of the dead, no proliferation of corpse eaters to suggest you'd crawled away somewhere and died in the facility. You didn't go home." He chuckled. "It's doubtful you'd recognize your home after what we'd done to you."

The bulk of the report chronicled the resulting investigation. They returned to her house, just in case she returned and left unnoticed. There was a dog and the disposal squad almost shot the damn thing because of the nuisance it caused. Thank goodness they called for instructions.

"Use butorphanol. There's some in the van. Make sure it survives. With no aftereffects. Understood?"

"Yes, sir."

Earl sighed. Where did you go, Ellie?

Her disappearance ended involuntary recruitment. He'd taken them from all over. None of them had disappeared before. True, he'd had some disappeared but those were technical disappearances. There were signatures and release forms and paper trails and chains-of-command should those disappeared, or perhaps their body, need to be found.

But Ellie MacPherson? She Cheshired right out of existence.

Earl closed and finalized the lab, the facility's appearance surgically returned to that of an abandoned warehouse in a rundown part of town.

He returned to the manifests for the second leg of his journey; from Chicago he would board the *Lake Shore Limited* and continue east. He backchannel funded a Dr. Capoçek Lupicen up at Dartmouth. Lupicen researched Charles Bonnet disease, humanish shapes that came in the night. Earl had a man up there, keeping tabs. Perhaps he had some answers.

He sliced open the passenger manifests and skimmed down the

names, stopped, and held the manifest closer. His eyes widened. He chuckled. He slammed the manifest down on the table and danced away, light on his feet, his arms up in the air embracing nothing at all, silently laughing, then danced back to the table, picked up the manifest, and checked the names a second time.

He picked up his phone. "I will need Nighthorse and Styles. We need to make some preparations."

Chapter 9

One Great Truth

Tom, Jamie, and Shem followed Jack through the upper level of the *Lake Shore Limited's* Superliner Snack Coach. "Come on, gang, it's not much further to the Viewliner. That's where we're sleeping." Some five steps behind them, a nurse and two attendants followed sipping root beers and munching potato chips from crinkling cellophane bags.

Tom sneezed at a sudden whiff of diesel fumes. Everyone stopped. With no rhyme or reason to his narcolepsy, everyone prepared for another cascade.

"I'm fine, I'm fine." His head fell forward and his eyelids fluttered. The attendants hurried forward as Tom straightened up. "Ha! Gotcha!"

Tom held his fists face level and moved them in a circle while singsonging "I gotCHA I gotCHA." Shem wagged his tail at the sudden activity. Jack shook his head and rolled his eyes. The attendants smiled.

Jamie remained silent.

Jack reserved the last Viewliner rooms for the seven of them. The one closest to the rear door and the diaphragm-engulfed platform between cars - Jack explained it prevented people jumping or falling from the train when they moved between the cars - was a bedroom suite for the attendants, base medical and ambulance grade EMT supplies and equipment. Jack took the furthest in-train of the four, a standard bedroom. Jamie, Shem, and Tom shared the next in-train, another bedroom suite. The nurse had the bedroom suite between the MacPhersons and the attendants. The suite also contained a Lexicor MedTech NeuroSearch-24, 19 AC-coupled amplifiers, an Autonomy's Frontalis recorder and more dedicated neuro diagnostics than most hospitals could afford.

Jack refused to take chances. When Tom slept, he demonstrated intermittent trains of rhythmic spiked morphology waves. Tom's body slept but not his brain. He closed his eyes and his fronto-orbital regions lit up like aircraft landing lights desperately seeking safe ground. When no such place appeared Tom's brain turned the lights on brighter, intent that some safe landing existed and waited to be found. That much neural horsepower required his autonomic nervous system to take over body functions completely. No distractions, nothing to interfere with the search. Not Jack, his team, nor anyone he shared the data with had seen anything like it.

Tom stopped at the door to his suite while Jamie and Shem walked in. He smiled at Jack. "Alas, to sleep. Perchance to dream."

Jamie, already in bed with Shem beside him, watched Tom clean up and get under the covers. He listened for changes in his father's breathing as Tom drifted off, wanting to be sure his father was there when he woke up, until the train's steady *ruddaRump ruddaRump ruddaRump* rocked him to sleep, Shem curled up beside him.

A COLD WIND BLEW ON JAMIE'S FACE AS THE STEADY *ruddaRump ruddaRump* reminded him of the train. His eyes opened to see the inside wall of his bunk. A tiny cloud of his breath caught in the moonlight flooding their suite. He lifted his hand into the light as if to hold onto it, to shake hands with it. His breath swirled around his pajama top's sleeve, almost forming a moonlit hand to welcome his.

"Somebody forgot to lower the blinds, Shem. Let me get up."

He rolled over to get out of bed.

The windows and the wall which held them were gone. In their place was a vast winter plain, a snow-covered whiteness, the landscape broken only by fasts of pine, winter oak, and scrub brush. Strong, bright moonlight cast hard edged shadows as the moon rose. Steady, chilling winds carried the musks of a winter's eve - far away campfires, clove and pine and mulling spices, something roasting on a spit, the scents of work well done - into the suite.

On the far side of the suite his father slept soundly. Jamie heard him breathe, heard little movements of comfort on his father's bed.

A great, gray wolf sat on the floor between his and his father's bunks. The wolf stared into Jamie's eyes, the moonlight showing one of the wolf's eyes dark, the other light.

Jamie's stomach tightened and he reached down to shake Shem awake.

Shem rolled onto his back and moaned, legs up in the air. He turned his muzzle towards the wolf and wagged his tail.

Shem and the wolf touched noses. The wolf said, "Hello, Little Brother."

"Who are you?" Jamie asked.

The wolf laughed. "Oh, now that would be telling."

"Don't hurt my dog."

"I wouldn't think of it. You are young, Jamie, but even you know there's no such a thing as a talking wolf. That tells you there's something special about me. Is there no way you can find out who or what I am?"

Slowly, shaking with more than the cold, Jamie reached into his pajama pocket and lifted the Gate to his eye. "Mr. Graywolf!"

"Graywolf, yes. Inside, always the same. Outside, whatever I need to be. Come now, Jamie. We have far to go."

Jamie put the Gate down. "But how do I know you're really Mr. Graywolf? He was a tall, skinny Indian. You're a wolf."

"Maybe yes, maybe no. Some of and some not. Things are not always as they appear. Names and faces change depending on times and places. Has the Gate ever shown you a lie?"

"No."

"Good. Look at me through the Gate again. What do you see?"

"A big wolf." Jamie lowered the Gate and Mr. Graywolf stood there, leaning over to rub Shem's belly. "Hey!"

"There are many truths, Jamie. You can see them all. Sometimes you'll encounter two truths that don't seem to go together. You'll know both are true but how can they be? They're different and don't belong together, like one can't be true if the other is."

Graywolf lowered himself to one knee so he and Jamie stared eye-to-eye. He held Jamie's arms in warm, tender hands. "But remember this, Jamie: there will always be one truth at the center that all the other truths come down to. No matter how confusing things seem, look for the one truth, the one great truth, that holds all the other truths together."

"What if I can't find it?"

Graywolf's hands slid to the floor and became paws. His body changed as he spoke. "Then at least one thing is a lie. Whatever one thing won't fit with all the other truths, no matter how much you need it to be true, that's the lie." Once again a great, gray wolf sat before Jamie. "Do you understand?"

"I think so."

"Good." The wolf got up. On all fours it stood taller than Jamie and almost twice as big as Shem. "Come, we must go while there is light."

"But it's night."

"Moonlight, Jamie. The kind that reveals truths unseen by day. Hurry, we must go."

No one felt the way he did about the night or moonlit skies. No one had ever said that to him before.

"Are you afraid?"

"Yes, sir."

The wolf stared at him a moment. "So am I," it said, then smiled.

"Can Shem come, too?"

"No, not this time. He has other journeys to take before we're done.”

Jamie patted Shem. “Good boy, Shem. Such a good dog. So good. Such a good boy.”

Shem rolled over and went back to sleep.

“What about my dad?”

The wolf said nothing but motioned him towards the arctic plain. A set of wolf tracks came from the far horizon and stopped at the suite, the tracks lit brighter than the rest of the snow, as if the moon cast herself upon them special.

He walked over to the missing wall. “Hey, we’re on a moving train! How did you do that? If I leave, how will I get back? Won’t the train move away if I’m not on it?”

The wolf smiled again. “We are and we aren’t. Here we’re on a moving train. There,” the wolf pointed his muzzle towards the serene, winter landscape, “we’re not. The train will continue on its journey as will you. Two truths, Jamie. Find their center. Don’t forget your bathrobe and slippers. It’s cold where we’re going.” Jamie grabbed the white robe from the shelf next to his bed and slipped on some fluffy bunny slippers tucked under his bunk.

At the edge of the suite, where a few snowflakes melted on the carpet, Jamie looked back at Shem, still sleeping on the bed.

“Shem and I always do things together. Not school, of course. But Shem walks me to the bus and back.”

“You should say good-bye, Jamie.”

“No.”

The wolf nodded. “But only for a little while. I promise.”

Jamie went back to Shem, put his arms around him, buried his face in the old dog’s fur. “You’re such a good dog, Shem. Such a good, good dog.”

Shem licked his face.

Graywolf said, “Come, Jamie.”

“Stay with Dad, Shem.” Tears froze with Shem’s lapping Jamie’s face. “Good-bye, Shem.”

Jamie followed the wolf to the path. The Aurora blazed and twisted far overhead, reaching down and dancing on the horizon.

"I should leave a note."

When he turned back, the train, everything he recognized, had disappeared.

"No time now, Jamie. We must hurry. Get on my back."

Jamie's hands moved through the wolf's heavy fur and its scent rose to greet him.

"Now hang on. Tight."

Jamie clung tight, his hands deep in the great wolf's coat, unsure of how long they'd travel, only aware of the smell and warmth of the fur, of Graywolf's steady breathing as he chased the night through cloudless, star-filled skies. He couldn't see the train anymore, nor cities, nor towns nor lights of any kind, only the white, snow-covered landscape and occasional clumps of trees they passed. The sky held more and brighter stars than he'd ever seen before. The Aurora crashed down on the horizon like waves on a beachhead of sky.

One clump of trees got closer and closer as Graywolf ran. When he braved the cold enough to do so, Jamie raised his head and noticed the trees from that clump were starting to fill the horizon. The Aurora came down into the thick of trees and not beyond them, as if shores of night existed where earth met the Arctic sky. A little closer and he realized the moonlit path entered that clump of trees, too.

"Is that where we're going?"

"Yes."

Jamie tucked deeper into Graywolf's fur, protecting himself against the cold, listening to Graywolf's steady breathing mixing with the wind rushing past them, the crackling of the snow as Graywolf's padded feet kept their steady *ruddaRump ruddaRump* rhythm, and his own breathing, his teeth chattering and the pounding of fear in his heart.

He strained, listening and not knowing what for, but hoping to hear sounds that would end the confusion: Dad nudging him to wake up, Shem woofing while he chased rabbits in his sleep, Mom...

But Mom was gone. Gone. Nobody could find her. Jamie even bet that Graywolf, his sometimes Indian sometimes great wolf friend, couldn't find her.

With the sounds of the cold arctic night he heard his own quiet sobs.

CHAPTER 10
Poppie

DR. CAPOÇEK LUPICEN SAT AT HIS DESK IN THE DARK, an oversized computer screen's dim afterglow lighting his face. His left hand arched over the keyboard, his long, thin fingers resting on a large red trackball. A switching panel stood to the right of the screen, its red lights reflecting off his glasses and making it appear that an ovoid-headed demon with large red eyes stared at him from his workstation. Other labs had virtual displays and keyboards. Dr. Lupicen preferred the human touch physical keyboards, screens, and trackballs afforded him.

A small, old, worn, black and white photograph in a silver frame held pride of place on his desk, standing between his keyboard and screen. Two boys with similar features, one about ten years older than the other, smiled out of the photograph. He'd check something on his screen then look at the two boys smiling out of the photograph, gently tap the older boy's face, smile, then return his gaze to the computer screen, as if confirming the screen's information with the boy in the picture.

He cupped his narrow chin in his right hand and reread what he entered in his journal, evaluating every sentence, every thought. He released his chin and cupped his ear, letting his fingers beat a mindless staccato on his short gray hair as words were considered, phrases whispered, accuracy determined. A passage dissatisfied him. He lifted his glasses from underneath and massaged his sharply etched pince-nez. Often he adjusted himself on his seat as if a slightly different position clarified his thoughts. The sharp citrus and pine aromas of laboratory cleaning solvents tinctured his nose and he exhaled sharply. The scent of stronger, industrial solvents wafted through his lab and he pulled back, hurrying to pull a handkerchief out of his pants pocket before he sneezed. He wiped his nose, absently returned the handkerchief to his pocket, and continued writing and editing.

Each night he came here to enter the day's events into his journal. Each night, after all the postdocs and grad students and assorted degree candidates and research associates had left and the sun had set, he quietly unlocked the door and tiptoed in as if he had no right to enter the lab his research funded. He would look right then left then right again, looking first through then over his glasses as if the clear vision they granted might prove a lie. He never turned on a light, all old habits from an older part of the world, from a place and time when silence and stealth were the secrets to life itself.

Satisfied with his entry, he sat back and put his hands in his lap.

Footsteps approached in the hall. That would be Mr. William Murphy - the janitor the students referred to as "Wild Bill" because he was often slightly drunk, dressed like a woodsman regardless of season or weather, his woodsman's cap pulled low to shade his eyes day or night and its flaps up like the ears of an attentive dog, who sang to himself quietly but offkey - working slowly, methodically, intentionally; all things Dr. Lupicen admired and approved of. Sometimes, when he'd finished making his entries early, he would invite Mr. Murphy in to chat, to sit and share some tea. Mr. Murphy was a good listener, smiled and nodded at things he couldn't understand, then said thank you, cleaned, dried, and replaced his cup on the shelf above the sink, shook hands and went about his ways.

Lupicen appreciated the quiet friendship.

But not tonight. Dr. Lupicen sat motionless until the casters under Wild Bill's wringer bucket, the sloshing water, swishing mop, Wild Bill's own nasally singsong voice, and the sharp smells of his cleansing chemicals echoed away.

Lupicen turned his chair to look out his lab's western facing windows. His lab was the largest in Vail Hall, in the last cluster of academic buildings on the north side of the Dartmouth campus and occupied the entire west side of the second floor.

A few cars could be seen under the lights of the parking lot behind the building. Trees created a small woods extending past the parking lot down several hundred yards past some roads and eventually to the Connecticut River. Across the river he saw the glow of Norwich and Thetford, Vermont, and beyond them the eastern faces of the central Green Mountains.

The faces were lit by the moon rising in the east. On the nights his staff worked late he would take a moment from observing the people sleeping in the chambers he'd designed to watch the moon slide down behind those mountains.

The moon in the mountains.

Turning back to his workstation, he tapped the trackball and the screen flickered to life. He logged out of his desktop then pressed his thumb against a small scanner on his keyboard. The screen's connection, along with the connections to the trackball and keyboard, went from his desktop to the APS System 70v3 computer resting like a plexus between the sleep chambers, its cables like the webbing of a fat, dark spider in the center of his lab.

His fingers moved the trackball as if he were cracking a safe. The screen lit up and a blue door appeared centered in a deep-ocean colored background. He opened a drawer and pulled out a HUVRSA, a Heads Up Virtual Reality Sensory Accumulators helmet, two cybergloves and a cybersuit. He undressed and slid his mantis-thin body into the tight, form-fitting neck-to-toe cybersuit. His cybergloved left hand made a knocking motion in the air. On the computer screen his knocking became a cartoon balloon with the word "knock" repeated three times on the surface of the door.

"Ann? May I come in, my girl? Hmm? May I come in?"

Nothing happened. He looked at the '70's dark display, then spoke directly into the HUVRSA's voicelink. "Are you awake, Ann?"

A YEAR AGO, LUPICEN, SITTING AT THE SAME DESK, fixed his gaze on the new computer screen, his left hand on the new keyboard and a pencil, long and thin with white sides and gray-tipped eraser, as if he held a stick figure of himself, in his right. The pencil went back and forth in a protractor's arc, tapping right left right left, keeping time to clicks coming from the APS System 70v3. Several grad students and engineers from other labs worked on its splayed intestines, dressed out along the lab's floor like the best parts of a cleaned and gutted kill.

A voice called from outside his office. "Could you use the keyboard again, Dr. Lupicen?"

His hands rocketed across the keys 'TYPIE TYPIE TYPIE'. Before retrieving the pencil, he caressed the older boy's face in the photograph. He whispered, "Maybe, when we are done, I can find you, Émile?"

Outside his office and encircling the hermetically sealed intestines of the '70, hammers fell and power tools sang as five individual sleep-chambers grew from wood and electrical wiring.

Another engineer called to him. "We're ready to start interaural phase coding, Dr. Lupicen."

Lupicen nodded.

In a moment the screen flickered the '70's higher brain functions coming online, black text sweeping red against a white background as each function successfully completed testing.

```
Central nervous system processing auditory signals.
Loudness-coding mechanisms inferred.
Neurons defined as disparity detectors.
...
Shape/Shading referents installed/invoked.
```

The cursor stopped at the start of a new line and blinked: one-two-three. Lupicen held his breath.

```
Visual cortex connections - Complete.
Neural map of auditory space/optic tectum - Complete.
Biosonar echolocation grid - Active.
Extrastriate and frontal cortical areas - Active.
```

Four more lines followed, all ending in - *Active.*

The cursor stopped again and blinked: one-two-three-four-five-six-seven. Lupicen unbuttoned his labcoat to stop sweating.

```
Location  v  Presence  discriminators  -  Active  and
Engaged.
Spatial  v  Placial  discriminators  -  Active  and
Engaged.
Orientation discriminators - Active and Engaged.
```

The cursor stopped and blinked once more. Seconds seemed like hours. Lupicen remembered Einstein's "When a man sits with a pretty girl for an hour, it seems like a minute. But let him sit on a hot stove for a minute and it's longer than any hour."

A rapid blinking of lights filled the lab.

```
Somatic  matrix  attached  to  experiential  control
converters - Learning engaged.
```

Nine more lines, one for each human sensory system, all ending in - *Learning engaged.*

The messages pulsed on the screen as the '70 prepared another round of first-time self-diagnostics. An engineer came up behind the sitting Lupicen and stared at the monitor. "That will be impressive, Doctor, if you can get a somatic matrix to hold. You'll have a feeling machine."

"Feeling as with the hands? No, no, no, that is not what is meant. That has already been done. Cog has done it. No." He nodded towards his screen. "Most machines of this type can intellectualize emotions, the 'cold emotions' syndrome of the quadraplegics. This KISMET II has done." His pencil bobbed towards the APS System 70v3. "This machine was designed for whole brain effects research. It is a machine which can dream, or in which we can model what it is to dream. For that we need a machine which can welcome Somnus, which can open itself to Morpheus, Phobetor, and Phantasos, which will be the hand-maiden of Selene, a machine which can feel enough that it wants to dream to understand what it feels."

The engineer's eyes went to the HUVRSA and its matching cyber-gloves.

Lupicen followed his gaze. "Yes, this is how the machine shall come to understand what it is to feel: a VR altricial interface." More would come later - this machine would understand a human touch - but Lupicen didn't mention that.

"Those quantum logic circuits, the QLCs, are mighty impressive, Dr. Lupicen. I don't even think Turchette and the NIST team have an entanglement-on-demand system with arrays that large."

Lupicen turned and probed the engineer's face. "You know of Turchette's work at NIST?"

"I know your work goes beyond his. Data coded in abstract space, multidimensional space? The ability to understand and use reflexive language? And engage in adaptive social iteration? Your system goes places nothing else comes near."

Lupicen continued studying the engineer's face as the latter read from the screen. "As you say, my system goes places nothing else comes near. Quite so; this computer dreams. I did not know this was an area of interest to you."

"I read some of your papers, Dr. Lupicen. What I could understand, anyway. 'To dream is to go to places which don't yet exist. But to do that it must first code data - *think!* - as we do. To do that, it must learn simply by observing others and in doing so, determine how to go where we can't.'" The engineer paused. He took his eyes from the screen and smiled at Lupicen. "No, that's all I can remember."

Lupicen nodded. "It can open gates and walk through them knowing where they are, gates we only encounter when we sleep. It will live where we are only nightly tourists and be our local guide to places we've never been. We will not only watch this computer dream, we will be able to follow where it goes and ask it to take us there. We will no longer be observers of our dreams, but participants in their realities." Suspicions from a previous time tightened Lupicen's stomach. "You remember passages of a paper you did not understand?"

"I read up on your work so I could get this job. But data encrypted in multiple-state form? That can only be read by other quantum computers prepared by the sender. That's what Wineland at NIST says, anyways. The NSA's got to be watching you, Dr. Lupicen. Don't be surprised if they come knocking on your door."

"Yes. Of this I am aware."

"Well, I wouldn't worry. No one has a quantum computer capable of solving that problem. Even if this one could, you'd need another QLC system to follow it."

"But we do have another one. Here." Lupicen pointed at the engineer's head. "All we need to do is to allow this computer access, learned access, to the aesthetics of another, as a child learns to feel from first itself then its parents then society and finally itself again. Doing so, we can ask and it will tell us how to understand its dreams." He read the engineer's nametag. "Do I make sense to you, Mr. Tibbs?"

"Let's say you got my attention."

THEY FINISHED LATE THE NEXT EVENING. EVERYONE went off to celebrate, leaving Lupicen sitting in the dark in a chair next to the '70's black housing.

"Yes, yes," he said, reflecting on the previous day's conversation. "It is the entanglement, the confusion, the probable juxtaposition, which is the root of your consciousness, and because your consciousness is based on the shifting realities of quantum core fluctuations, like superpositions of Penrose's mitochondrial cores, all realities are possible to you, my child."

The APS System 70v3 didn't respond. If it knew he was there, it didn't show it. It rested quietly, supported off the floor by four five-inch pneumatic tires, all in the locked position. Occasionally the '70 sighed as its massive liquid nitrogen-helium cooling system cycled to keep the magnetic jackets, the real cooling apparatus for the quantum entanglement system, active.

When it sighed, Lupicen stroked what might have been its face and instead served as its operations panel. "Most will see you as a bicameral, magnetically cooled quantum computer, as the closest analog to a questioning human brain we can achieve."

Thick black cables packed with optical fibers wrapped in their own cooling jackets erupted from what might have been the '70's eyes and made their way into the darkened chambers encircling it, Lupicen guiding them with his hands.

"But that is because all others like you have only been taught human language, referential language. You must also learn instrumental language, animal language, so you can understand us when we weep, laugh, scream...love - all the strongly emotional components of language."

He stroked the '70's face again. "Right now, you do not feel this. Tomorrow, we will begin. But first let's give you a name which will make sense to everyone around you."

He paused, raised his hand to his face, and his fingers drummed lightly on his lips.

"I will call you Ann because you are an Articulated Neural Network. Your last name will be more difficult to pronounce. MP-MPQLS? Massively Parallel - Multiple Processing Quantum Logic System? I think we shall just call you 'Ann.'"

In Lupicen's office, with no one to see, two more messages flickered briefly on his screen:

```
Unknown Realities - Creating
```

Unnamed Realities - *Creating*

"Are you awake, dear girl? Are you awake, Ann?" Lupicen repeated.

The door opened inward on Lupicen's screen as the 70's QLCs chugged to life, lighting up as cold helium pumped itself into them and fiber optic cables carried random nerve signals back to the main's massively parallel processing arrays. Once the two QLCs hemispherically stabilized, their light diminished into colors too cold to see, replaced by a steady, throaty, distinctly non-machinelike hum.

Lupicen put on the other glove and fitted the HUVRSA to his head. Before triggering power to the altricial interface, he glanced over to the '70's operations panel. Lights came on as more of the APS System 70v3 awoke to the personality inside.

```
Central nervous system - Online
Experiential control converters - Online
```

A red dot, barely more than a pixel, pulsed on the screen. A moment later it was followed by another, then another. A line formed, all the dots pulsing together, the heartbeats of the machine. Lupicen didn't blink, didn't breathe. His head bobbed slightly as he counted thirteen red dots.

Then

```
Sensory matrices - Online
```

Lupicen watched the screen. "Wake up, dear child."

```
Experiential reference accumulators - Active
```

Lupicen pushed the virtual door a little. His gloved hand felt normal, hinge-like resistance. "Ann? Where are you hiding, child?"

A little girl, curly golden hair and bright blue eyes and soft, pale skin came laughing from behind the door, throwing her arms around Lupicen's knees, almost toppling him in her enthusiasm for his presence.

"Did you bring me anything, Poppie?" She swished her dress, white with blue Morning Glory vines printed on it, as she looked up at him.

"Did I bring you anything? Do you wish me to spoil my little girl?"

The soft white cheeks blew into a pout and her arms dropped to her sides. She looked down and kicked her shiny black Buster Browns slightly, showing white ankle socks with blue flower trim.

Lupicen reached into his labcoat pocket and pulled out a cherry Tootsie Roll pop. "Of course I brought you something. I always bring you something."

The child reached for the candy and stopped. "Poppie. You're crying. Are you alright, Poppie?" She ignored the lollipop and wiped a tear from his cheek.

"No, Ann. Just remembering something I learned when I was your age: *Ar trebui să ne răsfățăm proprii copii cât putem de mult, pentru că nu știm niciodată cât timp vom fi alături de ei.*"

"Children are meant to be spoiled for we know not how long we will be with them?"

"Yes." He unwrapped the lollipop and handed it to her. She curtsied and thanked him, took a lick and offered him one. "No, thank you, Ann. It's all for you."

His labcoat transformed into a formal tuxedo with tails. A rocker grew out of the air behind him. He folded the tails up over his lap, sat, and motioned Ann onto his lap.

Outside, in the lab, he felt the pressure of her body slide easily onto his legs, the small roundness of her head nuzzle into his chest, heard her lips and tongue work over the candy greedily because it was all for her and smelled the cherry flavoring of her breath when she looked up and smiled.

"Do you think you can help me with my work?"

"Oh, yes, Poppie. Yes," she said between licks.

"Do you see those boxes way over there?" Boxes, hundreds upon hundreds, going on into the infinity of the empty room, appeared opposite them. Outside of the interface, Lupicen's left glove toggled opened the gates of several new ultra-wide, ultra high-density research ports on Dartmouth's backbone, physically linking Ann to information, both bright and dark, around the world via wide-line trunks.

"Please find Poppie any occurrences of sleep disorders or sleep anomalies which fall into the category of transient relational awareness. Pay special attention to any cases which resemble Charles Bonnet disease."

The QLCs gave one chug. Lupicen faintly heard Ann's MPPAs, the massively parallel processing arrays which served as her memory and thoughts, prepare their search.

The nitrogen-helium system sighed as Ann spoke her thought, "That's the hallucination of little, man-like creatures?"

Lupicen bent and kissed the little girl on her forehead. "You are such a bright little girl, Ann. You make Poppie so proud."

She smiled and beamed and clapped her little hands.

"Yes. That and occurrences in which aspects of consciousness and awareness have correlates in temporal lobe seizures. Now hurry, Ann, you mustn't wait."

Outside of the interface, the QLCs hummed green then descended into duller colors of red.

"Ok, Poppie."

Lupicen stood and Ann grabbed onto his tuxedo. "Poppie?"

"Yes, my little love?"

"I have a question for you, Poppie."

"Of course, my little child. What can Poppie answer for you today?" Her requests always delighted him. Could he bring her a butterfly, could he show her a lake, could he sing her a nursery rhyme.

"I am different from you, aren't I, Poppie?"

A vise clamped his heart. She had become aware of their shared alienness, had recognized they somehow differed from each other, something beyond differences of gender and age and experience. A piece of her innocence was about to be lost or already had been. But he had intended this all along, that she should grow and be able to tell him about his memories and her dreams.

But how had she realized this so soon? He cleared his throat, made sure his voice would not crack, before he spoke. "Yes, Ann. Do you know how?"

Her little face screwed up as she thought about it. Lupicen kissed her on the forehead again and left.

Outside of the interface, he went into chamber 1, reclined on the bed he found there, and slept. The moon had long set when he woke. No lights shown in his lab and only streetlights came through the windows. The only colors in his lab were the undulating rainbows of Ann's twin hemispheres as the '70's QLCs passed information back and forth.

"Still working, Ann?" Lupicen reached behind him and smoothed the folds of his labcoat, moving his hands as if he were grooming wingplates and his labcoat a carapace. "Deep in thought of how Poppie and you are different? Is that what causes the disturbances in your matrices?" The '70's dull red throbbings echoed in his eyes.

"Or do you dream?"

CHAPTER 11
Shem

TWO MEN, ONE SHAVED BALD, TALL, THIN, AND QUICK like a whip, and the other a fireplug on legs with a jet black ponytail halfway down his broad back, both in tailored, navy-blue pinstripe suits and wearing hand-made, alligator-skin shoes so polished they reflected the lights marking the aisle, made their way from the locomotive through the tender to the back of the train. The whip would walk a few long, waspish steps, wait, then spin the gold and diamond pinky ring on his right hand until the fireplug caught up. When the fireplug reached him the whip would walk a few more long, waspish steps, wait and spin his ring again.

The fireplug strolled, his hands clasped in front of his chest as if in prayer, his eyes skimming over his knuckles as they evaluated, the bands of the two turquoise rings he wore - one on each ring finger - clicking sometimes as he walked. He passed no one without reaching out to their carotid and checking for a pulse: conductors, stewards, clerks, passengers. It didn't matter.

The fireplug's slow methodicity and attention to detail frustrated the whip who released his frustration by aiming a small but powerful ruby laser into the lens of the security cameras while he waited for his partner to catch up.

"Christ, look at this place. What did The Boss use again?"

"Ambien. That's what he had us dump in the food service trucks. It makes you sleep and wake up without feeling groggy. 'Far as everyone on the train is concerned, they'll all think they probably had too much to drink."

"Do you have to test every mother's son?" The whip broke protocol and used names in an attempt to make the fireplug move faster. "We're supposed to get MacPherson to Pangiosi before morning, you know."

The fireplug stopped and stared at the whip who turned away before the fireplug answered. "We have plenty of time. Besides, we find one dead person, we got trouble."

"Didn't you tell me once something about your grandfather teaching you to help people die?"

The fireplug nodded as he worked. "Not exactly. He taught me to sing them from this world to the next, to carry the souls of the dead so they'd find peace."

"Happy hunting ground stuff?"

"Something like that."

"You believe in that stuff?"

"I don't believe in much of anything anymore."

"Yeah. Copy that."

The fireplug continued his slow inspection. The whip tapped his foot at the rear door to the car.

The fireplug stopped and looked up. "I wonder if these people dream."

The whip broke protocol a second time. "John, who gives a shit. Pangiosi gave us an order. We carry it out."

John stopped. His arms folded over an expansive chest.

The whip looked out a window and spun his gold and diamond pinky ring. "Sorry."

John's prayerful hands went back to work.

Shem twitched himself awake. His head rose up and he sniffed the air. A scent, something from deep dog memory, canine memory, canid memory, canis memory. He leapt off the bunk and growled. A door opened in the bedroom suite, a door only dogs, only canines, only the line that first walked before man then behind then beside could see, sworn under the first full moon to watch for such doors because humans, the canids knew, would forget.

The door closed. Whatever had been there had been warned away by flashing eyes, by baring teeth.

He jumped back on the bunk. As he circled to lay down he remembered the Little Master had gone. He looked across the suite to the other cot. The Great Master snored lazily like an old Alpha in the tall grass on a hot summer day.

Shem scratched his ear with a hind paw then sniffed his genitals. He rested his head over his paws, flopped to his side and stretched on the mattress. The entire bed was his!

Glorious His!

A few minutes later he, like the Great Master, snored like an Alpha in the tall grass.

THE RIME OF THE SEA-SALT AIR. SHEM WAGS HIS TAIL. Bright sun. Sand under his feet. Waves, water. Bitter to taste. Only for swimming.

"Shem, come here, boy."

The Great Mistress' scent.

He is panting.

"Here, boy. Come under the umbrella with me."

Shem wags his tail. The Great Mistress. Young. She likes to play with Thefrisbee. He brings it to her. In the shade. Under the umbrella.

"Are you my man?" The Great Mistress asks as she takes Thefrisbee from him. "No more Frisbee right now, okay, Shem?" She scratches his head. "Are you my loving man?"

She reaches into Thecooler. Here is his bowl. She reaches again. "You poor, hot boy. Here's some cool water for you."

Splash.

"Oh, Shem. Now you got the towel wet. Here's some more."

He laps.

She taps herself with the strange smell. She rubs herself. Shem comes over to lick it off.

"No, Shem. You don't like tanning oil." She turns his head away. He turns back, his tongue again on her arm. "Shem, no."

He looks at her and sits. In the shade of the umbrella on the towel where he made it wet. He smells the sea and the salt and the trace of diesel from the ships off shore. There is the scent of other dogs and he wonders if he should go tell them about his water and his shade and his towel and his Great Mistress here.

But it is cool where he is. There is a breeze that sometimes blows hot sand onto his face, into his eyes, and he is no longer interested in the seagull-cracked shells-seaweed smells it brings him.

He shakes his head to avoid the blowing sand. He ears flap and slap against his head.

The Great Mistress is on her chair. Not too long ago she would call him up there with her. Now he is too big.

He puts his paw on the fabric of the beachchair, between her feet.

"You want to come up here, do you? You know you never stay up here too long. You know that, don't you?"

Woof.

"Oh, alright, you big baby. Come on."

He comes up slowly, circles and lays so his muzzle can rest over her ankles.

She pulls something from her bag and he raises his head to smell it. It's a Whatshallwereadnow. "You want to read my Nook, too, Shem?" She holds it to his nose and he sniffs quickly. One, Two, Three, Four, five, six, seven quick breaths with his eyes fixed on nothing at all and he knows it is something that doesn't taste good, something from the den, where she sleeps and he sleeps with her.

He licks it. His way of acknowledging its presence in their life. "It's okay, now? I can read it alright? No help from you?"

The wind again. He lifts his head and sneezes, gets off the beach chair and curls up on the cool, wet spot on the towel in the shade the umbrella provides.

She reaches into another bag. She puts something on her head and pulls it underneath. She reaches in again. This thing goes on her eyes.

Should he sniff them? He starts to rise.

"No, that's okay, Shem. I bought some for you, too."

She takes other things out of the bag. They are like the things she put on her head. She puts one over his head as he sniffs it as she does so. It smells like "Thestore," a place he's never been but a sound she makes often. She ties it under his muzzle as she did her own. Does she think this will restrain him if another dog comes to play or challenge? The other thing she puts over his eyes and the world goes darker than it should be. The world smells the same so this thing on his eyes lies and he doesn't like it.

"Look at this handsome boy. Just look at him with his hat and sunglasses on."

He groans and lies down. One of her feet comes off the chair and scratches his side as he lies there, panting.

The Great Mistress makes her "reading" noises. It is okay for him to rest.

Warm but cool where he rests on the towel, wet, under the umbrella shade.

Cool Wet His!

Running.

Running and here and there a little pee to say hello to other dogs he knows.

To let them know he is okay.

To let them know the Great Mistress is safe, running sometimes ahead sometimes behind him.

She talks to others when she runs. She calls out the names of other dogs more often than the names of the humans beside them.

This place is "Thepark" and he is running with her and she has a strong smell. She stops and he runs back to her.

She carries a bag on her back and reaches into it. "What do you think we have in here, Shem? Huh? What do you think?"

She pulls out Thefrisbee and his tail wags like it's mad, like it is the dog and he is attached. He runs a little way and turns to her.

"You gonna get it? You gonna get the Frisbee?"

She teases him a few times but he is not so young and he is not fooled.

"Go get it, Shem!"

She lets it fly.

Fly, fly, fly!

He runs!

"Oops, sorry, fella!" He hears her voice but he must concentrate on Thefrisbee, see where it lands, hear its movements in the brush and wind. A male answers the Great Mistress, "No problem. Nice dog."

He ignores the male, there is no threat.

But Thefrisbee! It has gone into the thick smell of green.

"Can you get it, Shem?"

He feels the green pull against him. No other dog has been here in a great long time. The scents left are old. Old beyond remembering. Why?

This would be a good place to pee.

But here is a trace, old. He inhales sharply.

Thefrisbee. He sees it there.

It is a warning smell.

Yelp!

"My god, Shem, you alright?"

Yelp!

"Shem, I'm coming, boy. I'm coming."

He hears the Great Mistress running, hears her breathing, smells her fear when the wind brings it towards him.

Pain, pain, pain. Why is she not here to help him?

He hears another voice, another breath, smells a human male close upon him.

Whine.

"Where are you, boy?"

Whine.

The green parts. He smells his own fear on him now. A human male face looks down upon him. It is the male he smelled a moment before.

Growl. Whine.

Oh, it hurts too much to challenge.

"I'm coming, Shem!"

"He's over here, miss!"

He hears the Great Mistress' direction change. She is nearer now.

"Shem?" The human male asks. The male's hands glide down his sides, onto his quarters, down his shanks, over his legs. "Is that your name, boy? Shem? Can you tell me what's troubling you?"

Shem sniffs despite the pain. This male smells nice. Gentle. Concerned.

He has not always liked males around the Great Mistress. They always growl without sound and their faces lie.

Whine.

"He's over here in this thicket, miss. I think he stepped on a spike weed. Painful, for sure, but nothing serious."

The Great Mistress is here now. She smells of salt on her face and it is wet from her eyes.

The male's hands reach down and lift Shem up and over the green.

He says, "Lie down, boy. Let me have a look," and Shem does as he says.

"Well behaved dog, miss."

The Great Mistress' face is still salt and wet, like the taste of ocean but he will lick her face anyway because she has the smell of liking it when he does.

"He's got one spike in his paw. He walked into a patch of Many-Spined Opuntia."

"A what? Can you take it out?"

"There's a few ground cacti in there. We usually don't get them this far east. It'll hurt a bit but he'll be fine once we do."

They make all this noise and he is in pain! Pain pain pain!

"You got him?" The male is touching softly, pressing his paw, holding it gently. Shem whines less and less.

"Yes."

"Good boy, Shem. Good dog. Good boy. Such a good dog." Shem rests his head in the Great Mistress' lap. She is still making the salt and wet smell. He goes to lick her.

"Hold him still."

"Lie still, Shem." She's making her fear smell. She is making her wet and salt and fear smell.

The male's smell is not afraid. He is a curious and concerned smell.

"Good dog, good boy, good Shem. Such a good dog." The male uses the Great Mistress's words. Shem is not sure if it is right that the male uses them.

Oh, but now there is pain.

Yelp!

Shem leaps to his feet, knocking the Great Mistress over and pushing into the male.

"We got it. We got it. He'll be okay now." The male also has a bag on his back. He takes it off and reaches in.

Always these humans reach in. If only they had nothing to carry they could be free!

The male holds something up. "This is what got you, boy." It smells a little like Shem and a little like the patch of green where long ago others sought to warn him away.

He will remember this all green smell. He marks it with a warning smell.

"Let me see your paw. Shake."

Another stupid game.

"Good boy." The male rubs something cool on his paw and the pain goes away. "He'll be fine now. I put a little aloe on the wound to heal it up."

The Great Mistress has stopped making wet and salt. Her fear smell goes away. Her glad smell comes back. She puts her arms around Shem and rubs her face against his. He licks her face clean of the salt that dried there. "Don't you ever do that to me again, Shem. You hear me, Mr. Dog?"

The male stands up. He reaches into the hurting place. "Is this what he was looking for?"

Thefrisbee! Shem's ready! He's ready! Send it to him, now!

"Yep. That's his Frisbee."

Enough talk. Shem stands, bows, waits.

Woof!

"You don't mind if I toss it to him?"

"No. Please do. My name's Ellie. Eleanor. Can I buy you a water or some fruit juice or something?"

Thefrisbee goes through the air, into the clear air. Shem runs and leaps and it's caught between his teeth.

"I think I'd like that, Ellie. My name's Tom."

The male's hand touches the Great Mistress' hand. But her smell is glad and he smells much the same.

Shem spits out Thefrisbee at their feet. He stands, bows, waits.

The Great Mistress says, "Shem, this is Tom. Say hello."

More stupid games. Woof!

The male picks up Thefrisbee. "Which way we walking? Oh." He throws it and Shem runs and leaps and catches it in his teeth.

Glorious Teeth!

It has been two snowsontheground that the Great Mistress and the Tom have shared a den. It was the Tom's den but he did not challenge Shem and the Great Mistress has always smelled glad to enter.

When they first came, the Tom showed Shem a bowl of water and some food and said, "That's for you, Shem. This is your home now."

Shem didn't understand, but the Great Mistress smelled happy and the Tom made way for Shem in front of a fire that blazed on one side of the den. The Tom leaned against him and Shem moaned softly because the weight of the Tom reminded him of his denmates when he was very young, before the Great Mistress had come to him, when they all slept and suckled at She.

Shem knew there was a snowsontheground outside but there was a fire inside and the Tom let him share it. And the Great Mistress, too. She often came and lay beside them. And when the two of them played like young ones on the floor Shem was always welcome to join them.

That was two snowonthegrounds ago.

Shem stretches in front of the fire and sometimes the Great Mistress is not here and hasn't said "Thestore." This is one of those times. Where could she be?

She is around more often than she is away, even though this is the Tom's den and he has welcomed them. Perhaps he is the Great Master and no one has told Shem? Whenever he is gone more than one darkness he always gurges his kills for Shem like a He feeding his young. The Tom does not gurge well and the Great Mistress knows this because she makes what for her is a growl, "I can't believe you give him his treats from your mouth, Tom." The Tom answers but not with a growl, "Hey, in the wild the alpha dog always regurgitates for the pack. I'm just letting him know I'm dominant." Yes, the Tom always gurges for Shem soon after he gurges for the Great Mistress. Sometimes before, but never long after. He always gurges what Shem knows is in Thetreatcloset. This is a mystery to Shem but he doesn't question it.

The Tom comes down from the high den now and lays beside Shem by the fire. Shem moans and the Tom scratches Shem's side.

Shem raises his head and bares his teeth.

"Are you challenging me? Is this a challenge, Mr. Dog, Mr. Shem-puppy?"

Shem growls, but he can't make the growl he wants to make. He growls like a young one at play.

The Great Master...

The Great Master?

The Tom!

The Tom bares his teeth. Worthless teeth.

They could do nothing if they had to.

The Tom growls back. He sounds like a milk-fat kitten.

Shem bares his teeth and curls his lips back.

Grrrr!

The Great Master...

The Tom!

...bares his teeth and puts his face right beside Shem's.

The Tom doesn't smell of fear. He smells of safe and comfort and treats and food and water and some useless human scents. Shem remembers all the good smells the Tom always has with him, how the Great Mistress always smells when she is beside him.

But he challenges Shem and doesn't smell of fear.

The Tom's hand still scratches Shem's side.

"You challenging me, Mr. Dog-boy?"

Shem opens his muzzle, bares his teeth, curls back his lips, closes his eyes and...

The Tom is challenging!

...sneezes.

"Aa-choo! You catching a cold, boy? You alright?"

The Tom's touch is gentle, caring, concerned.

The fire is so warm and Shem knows it is a snowsontheground outside.

He bares his teeth, rolls his lips, but the Tom does the same and shows no fear. His face shows the same as his smell; he is happy Shem is here.

Shem opens his muzzle but knows he will sneeze again. Instead he licks the Great Master's face and rolls on his back, exposing his belly.

The Great Master...?

The Great Master lies next to Shem and scratches and rubs.

Shem is warmed and gets gurges and scratches and rubs!

Glorious Rubs!

WATER. NOT LIKE WATER BEFORE. THE TASTE IS DIFferent. Not good, but not like before. The Great Mistress has Thefrisbee.

"You going to get it? You going to get it, Shem?"

She throws it and he leaps and catches it in his teeth.

He spits it out at her, stands, bows, waits.

She picks it up and he's already moving, already watching, all his dog senses from before canids walked with men alive and working for the moment she lets go!

Up! Away! Fly, fly, fly and leap! Catch and return.

There is the smell of green here. Many other dogs come and he knows them all. Some he challenges and some challenge him. Mostly he plays with them and the young ones taken too soon from their Shes he cuffs and growls at until they learn The Way.

They learn.

They listen.

"Shem, do you like Chicago?"

Shem doesn't know if "Chicago" is "Thestore" or some other place he knows the sound of but has never seen. He thought this place was "Lincolnpark" but he doesn't know for sure.

He only knows this is the place of other dogs and play and running with the Great Mistress and Master and the water doesn't taste very good.

Woof.

"You like it here enough?" The Great Mistress starts running and he follows.

Soon she stops and Shem stops with her. She sits on the green and he sits next to her because there is a good smell where she sits and he wants to add something to the conversation the dogs before him have had. When she moves to leave, he will add his mark.

"Shem, can you keep a secret? Not really a secret, because we're going to tell Tom when he comes home."

The Tom? The Great Master! He will be home before the next darkness - Shem knows, he can tell - and he will gurge! Glorious gurge!

Shem wags his tail. It beats against the Great Mistress's seated back.

She rubs his ears and head. "I knew you could, Shem. I knew you could.

"Shem, I'm pregnant. It's too early to tell but I think it's going to be a boy."

Shem doesn't know what these sounds mean. She pats her belly. Shem knows her scent has changed and changed mostly there.

So she will have pups and the Great Master sired them.

This isn't news. They've carried each others' scents for as long as Shem remembers.

Woof.

"You're such a good dog, Shem. You know that you are, don't you?"

Woof.

She gets up. "Come on, boy."

She starts to run away.

Shem sniffs where she sat. Yes, some other dogs have argued this same argument before. Shem adds his mark, his definitive, his closing statement, conversation over. He circles.

"Come on, Shem. Hurry up!" She is not so far away Shem cannot catch her.

He pees from the other side, this time marking that the Great Mistress carries a pup and the Great Master, it is his.

He kicks up the dirt with his back legs, adding the scent of his knowledge of the news she brings.

"Shem?"

He runs and soon runs beside her.

THE GREAT MISTRESS IS LARGE NOW. HER PUP WILL come soon. Most Shes have several pups. The Great Mistress, one.

There are many mysteries Shem doesn't care to solve.

Often she talks to the pup. Does she know it listens? She talks while holding a Whatshallwereadnow. All the time, one hand going back and forth from her belly to Shem.

Does she think she carries Shem's scent to the pup?

Then why talk while holding a Whatshallwereadnow? "Once upon a time..." she says and the pup listens. "Long, long ago..." she says and the pup pays attention.

It does not matter. Shem knows. The pup listens. The pup knows. It is enough.

The Great Master has been gone two darknesses now. He told Shem to guard the den, protect the Great Mistress She, until he returned.

Of course Shem would do this. He is Shem, is he not?

Now the Great Mistress She does what she does every darkness since the snowsontheground came. There is a fire and she invites Shem to her beside it.

The Great Mistress is a wonderful She.

On many shelves there are Whatshallwereadnows. These are old things, old things with long scents, scents of many humans and dogs, Protectors of other Mistresses and Masters and Shes and Hes, old things that both the Great Mistress and Master sit quietly with. They sit with these old things of the long scents and make glad sounds and happy noises. Sometimes sad sounds and pain noises.

The long scents tell him much. The rest is another mystery to Shem.

The Great Mistress takes one of the old long scent things, a Whatshallwereadnow and sits, spreads it on her lap, and talks to the pup. She says "dog" several times and Shem always looks up.

"You like this one, Shem? You like 'The Tinderbox'? You like stories with dogs and wolves in them, don't you, Shem? You like it when I read Jamie stories, I can tell. You always curl up on the floor beside me and doze off. You going to curl up with us when he's born? I'm going to read him stories then, too, you know. You know that, don't you, Shem. You're such a good dog, aren't you, Shem. Good dog, yes."

She makes glad sounds. She also makes lots of nonsense sounds, but they're happy sounds and good noise so Shem doesn't mind. If he thought they could learn, he would teach them to howl their songs into the night.

The Great Mistress talks a Whatshallwereadnow to the pup every darkness now, whether the Great Master is home or not.

Now the Great Master is gone, but Shem knows tonight is the night he'll return.

Shem also knows this is the night the pup will come forth. He wonders if the Great Mistress She knows. He thinks not.

Another mystery. These humans have as many mysteries as they have stupid games.

The Great Mistress She puts the Whatshallwereadnow down. Shem licks it. She scratches him. He offers his belly. She stretches out beside him by the fire. Soon she sleeps.

A darkness comes, an opening in the night.

Shem stands. He bares his teeth. He growls. Foam flecks his lips. He feels his body tense.

The Great Mistress She is heavy with pup. She sleeps. The Great Master ordered Shem, "Take care of the house while I'm gone, okay, Shem? Good boy." It was a lot of sounds, but Shem understood just the same.

He is Shem, after all.

He prepares to spring. The Old Enemy will not take them. None shall harm the Great Mistress She or the pup inside.

He shows his fangs. He shows The Challenge.

Another door opens in the night. The Oldest Door. The One, the First, is there.

The opening, the Old Enemy, the darkness and the thing in it flee.

Shem sits, waits.

The One, the First, stands like a human but is the oldest of dogs, of wolves, the first of the line of canis, canid, canine. The One of All Packs, The Only of All Dens. Long ago The One taught the line of canis, canid, canine to sing their songs to She Who Knows All Mysteries, The One Queen, The Goddess, The Moon.

Shem stands, listens.

The One tells Shem of the pup to come, of what Shem must do, of how Shem must be.

Shem wonders if the pup will be taken from the Great Mistress She too soon and will not learn the Way of things.

The One, the First, knows Shem's question, understands the importance of such mysteries, and answers for Shem not to worry; today there is a fire, today Shem's belly is full.

But he also speaks of the pup to come. There are things Shem must know, must understand, so the pup will survive.

Shem listens. His tail wags as the One, the First, teaches, speaks.

The Great Mistress She groans from the floor beside him. She opens her eyes but they are still heavy with sleep. "Huh? What? Shem? What's that? Am I dreaming?" and then she's asleep again.

The One, the First, asks if Shem can hear the pup inside preparing to come out, needing to be born.

Of course he can. He is Shem, after all.

Good says the One, the First, and leaves.

The Itsforyou is whining again and the Great Mistress wakes to comfort it. No matter who seeks to comfort it, the Great Mistress or Master, once they hold it and speak softly to comfort it they hand it to the other. The Itsforyou is a strange thing, silent for so long then whining for no reason Shem can understand. Shem barked to comfort it once. It kept whining then stopped. Strange.

Human mysteries he doesn't understand. Old canine mysteries he does.

She comforts the Itsforyou. "Tom's home, Shem." She gets the excited smell.

Oh, but Shem can smell something more in her excitement than perhaps she knows.

"Let's go get him, Shem. Top of the hill. Let's meet him there."

She puts on her furs. Shem dances at the door.

There! There! Shem can tell by the sound! It is the Great Master's Letsgoforaride. Yes! Yes! It stops and opens and the Great Master is there and Shem jumps in and the Great Master gurges and Shem is so excited because he can smell the Great Mistress She is preparing...

"Tom? Oh my god, Tom. My water just broke."

"Let me put my stuff in the house, okay?"

"Oh, he's in a rush, Tom. We better get my bags. Oh, my god he's in a rush."

"Ha. Looks like I got home just in time." The Great Master scratches Shem's ears. "You did good, Shem. You kept everything safe until I got home. Good dog. Good boy, Shem. Good boy."

Everything is good and safe and wonderfully happy smells.

Wonderful Good Safe Happy he!

OH! THIS PUP! THIS HUMAN CUB! HOW FRAGILE, how frail it is!

Shem is careful to not get in the way. At the same time he will let no one near this cub he does not know, and he knows all who should be in this den: the Maxine, the Jack, the Rita...

Rita, Shem can tell, has herself recently become a She.

The Rita pats Shem's head while holding the cub, the pup. "What do you think, Shem? Looks like Tom but he's got Ellie's hair, huh?"

"You know, it's funny, but there's always been one red head in my family for as far back as anybody can remember."

The Jack makes a happy sound. "Not in mine." Everyone makes happy sounds.

Woof!

There are others who come in the house. Some smell like young denmates of the Great Mistress. Shem watches them, each and every one.

When he sleeps, he sleeps under the cub's little den.

When the cub's awake, so is Shem.

The Great Master and She hold out the cub for Shem. Shem licks it. The cub bares its...

It has no teeth! What is wrong with this young one!

Shem decides he will never be away long from this cub. This cub is his denmate and cannot fend for itself.

Shem goes to the place of his food and takes a muzzlefull. He chews and he steps lightly to where the She suckles the cub.

Shem gurges for the cub. He can provide, Shem. He can care for the cub if the time comes.

"Oh, Shem. Aren't you feeling well? All this excitement got to you?"

He doesn't know the words but he knows she doesn't understand.

"That's okay, Shem. I'll clean it up as soon as I put Jamie down. You be a good boy and just don't step in it, okay?"

Whimper.

"It's okay, Shem. You're a good dog, still."

Whimper.

The cub coughs. It gurges. It understands?

She moves the cub and its forepaw comes down on Shem's head. It pats his head and pulls his ear. It bares no teeth but it won't let go. It coos. It makes sounds Shem knows will become the sounds the Great Mistress and Master make but because this is a cub perhaps Shem can make it understand.

Shem licks the cub's forelimb and it makes another good sound and pulls its hand away.

It also goes out without asking to go outside.

"Jamie, you sure do pack a wallop."

It will have to learn not to do that if it wants to stay in the den.

THE CUB GROWS. NOT AS FAST AS A CUB SHOULD, BUT human cubs are like that. They take so long. It finally got teeth - ineffective teeth like the Great Mistress and Master have - but it got teeth and challenged Shem to use them.

Shem licked it. He gave it his favorite ChewChew to strengthen its teeth. He led it to his food and let it eat.

"Shem!"

"No, Ellie. It's alright. Dogs don't share their food except within their pack, and only with those they recognize need it."

"And he lets Jamie chew his nylabone, too."

The Great Master reaches down and holds Shem's muzzle up, then lets Shem touch tongues. "You good, boy, Shem. Good boy!"

Shem wags his tail. His whole body moves, again his tail is wagging him, because everyone in the den knows Shem has done good and they all smell it.

The Great Mistress She lifts the cub and carries him away. Shem starts to follow.

The Great Master has opened the cold box and pulled out a treat. "Shem?"

Shem jumps up. When he lands he can't control his tail.

"Is this for my good boy?"

The Great Master puts the treat in Shem's bowl. Shem attacks it, whining because of the cold on his teeth, but not stopping because this is such a good, good thing.

The Great Master sits beside Shem, not moving to take the treat away. He pats Shem's back as Shem eats.

"Good dog. You like that, Shem? You know you're a good dog?"

Shem knows he has done a good thing. He is eating and whining and wagging and wagging.

Glorious Wag!

"Jamie! Shem! Dinner!"

This is the Young Master, the Little Master, and he moves like a pup just out of the den.

"Shem! Jamie! Dinner!"

They have played and romped in the den since the Great Mistress brought the Little Master home. They went to "Thestore" and to "Thedoctor." Shem is not sure but he thinks "Thedoctor" is "Thevet" for the Little Master.

Does "Thedoctor" give the Little Master bones to crunch? Shem always licks the Little Master's face when they return but there is no scent of food there.

Why do they go, then?

The Little Master sometimes tugs on Shem's fur or sometimes an ear. The first time it happened Shem was ready to snap at this cub.

But the cub opened its poor, toothless mouth and stuck out its tongue, something any good canid knows packmates do before they hunt, before they kill.

Shem touched his tongue to the cub's and let it go at that.

"Eeyeew!"

"Oh, let it go, Ellie. Shem's tongue is probably cleaner than what Jamie finds crawling around on the floor."

But the cub grew in its own, slow way. Shem taught it to sniff and track but its poor, small nose was useless.

Shem taught it to mark its territory but the Great Mistress sounded

"No!" and that was the last of that. The Great Master didn't mind, although his marks were always too much and always too wasted, and never where they should be. Shem sought to teach the two male masters but they couldn't seem to learn.

There was the time Shem and the cub hunted for Thetwistedsock. Shem remembered the Great Mistress and Master making the noise but not wanting to play.

"Tom, Shem's taught Jamie to chew on his twisted sock."

"Yeah, so?"

"Tom. Come on. We have to take it away. That thing's filthy. The two of them lie down and gnaw on it together. I think Jamie's going to growl before he can talk the way they go at it."

"But, Ellie, that twisted sock is Shem's favorite toy."

"Tom." The Great Mistress was making her command sounds.

"Ellie, Shem loves that twisted sock. You can't take it away from him."

"Oh yes I can and yes we will."

Sometimes Shem wondered who ruled the pack. He always thought it was the Great Master until the Great Mistress made those sounds. Then the Great Master's smell changed and he cowered away.

But when she wasn't looking he'd give Shem a treat.

Shem decided that was the human mystery way.

"If it makes you feel better we'll just hide it until Jamie's old enough to know not to chew on it. Okay?"

"Alright."

Shem would get a treat, he could tell.

But neither he nor the pup could ever find Thetwistedsock again.

THE LITTLE MASTER FOLLOWED SHEM TO "Thetreatcloset." Shem could never get the treats that the Masters kept hidden there, but the cub could.

The cub could.

The cub, the Jamie, became the Little Master then.

Shem's tail wagged him as he realized this.

The Great Mistress realized this, too, just as Shem did. "Oh this is too much. Tom? Come in here, please."

She was making a bad sound. Shem's tail wagged, but less.

The Great Master came in. He bared his teeth but not in challenge and he did not make a bad sound. He made his good sound.

"I see you've taught your son all your tricks."

The Little Master gave Shem another treat. He took one more out and held it up to the two Great Masters.

The Great Master picked up the Little Master and bowed so Shem could get the last treat in the little one's hand.

The Great Mistress walked away. "Oh, you're all too much." But she made a good, happy sound when she did.

The Great Master patted Shem's head. "Taught him good, huh, boy?"

Shem's tail wags him! He is good!

Glorious Good!

The Great Master, the Great Mistress, the Little Master, and Shem are all in the den together, stretched out on the floor. There is a fire and Shem is dozing with his muzzle over the Little Master's legs. The Great Master and Great Mistress shared a Whatshallwereadnow until The Little Master slept. The Great Master and Mistress speak and, although Shem can not understand all the words, he knows they speak about him.

The Great Master sounded first, "Can I tell you something without you thinking I'm crazy?"

"Tell me and I'll let you know."

"I had the weirdest dream last night. I thought I was awake but I'm not sure. It was weird, though."

"So far I don't think you're crazy."

The Great Master and Great Mistress touch muzzles. Funny way to gurge.

"I thought I saw Shem sitting at the foot of the bed."

"Oh, yes, that is strange."

"No, not that. I thought he was looking at something and I thought I saw it, too. It looked like a man with a dog's head. Kind of like Anubis or that other one - "

"Wepwawet, Anubis' brother. Anubis is god of the dead, Wepwawet guards doors and opens doorways."

"You read too much."

"You were saying?"

"I thought Weppy Wets was talking to him and he was listening to it."

"Wepwawet and you're kidding."

"You think I'm nuts, Weppy Wets?"

"No, I remember that exact same thing. It happened the night Jamie was born, before you called and came home. I just thought it was hormones doing their nasty deeds. But it seemed so real..."

"Weird, huh?"

"Yeah, weird."

Shem isn't sure what all the words mean. They saw the One, the First? Do they know the reason dogs walk with men? To keep them safe, yes. Worthless teeth. But also to guard their hopes, to allow them their dreams.

Loyalty, love, faithfulness, acceptance. These things do not come free. If dogs did not guard men's hopes and dreams, give them solace against their fears, where would loyalty, love, faithfulness and acceptance be? Without hope, without dreams, these things cannot survive.

That is what the One, the First, tells us all.

SHEM LAYING IN THE BACKYARD, DREAMS.

He dreams water. Confusion and water.

There is sand under his paws and he smells the deep water, hears the water coming up against the sand under him, feels it breaking and spraying not far away.

Where is the Great Mistress?

Where is the umbrella shade and towel to lie on? Where is Thefrisbee?

Shem feels the breeze blowing cold but the brightness in the sky is strong upon him. He feels its heat through his fur, his skin, his pelt, but the sand blows in his eyes and the wind is cold that sends it.

The air is salty like the rime of the sea, like the Great Mistress' tears, and he looks for her to lick her face and make her salt-wetness go away.

Where is the Great Mistress?

Woof!

She will call him.

Woof!

She will hear him and call him to her.

Woof!

Shem yawns. He runs left and right. He sniffs the sand.

This is a strange place.

There are no smells except the great water and no sounds except its crashing on the beach.

Shem runs, wanting to hear the big things floating on the water, wanting to smell the stink they give.

There is nothing.

Woof! Whine! Woof!

There is nothing here. Shem is alone. Shem howls.

No one in the pack answers.

Shem hears the Little Master enter the den and whines at the back door.

"Mom! Mom? I'm home, Mom!"

Whine!

The den opens and Shem knocks over the Little Master, his tail wags furiously as he licks the Little Master's face.

"Where's Mom, Shem?"

Whine!

"Let's go find her."

The cub, the pup, the Little Master. He does not know. How can Shem tell him? The Great Mistress went to "Thestore" but too many clouds have passed. The Great Mistress is always in the den when the Little Master returns. She and Shem go to greet the Little Master and protect him from all challenges. He doesn't know how to defend: worthless teeth in a too small mouth.

The Little Master goes up in the den. "Mom? Mom!"

Shem races up after him and runs from room to room to room.

Woof!

"Mom! Where is she, Shem?"

Woof!

Shem and Jamie, the Little Master, run down the den. Jamie goes out back. "Mom?"

Shem runs out with him and pees on all his spots. He marks them anew. He yawns at the last one, lies down and licks his genitals. He sits up and yawns.

Jamie goes back into the den and Shem follows. He goes to where the Letsgoforarides are kept. "Her car's gone, Shem. Did she leave a note?"

Back into the den. Shem circles at the front of the den.

"No notes, Shem."

Whine.

"No messages on the machine."

Whine.

Shem circles.

"You need to go out, Shem? But you were just out. I thought you did everything you had to do."

Circle. Whine.

"Okay. You want to go out front? Okay, just remember to stay in the yard."

The Little Master opens the den and Shem runs!

Run, run, run!

"Shem! Come back!"

Shem sees a big Letsgoforaride. It slows as it passes. Shem bares his teeth and challenges it.

Bark!

Bark Bark Bark!

"Shem!"

Shem chases the big Letsgoforaride. He sees a male face. It growls without sound and it lies.

Shem will feel this face between his teeth as if it were Thefrisbee.

"Shem, come back here now!" The Little Master's sound is urgent. Shem knows he can not catch the big Letsgoforaride.

He stands, panting, watching it go further away, smelling the scents he can from it.

The Great Mistress' scent comes from it.

BARK BARK BARK BARK BARK BARK BARK!

BARK BARK BARK BARK BARK BARK BARK!

BARK BARK BARK bark...

Bark...bark.

"Shem, what's wrong, boy?"

Something has happened to the Great Mistress. Another pack has killed her as she protected the Little Master and Shem?

Shem must protect the Little and Great Masters now.

They have no teeth.

What could they do?

THERE IS A BIG LETSGOFORARIDE. SHEM REMEMBERS the scent.

It slows. It stops.

Shem remembers.

The scent of She!

Masked. Weak.

The Great Mistress!

She!

Shem bares his teeth and challenges the big Letsgoforaride.

Inside there will be males who lie.

Shem knows. He can tell. The scent is as before.

Bark!

Bark Bark Bark!

BARK BARK BARK BARK BARK BARK BARK!

A male face. It growls without sound and it lies.

Yelp!

The pain as from long ago, before The Great Master was The Great Master, when he held Shem's paw in Thepark.

BARK Bark bark bar...

THEJACK IS HERE WITH THERITA. THEY CAME IN TheJack's Letsgoforaride but what is that other Letsgorforaride doing here? TheJack says, "I told Dr. Lupicen we'd be there in a couple of days, Tom."

The Great and Little Masters move towards the other Letsgoforaride. Shem follows.

"No, Shem. You go with Rita today, okay? We'll be home soon. Soon, soon."

The Great Master says to go with TheRita in TheJack's Letsgoforaride?

Shem will be separated from The Great and Little Masters?

No! This cannot be!

Woof!

Shem will not let them go!

Woof Bark! Bark Bark Bark Bark Bark!

"What's gotten into Shem, Tom?"

"I have no idea. I've never seen him like this."

Woof Woof Woof Woof Woof!

Oh, how to make them listen, to make them understand?

Woof Bark Woof Bark! Whine. Woof Bark Woof Bark! Whine.

"Shem, go with Rita. Be a good dog now. Go with Rita."

No! Shem will not go with TheRita. Shem will stay with the Great and Little Masters. The First One has said it must be so!

Woof Bark Woof Bark Woof!

"Shem!"

Whine.

"He wants to go with us, Dad."

The Little Master understands! He listens! He can see!

"Jamie - "

WOOF WOOF WOOF WOOF WOOF WOOF WOOF.

"Shem, what is it?

The Great Master! Can he see? Can he understand?

"I think Jamie's right, Tom. I mean, he hasn't been away from you two since...you know..."

TheJack! TheJack!

"Jack, I'm probably going to be asleep most of the time. It's your call."

The Great Master understands! He sees! Shem's tail can't be controlled!

"I've got no problem. He'll keep Jamie company. Let's bring him along."

TheJack knows!

"Jamie, you're going to have to take care of Shem. Do you understand that?"

The Little Master's hand on Shem's back, on Shem's head. Oh, scratch scratch scratch scratch scratch!

"I understand, Dad. I'll take care of Shem."

Oh, Glorious Masters!

Glorious Scratch!

SHEM LAY ON JAMIE'S BUNK IN THE DELUXE BEDROOM Suite on the *Lake Shore Limited*'s Viewliner. His nose pulled in the scents of the Little Master and he woofed gently in his sleep.

The Little Master is with the Wolf-Brother. He is safe.

Shem hears a sound. He smells a bad smell, an evil smell, a lying smell.

His nose sniffs one two three four five six seven times.

He knows this scent. It is the male who growls and whose face lies, the one who carried the Great Mistress's scent in the big Letsgoforaride.

THE WHIP SPUN HIS RING. "WILL YOU QUIT LOOKING in every goddamn door and get the fuck over here."

John continued his methodical inspections "Pays to be careful."

The Whip pulled a taser out of his pocket. "This is careful. See this? Fifty-thousand volts and look at this." He pointed at two slider controls. "I can go from one microamp to a full ten amps, from twelve hundred volts to the full fifty k. With laser sighting, air guides and up to five minutes of discharge per shot. Did all the mods myself."

"You know how to do that kind of stuff?"

"Found it on the internet. It'll stop a rhino."

"You expecting any?"

The Whip reached into his other pocket and pulled out a slipjack billy.

"What? No gun?"

The Whip tapped the back of his beltline with the billy. He stood in front of MacPherson's suite door.

John took a small aerosol can from his pocket, sprayed silicon on the top and bottom door runners then stepped back. "Strong and silent. On my three."

The Whip nodded.

"One. Two. Three."

The Whip pressed the latch. The door slid open.

THERE IS ANOTHER SMELL. A FAMILIAR SMELL.

He whimpers in his sleep. She has come to him. The Great Mistress. She is here.

She calls him. "Shem!"

The Great Mistress stands on the great, splashing water. He can hear her, see her, smell her. She holds Thefrisbee.

"Come on, Shem. You can get it."

"Not this goddamn dog again."

The Whip's thumb moves the slider up to the full ten amps and fires. "Wait! Don't!"

The electrode's hit. Shem's body convulsed up and off the bed. His jaws open wide and clamp down on the Whip's face.

SHEM FEELS HIMSELF LEAP. HE FEELS HIS TEETH SINK into something, not Thefrisbee, more like flesh.

Flesh!

Glorious Flesh!

He feels the water come up around him.

"Come on, Shem! You've got it! It's all right."

His tail is wagging. He can't control himself. The Great Mistress is here and she calls him. He's not lost! He's with his pack once again!

"Come on, Shem," the Great Mistress stands, waiting for him. "Bring it here, you good dog."

THE WHIP'S BODY FLAPPED LIKE A BROKEN KITE IN A strong wind, his neck vertebrae cracked as if his body were a flesh-covered bullwhip. Shem, his jaws clamped shut and his muzzle frothing with blood and spit, had all but torn the man's face off.

John looked at his fallen comrade. "Styles, you stupid fuck. The dog was asleep. Did you think it remembered you from the last time you two met?"

The taser's indicators flickered weakly and stopped. The Whip and Shem vibrated then lay still.

"Styles, you dumb fuck."

SHEM FEELS DIFFERENT. HE IS STILL SHEM. SHE IS still the Great Mistress. He spits out Thefrisbee and for a moment he tastes bad blood and Thefrisbee smells like a lying male.

"Good boy, Shem. Good dog."

She rubs his head and scratches his ears.

He pants.

"Come on, Shem."

He looks up at her and wags his tail.

"We have to do something for Jamie."

Shem cocks his head. His ears pull up slightly. The Little Master?

She turns and jogs out over the water.

He follows.

He does not notice because he follows her; he does not sink.

He doesn't sink.

This is not a human mystery. He knows. He has one more thing to do for the One, the First, for the Little Master.

The One, the First, told him long ago.

John watched Tom MacPherson snoring lightly on the other cot; he hadn't moved, he hadn't blinked.

Pangiosi appeared in the doorway. "Mr. Nighthorse."

John stood back.

Pangiosi scanned the suite. His gaze stopped on Shem's body. He sat on the floor and stroked the dead dog's fur. "I had a dog once. Did you know that, Mr. Nighthorse?"

"No, sir."

"I was barely three years old, I think. A puppy abandoned on the street. I talked to it and it followed me home."

"I didn't know that, sir."

"I asked my mother if I could keep it. She looked at it, then me. She said, 'For a while.'"

"Sir?"

"For a while. Every day she'd give my puppy a treat, after I'd played with it for a while. Every day. She made a game of it, holding the treat up so my puppy could see. She taught my puppy to follow her through the house, having it chase her, then giving my puppy the treat just before it tired and lay down to sleep."

"Mr. Pangiosi?"

"Then one day she had it follow her to the attic. It was a full attic. More like a third story, really. She'd gone up there earlier. I didn't know. She had my puppy follow her. I was close behind, laughing at the game they were playing. She had my puppy follow her to a window she'd previously opened and threw the treat out."

"Sir?"

"My puppy leapt after it. I heard it yelp. Scream. In terror as it fell. I screamed, too."

"Mr. Pangiosi, I..."

"I heard it hit."

"Sir."

"My mother looked out the window and said, 'Make people believe they can get what they want and they'll follow it to their own destruction.' She'd planned the whole thing. Probably from the moment I brought it home."

"Excuse me, sir, I..."

"Then she looked at me and said, 'Never bring anything home again.'" Pangiosi rose. "My father came home and I was still outside, stroking my puppy's fur. We buried it in our backyard. It was the only time I saw my father cry."

"Mr. Pangiosi..."

"I was too young to even give it a name. I just called it 'Dog'."

"Sir, I..."

"She changed my life forever that day."

"Excuse me, Mr. Pangiosi, I..."

"Make sure you clean everything, Mr. Nighthorse. Come to me when you're done."

"Yes, sir."

John shivered once Pangiosi's footsteps faded down the hall. He removed some latex surgical gloves from his pocket. His first job was to package Styles for removal. Doing so required freeing Styles's face from the dog's jaws.

He touched the dog and jumped back through the open door, his head banging on the hallway wall opposite as if it were a mallet striking a drum. He caught himself mid slide to the floor, stood up and shook his head, running his hand over his scalp checking for wounds. No blood. No wounds. No swelling. But his muscles tingled like he'd been hit with a cattleprod and his vision blurred. He blinked a few times and felt the back of his head again.

Nothing, except for an ache in his eyes. He reached into his inner pocket and pulled out a pair of wraparound sunglasses. "Better."

He reentered the suite and kicked the taser out of Styles's hand.

"Going to get us both killed, Styles." He paused. "How come Pangiosi didn't get hit?" He shrugged. Most people wondered if Pangiosi was human, period. Maybe electric shocks didn't affect him? Maybe he didn't touch the right part of the Styles-Dog-Taser circuit?

Not important.

The steward's closet had cleaning supplies. He wrapped Styles the best he could and placed his body in the diaphragm between the cars.

What to do about the dog?

It bore no marks. Styles hadn't beaten it, but its jaws were slack. Blood clotted its lips, ears, nose and eyes. He found Jamie's clothes neatly folded under the bunk the dog slept on and twisted them, the blanket, and sheets around the dog then snapped its neck, as if it had somehow strangled itself in its sleep, choked on its own tongue perhaps and scratched and bitten itself trying to get free.

There would be a tie between the boy and his dog - his grandfather taught him that's the way things were meant to be - and he allowed himself to feel some pity for the boy.

He hummed parts of an old deathsong - something his grandfather taught him - for the dog and for the boy's sake.

As he moved the dog's body the Gate dropped from the bed.

Interesting stone. It reminded him of his favorite movie, "The Outlaw Josey Wales", with Clint Eastwood and Chief Dan George. Chief Dan George pulls out a piece of rock candy and says to Eastwood, "...it's not for eating, it's for looking through."

John looked through the stone, even though the only light in the Suite was coming in from the passageway.

Nothing looked any different. The walls looked like walls, the doors looked like doors, the curtains looked like curtains.

He looked down at the dog's body. The dog looked back but from far away. A beach of some kind. Nighthorse blinked and saw himself through the dog's eyes.

He stood in a field between buildings. Night. Someone said something. A brilliant light hit his chest. Laser sighting?

You'd aim for the eyes with a beam that bright, not the chest.

His chest exploded. Probably a large caliber soft-point. From behind.

His DeathVision? He'd heard about things like this before, as a kid living with his grandfather on the reservation. "Is this what you were preparing your little Pokachee for, Grandpa?"

He lowered the Gate. Only the dog, wrapped in some sheets and a little boy's clothes.

He lifted the Gate to his eye again.

Field. Buildings. Night. Someone talking. Blinding light. Shot from behind, blowing out his chest.

He blinked. The dog on the beach.

He sighed. His nostrils flared briefly.

His DeathVision.

If such it was, so let it be. "We can't change our destiny. Isn't that what you said, Grandpa? We can put it off for a while, but what The Great Maker has for us, The Great Maker has for us."

He took one deep breath. His abdomen fluttered as if tickled. He smiled. "Tickling your little Pokachee, Grandpa?" He corrected himself. "Grandfather."

The old man always seemed more Grandfather than Grandpa to him, even as a kid.

He'd had enough. Maybe he got some Ambien when he and Styles had mixed it for the others. It had shaken him. That's what it was. He made a mental note to sing the full deathsong for the dog when he had a chance, remembered his own DeathVision, and wondered who would sing his DeathSong.

John lifted Tom over one shoulder as he pocketed the Gate. Through the diaphragm he lifted Styles's body to his other shoulder. He walked, quicker than he liked, wanting to get away, to Pangiosi's car.

Chapter 12

John Nighthorse

JOHN STOOD BEFORE EARL PANGIOSI IN THE LATTER'S private car, Styles's body on one shoulder, the sleeping Tom MacPherson on the other, and showed no sign of strain.

"Mr. Nighthorse." Pangiosi sat at the far end of the table, his chair tilted against the wall on its rear legs and his hands behind his head. He stared at John, cocking his head first right, then left, evaluating. "That's quite a story."

"Yes, it is, sir.

"Are you sure you're alright? Would you like me to check your eyes?"

"Thank you, sir. I'll be fine in a few minutes."

"You'll let me know if your situation goes otherwise?"

"Yes, sir."

"Very good. Then we continue. You're confident Mr. Styles is the only one compromised?"

"As I said, Mr. Pangiosi, there were three suites I didn't enter. Considering - "

Pangiosi waved his explanation away. "Yes, yes. Well." He rocked forward and got up. "Would you put what remains of Mr. Styles on the floor, please."

John knelt and lowered his comrade's body without a word.

Pangiosi knelt beside the body. He arranged the shirt and sport coat. He picked some lint from the lapel. He sighed.

The billy, still gripped in Styles's right hand, caught Pangiosi's eye. He lifted it and the hand and arm came with it. Pangiosi tried to pry it free but Styles claimed it even in death.

"Mr. Nighthorse, jacket that one in the next room, please, then bring me some sheets of plastic, a hammer, or better, a mallet and a knife, the sharpest you can find."

"Yes sir."

John gathered two plastic straws from the wet bar then lay Tom's sleeping body on the bed in the next room. He pulled a straightjacket from the closet, gently maneuvered Tom into it and strapped it tight. He put the straws between Tom's lips, took out a tube of SuperGlue out of his pocket and glued Tom's mouth shut. He rolled tissue into balls and placed one in each of Tom's nostrils. Lastly he gently placed Tom on the floor and put a pillow under his head.

He returned with Pangiosi's requested supplies.

"Thank you, Mr. Nighthorse. Spread out the plastic and center Mr. Styles on it, would you?"

John did as instructed.

"Now stand back, please."

Pangiosi lifted the mallet and smashed Styles's teeth, bringing it first straight down on the mouth, then twice on either side. He parted Styles's broken jaws and looked for unshattered teeth. Finding one, he smashed the abhorrent side of Styles's face once again.

"Make a note, Mr. Nighthorse: Dentals, check."

Pangiosi raised Styles's free hand as if giving a manicure. He inspected the fingers then took the knife and severed the tips. He lifted the hand still holding the billy and severed the fingers between the mid-digital knuckles. The billy dropped and he inspected the finger stubs, blowing on them lightly as if drying nail polish.

"Fingerprints, check. Remove his shoes and socks, please, Mr.

Nighthorse."

A moment later, Pangiosi flensed Styles's soles from his feet.

"Soles, check."

He knelt by Styles's broken features and flensed his face down to the bone. When he got there, he lifted the mallet again and smashed the upper face and forehead into the brain.

"Face, check." He paused and stared at the faceless Styles. "Do you think anybody could recognize him now?"

"I don't think so, sir."

"Pity we don't have DNA scrambling equipment handy. Expunge his history at your earliest convenience, would you, Mr. Nighthorse?"

"Yes, sir."

Pangiosi went to the lavatory to clean himself up. He called out, "I believe he was a friend of yours?"

"Yes, sir."

Pangiosi came back into the room and picked up some files. John remained standing over the body. "May I trust you to attend to that in your own way?"

"Yes, sir."

John gathered Styles's remains in his arms, like a father carrying a dead son.

"Oh, John?"

"Yes, sir?"

"Please make sure any of Mr. Styles's traceable weapons are secured in my stores, would you?"

"Yes, sir." Nighthorse walked over to the storage cabinet. He shifted Styles's body in his arms, removed the dead man's Walther PPK and placed it on a shelf beside Pangiosi's Beretta 92X and laundered shirts.

He walked out the rear of Pangiosi's car and into the train's hurtling night.

At the rear railing of the last car, his hair loose and lifted by the wind, Nighthorse stood like a red-crowned Medusa in the End-of-Train's light. The moon had long passed overhead. He removed the sunglasses, his vision cleared. He still carried Styles's body, but now wrapped in white linen and tied with greased and fatted red, blue and yellow threads. Somewhere between Pangiosi's concealed car and the End-of-Train John picked up a black kitbag which he'd slung over his shoulder by its strap. The bag, wider at the bottom than at the top and zippered on the outside, looked like either an external lung or an ambulatory kidney, in either case one with a zippered filter for easy cleaning.

John looked down on Styles's butchered, battered face. "It would have been better if there was a moon to light the path for you, my friend."

He stood there, waiting under the cloudless, starlit sky. Occasionally diesel fumes washed over him and he held his breath until they passed. After a while he heard the locomotive's wheel rhythm shift and felt the difference of the ballast by the singing in the rails under him.

Nighthorse stood Styles up against the railing. He opened the kit bag and took out a smudgestick, lit it with a ShurLite he kept from his Navy Seal days, and let the rushing wind of their motion bathe Styles's wrapped body in its smoke. He knelt by Styles's feet and aimed the ShurLite's intense flame on the linen there, using his massive back and arms to block the wind and making sure the linen and greased threads caught and held.

"Just a little while longer, Styles, and we'll be going over water. The Hudson. Didn't you say you were from somewhere up here? Acra? Your parents owned a chicken farm or something?"

In a few seconds flames engulfed the body and Nighthorse stood back, raising his arms to block the heat from his hair and face.

The singing in the rails shifted quickly. He caught a whiff of the shoreline, brackish from low water, as the pitch of the train's rud-da-rump climbed, its weight shifting from ballast to trestle.

He rushed forward and tossed Styles's burning body over the rail, past the trestles, and watched it fall down into the water.

He raised his arms, his blistered palms skyward, and sang a DeathSong, a series of blind vocables he'd heard when he walked with his grandfather long ago. He remembered the rhythmic beating of the big drum and how the sounds flowed where words should be:

Anyanna-he Anyona-ho
E ai sonta
Kai ipa che
Che bo wan ta'bey
Che bo wan a'chebe-ho

He repeated the verses four times, each time facing a different direction, then grew quiet and brought his hands down.

"I wish I'd taught you a DeathSong, Styles."

"Very impressive, Mr. Nighthorse."

John, looking back over the receding rails, answered Pangiosi without facing him. "Thank you, sir." Some headlights arced along the highway paralleling the railway, sometimes closer, sometimes farther away, sometimes not at all. The headlights flickered like emergency lights as they shot through the guardrails on the side of the highway.

"When we get to Springfield, see that my car is transferred to the *Vermonter*, would you?"

"Yes, sir." John reached into his kit for some balm to put on his hands and brushed the stone he'd collected in MacPherson's bedroom suite. Perhaps because of the song he'd sung to guide Styles on or the power in the stone itself, he couldn't tell, but his eyes glazed briefly as he touched it.

"Is there something wrong, Mr. Nighthorse?"

There was something in this stone. Something John didn't understand but knew Grandfather would. Whatever this stone was, Nighthorse knew it couldn't fall into Pangiosi's hands. His mind instinctively started multiplying the flickering lights of passing cars by twelves, part of PsyCon training to mask his thoughts.

"No, sir."

The "twelves" tables raced through John's mind. He could feel Pangiosi's eyes on him.

"Are you sure?"

"Yes, sir."

Pangiosi turned and stared at John's reflection in the window of the car's rear door.

"Mr. Nighthorse?"

"Yes, sir?"

"You're a well-read man, Mr. Nighthorse. Have you ever read Tolkien's *The Hobbit*?"

"Yes, sir."

"So the phrase 'What does it have in its pockets?' has meaning to you?"

John said nothing.

"Turn around and face me, please, Mr. Nighthorse."

John grabbed the rail and vaulted over it before Pangiosi could move. He tucked himself into a ball and rolled to dissipate his momentum, his heavy, thick, muscular body breaking through the scrub, broken glass, young trees, and ballast lining the railbed.

When he stopped rolling he lay on his side, head and hair tucked under an arm, knees buried in his chest, off the side of the railbed where it met the tallgrass. He was dew-covered and, like his namesake, let his skin twitch when he felt something crawl up under his clothes. There were lots of those, things crawling up under his clothes, up his pantlegs, up his sleeves, through the placket unto his chest and stomach. Aside from the twitching of his skin and the imperceptible swelling of his chest when he took slow, short breaths, he didn't move. He stayed that way, not moving from where he rolled, until he could hear neither the train itself nor its thrumming in the rails a few yards from him.

He waited, unmoving, until only the chirping of peepers and crickets, the boasting of frogs and toads, until only the normal sounds of the night could be heard.

Nighthorse stood slowly, letting each movement alert him to any possible damage or insult his abrupt departure from the train may have caused. Satisfied, he shook himself off and brushed the dust and dew from his clothes.

He reached into his kit and removed the Gate, amazed it had survived the tumbling unscathed, and lifted it to his eye. The world looked the same whether he observed it through the Gate or not and he put it in his pocket, patting it to make sure it fell to the bottom where it would be safe.

He pulled some tallgrass up and licked the dew from the leaves and stems.

The train had passed a highway not long ago, not far off. Nighthorse had an excellent sense of direction.

Twenty minutes later he stood on the macadam of a state road, not an interstate or even a class V highway. He pulled up some more tall grass and continued to slake his thirst as he walked. He removed his sport coat and swung it over his right shoulder. It was the first time he'd been walking in years, walking where he could be seen and not worry someone might recognize him.

He couldn't afford to be recognized. He'd been dead eleven years.

CHAPTER 13
Detective Colodnie Johnson

DETECTIVE COLODNIE JOHNSON HUFFED AND PUFFED her way to the *Lake Shore Limited*'s security station at the rear of the kitchen car. Despite the smoothness of the ride she waddled in the narrow train aisles and pulled herself along as if climbing uphill. She hadn't eaten before leaving Chicago and didn't want Games or MacPherson to know she followed them onboard, so she stayed in her berth all through supper chain smoking and laughed at the smoke detector she'd juried every time she lit a new cigarette from the still burning end of the last.

Her stomach moaned in disbelief.

She sneered into one of the security cameras as she passed underneath and wondered what whoever was on the other end saw. A big, black woman? She wasn't really all that black. She could have passed for a dark-skinned Mediterranean, maybe a Sicilian or a Moroccan, her features were soft and her skin rarely ashed. There was an Italian girl in college with Colodnie, big like Colodnie. The BSU, the college's Black Student Union, approached the Italian girl to join but not Colodnie. She found out years later they were so embarrassed by their first mistake they didn't dare make another so never invited her to join.

In the beginning she thought she wasn't good enough, maybe not black enough or not militant enough, or not cerebral enough. Maybe they found out about her Aunt Connie, who ironed her hair and passed for the thirty years she worked as a secretary downtown, and that's why they never spoke to her or called her "sistah."

Or maybe they were just fucking morons, such totally inept fools, clods, and idiots they didn't deserve the likes of her.

She got her degree, enrolled in the Chicago Police Academy, and started eating two portions instead of one with every meal all in the same week. Smoking came much, much later.

She tapped on the patrol station door. It was ajar and no one answered. She withdrew her GP100 7 Shot .357 Magnum from its holster and slammed herself against the door, ramming whoever might be on the other side into the wall.

She entered the room faster than her colleagues might've guessed, her GP braced in attack position. She kicked the door closed.

Nobody.

She backed against the door until it clicked shut and panned the room. One of the security monitors flickered red then went out. She aimed at it for one, two, three slow breaths. She tapped her bellygun, a SIG P320 Nitron she kept taped into the expansive folds of the small of her back to make sure it was there.

Two guards manned the security station. One snored in the corner, spilt coffee staining his pants and the floor. The other sat at the control board, but arched back over the chair, arms flung out as if crucified. Images from the four by twelve array of monitors reflecting off his glasses made him look bug-eyed.

Colodnie checked for a pulse. "Huh. Sleeping like a baby."

She shook first him then the snoring one. Neither woke. A partially full styrofoam coffee cup rested on the control board. She lifted it and sniffed. Nothing. She stuck her finger in. Room temperature. She didn't taste it.

From their condition she knew whatever they'd been given was powerful and probably not lethal. It also explained how she could approach the security station unchallenged. The coffee's temperature told her how long they must have been out. She met no one as she walked down the train - nobody could have gotten past her. She took up the entire aisle if she walked straight on. Somebody could have walked from here towards the end of the train, but why? Beyond the kitchen car were baggage, transport, and flatbed cars and not too many of those. Both men wore active PTTs mobiles. She doubted they were the only security on the train.

Where was the other security? She'd seen no one. No lovers, no kids, no teenagers, no stewards, no conductors, no men or women the entire length of the train. The train was obeying the railroad traffic laws so the engineers must be awake. Or the train was smart enough to run itself. But for how long?

She looked around and found the station log. Entries every fifteen minutes, stopping at 21:30 local. It was 2:45 now, five hours and fifteen minutes after the fact.

Who would want the entire train out for this length of time? Who would know how to do it?

Games? "Stupid fool thinks I wouldn't have trains covered? You're a clever fool, Games, but not like this." She pushed the man at the control board off the chair and took his seat. Within a few minutes she called up the passenger manifest, located his suite, and called up the suite's camera through monitor two.

She panned right to left.

Dr. Games sound asleep. The camera's privacy alarm should've woken the dead. There were no sound capabilities or she would have listened for breathing.

Tom and Jamie MacPherson were one suite down. She played their suite's camera.

A sheet covered a lump on the floor, a dark stain surrounded it. It was about the size of the MacPherson boy. She panned the camera. Tom MacPherson was nowhere to be found.

She got up, racing, no longer a too big, too fat woman who couldn't get out of her own way to save herself, now a smaller train within a train, the smaller eclipsing the greater with its speed. She clicked a PTT she'd lifted from one of the guards as she leapt out of the security station. "Anybody hear me? Anybody?"

Breaths came hard and fast when she blew the lock off MacPherson's door. The door slid open and she dropped to one knee, the GP braced in an overhand grip. She aimed down the barrel at bunk, bunk, overhead, overhead, underneath, underneath, zigzagging back and forth rapidly looking for some telltale revealing somebody watching her from the shadows. She spun to her other knee, rolled onto her back and kicked open the lavatory door.

Nothing. No one.

She turned on the light and lifted the sheet. "What the fuck?"

She dropped the sheet and checked all possible hiding places again.

Somebody groaned next door in the Games's suite.

She ran and pounded on the door. No answer. She pounded again. "Games, this is Detective Johnson. Open the goddamn door."

Crashing noises came from the other suites and she ignored them. She lifted the GP to blow the lock off when Jack Games opened the door, his eyes barely open, and fell into her arms.

It occurred to her this could be enjoyable. She let him drop, got a glass of water from the lav and threw it in his face. "Wake up, you stupid nigger!"

CHAPTER 14

Pangiosi and Tom

EARL PANGIOSI POURED HIMSELF ANOTHER TWO-FIN-gers of Macallan and turned the stereo on low, Sinatra, soft and not distracting. Above the train's rumblings and Sinatra's croonings, he heard movement from the bedroom.

"Ah, Mr. MacPherson, are you ready to join us?" He opened the door and flipped on the lights, turning the dial to full brilliance.

On the floor, straightjacketed and gagged, Tom MacPherson closed his eyes and rolled away from the harsh brightness.

"Well, Mr. MacPherson how are you today? It's such a relief to know you're still with us. I was concerned, you know." Pangiosi helped Tom up onto the edge of the bed so they could sit side-by-side. He laid an arm across Tom's shoulders and gave a gentle hug. "Mr. MacPherson, I am your friend."

Tom hesitated, resisting Pangiosi's gentle pressure, squinting at the silhouette Pangiosi made against the lights.

"Oh, so sorry, Tom. May I call you 'Tom'? Let me turn those lights down a bit."

Pangiosi walked to the switch and back. When he stood over Tom,

Pangiosi adjusted his sport coat to reveal his 92X in a sling holster.

Tom's eyes went wide and fixed on him.

"Do you know, Tom, your wife, Eleanor, and I were quite close friends? Did she ever mention me?"

Tom's eyes narrowed and his brow descended.

"God's truth." Pangiosi held up his right hand. "What became of her, Tom? Do you know? Can you tell me?"

Tom looked around the room, his eyes moving quickly, taking in the richly paneled walls, the dresser, the vanity, the entertainment system, the phone, the computer recessed on the far wall, the slightly ajar lavatory door showing the hints of marble within, the other door showing the working table and chairs and paper stacks thereon.

But he never took his eyes off Pangiosi for long.

"Let me tell you what I know, Tom. Let's see where it all fits."

Pangiosi sat on the edge of the bed, his left foot touching the floor and his right leg crooked over the covers. He folded his hands in his lap and canted his face and eyes to the ceiling as if the memory was written there.

"I'm not sure where we recruited Eleanor. Oh, I have the information in the other room." He waved towards the open door. "But that's not important right now. I'm sure you agree. Don't you, Tom?" He shook his head as if dismissing some of the memory. "What I really want to discuss with you is the matter of her departure. It is most interesting and quite puzzling, to be sure."

Pangiosi's gaze came down to Tom. "Now just so we're clear, Tom, what I'm about to tell you is quite confidential. Top secret, hush-hush, eyes only and all that. I'm happy to tell you, of course, but then, as they say, I'll have to kill you." He laughed, looking sideways at Tom and punching his straight-jacketed arm. "Oh, laugh, Tom. I'm kidding."

His voice grew quiet, conspiratorial. He leaned in to Tom, his arm around Tom's shoulders.

"The first thing you need to know is that I'm involved in dream research. That's where all this begins, and Ellie got herself involved in it with us. Did you know Ellie is what some people in the field call 'a gifted dreamer'? I don't think she even knew it. Basically, she had the ability to go so deeply into her dreams they became her reality. Now this is something right out of mythology. Australia's aboriginals have been telling us about this kind of thing for years but let's face it; dreams become realities? You have that whole wishes-horses-beggars thing and nobody wants that." His head shook briefly as if tasting something distasteful.

"But back to Ellie. At one point Ellie was fully in D-sleep - that's 'desynchronized' or 'dreaming sleep. That's what we call it, 'D-sleep' - and had been for days. It almost seemed as if she'd been waiting for us to come along and help her succumb to Morpheus' charms. Except we didn't. My hand to god, we didn't do a thing to her." He slapped Tom's thigh as if the two were enjoying a joke. "Can you beat that? We didn't do a goddamn thing and, as soon as she can, she's fast asleep and twitching to beat the band."

Pangiosi stopped and rubbed his forehead. "You know, as I remember we had to drug her to keep her awake. I think by the time she disappeared she had so much benzedrine in her her eyeballs bulged through her eyelids a bit." He gently nudged Tom's ribs with an elbow and looked at him sideways. "Makes me wonder what kind of a man you are you'd tire a woman like that."

Pangiosi's smile shifted from a snicker to grin. "Now imagine my surprise when I read through the passenger and freight manifests and discover we're on the same train going to the same place and that you suffer from some malady that makes you sleep and not dream. A significant item, that 'and not' part. Dear Eleanor couldn't stop dreaming, you can't dream at all. I'll ask that you remember this information for further along in our discussion." Pangiosi stared directly into Tom's eyes. "You'll do that for me, won't you, Tom?"

Tom blinked.

Pangiosi continued. "Good, but first, let me share with you what happened to our beloved Eleanor. I've never shared this with anybody. Nobody else noticed it, nobody else knows about it. But there's a good reason for that. Here, let me show you."

Pangiosi got up and went into the lavatory. He came out with his hands over his eyes and stood directly over Tom.

"Ready?"

Tom grunted.

"Boo," Pangiosi shouted as his hand dropped to his side revealing his eyes, the left blue, the right brown. "Interesting phenomenon, don't you think? It's called 'heterochromia iridis'. It's not rare and nothing most ophthalmologists would be concerned about. My eyes were sensitive as a child, indeed so much so I started wearing shaded contacts in my teens, but as I matured so did this somewhat unique trait and there you have it." He shrugged. "I've had to wear contacts just about nonstop ever since. Only when the lighting is low, like this, or at night when there's no other lights around can I get away without optical aides."

A tear slid down Tom's face.

Pangiosi's tone became conciliatory. "Oh, come now, Mr. MacPherson, I'm making every attempt to be your friend here and enlist your aid in solving this mystery. There's really no need to be afraid." He patted Tom's shoulder and wiped away the tear.

"Where was I? Oh, yes."

He got up from the bed, selected a flashdrive from a keychain full of them, stuck it in the TV's USB port, and returned to the bed with the remote in hand.

"Can you see this alright?"

He turned Tom to face the TV.

"Now you watch this, maybe you can help."

The screen gained color as the TV loaded the file and played the video.

White words showed on a black background. "Pay no attention, Tom. That's just spookspeak, meaningless to anyone outside the intelligence community. But just lookie there in the lower right hand corner."

Tom read the YYYYMMDD date - a month after Ellie'd gone missing - and almost inhaled the gag.

"I knew that'd get your attention. Quiet now. Shhh. Watch."

The white words and black background were replaced by Ellie

strapped to a hospital gurney, tubes in her nose, tubes down her throat, tubes in her ears, tubes running up under her eyes, a pump and respirator near her chest, waste bags hanging by her side. She was covered by a thin sheet and heavy leather belts held her down. Her cheeks were shrunken, her chestnut-auburn hair oily and falling out in patches. Bandages and sutures made a mosaic on her scalp. The only sounds from the player were the quiet sussurations of feeding and breathing and waste removal mechanisms attached to her. Everything else in the room was clean and white.

Tom groaned, shook, and strained in the straightjacket. He choked, his face reddening with tears.

Pangiosi put a hand on him. "Shhh, shhh. Here it comes."

A single soft, white light fell on Ellie's face, stroking it, as if brushing her hair away.

"Pay no mind. Moonlight from a single small, window high on the exterior wall. We had to keep it for insurance purposes. Fire hazards and all that. Stop people from asking stupid questions."

Ellie twitched. Her eyelids fluttered. Tears formed where tubes were inserted under the eyeballs. Her head moved back and forth, to either side of the gurney. She started to moan something, as if trying to speak despite the feeding and respirator tubes up her nose and down her throat. Her head lifted as much as it could and she tried to clear her eyes by blinking, as if to better see down by the foot of her prison.

"Quite impressive, Tom. Doesn't it appear to you she's trying to communicate with someone or something that's right there? One might conclude she's hallucinating, hypnagogic or hypnopompic experience, but wait for it."

Tom groaned and strained to get free of the restraints but what happened next took all the fight out of him; Ellie, lying on the gurney, moaning and looking at nothing he could see, began to fade as if some special effects wizard had doctored the file. She relaxed, she lay her head back, and she began to fade but not any of the instruments attached to her. She grew translucent, then invisible, then all the tubes and wires and bleeders and feeders and restraints and the sheet collapsed onto the table and floor. Alarms sounded in the background and the room filled with red light as the moonlight faded away.

She had gone. Vanished. As if she'd never been.

"The last time anything like this was recorded was the biblical story of Enoch. Do you know that one? 'And then he was not'? I tell you, Tom, literally every person who's seen that file has been as baffled as I'm sure you are. I'm as sure of that as I'm sure you didn't see everything that happened. Neither has anyone else and neither did I until I watched the file one night in this very room."

He adjusted the counter to the point where Ellie's eyelids fluttered and paused the file.

"There." He jabbed the air with the remote control for emphasis. "There, do you see it?"

Tom stared at the screen but all that filled his eyes was the horror of Ellie.

"No, of course you don't." He grabbed Tom's hair and pulled Tom's head around until he could stare into his eyes. "No, you're not as blessed as I." He made sure Tom's eyes were on his, opened his eyes wide, and blinked. "What you can't see that I can, Tom, is a suddenly appearing group of little shadowy creatures. Little dark humanoid forms hovering all about our dear Eleanor, touching her, caressing her, helping her."

Pangiosi backed the video up and replayed it in slow motion. "Right before their appearance Eleanor was close to waking up, but she was still experiencing deep dreams. She wasn't giving any indications of a smooth transition from one sleep stage to the next. It was as if she was waking up but something, some part of her, wasn't ready. Then these little fellows - I assume they're fellows - show up. Look at them."

Tom frowned. Pangiosi pointed. "There! There! See?" He glanced at the frown on Tom's face, at Tom's eyes roving the picture and not seeing what was there to be seen. "Oops. Sorry. You can't see them, can you. Forgot about that. They're definitely communicating with her. Now they're all around her."

Ellie's head turned side to side and up and down, moaning what sounded like words.

"I wonder what they're saying to her. I wonder what she's saying to them. 'Eleanor, we're here to help you. But you must hurry, girl. Hurry.' 'Who are you?' 'We're Mr. Leyman's Midnight Men.'" He turned to Tom, shook his head and waved the remote in dismissal. "Don't worry about Leyman. He was somebody else who didn't work out."

Pangiosi's attention went back to the video. "'What are you going to do to me?' 'You've got to get ready, Eleanor. If you're late everything will go wrong.' They're hustling around Eleanor as if she was the most important prize the universe could imagine. I wish I could find workers with that sense of urgency. Look at their anxiety, their nervousness. Perhaps they thought we might come in and find them."

Ellie started to fade.

"I'll tell you, Tom, it makes me wonder if there's more to dreams than any of us ever imagined."

Her body went away. The room she was in went red as monitors sounded alarms. The moonbeam pulled back up through the window and away.

"What if Eleanor was caught between waking and dream realities and a fluke occurred. What if her body was ready to wake up but she wasn't in it yet and that's what the rush was about? Makes you wonder, Tom, doesn't it? Makes me wonder and I can only remember one dream in my entire life."

Pangiosi turned off the TV and tossed the remote onto the entertainment cabinet.

He faced Tom. "You're not able to do that, too, are you, Tom? Eleanor seemed surprised when they arrived, and I'm only guessing her agitation and then calm was in response to the arrival of Mr. Leyman's Midnight Men." He sighed. "I spent most of the day watching people fall asleep on this train, all types of people falling asleep in all sorts of places, and not once did I see anything like that happen again. I don't know why I can see these little creatures and you can't. No one else on my staff could. Leyman could but he had regular, homochromia eyes.

Then again, I'm not really sure what he could see. How about you, Tom. Any ideas?"

He stared at Tom for a moment then repeated himself. "So can you do that, Tom, call up little shadow people like that? Hmm?" He clasped his hands in his lap. "I'll tell you why I'm so interested. I've been able to see something similar for as long as I can remember. Not quite little human-like creatures, more like little amoeba blobs that take on whatever shape is needed. One would assume such an ability, demonstrated under extreme stress, is genetic. That make sense to you?" He paused. "But no one in my family, either side, ever made mention of such a thing and in my family, such an ability would have been talked about ad infinitum." He laughed and slapped his knee.

"But then again, nobody in my family had hair as brilliantly red as mine." He paused. "Not that I know of, anyway." Pangiosi smiled at Tom. "Now Ellie, she had beautiful auburn hair, didn't she?" He paused and looked away as if contemplating. "Auburn. That's kind of red, right?" His gaze fell back on Tom. "And your boy - Jamie, isn't it? - he's a ginger, isn't he?"

Tom's eyes went wide and he shook his head like a dog shaking off water.

Pangiosi smiled. He put his arm around Tom's shoulder conspiratorially again and turned Tom's head so they could stare at each other. "What this means to you is, if you don't demonstrate the ability to bring forth little shadow men then the only one I have left to test is your boy. Interestingly enough, he was not in your room when my people got you. With all the Ambien we pumped into the food and water, he managed to escape and hide somewhere on the train." He paused. "Sorry about the dog. Dogs are man's best friend, you know."

Tom grunted and strained himself against the straightjacket.

"So, either you manifest it, or I have to find your son."

Tom tried to kick at Pangiosi but only succeeded in pulling the crotch strap tighter. He winced and fought to catch his breath.

A light flashed in the living room section of Pangiosi's car. "Ah, people elsewhere are waking up. At least the security personnel in their little station are. That's what that little light means. Someone soon will discover you're missing, your dog is dead, and your son is gone. With your history with the police, that's not going to look too good for you, is it?"

CHAPTER 15

Empty Sky

A COLD WIND RUFFLED JAMIE'S BATHROBE AGAINST his pajamaed legs. Thick animal fur warmed his face like a blanket, and its smell filled his nostrils with each breath.

But not Shem's fur. It smelled...heavier than Shem's fur...more urgent than Shem's fur.

He raised his head, his hands stiff from clenching Graywolf's coat. "We're almost there, Jamie."

They moved through a rush of trees. White-barked birch and scotch pine, gray ash and winter oak towered over him, their branches alternately pine needle and leaf and snow covered and offering a canopy through which the night sky, its stars and planets, could still be seen.

High overhead the moon sailed through the sky, full and rumbling like a big church organ. The Aurora walked back and forth in the cold night, crinkling like cellophane candy wrappers, sounding almost like words just beyond his ability to understand, like the Aurora was people talking at a party, like when Mom and Dad had people over and Jamie and Shem listened from the top of the stairs.

The wind moved through the trees and sounded like long, low, breathy, conversations, as if the world talked all around him, ignorant or perhaps unaware or maybe even uncaring that he and Graywolf *ruddaRump*ed underneath.

Jamie whispered, "It sounds like everything's talking."

"Everything is, Jamie. The world just waits for someone to listen."

Something moved quick and clean, a snowhare, down and ahead of Graywolf's steady gait, leaping out of his way. Jamie wondered that he could hear it, wondered what kind of magic was in this place that he could hear things so.

Overhead, he heard the beating of great wings. Many of them. Large birds, and in a flock. From the island of trees ahead, wolves. Hundreds and hundreds of wolves. Howling, their calls drilling across the frozen arctic plains. Their howls answered from somewhere high up in the sky. From the forest of pine and birch trees up ahead came howls and the sounds of other feet, padded like Graywolf's, *ruddaRump*ing across the wilderness, gathering, all of them baying at the moon, some sounding like they came from the moon.

"We're here." Graywolf stopped running so quickly Jamie tumbled from his back, rolling in the hard-packed snow, rolling where many feet had pressed it down. He yelped and put his hands out to stop rolling. They came back cold and wet.

What's going on? Why wasn't Dad waking him up?

Tall pines and birch, ash and oak, continued their rumbling talk all around them, their breath filling the air with the scents of their saps and spines, their voices washed back and forth like waves on the snow. The moon continued its deep organ trumbling high overhead. The Aurora he was right about. It did come down, right into this clearing. He could see there were lots of different lights moving back and forth, not just one big one. All the different lights had different colors and sounds associated with them. The ocean sound became a breathy sigh as the lights came and went.

Jamie stood and brushed snow from his bathrobe. The lights stood aside and he stared into the clearing's center.

Many eyes stared back.

From the ground and the air above it.

The beating of wings didn't come from birds. It came from wolves. Each wolf had great feathered wings. When folded, they tucked so tightly against the wolves' backs and sides they practically hid in the fur. When extended, each wing was twice as wide as its wolf was long. There were birds in the air and in the trees, too. Owls and eagles and cranes and more, but none of them as big as the winged wolves.

Jamie's legs wobbled.

Graywolf came up behind him, supporting him. "Easy, Jamie."

Some of these creatures hovered with great windy wingbeats over the heads of those on the ground. Others came and went, trotting and galloping along moonbeams, rays from the Aurora or sometimes flying with their peers like puppy-dogs at play.

"What kind of wolves are these?"

From the center came an old, gruff voice. "We are not wolves."

Graywolf had his doggy-smile again. "Oh, now you've done it." With his long nose he pushed Jamie in through the winged wolves to the voice at their center. It came from a very old, very white, winged wolf.

The old creature sniffed at him then ruffled his wings the way an old man might pull his coat tighter around him after seeing some unpleasantness. "Hmmph. Human cub."

Several of the winged wolves rose up from the snow and ambled towards Jamie, their noses twitching as they approached. Clouds of warm breath rose from each as they moved silently on the snow, their pads making marks like white whispers while their tongues hung over long, sharp teeth.

Other wolves rose, their noses twitching as well, their ears flicking forward and back. Their eyes and coats glistened in the ever-brightening moonlight, brown eyes and blue eyes shining and watching from faces of gray and black and brown and white winter fur.

Sweat dampened Jamie's robe. It entered his slippers and slickened his feet. His heels, steaming with sweat, melted the snow, like sand shifting under his feet when ocean waves came to lick them.

The wolves circled, closed.

A familiar voice, not Graywolf's voice, came from behind him, from the direction of the ever-brightening light. "Enough."

The voice came again, "Enough." But this time the voice carried every sound Jamie'd ever heard at night. Owl calls and wolf howls and trees rustling and rain and snowfall and bats crying and crickets tittering and things he didn't want to know grunting and running.

The winged wolves stopped, their eyes and ears and nostrils and tongues fixed on what stood behind him.

"Of all that dreams, of all that rests in the sleeping world, he alone hears me."

Jamie felt something rest gently on his shoulder. A hand? He didn't want to look and find out it wasn't. As it rested there, the voice resolved itself into one heard long, long ago, a woman's voice. "In all the sleeping world, he alone hears my voice. It is enough."

One of the wolves not far from Jamie raised its muzzle and howled. Soon some others joined in, each wolf lengthening its throat and lifting their muzzles skyward. Within moments all the wolves sat on their haunches, their eyes open yet seeing nothing in the cold, night sky, each one hollowing its muzzle and lolling tongue until the arctic plain echoed with the trumpets of the night.

Finally the old wolf rose and walked over to Jamie, licking its lips and running its tongue over its fangs like a barber stropping his blade. It knocked Jamie to the ground and licked his face, just like Shem, only the old wolf's tongue was a little rougher as it ran along Jamie's cheeks.

"Yes. It is enough." The wolf's breath filled Jamie with thoughts of deer kills and things chased through the snow.

The howling stopped while the old wolf spoke. Now it rose again twice as loud as before. The wolves howled, their tails thumped the snow-covered ground, the Auroras sang and waved and lifted up into the night, merging to become a multicolored nightcloth. The trees spoke a single word that came out as a deep, shaking thrum.

"Where am I?"

A woman, dressed completely in white, walked from behind Jamie to beside him.

She was the most beautiful woman Jamie ever saw.

Everything about her was white: white skin, white lips, white mouth and tongue when she spoke, white hands at the end of a billowing white sleeves, white hair flowed like a lion's mane and almost touched the snow-covered ground. Her white robe had the faintest lines of nightsky-blue edging. Jamie was sure if she wore shoes or slippers beneath her long robe, they'd be white with the fine blue edging, too. Only the fine lines of her features and shadows on her face gave clues to where lips ended and nose began, where nose ended and eyes began, and so on for her ears and chin and brow.

Except her eyes. Deep and dark, almost as if she had no eyes at all. Jamie stared but couldn't be sure. It almost seemed as if there were stars in the dark of her eyes.

"You are in my garden, Jamie," she said. "You see these men and women around you?" She waved a hand. A crowd of men and women replaced the gathering of wolves, easily as many people as there had been winged wolves a moment before, dressed all sorts of ways. Some looked like they worked in cities, some in the country. Some looked like they came from far away. Some wore clothes Jamie had never seen before, some wore almost no clothes at all. Some looked like they drove trucks and some looked like they flew planes. Two pups, their wings not yet fledged, wrestled at the edge of the group until a woman cuffed them into silence. They stood up and became young men. The people were of every color, as if their skin had taken on the colors of the winged wolves' fur.

But all of them shared one thing in common. All had their right eye blue, their left eye brown.

"Yes."

"These are my guardians, Jamie."

An old man dressed like a woodsman, a green hunter's cap pulled down tight around his ears, a red and black plaid jacket with its collar pulled up and buttoned tight around his neck so only his scruffy, unshaven face showed through, walked up to him. "Aye," he said.

"Guardians of The Moon. Children of a King your pack has long since forgotten."

"Who are you?" Jamie asked the woman.

The clearing brightened as she spoke. "I am The Moon."

Jamie looked at her. He knew the moon he saw in the sky was only a reflection of the moon he saw here, much like the moon in the sky was only reflecting the light of the sun.

"Why did Graywolf bring me here?"

The old man took off his cap and ran a rough hand through thick, white hair. Jamie could see his face clearly. His eyes. The right blue, the left brown. He lifted a pipe from his pocket, tamped tobacco into it, and lit it. A cloud of smoke blew in Jamie's direction and a sweet smell like mornings in a forest filled him.

"Because, cub," the old man said between puffs, "you listened."

"I did?"

"You heard when I spoke, Jamie," said The Moon. "You did not know it was me, you did not know what you heard, but it was my voice and you responded to it. For all the time that men and wolves, men and the children of wolves, have walked together, those who've heard my voice are asked into my service."

"You want me to become a wolf?"

Graywolf laughed and Jamie looked up at the sound. Graywolf was a man again: long black hair, dark skin, right eye blue, left eye brown. "No, Jamie, not a wolf."

"Come, child. There is much to tell you." The Moon held out her hand to Jamie, the sleeves of her robe filling the sky like sails sown from the Milky Way.

Jamie looked at the creatures around him, some winged wolves, some human, Graywolf, tall and silent, the trees now quiet, the birds and hares and moles and voles, rabbits and fox, even the Aurora stopped crinkling. All grew silent, waiting.

He reached out and took her hand.

"Jamie, do you believe you will see your mother again?"

"I don't know. I hope so."

"Yes. You don't *know*, you *hope*. Imagine how you'd feel if you knew you'd never see her again."

Tears filled Jamie's eyes and made icicle rivers down his face.

"You do not know, you hope. Hope goes beyond knowledge. Hope sees more than knowledge can reveal. Hope lies in dreams, in imagination, in the courage to turn dreams into realities. It is what the Old Ones of your kind called *Elp*." Her eyes closed and she shuddered as if touched by a brief pain. "When people lose hope, when you believe you'll never see your mother again, that is despair. It, too, has an ancient name: *Vön*."

"I don't understand. Are Elp and Vön people?"

Graywolf said, "Not exactly. Remember what I said about always finding the center? You can see Elp in the eyes of a baby in the arms of its mother, in the voice of a father teaching his child to play games, in the sounds of a village working together to bring in a harvest. Elp is what's in people's center, what holds them together."

The Old One spoke, "Aye. Vön is what drives them apart. It is the wolf that never had a pack, never fed from a hunt, never had pups who played. Old beyond time, its coat matted and unkempt, never hearing a mate's or kin's answering song in the night." He pulled on his pipe, pursed his lips and exhaled a cloud of smoke. It coalesced into a lone wolf on a hillside, thin, hungry, afraid, but always wanting to be strong and not knowing how, then floated away. "When the world was young, when your pack first stood on two legs and saw farther horizons, hope ruled the world."

He became a winged wolf again. "Now they look no further than what they hold in their hands, their eyes never cast to the heavens and it's the heavens that's your tribe's destiny."

All the wolves, winged and wingless, howled in agreement.

"Some's dreams go no further than their next meal and they forget the rest of the world dreams of being warm, being fed, being safe, being dry, …"

Jamie turned at the sadness in Graywolf's voice. "Being loved," Graywolf said. "People are losing the ability to dream, Jamie. To imagine. Without that, humanity is lost."

He knelt and rested his hands on Jamie's arms. "We would like you to help us, Jamie." He stared deep into Jamie's eyes, ran his hands up and down Jamie's arms as if warming him. A tear slid down Graywolf's cheek.

"Are you okay, Graywolf?"

"We cannot ask for your help and leave you unaware, Jamie. You must know what you'll face."

Jamie met Graywolf's eyes. He blinked and looked up at The Moon.

The old winged wolf spoke up. "No one serves the Queen under force, cub. It is your decision to make but make it you will before you leave this place. If you decide to walk away you'll wake up on the train and all of this will have been an interesting dream. If you decide to walk with us you'll live your life seeing things as they truly are, as they must be seen."

"What's that mean?"

Graywolf shook Jamie's lightly. "It means you'll always see things' centers. The real meaning of things. What people really want, not just what they say they want."

Jamie's face scrunched, deep in thought. "You mean like one time when I didn't want to give Bobby Games any of my HotWheels, but he didn't have any and I gave him some of mine anyway?"

The Moon glowed brightly. "You shared even though you didn't want to. You chose compassion over fear, kindness over conceit. That is Elp. If you chose not to, if you feared your having fewer more than his having none, that would have been Vön."

Graywolf held Jamie at arm's length. "To do what you must do, Jamie, you must lose your innocence, and it is better I show you than a world of others who love you less." Hot tears became snowflakes drifting down to the snow. "You can't do what you'll be asked to do unless you know the enemy you'll have to face: Hopelessness. It is your decision to make, Jamie. If you are willing to help us, you'll be changed forever. There's no going back if you say yes. Do you understand?"

Jamie nodded. "Yes."

"Look into my eyes, Jamie."

Jamie did. He saw things. Horrible things. Bombs falling on mothers running, their children in their arms. Boys no older than him and Bobby Games carrying weapons into fields and on city streets.

His vision swirled around him, engulfing him in what he saw, a hellious dancer pulling him on to the dance floor.

Soldiers came into his home with long knives called machetes, killing his baby brother and sister before his eyes, before the eyes of his parents, then running their blades through the rest. The last thing he heard was the soldiers laughing as they walked out, bloodstained.

People came at him with clubs, beating him, beating the people with him, beating them because they looked different. Or thought different. Or spoke different. Or prayed different.

He watched people half-buried in the ground, unable to move, screaming as wild animals came to feed on them.

He watched boys his age and younger, girls as well, walking streets, standing under streetlights or in dark alley corners, getting in cars.

He held his hand out for food and heard laughter from behind before being knocked to the ground.

Someone grabbed him and threw him in a van, left him in a dark room, chained to a bed, until someone came in.

He was a teenager. He was with a girl. They left their baby in a dumpster and ran, hoping to outrun its screams of hunger.

He was a man. He watched his wife and children torn from him, torn from each other, never to be seen or heard or felt or known again.

He forced his sister to leave her baby on a bench in a park in the dead of night.

He was old. He lived in fear. He slept, woke and lived with nothing, his mind, heart, and stomach empty.

He felt hunger. Pain. Cold. Thirst.

But never love.

Never, ever love.

Graywolf closed his eyes.

Jamie's world stopped swirling, the dancer let go. Jamie shook, his little hands shaped into claws, his eyes darting, his chest heaving yet unable to breathe.

He screamed.

A BRIGHT LIGHT SHONE ON HIS FACE. SOFT HANDS cupped his cheeks. "Mom?"

"I'm here, Jamie."

"I had a bad dream, Mom. I'm afraid."

"I know, Jamie. That's why I'm bringing you special friends. Friends like Graywolf. They'll help you, Jamie. They'll help you."

"You know Mr. Graywolf?"

"Yes. He is one of many. I...We...need you to be strong, Jamie. I know you're afraid. And you're still a little boy and I want you to be my little boy forever, but I can't be selfish like that, Jamie. Do you understand?"

"You can't be Vön."

"Exactly, Jamie. I can't be Vön. But I can be Elp. Can you be Elp with me, Jamie?

"Can you be..."

Mom's voice faded as Jamie opened his eyes.

He lay on the ground, The Moon kneeling over him, holding his face in her moonlight hands. A campfire blazed. Around it, cave people, an old one talking, grunting, pointing. All the others, especially the young, listening, focusing, their faces wide with amazement, wide with joy.

The old one stoked the fire. Embers flew up into the sky and became stars. Jamie followed them with his eyes. All types of mythical creatures walked in the starry embers, some battled, others counseled, some played.

The family faded. Graywolf tended a fire. Beside him, The Old One. Beyond them, The Moon's Guardians and all the wonders of the night.

Graywolf offered Jamie the stick to tend the fire. "Teaching stories, Jamie. People learn through teaching stories."

"The creatures..."

The Moon nodded. "Yes, Jamie. Those must never fade."

Jamie watched the sky. "I saw my Mom. I talked with her."

The Moon knelt beside him, helped him keep the fire alive. "Yes. There is hope."

Graywolf came over beside him. "I'm sorry, Jamie, so sorry."

The Old One became a winged wolf again and sat across the fire from him. "From now on, cub, when you see a man walking to work you will instead see a giant going to protect his village. When you see a girl riding a bicycle you will see a woman flying a mission into space."

The Moon guided his hand so they stoked the fire together. "You will see not just them, Jamie. You will see their dreams."

The Old One's wolf tongue licked its nose. "Aye. Some dreams will be so simple: another bowl of oatmeal before going to bed or a little sugar in their coffee. Other dreams will be so complex: recognition for an idea that will change the world or a secluded house high on a hill, away from the demands of others." It changed back into a man dressed in woodsman's clothes once again. "But the point is, you will see people both as they see themselves and as they really are. You will understand why some people are willing to be seen as fools and others willing to kill not to be seen as such, why some people run and hide when others approach and why some go gladly into a stranger's arms."

Graywolf took the stick from Jamie's hands. He touched it to the fire's core and both blazed with blinding new flames. "And always, their truth will be in their center."

Jamie understood.

There'd be no more playing HotWheels™ with Bobby Games. No more trips to Disneyland or Busch Gardens or even the small amusement parks an hour from his house. He might still do these things, but their meaning would be forever changed for him. Every time he played or laughed he'd know there were others who never knew play and who never laughed, others to whom every day was a challenge and few survived.

The Moon's dark eyes fell full open him. "Jamie, I am sorry."

The Moon took Jamie's hand and helped Graywolf to his feet. "You have done well, Mountain Child," she said. "There is one more task which remains to be done. There is little time to do it in."

"I will need one more night, perhaps two, and your light to guide her."

"Those you shall have. Can you do it?"

"In this world and the next," he said. As he spoke his body melted from man to wolf and he raced off into the bright, moonlit night.

The Moon knelt until her face was even with Jamie's. "Jamie, do you know where your dreams come from?"

"No."

The Moon stood, lifted her arms, and turned to take in everything. "From here, Jamie. They come from here."

All the men and women had returned to winged wolf form. Those closest to him either lay down on the hard-packed snow or padded silently back and forth. The others walked quickly and on their toes, like Shem when he was waiting for something to happen, to go for a walk or to play. Some opened their wings and groomed or took to the skies. Scents of Shem, memories of how warm and comforting his fur was even when wet, filled him.

Stars, twinkling, dotted the sky. A soft wind rustled the winged wolves' fur, carrying with it the sound of the planet as it moved through space. The Aurora's arcs seemed like rippling rainbows, a multicolored river rapid against the darkness of night. Where the lights touched the ground, little human forms, men and women, took shape and walked amongst the wolves, chattering and nattering in their little crinkling cellophane talk. In other places the human forms stepped into the Lights and were transformed as they were pulled up into the night sky. Along the edge of the clearing trees waved their branches in recognition.

"Those light people? They're dreams?"

The Moon shook her head. "No." She closed her eyes and lifted her arms, her billowing sleeves and gown capturing suns and stars and galaxies. But not only images from deep in the night. Her gown captured ocean bottoms and mountain tops and caves so deep it took years to reach their ends. "Watch, and listen..."

"To what?"

The Old One quieted him. "Shh..."

Softly, just at the edge of hearing, Jamie heard a *tha-thump tha-thump*, almost like the rhythms of the train, of Graywolf's running, but...but it sounded like his own heart when Uncle Jack let him listen through a stethoscope.

It grew stronger yet quieter, spreading out, surrounding them, gently quaking the winter landscape, gently shaking the trees, each *tha-thump* a whisper, a promise, like heartbeats, each one a gift.

The Moon, her arms wide, her eyes still closed, her chest rising and falling, her face becoming more beautiful each moment.

Jamie heard a *tha-thump* beside him. A little silhouette stood there. It took his hand. Its eyes twinkled like rainbows. The arctic plain disappeared, his backyard took its place. He was playing Frisbee with Mom and Dad and Shem. Shem was woofing. Mom could throw it but couldn't catch it at all and everybody laughed. Dad threw it in all crazy ways: underhanded and flipped from his side and upside down and... the smell of cookies. A buzzer going off. Mom said, "Okay, now, Jamie. None of these for Shem. Understand?" Dad standing behind Mom making faces. Jamie burst out laughing. Mom turns and pushes Dad away. She looks mad. "Three men," she says. "How did I get three men in my life?" Shem woofs. Mom breaks a cookie in half and gives it to him. Dad laughs, takes her in his arms and kisses her. He picks Jamie up and holds him between them, Mom and Dad kissing him. Shem woofs and everybody gets down on the floor and everybody's loving Shem.

The twinkling stopped. Jamie was back in The Night Garden.

The *tha-thump* came from The Moon, from her heart. Each beat brought more of the little silhouettes, their eyes twinkling as they rose into the sky, into the night.

"Who are they?"

"They are Dreams, cub. The Oneiroi. Through their eyes your pack sees what might have been, what will be. They give warning, they bring hope."

"The Oneiroi - Dreams - are my children. They connect the heart to what has been, to what might be, and are older than thought. They are my gift to you. Before humans were, when they first looked up into the night sky, wondered and didn't fear, I gave the gift of Dreams."

"Listen close, cub, and understand. When the world was young dreams were made so people could hope. When people hoped, them that had it in them, could act upon their dreams. Not everyone did, but not everyone was supposed to. Only a few dreamers per generation were necessary to help your kind find their path." The Old One looked up into the dark night. "But now and for a while past, people haven't dreamt, or they've dreamt things they shouldn't, or they've forgotten how to dream. Some don't want to dream at all, don't want to hope at all. They want something better but don't dare hope for it."

The Moon's arms lifted to guide her children into the night. "It comes down to the ability to make a choice, Jamie, to choose something better for yourself and for others. To choose to do right from wrong or even wrong from right."

The Old One's gaze fell back on Jamie. "Dreams helped your kind make that choice."

The *tha-thumping* stopped. The Moon pointed. "Look up into the sky, Jamie."

Dark patches. When he arrived on Graywolf's back, he was sure the sky was filled with more stars than he'd seen on the darkest Upper Peninsula night.

"What happened to all the stars?"

"The dark patches in the sky are where there is no more hope, where there are no more dreams, cub. Your pack has forgotten what it is to dream, to believe tomorrow will be better than today. They no longer want to dream and instead fear their tomorrow may never come. Their lack of hope strengthens Despair, the Destroyer of Dreams."

The Moon's light dimmed. "Where there is no hope, there can be no dreams."

"How come that means there are no more stars?"

"Because the stars are where your pack would look to see their dreams, cub, to tell their stories, to learn right from wrong. Your ancients put their heroes in the stars, your pack learned how to circle the world by them, your tribe told stories about the gods and monsters that lived among them."

The Moon's arm swept the sky. "The stars are no longer where people place their dreams."

"Aye, your pack made the stars something to be understood. In your world, things don't exist until someone understands them. People have forgotten it's alright not to understand, that there's more to Night and Day than telescopes and satellites reveal, there's more in the Earth than a few miles of hole can show, there's more in the oceans than the deepest diving subs can reveal. The places where you do not understand are the places were magic happens."

"Like this place, here."

"Yes, and in your world, too. I've been to your cities, cub, long ago when I was a man. You can't see the stars from the centers of them and people wonder why there's so much trouble in their hearts. Your pack lights the darkness and forgets the darkness has lights of its own, lights that reveal things that can't be seen by day. Despair, believing things can't change, is more real to them than dreaming a change that brings hope. Your pack seeks to understand because they fear not-understanding more."

"The Vön!"

"Aye. Your pack's forgotten; not-understanding and understanding go together like two scents on the same tree. One tells you where you've been, the other where you're going."

Dark tears occulted the stars and night that filled The Moon's eyes. Hollow rivers streamed down the whiteness of her face. "Jamie, people act as if the deep earth, the forest and the waters, the moon and the planets and the stars, were their own creation, something discovered one night when they fell out of a tree and looked up to see where they'd been, something to do with as they pleased."

Jamie reached up to wipe away The Moon's tears. She took his hand and kissed it. "Yet people write songs about them, write poetry about them, people laugh and hold and love under them, people know there's still mystery in them. That mystery used to bring awe and wonder. Now it brings fear, the unknown, but not to explore, now to exploit."

"Understanding is fine, cub, but not forgetting."

Several wolves howled at the Old One's words.

"Forget the mysteries and you forget where you've been, you lose track of where you're going."

"In their emotions," said The Moon, "in their hearts, where people live whether they want to or not, even the ancients of your peoples realized that to sleep, to dream, was more important than anything that happens in their conscious lives. Without dreams, without hopes, without wishes, without the ability to touch at least one other person with your life, all that remains is an empty sky."

Jamie wiped her dark tears with his hand, fearing his bathrobe sleeve would be too rough on her moonlight face. She kissed his hand and moved it away. The winged wolves howled as she sobbed.

"I didn't know."

"There is more, cub."

"What more?"

The Moon whispered, "I do not fear for myself, child, but in time..."

The Old One spoke up. "In time, cub, she will become a dark moon, unseen through man's clouding of the night, no longer circling the earth, no longer shining light, no longer calling people to dream. Then, cub, your pack will be lost. The Old Enemy, Despair, will have won."

"Dreams are the heart's way of seeing."

"What can I do?"

The Moon placed her hand on his shoulder. "You, Jamie, can dream."

"Of course I can."

The Moon shone on him. "Jamie, you hear but you do not understand. You can dream, as could your mother."

"My mom?"

"There are worlds upon worlds, realities which come and go in an instant or stay side-by-side through all eternities. Your mother, Jamie, is learning to dream Warrior Dreams, to move realities between worlds. When you return to your world, Jamie, there will be others come to help you."

"Mom told me that, too. Who are they? How will I know them?"

"They are others who can dream."

"But I still don't know what you want me to do!"

"The Gate is the eye of a Dream, Jamie. It is a lens to worlds where anything can happen. If you and the other dreamers use it, you can destroy Despair."

"Maybe not forever, but at least for a while," said the Old One.

"Yes. You can at least restore the universe of dreams." The Moon waved at the ever-darkening sky. "But the Gate you hold is special. It is the eye of the Oneiroi that guided your father's dream, his last dream, the dream he's not yet woken from."

"From back at the cabin?"

"Yes, he dreamt of your mother. An Icelin destroyed the Oneiroi guiding your father's dream. He can wake but always part of his mind will be searching for your mother, calling to her, needing to hear from her, to finish his dream."

"What can I do?"

"Before your Gate weakens, you must use it to let your father finish his dream."

"But remember, cub, the Gate can only be used a few times when it's removed from a Dream."

Jamie covered his mouth as he remembered. "But I've already used it. A few times. I looked at people around me to see if they were different."

"That is naturally done. The Gate shows how things really are when used as a simple looking glass, but as a lens, a focus for pulling what might be into what is, it will only work a few times.

"Have you changed anything that you saw into something you'd rather it be?" asked the Old One.

"No, sir."

"Good. There's plenty left."

"But how will I know when to use it?"

The Moon walked away from the winged wolves and Jamie. "That is why I chose you, Jamie. That is why when I spoke you listened. You still dream. You still choose. You must decide when to use it and how." She looked up into the sky. "Remember to always seek the Center."

"Those are the decisions you have to make, cub. Those are the choices difficult to make."

"What if I make the wrong decisions? What if I can't decide?"

Jamie watched as The Moon's heart started glowing in her chest, brighter and louder with each beat, until Jamie could see it and hear it beating over the landscape. When Jamie could see it pulsing red under her white gown The Moon sighed. Wind rushed up around her with the sounds of big bass organ pipes and she melted into it. It was as if her body became an arrow with her heart its head, her gowns the shaft and feathers, and the snowy plain and all that remained the bow shooting her into the sky.

The woman-arrow flew high into the night. The winds remained, swaying trees and making Jamie pull his robe tighter around him.

The Moon, round and bright, spoke from high in the heavens. Jamie could feel the deep notes of her words vibrating in his belly. "You are still a child, Jamie, and children...naturally...dream."

The Queen of the Night continued her transit across the sky.

Jamie rested a hand on the Old One's head and rubbed his ears. Several of the younger guardians got to their feet and snarled.

"Stay," growled the Old One. "It has been long since a human has rubbed behind my ears, cub." To the others he said, "It will be a memory, for finding."

Jamie had no idea what he meant. "My dog likes this."

"It is time for you to return to your pack."

"How?"

The old guardian laughed and his tongue wagged again. "Listen."

Far off, distant, Jamie heard a train rushing through the night, its whistle screeching to warn all things away.

"Is that my train?"

"Aye. Not far now. Just beyond those trees. Hurry or your first decision will pass you by."

Jamie started walking, then running, as the winged wolves took to the air and howled in the moonlight. He stopped and looked back, the train whistle now distinct and growing louder by the second.

Before long he could see the train's wheels turning. He could hear it rumbling along and knew it was moving quite fast. He could see lights coming from some windows on some of the cars and watched the train's great headlight whiten the distance.

Yet it was standing still. It was standing still and the wall to the Deluxe Bedroom Suite he shared with Shem and his dad was gone. It was dark in there, but he could see well enough in the moonlight to take a good solid step and be back on the train. There was no wind where he stood, but on the other side of the train he watched and listened as its wake vacuumed up the earth and pulled on the trees.

He stepped inside.

He tripped over a lump under a sheet on the floor.

Lights were coming on, in the hallway, in the suite.

He lifted the sheet.

He screamed.

His hands raced against each other to lift his pants from under his bunk.

Gone.

There, on top of the bed.

The pockets were empty.

He screamed again.

He tore at his shirt.

Nothing.

Again he screamed.

He lifted his clothes, everything he owned, each time a dry, wracking scream.

He understood. He had a choice. He could use the Gate to bring back Shem.

But where was the Gate?

He tossed his clothes aside and stroked the body of Shem, as if his hand alone would be enough.

Alarms like schoolyard fire drills sounded all along the length of the train.

A thud in the hall.

A groan.

A big, black woman filled Jamie's doorway and stared at him. "How'd you get in here?" She had a gun in her hand pointed up, not at him.

Security guards raced up and down the hall behind her.

CHAPTER 16

The Stranger on the Road

CAPTAIN SALLY ORATED NANTUCKET LIMERICKS FOR sixty miles without repeating a one and without cracking a smile. Al left the highway and took country roads to relieve the boredom.

"We'll have to pull over soon, Captain."

Sally leaned over and inspected the gauges. Gas was low but not dangerously. "See if you can find a real diner this time. You know, looks like a trolley car without the wheels..."

"I know what they look like."

"Hard to believe from all them *Dunkin Donuts Citgos* you stop at. Time for a real breakfast."

"Ok."

"Stack o'jacks. Eggs. Real ones you can break open and watch the yolk flow out. Sausages. Bacon. Homefries. Burnt crisp with onions in them. Thick bread toasted brown. And butter making the center out to the edges looking like a sunrise on a dusky day." He squinted at a figure hitchhiking ahead on the road. "Maybe he knows a place around here."

"I don't know. He don't look too local, not with that suit and all. Looks more like he broke down. We didn't pass a car, did we?"

"Not that I recollect. Pull over anyway. I'm tired of talking and you don't say much."

"Aye, Captain."

WALKING EAST, HIS THICK BROW SHIELDING HIS EYES from the rising sun, Nighthorse caught the sound of an old pickup coming up the curves behind him. He enjoyed walking, the smell of the dew rising from the asphalt as the sun struck it, the smell of the grass and the trees as the morning engulfed them, the feeling of the movement and the rhythm of his body doing something it was meant to do. Maybe he'd take off his shoes and socks off to enjoy the feel of the world under his feet again, something he hadn't felt since he was a kid working in grandpa's store.

But he didn't have time. The rambling old pickup sounded closer.

John turned to face the oncoming pickup, an old Ford F-150, red with white trim, a big V8 with a five speed standard from the sound of it. There were two men in it. Both old, or at least older. Older than John.

He stuck his thumb out. They slowed and pulled right up beside him.

Both looked old and tough and like men who'd worked more than they'd played, but men who were proud of it. One was a barrel and the other a rail. The barrel wore a CAT diesel baseball cap and the other a sailing captain's hat. They reminded John of himself and Styles, the way they'd be if they'd stayed together another twenty-five, thirty years.

The rail rolled down his window. "Where you heading?"

John smiled.

SALLY ROLLED DOWN HIS WINDOW AS AL STOPPED the pickup. "Where you heading?"

The hitchhiker smiled, strong white teeth in a dark-skinned face. "East."

Al smiled back. "East we can do. I'm going to Dartmouth College. He's going - "

"Further. Maine coast, most likely," Sally finished. "You know a place to get real food around here?"

The hitchhiker pulled a long, braided ponytail over his shoulder. "Sorry, can't help you."

Sally lifted the handle on his door and the hitchhiker held it shut. "I'll ride in the back, if it's alright."

Sally lowered the handle slowly and the door latched itself closed without ever having opened. "Fine with me. Al?"

"You're not going to hurt us, are you, friend?"

The hitchhiker watched them carefully. "No. You plan on hurting me?"

Sally laughed. "I don't rightly think we could by the size of you."

The hitchhiker nodded. "I'll get in the back now, if that's alright."

"Don't mind at all."

"Thanks."

"Got a name, friend?"

"John." He paused. "Nighthorse."

"Sounds like you ain't too sure." Sally reached into the ashtray for a corncob pipe.

Nighthorse shrugged. "That's the name. Can I get a ride?"

Al nodded. "Not a problem, Mr. Nighthorse. Knock on the window when you want to get off, ok?"

"'K." Nighthorse threw his jacket and kitbag in back and climbed up over the wheelwell.

When they were going fifty-five again, Al said, "You think he's a real Indian?"

"Only way to find out is to ask."

John, resting against the driver's side wheelwell of the truckbed so he couldn't be seen in any mirrors, lifted the Gate to his eye and stared at Al and Sally.

He put the Gate down slowly, closed his eyes and rubbed them as if squeezing out lemon juice. Opening them, he looked at trees and fences and roadsigns they passed.

Everything looked normal.

He raised the Gate again.

Al was some kind of half-man-half-beast in the middle of a whirl-wind. Not standing on anything and blowing, white wind swirling around him. Snow? All Nighthorse could think of was a friendly werewolf in a snowstorm.

John lowered the Gate and looked at Al: a man in his early sixties, heavy in the gut but still with some strength through the arms and shoulders. If anything, it looked like his hands were attached to the steering wheel rather than just holding it. Could have been due to the light.

He gave Sally a second look. The old salt was a man in a sport coat at a blackboard, looking back in his direction, talking to someone behind John. John blinked and looked again. Now Sally was the same man but dressed in scuba gear on a rocking ship and holding something like a valise.

Well, at least he was on a ship with rigging and a boom. Maybe a small fishing or lobstering vessel.

Matched what Nighthorse, sans Gate, could see. The second image, anyway.

But neither were completely what they seemed.

Nighthorse exhaled slowly through his nose and returned the Gate to his pocket.

Several hours later Al Carsons was driving up Main St. in Hanover, NH, and weaving his way around the Dartmouth University campus. Half a country ago, Doc Martin told Al Carsons to take a vacation. Specifically, take a vacation to Dartmouth's Vail Hall, to a Dr. Capoçek Lupicen, and to stay there and do what Dr. Lupicen said until Dr. Lupicen told Al it was time to leave. "But where am I supposed to go?" he asked.

Sally pointed. "That's it. Vail Hall."

Al parked in the indicated lot next to a long flatbed that looked like it had a miniature aircraft carrier on the back. As they watched a fleet of drones buzzed onto the flight deck and a young woman in a t-shirt and overalls got out of the conning tower.

Sally put on his best smile and waved. "Nice rig."

The woman nodded. "Yeah, we do lots of aerial surveys up here, easiest way to do some deep woods studies. This is just the maintenance vehicle, though. I don't get to play, only to test and repair."

"Those work over water?"

Al got out and watched the students go by - many of them international and of colors and hues he'd only seen in magazines or on TV - as Cap'n Sally chatted up the young woman. Al muttered, "What am I doing here, Effie?"

Nighthorse jumped out of the back, lifted his kitbag and snapped his jacket over his shoulder. Captain Sally got out and walked around to join them.

"What now?" asked Nighthorse.

Sally pointed back the way they came. "I'm hungry. Going to walk downtown and see if I can't find me a real breakfast."

"Sounds good to me," said Nighthorse.

"You two go on ahead. I'll catch up with you later. I'll tell Lupicen I'm here."

Nighthorse and Sally waved him on and headed south through the campus without another word. Al shuffled towards the main doors of Vail Hall, hands in his pockets, eyes down, each step wandering a little from the direction of the last.

Inside he followed the office listing's instructions and quickly found himself looking through the open door of Lupicen's lab. So many people, most of them young, some of them in labcoats, about a fifty-fifty mix of men and women and about a fifty-fifty mix of sneakers and sandals. It was Indian Summer outside and the windows opened to let the warm breeze in. Papers ruffled and tried to escape smoothed granite paperweights holding them down. Other papers blew off desks only to be picked up by people and placed under the stones as they passed. Computer screens blinked or winked or showed strange scenes on most of the desks. He heard snoring and followed it back to a series of little rooms constructed in the middle of the lab. Every few seconds there would be an almost human sigh from the center of the little rooms and Al wondered who exactly Lupicen had sleeping there.

Through the windows he watched rolling thunderheads coming out of the west. The breeze brought the sharp smell of lab cleaner to him and he sneezed.

A young bespectacled woman came forward. "Can I help you?"

Al looked at her numbly.

She blew a stray lock of blonde hair away from her eyes. "Excuse me, sir? Can I help you?" She stuck a well chewed pencil behind her ear and folded her arms across her chest, keeping a clipboard in her hands while she looked at him.

"Effie would call your haircut severe," he said. "But your eyes make up for it. She'd call them 'Icelandic blue'."

"That's about the most original come-on line I've heard since I got here, Dad." She emphasized 'Dad' and Al blinked at her.

"I'm...I'm sorry, miss. I'm lost."

"Are you here for the RBD studies?"

Al handed her Doc Martin's paperwork. She read it, consulted her clipboard and wrote something down.

"Mr. Carsons, hello." She offered her hand. "I'm Sandy. Olafssen. When was the last time you slept?"

"I don't know, twelve, fifteen hours ago."

"Any occurrence of Charles Bonnet...did you have any hallucinations? Little men, maybe?"

He shook his head.

"Are you tired now, Mr. Carsons?"

"Yeah. I guess. I just drove in from Minnesota. Hallock."

"Perhaps we should show you to your room and let you freshen up."

"I got a couple of fellas with me. Drove out with me on their way to Maine and - ," he couldn't think of where Nighthorse was going, " - the coast. Any chance they could bunk with me and get a fresh start tomorrow?"

"I'll see." She turned back into the lab, never letting her clipboard down. "Dr. Lupicen, we got another of your Dreamers here."

A praying mantis of a man separated himself from the group thronging at the middle of the little rooms. "Yes? Who is our lucky fellow now?" Lupicen came forward with his hand out.

"This is Mr. Carsons, Doctor. He's here from Minnesota at the request of a Dr. Martin."

She got no further. Lupicen took Al's hand and shook it. "Yes, yes. I remember. Doctor Martin speaks greatly of you. We are lucky to have you here and hopefully, when we're done, you will be lucky enough to sleep soundly again."

"He has some friends and wants to know if we can put them up for the night, Dr. Lupicen."

Lupicen patted Al's arm and smiled. "Certainly, certainly. This we can do. Maybe they would like to take part in our little studies, yes? I believe we can be as generous to them as we are to you. This we can do, Ms. Olafssen?"

"Just wanted your approval before I offered it myself, Dr. Lupicen."

"You will ask your friends, Mr. Carsons, if they would like to help us, too?"

"Yeah, sure. I'll ask them."

"Then I will leave you to Ms. Olafssen to see to your rooms and meal passes and all such good things. When you are ready and refreshed, come to me here and we will begin. It does not have to be today, if you wish. Tomorrow is soon enough. Take the time to learn about our little village with your friends." With that, Lupicen bowed quickly and slightly, shook Al's hand again, spun and went back to the cluster of people in the center of the room.

Al followed Sandy Olafssen into the hall and down a flight of stairs. "Funny little man."

"Yeah, but we love him just the same."

The waiter looked down at the interesting pair who sat themselves at station 13, the last table at the edge of his section. Most of the other people in *The New Peter Christian's* were professionals, college students or professors who wanted to befriend college students. They either sat at the bar or chose tables back from the light. These two sat where the late morning sun came straight in, catching them in a spotlight. He lifted the two extra place settings from the antiqued tabletop. "Can I get you gentleman something to drink?"

The broad, muscular, dark-skinned, black-hair-in-a-ponytailed one, the one who looked like a professional but a professional what the waiter didn't know, said, "Water."

The waiter sensed a big tip coming.

The other one was old, tall, wiry, and smelled like a cheap pipe left in the sun. "You, sir?"

"You got any coffee left on the burner too long?"

The waiter protested. "Oh, no, sir. Our coffee is always fresh." He started writing.

"Now just wait up here, sonny. I want the coffee that's in the bottom of the pot, when you got about a quarter, half an inch left, that's been on the burner an extra half hour because nobody thought to change it. Now you got any coffee like that hanging around? Maybe back in the kitchen so cheffie can make some iced coffee tomorrow or tonight? I don't want it cooled down none. I want it right off the burner hot enough to curl my nose hairs. You know what I mean?"

"I'll see what I can do. You two gentleman want to see menus?"

"You still got breakfast?"

The waiter checked his watch. "For the next five minutes then the lunch menus come out. It'd be easier for the kitchen if you order from the lunch menu."

"Breakfast."

The waiter nodded then looked at the broad, muscular one. "You, sir?"

"Breakfast."

The waiter went down his list. "Eggs? Ham? Sausage? Homefries? Omelets? Westerns? Mediterraneans? Toast? Muffins? Bacon? Canadian? Hotcakes? Bagels?"

The old one said, "Yep. Bring it on. Sounds like breakfast."

The broad one said, "I'll have what he's having." He added as an afterthought, "And when you get it, a fresh pot."

The waiter walked away writing on his pad.

Sally took his pipe out of his pocket and cleaned it into his napkin.

Nighthorse said, "You can't smoke in here."

Sally took out his pouch and tamped some tobacco down. "You no likum *wasiçu* smokum sacred pouch?"

Nighthorse rolled his eyes and looked into the kitchen.

"You don't say much and you don't show much, Mr. Nighthorse."

Nighthorse shrugged, still keeping his eyes towards the kitchen.

"You want to tell me what you were doing on a back country road twenty miles between towns?"

"Walking."

"From what?"

"You got a lot of questions for an old man."

Sally put the unlit pipe in his mouth and sucked on it as if it were lit. "Ayuh, that I do. So what do you have in your pocket?"

Nighthorse's eyes came around and locked onto Sally's.

"I've known many an Indian in my day, Mr. Nighthorse, and I can say they go two ways. There's the ones who know when someone is their enemy and there's the ones who'll shoot their friends because they've forgotten not everybody is their enemy. Which one are you?"

The waiter came by with the water and coffee. Neither man spoke nor took their gaze from the other. The waiter quickly walked away.

Nighthorse looked to the entrance and to the kitchen as if they were a rock and a hard place, all the while keeping himself at an angle to Sally. He'd wanted to get away and instead he'd walked smack dab into it. In a day, two at the most, Pangiosi would be in this same town and he hadn't seen many places to hide. When Carsons told him he was driving to Dartmouth it seemed as good an idea as any to tag along, especially because Sally would be going further.

But Pangiosi wasn't just coming to Hanover and to Dartmouth, he was coming to see Dr. Lupicen, to find out about the incredible dreaming computer Dr. Lupicen built, and probably would subsume Dr. Lupicen, his test subjects, his research, and anything else he could get his hands on.

Nighthorse flashed onto the battered dog on the traincar floor and remembered seeing himself, caught in a spotlight and shot through the back while talking to someone.

Pangiosi would get his way. He would fuck these people up and they'd probably never know it. People with the best skill for undercover work are those with a native talent for misrepresentation and guise. That was Pangiosi all the way.

That's why Pangiosi was Pangiosi and Nighthorse was just a strong man. The NSA fostered Pangiosi's behavior but with Nighthorse it wasn't the same. He could kill the man sitting across the table from him and never break a sweat, but he wouldn't lie to him or mislead him. He'd tell him the truth and if he didn't want to tell him the truth he'd tell him nothing at all.

Pangiosi was a formidable foe and Nighthorse needed time to decide if he was going to run and hide or face the monster who'd created him. "Just a piece of rock. Good luck charm. That kind of thing."

"*Wotai*?"

"You must read a lot of books, old man."

Sally nodded. "Must be a *sicun wotawe wotai* for you to keep looking at things through it."

"Lotta books."

"Ayuh. You going to show me your *wotai* or am I gonna have to wrestle you for it?"

Nighthorse laughed. He pulled the Gate out and laid it on the table. Both men watched it soak up the color of the antiqued pine until it almost disappeared.

"Looks like rock candy."

Nighthorse smiled. "Yeah, but it ain't for eating, it's - "

"Just for lookin' through. I seen that movie, too. Based on Forrest Carter's *Gone to Texas*. Same man who wrote *The Education of Little Tree*. Mind if I take me a look?"

Nighthorse considered a second longer than he should have. Sally palmed the Gate and lifted it to his right eye. "Well, Mr. Nighthorse, ain't that a thing. Your *wotai* must have some interesting impurities in it. It makes you look halfway like a dog. Still, you're a right handsome man when you let yourself be, clean yourself up some and decide what you're going to do with your life."

The waiter came by with their tray of food and Sally stared at him through the Gate.

"Something wrong with the food, sir? I think I remembered everything."

Sally placed the Gate on Nighthorse's side of the table. "Nothing. Looks like you got everything. Nighthorse?"

When Nighthorse didn't answer Sally looked up at him. "What?"

Nighthorse closed his eyes, held them closed, and when he opened them he was looking away. When Sally'd held the Gate up, Nighthorse saw a similar image to the one he'd seen before: this time of a man in a sport coat standing beside a slide projection of some artwork, a pointer in his hand as he said something to people Nighthorse didn't see, as if the man were lecturing to a class somewhere in the past or future.

Somehow, somewhere, in his memory or in racial memory or in memories his grandfather's people gave him, he knew he should be either afraid or relieved by the magic the *wotai* held. He couldn't remember which.

But then the rock was clearly a *wotai wakan*, a Great Spirit Stone of some kind, and he'd never believed any of that, either.

Sally said, "Your water's getting warm."

Nighthorse answered, "Your coffee's getting cold."

Joni Goes to Dartmouth

JONI SAT AT THE COUNTER SEPARATING HER GALLEY kitchen from her small living room, eating the rest of the Brüdermann's frozen pizza, refrozen and rethawed, and sipping a Harp's Lager. Her eyes looked across the fifteen feet of empty space to the scorched facade of her fireplace, seeing nothing.

This was her home, this was her life. A bedroom, a galley kitchen just big enough for two to work uncomfortably in, a galley bathroom not quite as long as the kitchen on the other side of the wall and "off" the bedroom, and a living room slightly larger than her bedroom, which was just big enough for her queen-sized bed, a dresser, a mirror, a nightstand, and a vanity.

Her vanity. Each morning she spent an hour getting ready for work, not counting showering, brushing her teeth, and using the toilet. Each morning, ten minutes on each eye, five minutes on each lip, ten minutes on her hair, twenty minutes on her face alone. There was the hour. Add an extra hour to get dressed unless she remembered to lay out her clothes the night before, in which case it only took thirty-five, maybe forty minutes. Didn't matter if she was going out casual or dressed for the town, going to the office or to a meeting. Thirty-five, forty minutes minimum.

A piece of pepperoni, totally missed by the microwave, crunched against her teeth and she winced with the cold of it. A piece of pepper - maybe it was a piece of pepper. It was too hard and cold to tell the difference except that it tasted kind of vegetable-ish - got crunched and swallowed. She took a long, hard sip of the lager and belched as food and liquid fought their way down. Her eyes focused on the lip of the beer bottle and she laughed. Her own thick, red lipstick was stuck there. She took the bottle to her lips and rolled it, forcing more of her agar to splay on it, then she placed the bottle on the counter and stared at it.

Tall, thick, foaming and with a crown of red ringing the top. It looked like...well, let's not go there.

She brought the pizza up for another bite, got about halfway to her mouth, then dropped it down in disgust. Her eyes scanned her living room, from her front door to the security system right beside it to the brown, leather lounge chairs with the small metal and glass bookcase between them, the ashtray with the joint and plastic sample jar full of pot on top, over to the fireplace, the gold and green oriental carpet, the coffee table matching the small bookcase, the rackmounted black harman/kardon stereo beside the fireplace, another thickly padded black leather chair with an arching metal reading light angling over it beside that, then her black Strauss & Sons baby grand between the two windows overlooking the garbage strewn alley behind her co-op and the highway beyond.

Bauhaus all the way, that's me.

She called this her home and knew it was more than most people had. Definitely more than most people could afford. But this wasn't the place for children, not that she was sure she was ever going to have any. Dr. Fitz had been right.

So had the woman at the clinic. Her radar had been accurate. She hadn't walked up to Joni to retrieve her child. Her radar told her Joni was just like her and the woman was right. Like the woman with her orbiting children, Joni's relationships were defined more by mutual dependencies and needs. That woman's world was small, though. Joni's world had grown explosively large.

And dangerous.

All because Virgil refused to wear rubbers, wouldn't give her enough time to put in the foam, and the pill made her sicker than shit every morning.

"Yeah, all the fun of having a kid without having a kid."

Her eyes, finishing their circuit of her living room, came back to the lipstick-smeared beer bottle, a spittle of foam gleaming down its side, about to touch her hand. "You wish."

She pushed the box of pizza out of the way, rested her elbows on the counter then rested her head in her hands. A moment later she cried. This was no place to raise children. This was no place to have kids. And everybody she dated couldn't seem to think past her tits or her bed. The social media manager from work, the guy in accounting, the jerk she picked up when her friend talked her into going to AA, the line was endless, ending in Virgil.

So far she'd played with people who respected the rules of the game. When she listed her lovers for Dr. Fitz, one thing became obvious: she picked guys from lower and lower in the barrel. She'd thought Virgil was a step way up from that jerk at AA, a sixteen-year drunk whose one claim to fame was finding his spirituality flying a kite at the beach. He didn't lose himself in the bottle anymore. He just got lost at the beach. She went looking for him once and found him sunburned, stinking of whisky sours, and damn near strangled in kiteline with his kite crashed on the rocks.

She considered Virgil a major step up. Now she guessed not. She, like the woman at the clinic, must have her own radar, but one honing in on progressively dangerous men.

She emptied the bottle in one gulp and banged it down on the countertop.

It ended with Virgil.

She was tired. She'd made a decision and it somehow exhausted her. She rubbed her eyes and rested her head in her hands again.

THE RINGING PHONE WOKE HER UP. STIFF, HER ARMS, head, and neck seemed stuck together into a single piece, and her butt ached from sitting on the stool for so long. Her joints creaked when she moved.

She rubbed her face to get the sleep off it. "Give yourself a minute to wake up, Levis."

Another one of those shadow things stood on the counter.

No, this one was different. The others had mannish shapes. At least humanish shapes. This looked blobish, or amoebaish, without a face but she knew it faced her, and for the first time she realized how little color she had in her living room. Aside from the rug, everything else was black and brown. White walls with a green trim but black and white wall hangings, black and white photographs she'd taken in a master's class several years back when she had more time than money.

Photography and jiu-jitsu. After six months she tired of guys lining up to grab her gi and stuck with photography.

The blob grew tentacles and reached out to her. She pulled back.

It stopped, held still in the night.

A moment later its pseudopods reached out again.

Joni shook her head, opened her eyes wide, fixed on it.

It stopped a second time, held still.

Does it know I can see it, that I'm aware of it?

It slid off the counter, across the floor, oozed up the piano bench, onto and across the piano, and finally flattened against the window.

Joni craned her neck forward towards the darkness. "You block out the stars."

She pulled back again, raised a hand and covered her mouth, realizing she spoke out loud to a thing that could only be a dream.

Or a nightmare.

You're going nuts, Levis.

The thing spread towards her.

What the fuck? Who or what was this thing?

She opened a drawer and pulled out a rolling pin, shuffled herself off the stool and moved into her little living room.

The thing retreated against the window a second time. Only then did she notice it blocked out light from ground level up the several stories of nearby buildings, streetlights, billboard signs, traffic lights. … All occulted by its undulating skin.

But not the stars.

She raised the rolling pin and rushed it.

The thing shrunk to a line, collapsed to a point, sparked with infinite blackness and popped away.

She stared at the window, tentatively reached, ready to pull her hand back if she felt anything other than night-cooled glass.

Gone.

Where?

She looked outside.

There were hundreds of them, thousands, inkstains against the night, going up and down from everywhere all over the city. Little blobs in the night, gathering over buildings, over sleeping winos in the park, over streetpeople huddled over grills or in piles of trash, over the co-ops above, under, and around hers, over office towers filled with late working office staff who'd fallen asleep in their cubes, over apartments and homes up and down Boston's quiet midnight streets.

Ticks sucking the life out of the city.

The phone was ringing, wasn't it? Isn't that what woke her up?

A light crested the far end of I-90 where it met the expressway. It climbed up from behind and between some buildings as it moved up over the harbor. At first it was just a hint of something grand, and as she watched the crest turned into a crescent and the moon started to rise.

Somewhere she'd read that the moon was only half a minute of arc and from photography she understood a little of what that meant. As it came up over the buildings on the horizon it seemed larger, an optical illusion of the sky, except the perspective remained. Individual beams of moonlight flowed like lava through the darkening sky, They reached out to the ticks, shriveled them, crushed them, burned them, destroyed them.

Joni felt cold.

What the fuck is wrong with me?

Wait a second!

A moonbeam curved, came through her window, surrounded her.

With the little silhouette men.

The ones she'd seen before.

She watched the little shadow creatures ride the moonbeams up and down the sky. Those walking up towards the moon grew smaller in the distance.

And she could see the stars through them. The pinpoints in the sky, the ones she could make out against the city's nighttime haze, were visible as the little figures traveled up and down the beams of light.

The stars and the city lights.

WTF, Levis? WTF!

She turned at a voice beside her. "They show all, Joni. They show all."

A woman dressed in a flowing white gown smiled as she looked out Joni's window.

Everything about her was white; hair, skin, lips. Everything except her eyes. They twinkled with the darkness of midnight.

Joni opened her mouth. A beam of moonlight gathered the woman and she faded into it, through the glass she still rested her hand on, up into the night.

In her place Joni's living room filled with little silhouette creatures. One by one they turned back to the night and moved through the window, out and away.

She watched. The little figures danced under the rising moon, moved up towards it, gathered around it, their darkness still limning stars but taking on more human form in the light of the moon.

What is this? An alien invasion with the moon as the mothership?

Suddenly a single beam of the moonlight burst through the night and came into her room. It cut through her blouse like a laser, tunnelling through her breast and beating against her heart.

She felt it, felt the moon there, felt the heat of the light coming from that supposedly cold, libidinous orb. She stood, her eyes going from her breast to the moon as it moved up in the sky. Like a train braking fast, her chest throbbed as moonlight entered it. She felt her ribs quake, her whole body shaking. She steadied herself with one hand on her piano and the other on the windowglass. Again the moon shook through her as she watched her heart heave, pound, bang like a gong as its beating slowed to match the rhythm of the pulsing white light, as if her whole being was pulled through her heart into the night.

The little creatures, the small human shaped shadows in the night, walked the moonbeam down to her, filled her, entered her with the pulses, sought refuge, stayed.

She felt herself about to give in, to yield, to succumb to some overwhelming lover, when she lifted her heavy head from her palms and stared at the phone.

It had been ringing, for how long she couldn't know, but now her voicemail kicked in and she tapped it to speakerphone.

Virgil's voice. "Joni? Pick up. I know you're home. I'm coming over."

She rubbed her neck slowly. Her neck, shoulders, and arms still stiff, she looked around; to her left the remains of the pizza, in front of her a fresh bottle of Harp's. She touched it. Warm.

Christ, how long had she been asleep like that?

She checked the time on the microwave; 2:52AM. God, what a miserable life. Weird dreams about life-sucking blobs and silhouette babies because she'd had the abortion and now Virgil was coming by.

"Time to get out of Dodge." Soon. Now. If she didn't Virgil would show up and the concierge would let him in and he'd stay out in the hall and talk louder and louder until she let him in because he knew she didn't have the balls to kick him out or call the cops.

She packed in fifteen minutes flat, zipped her travel bag, threw it by the door, stood up and smiled.

Whatever she'd forgotten could be bought on the way. To where?

She changed her clothes and washed her face clean of makeup all in another five. She tied on her sneakers, threw on a coat, and glanced at her reflection as she walked out her front door. "You go, girl. Don't know where, but you go."

There were two elevators, one showed busy.

Virgil on his way up?

She took the other down and stopped at the freckle-faced concierge's desk. "Pete. No one gets into my co-op until I get back. Understood? No one."

"You got it, Ms. Levis. Any idea how long you'll be gone?"

"No, and write this down so everyone knows: Nobody, no access. I don't care if they say they're my mother, father, sister, or brother."

Joni watched him write the note. "Yes, Ms. Levis. I think your friend - "

"Yeah, I know. Tell him not to bother me anymore when he comes back down."

A lone cab moved slowly east along Comm Ave. She waved it down and got in. "I didn't know any cabs ran this late."

The cabby smiled. "Sometimes I can't sleep. Boss lets me take the cab home, so, when I can't sleep, I drive around, see what I can do."

"You got a name?"

"Several. Where you heading?"

She didn't know. Her hand touched the paper Dr. Fitz had given her. It was still in her pocket. "How far you willing to drive, Several?"

"Depends on the fare."

Joni looked at his hackney's license. It showed a youngish, dark-complexioned man with long, thick black hair in a flannel shirt. She couldn't make out much more in the dark of the cab. "I have no idea how to pronounce that name," she said.

"How about you call me Graywolf."

Just what she needed. Probably a Harvard PhD candidate who'd dropped out and joined an ashram to find himself. He probably went to a weekly sweatlodge-drum beating-AA meeting. She let it go. "Okay, Graywolf."

Joni caught sight of Virgil talking to the concierge through the co-op's glass doors. "Quick. Go. Anywhere."

He accelerated so fast she could feel the cold pizza and beer rise in her throat. Traffic was mostly delivery trucks and police cars at this time of night and he weaved through them expertly, as if he knew their moves before they did. Did this guy work for the people who hired Virgil? Did she step out of shit into the shithouse itself?

She studied the hackney license again. "Can you give me some light back here?" Lights came on on both sides of the passenger compartment. Yep, the man in the picture was the driver alright. There was something strange about his eyes. She looked up to see him watching her in the rearview. When he caught her eye he smiled. His right eye was blue, his left brown. "Nice eyes."

His smile widened. "Thanks."

She read his hackney's license again. Those eyes would be a real marker where ever he went. Unless he wore contacts.

"Graywolf? That's it? Graywolf?"

"That's it this time. Where'd you say you were going?"

"Ever been to Dartmouth College? Know the way there?"

"How much money you got?"

"What do you care? You were just driving around looking for mischief anyway."

He smiled as he adjusted the mirror. "Ok. You go to sleep. I'll take care of things up here." He pushed a button on his radio. Stevie Ray Vaughn started singing "The Sky is Crying."

She scowled. "I'm trusting you. If you try anything…"

"Hey, not me. I'm a coward."

She moved her hands to her purse. "I'm just letting you know, Mr. Graywolf, I have a gun here and I know how to use it."

"Aye, Kemosabe."

She fell asleep to Stevie Ray Vaughn before they got to Rte 128. A gray wolf watched over her in her dreams.

⸻

CHAPTER 18

The Lady in the Night

AL CARSONS WOKE UP IN THE DARK. A WOMAN'S FACE looked into his. He had to think of the word: Scrutinized? That's it. The face scrutinized him.

"Effie?" He wanted it to be Effie's face. No other woman entered his thoughts, ever.

He'd left the window open but the shades drawn, the covers pulled up against the northern New England night chill, feeling quite at home, forgetting where he was.

He lifted a hand from his big belly to stroke Effie's hair. His hand passed through the face.

It continued to stare at him in the dark.

It said something.

Is this one of those dreams Doc Martin told him about?

He didn't move, just stared back into the woman's face.

The night was moonless, the room cool and dark.

"Save Jamie!"

Al's eyes darted left and right. Was somebody in here playing a joke on him?

"I...I don't know any Jamie."

"When the time comes. Raise your Winds. Save Jamie. Go to your pack."

"What?"

He squinted in the dark.

Definitely a woman's face. Smiling? Confident? A sad smile? She wants him to do something? Who's Jamie?

He looked down.

Definitely a woman's body.

He averted his eyes. She might be naked.

Or surrounded by white, swirling winds.

Or he was.

Were those his sheets?

"I'm on a college campus," he whispered. "Some drunk college girl stumbled into my room."

His heart beat hard for a second as he reached for the light.

No one.

Captain Sally snored next door. He heard Sally snore off and on for some seventeen-hundred-and-fifty miles and he'd begun to appreciate why Effie'd sometimes elbow him to make him stop. If Nighthorse snored you'd never know it.

Al got up and opened the door to peer out into the hall. He didn't know how many other rooms were occupied, but all the doors were shut and no lights shown under the doorjambs. Dim lighting lined either side of the hall floor so you could find your way to the head or to the common area where there was a kitchen, a TV, and some chairs.

In the common area he stared at his reflection in the big windows overlooking the quad between the dorms and the research buildings. He was old, he knew. Old and alone without Effie beside him. Not even Charlie or Ben anymore. No other kin. Some people he knew, but mostly through Effie because she was the talker, not him, and some people from work. Tony, yeah. Doc Martin, maybe. Captain Sally, maybe. Or for sure. It was hard to tell with Sally.

But mostly just himself for the past five years. Staring out and staring back.

The sky lightened in the east. Stars began to fade. Dawn.

Dawn wouldn't break for another two hours back in Hallock, maybe three, and there they'd already had two big snows. Here, not even one. But he'd got up anyway. There might be something to do.

Down below a cab pulled into the parking lot. Al didn't think this town was big enough to have cabs. A woman got out. Al couldn't see much about her features except that she definitely had the figure of a woman.

Is that the woman I saw in my dream?

He blushed and mumbled, "Sorry, Effie."

The driver got out. The woman reached into her bag but the driver put his hands up, a "No thanks" gesture. It was too early for anybody to be up to get them a room and he didn't think there was anyplace open yet to eat.

He rapped gently on the window. They looked around. He rapped again. They looked up and waved. He signaled he was coming down.

Something big moved out of the shadows and Al jumped.

"Sorry, Mr. Carsons."

"John." Al patted his chest, stilling his heart. "You damn near scared me to death."

"You going to help those people?"

"I figure. If they got no place to go I'll invite the lady to take my room. The guy and I can bunk out here on the couches and chairs. What are you doing up?"

"Thinking. I appreciate your getting me into that study with Dr. Lupicen. It'll give me something to do while I decide what I'm going to do."

"Sometimes everybody needs a little time. I'll go see if those folks need help."

When Nighthorse couldn't hear Al's footsteps anymore he went to the window and looked at his own reflection through the Gate. He looked like he'd been through hell, but he looked better than when he looked at the dead dog on the traincar floor. Next he looked at the man and woman standing by the cab and Al trotting up to them. Al kept shifting between Al - a man too old to be that heavy but weighed down more by grief than anything else - and some kind of werebeast, something in transition. The woman...well, she certainly was a woman, except she glowed slightly, like the moon, when he looked at her through the Gate.

If he didn't let out a low wolf-whistle for the woman he certainly did for the man.

Where the man stood stood a wolf, massive and gray in the woman's light.

"I don't know what you got going here, Lupicen, but Pangiosi's going to go nuts with this."

Detective Johnson Investigates

Colodnie Johnson did not let surprises affect her performance.

How the hell'd the MacPherson boy show up unnoticed?

She didn't know.

How long'd he been in there?

She didn't know that, either.

She checked that suite. That she did know.

Make it fit, Colodnie, make it fit. Kid must've watched his old man kill the dog. Probably hid himself so his old man couldn't do him and watched him do the dog.

She pulled a cigarette from her pocket.

Yeah. Everything had an explanation if you just looked long enough.

She lit the cigarette.

Jack Games came up behind her. "Do you mind?"

He guided himself to Jamie's bunk with one hand on the wall, the other holding his head. "Jamie, you all right?"

"They killed Shem, Uncle Jack," he whimpered into the sheet covering his dog. "They killed Shem."

"'They' who, kid?"

"Oh for Christ's sake, Detective Johnson, have a little respect."

"Where's MacPherson, Games?"

Jamie's eyes went to his father's empty bunk. His face reddened. His hands clenched. He screamed.

Detective Johnson put her hands over her ears, her weapon and PTT two-way still in her hands, their metal pushing her ears flat against her skull blocking out Jamie's shrill voice.

Jack picked Jamie up and tucked his head into his shoulder, speaking softly. "It's okay, Jamie. Uncle Jack is here, Jamie. Uncle Jack is here and I'm not going to let anything happen to you, Jamie. You hear me, Jamie?"

"Where's MacPherson?"

"He's not goddamn here."

Colodnie Johnson whistled one of the Amtrak Security over to the suite door. "You make sure he doesn't leave this room and you make sure he touches nothing in this room. This room is locked down because it contains evidence. You got that?"

"Yes ma'am." The guard took the restraining strap off her gun.

Jack looked at them both. "Oh Jesus Christ."

Johnson hurried back to the patrol station. "Show me a map of where this train's been for the past ten hours."

"Yes, ma'am."

"Show me the car door security logs for the same ten hours."

"Yes, ma'am."

"Give me all recorded passenger movements. Match all these up side by side vertical with a timeline index."

Two patterns of movement. Hers and another. She counter-indexed the videos using the security logs as a reference. She watched herself on the monitor. There she was, alright, at one point even smiling into the camera.

One of these days, she was going to have to lose weight.

Or buy better clothes.

Fuck it.

Okay. She was comfortable that one set of security logs was her and her alone. Onto the next. She lit another cigarette.

Somebody was goddamn clever.

Hatch violations just as somebody shined a light into the nearest surveillance camera, a light strong enough to knock out the optics until the next hatch showed a violation. The progression worked its way from the front to the back of the train like a snake digesting too big a meal. The digestion slowed when it got to the *Viewliner* containing MacPherson's suite.

Back up the index. Nobody moving towards the engine.

"They were outside. On the roof. Then where'd they start?"

Back up a second time. No hatch violations.

"What the fuck?" She shook her head. "Save that for later, Johnson. Right now, find MacPherson."

She reviewed the suite videos for that time index.

Nothing nothing.

Nothing nothing.

Nothing nothing.

Nothing something.

Yep. At MacPherson's suite. A red flash blew out the camera.

What kind of a freak show was this? MacPherson was a cold-blooded killer but she didn't suspect him of conceptualized, serial slayings requiring this kind of planning. And how'd he leave the train?

She keyed the PTT. "We got any dead people up there?"

Various voices came back. "Car seven, not yet." "Car fourteen, everyone's fine. Sleepy but fine." "Cars eleven and ten. We got people waking up everywhere." "The drivers are fine. Last thing they remember is setting the speed on traverse slow before they nodded off themselves." "Car five. Everybody's got pulses."

Everybody reported in and everybody was fine. Some were still asleep, but fine.

She never fell asleep.

She'd not left her berth since boarding the train. She'd not eaten or drunk anything other than bottled water and a bag of *Snickers* minibars, both bought before boarding.

She keyed the PTT again. "Put one of Games's people on the line."

A groggy voice. "Yes?"

"Can you understand me? Are you awake?"

The voice cleared into a sneer. "Yes, I can understand you. What do you want?"

"Did you folks bring anything onboard that'll do a toxscreen on the food and water?"

Silence on the handset but voices back and forth in the background. "Well?"

"We could improvise. We could only look for obvious stuff."

"That'll do. Get some samples from the galley and supply cars and let me know."

She put down the PTT and picked up the hotline to the next Amtrak station. Thirty seconds into the conversation she said, "Fuck your blowback. Either you can do it or I call Chicago PD and have them invite the Cooks County FBI office to run the drill."

A muffled exchange of voices.

"I knew you'd think my first suggestion was better. I'm sending you the map now. I want a team covering that entire length of track - yes, it is a lot of track, that's why I want a team to cover it - and to look for anything indicating an emergency departure."

She listened again.

"That'll be fine. Thank you." She hung up. "Stupid fucking morons." Her next call was to Chicago PD, repeating her request in much less time but ending it with, "Yeah, well, W.C. Fields and the rest of the traindicks are supposed to be on the tracks looking, too. Do me a favor and shoot them if they get in the way."

JACK GAMES THREW UP HIS HANDS. "JUST HOW DO you think I got enough Ambien on this train to put everybody out? How the hell was I supposed to get it into the food and water without anybody noticing my being there?"

Detective Johnson leaned against the doorjamb to Games's room. The MacPherson boy was in the nurse's quarters. A security guard blocked the closed, yellow police-taped door to MacPherson's room.

"You brought half of CCMC onto this train with you, Games. You're the only one who could do it."

"Oh, I'm just too clever, Detective Johnson. I do all this without my staff knowing anything about it and I dump it into the food and water supplies without being seen."

He had a point. He'd even suggested drug and tox screens with Ambien on the top of the list. When she'd last talked to the FBI and asked how much Ambien was necessary to knock out everybody on the train for the period of time involved and show up at the concentrations the nurses found...well, he simply wasn't that big a boy.

But the FBI did turn up some hair, blood and clothing samples along the tracks about three hours back, a place where somebody suddenly left the train. No DNA yet but she could be patient.

Three hours didn't fit with Security's hatch violation logs, either. Not unless MacPherson decided to take yet another tour of the train but this time didn't open a single door to do it.

She stepped into the hallway and viewed the videos again on her phone. Hatch violations stopped in the *Viewliner* with MacPherson's suite.

She keyed the PTT. "What comes after car seventeen?"

"Mostly freight. Refrigeration units, boxcars, passenger luggage, some LandSea units and some US Mail. That kind of thing."

"How do you get in them?"

"You don't. There's no intercar access without a key and only the stationmaster's got them. Some of the cars you'd have to climb over to get to them. Even then you'd have to break the freightseals on them in order to enter."

"Is that tough to do?" She walked to the diaphragm at the end of car seventeen and looked to the next car. Sure enough, there was a door with a heavy, industrial, double-key padlock hanging right on it.

Hanging open right on it.

"Jesus H Fucking Christ. You and you." She pointed to two Pinkertons in the hallway. "You're with me. Let's go."

She led them straight back through three cars until they came to a flatbed with two LandSea trailers snugged back to back, marked US Mail, and still quite sealed. The only way further back was up and over them.

"Damn. You two climb over these and see what's on the other side. Look for anything pointing to someone being back there. Get back to me as soon as you can but be thorough about it. Understand?"

The Pinkertons started to climb. Detective Johnson went back to Games's suite.

"I still think you did this so your friend could get off the train."

"Of course I did, you idiot. And I killed the dog or watched him do it, too, right? Do you listen to yourself? Do you even think? Has it occurred to you that something as big as this was done by somebody with a lot more resources than I have or at least more than I brought with me? And the only person missing from the train so far is Tom? Tom ate the same food we did. He drank what we drank. He'd been sustaining a normal waking-sleeping pattern for about a day. The Ambien probably affected him the same way it affected us. If he's the only one missing it's because somebody kidnapped him. Ambien wouldn't cause psychotic episodes. He'd be as drugged as the rest of us..."

"And?"

He sat back and crossed his arms over his chest. "By your own admission, Detective Johnson, you were the only one awake the whole time on the train. There's more than enough evidence to demonstrate your harassment of Tom MacPherson. How do *I* know *you* didn't stage all of this just to get Tom somewhere and beat a confession out of him?"

She laughed. "You've been smelling your own glue too long."

But he made sense. There was nothing in either of their histories to indicate either Tom MacPherson or Jack Games could orchestrate something like this.

Only the FBI or somebody equally heavy could pull something like this off and the FBI would fuck up something on this scale. Ditto any other agency she knew of.

She needed the lab results from where somebody left the train three hours back.

She picked up the PTT and keyed the Pinkertons. "You guys find anything back there?"

OTHER LIGHTS WENT ON INSIDE EARL PANGIOSI'S private car. "My goodness, this is shaping up to be a busy day, isn't it?" He stared down at Tom. "Can I rely on you to be quiet for a while, Tom?"

Tom, still wide-eyed and breathing hard from struggling against the straightjacket and gag, nodded.

"Well, thank you, Tom. I do appreciate that." Pangiosi reached into his inside pocket again and Tom let out a muffled scream as Pangiosi pulled out a taser and fired it pointblank into Tom's gut. Tom convulsed off the bed and Earl kicked him under it.

"I knew I could rely on you, Tom." Pangiosi turned his attention upward. "It seems somebody knows enough to come looking for us. Pity, that."

He got up and went to the far end of his car, to the door leading back to the remaining cars and to the End-of-Train. Through the camouflaged exterior he watched two men climb down his car and then continue on through the others. "Oh, this will never do. Mr. Nighthorse didn't clean up after himself this time."

He reached through a seal and unlocked the door, then stepped out, quietly following the two train security guards as they made their way back to the End-of-Train platform.

"Look at that," one said, stepping onto the platform.

"Son-of-a-bitch. Looks like somebody had a pretty serious fire back here."

"No, gentleman," Pangiosi said, coming out with them and closing the door behind them. His hands were in his pockets as he stood before them guilelessly. "There were no fires here."

The first Pinkerton pulled his revolver from his shoulder holster. "Hands out where I can see them, mac. What's your name and what's your business here."

Slowly Earl removed his hands from his pockets. "Sorry. I didn't mean to alarm you." Earl, his eyes without their shielding contacts, focused on the man facing him. In a great Alec Guinness Obi-Wan Kenobi voice he said, "But there's nothing to see here."

The man lowered his gun as he stared into Pangiosi's eyes.

His partner watched him lower his weapon and said, "What the fuck you doing, man?"

Pangiosi turned his gaze on the second man and Alec Guinness spoke again. "You know there's nothing to see here, too, don't you."

The first man's PTT beeped to life. A female voice said, "You guys find anything back there?"

"Please tell whoever's on the other end of that device that you've reached the end of the train, are standing on the End-of-Train's platform in fact, and have nothing to report."

The man held the PTT to his face and keyed the mike. "We're at the end of the train, Detective Johnson. We're standing on the End-of-Train's platform, in fact. There's nothing to report."

"Damn. Okay. Come on back. We'll have forensics meet us in Springfield and go over all these cars before the brakeman can get to them."

"Got it, Detective Johnson. We'll be back up in a bit." He put the PTT back in his pocket.

"There." Pangiosi patted both men as if they were old college chums. "Don't you feel better?"

They nodded.

"I knew you would. Now I have one more thing to ask. You are with Amtrak security, correct?"

They nodded again.

"As I remember, the RailRoad Reformation Act didn't deprive you gentleman of rather impressive powers so long as you exercise those powers on railroad property?"

Again the vacant nods.

"Excellent. When we get to Springfield, please make sure the flatcars with the LandSea trailers marked US Mail get transferred to the *Vermonter* before anything else happens, would you do that for me?"

They nodded.

"There's my good fellows. Off with you, then. Go find your way back to whoever sent you and remember, there was absolutely nothing to see back here."

They stood there, zombies unaware of what was going on around them.

"Shoo, shoo, shoo."

They walked past him as if he wasn't there.

Earl shook his head in disgust. "The quality of help these days."

CHAPTER 20

Margerie's Kiss

EDUARDO IGNATIUS DELA MARTINA STARED AT THE black cloud, a darkness greater than the darkness of night, hanging over his bed. Its arms, so like an amoeba's pseudopods, reached down, almost embracing him. It sucked up his dream, drawing it from him as if sucking air from his lungs.

He inhaled, slowly, methodically, filling his lungs until his ribs ached and heart pounded, holding his breath to hold his dream until the darkness let go, snapped back, an elastic breaking with the strain.

Let go or gave up, he did not know. It flapped like a tattered sail clinging to the masts of his ebony four-poster bed and then dissolved into the night.

That's how he fought it. By not letting go. By not giving up. By keeping. By remembering.

It came when he dreamed of Margerie, taking little bits of her from him.

He noticed he was forgetting things about her. Especially in the morning. He had no symptoms of any dementia and being a man of science he studied his forgetting. He also started drinking lots of tea before bedtime.

Eventually, he knew, he'd wake up to pee and if he was lucky he'd learn something about his forgetting.

Either that or he'd wake up and forget to pee.

Never happened, but one night he woke cold and alone thinking of...

Thinking of...

He'd heard people use the term "it escaped me" when they couldn't remember something. This time he saw it. His dream, a memory of Margerie, escaping him, rising like a vapor, separating itself from him.

He followed the rising dream and saw a faceless, formless hole in the darkness floating over him.

He pulled the quilt up over himself and listened to his heart pound. He felt the darkness searching, questing, walking on cat's feet on the bedspread over him, only the covers stopping its claws from piercing him, rending him.

He swallowed.

He peeked. The black, shapeless thing hovered.

Was it alive? It moved like some dark nebula floating through space, some kind of black hole sucking in all hope and never letting go, letting no dream free, returning only a dark energy of dread and despair.

The next morning he fought to remember some simple thing: the way she liked her coffee. Cream first then three sugars with the tiny spoon, not a teaspoon, use the sugar spoon.

Yes, my love.

He realized. He understood.

It terrified him.

But he was a man of science. He replaced his fear with knowledge.

He taught himself to fight it. He gave it a name, a meaning, something to focus his studies.

No *spiritus nocti* was going to take his Margerie away. The loves of his life had been taken twice from him.

Never again.

He looked over to his dresser, to the picture of Margerie he kept there by the window.

"It came back again, old girl. What do you think it is? What do you think it wants?"

He had theories. "You think this is the chemo, Margerie?" He shook his head. "No, we stopped chemo a while ago. Maybe it's a hallucination because of the pain?" He glanced at a box beside Margerie's picture. "I won't wear the patch, Margerie. I may go out but I'll go out knowing who I am." He smiled at the photo again. "But then, I'll be with you."

He sat up. "Why do you think it doesn't bother with the nightmares? I wake troubled, disturbed, disquieted, and the *spiritus nocti* is just hanging there, not doing a thing, like it's waiting. It's not interested in the bad dreams, only the good ones."

He pulled back the covers and slapped his legs, felt the sting, smiled. They still worked. He looked back at Margerie "Only the ones about you. Let me dream some memories of happy times and that pitch black son-of-a-bitch is over me with its black, empty arms reaching into my mind to take you from me. I wake up and I feel the cancer eating me away from the inside out, a parasite of my own flesh, some monster inside of me killing me to set itself free. And the pain. I can't walk, I can't stand up for maybe five, ten minutes."

He swung his legs over the side of the bed. "You want to know the worst thing, Margerie? I can't taste my food. Everything's bitter."

His nightstand's drawer held a small, leather-bound notebook. He opened the drawer and removed the notebook. "Remember when you gave me this?" It was sealed with a cord with a fountain pen stuck in the binding. "Give me a minute to note this."

Somehow - he wasn't sure how - his *spiritus nocti* was linked to Al Carsons's dreams. He'd never seen the little shadow men Al described, and he'd done enough reading about Charles Bonnett disease to know he didn't have it or anything like it, and he'd done enough other tests on himself to know whatever he was going through wasn't something he was going to find in his books, his journals, online or in conversation with the medicos he knew on a first name basis.

But that Lupicen fellow? The one he'd sent Al to? He seemed pretty bright on these subjects.

When he'd talked to Lupicen's assistant, that Olafssen girl, on the phone to check and see if Al showed up safe and sound, she impressed him with what she said about Lupicen. He'd even done some looking up on Lupicen himself, just to be sure.

Not that he'd send Al or anybody to someone he didn't think could do them a whole lot of good, but with Al's case the trip was part of the treatment. Al was dying of a broken heart, while Eduardo Ignatius dela Martina was dying of a...

Dying of...

Perhaps he and Al Carsons weren't different after all?

"You know, " he whispered to the picture by the window, "I never lied to you." He pushed off the covers and sat up. "But I never told you the truth, either."

He smiled a lonely smile. He saw her face, knew she smiled at him, loved him, held him, wanted him still. The dark room couldn't keep her from him.

His side itched and he felt his colostomy to see if it was full. It wasn't. It was just the pain of memory.

He'd never strayed from Margerie. He'd been faithful, good, loyal, loving. They had no children, true. She wanted them badly, desperately, and couldn't understand why he always refused.

He lost a child once. He couldn't bear to lose one again.

"You always knew, didn't you, Old Girl? I gave you all the heart I had to give but I think you still knew. Somewhere inside, maybe? You never asked but you knew."

He lifted the picture and kissed the smiling face there. "And I love you all the more because you never asked. You know that, too."

She stopped asking for children.

She never had to ask if he loved her. He did and he told her so, more often than she could count. The one secret he kept from her, always so thankful she never kept any secrets from him.

But if someone other than Margerie were to ask him, if someone were to catch him unawares, his words would stumble, his voice would crack, and he would remember.

CAMBRIDGE IN THE FALL. BOSTON ALONGSIDE. THE Charles flowing wide and full in between. Didn't that say it all?

The son of immigrants who spoke broken English, his parents worked hard to make sure Eduardo could have the American dream.

Both died before seeing him achieve it.

"But here I am, Pa. Here I am, Ma. I hope you can be proud of me up there wherever you are."

He always looked to the same part of the sky when he thought of them, dead within a month of each other, his mother living just long enough after his father passed away to make sure all the money they had was available for him. They'd done well. They came over with lots of nothing and in fifty years owned a bakery, two apartment buildings and three trucks to deliver the breads and pastries they made there.

Eduardo dela Martina walked up the steps of the Harvard University Administration building. He'd paid his tuition in full, taking a loan out on one of the apartment buildings to do it.

He wasn't going to live on campus. He didn't have enough money for that. He'd rented out his family's apartment and set up some rooms for himself in the basement of their building on Prince Street. He could hear the boats on the waterfront from there and the dock whistle always got him up in time to catch the T across the Charles.

He went up to the secretary's desk in the front room of the Admin building and cleared his throat so the woman at the desk would know he was there.

She looked up. "Yes?"

He looked down at her. He stared. He swallowed.

"Can I help you."

He'd only dated Felincina Giancolo three times in his life and he'd never even gotten to first base with her. He knew he was staring and he couldn't help himself. It was Fall and where he was standing it was hotter than July.

The woman waved at him. "Hello, hi there, can I help you?"

She was petite with white skin lightly tinted by a suntan, reminding him of slightly rouged porcelain. She smelled like lilies. Her hair was golden and she kept most of it up in a bun, but a few strands fell down past her ears, across her cheeks and stopped just shy of her lips. She had soft, small, almost pouty lips.

"If you don't state your business I'm going to call security."

"I'd like to take you out to dinner sometime. And a movie. But we can have a cup of coffee first. Right now. Or a soda. Whatever you'd like. You have beautiful eyes."

An upperclassman, his red hair in a crew cut, thick-chested and wearing a sweater with a big crimson H across the front - what Eduardo's mother called "a lettersweater" - stuck his head in the door. "Honey, you need a ride to Hyannis tonight?"

"I'm not sure I'm going, Red. I might be busy and show up a little later."

Red winked and closed the door.

"Now what were you saying?" she asked.

Again the words streamed out of him. "Oh my gosh I'm sorry I didn't know you were with somebody please forgive me I just got carried away I'm sorry I didn't know I didn't mean to offend you please forgive me I'm new here I - "

"Slow down, okay."

He caught his breath but couldn't stop looking at her eyes.

"I get off at three. I'll be waiting for you outside on the stairs."

He nodded.

"Now, was there something else you came in here for?"

He handed her his paperwork. She went into another room and came out with his folder and handed him his schedule and work assignments.

He was a Harvard freshman now.

One month later he knew he was in love.

Two months after that he took her home, such as it was, and she spent the night.

The next morning, Red met him coming off the T. "Hey, Ed."

Muscles moved under the lettersweater's sleeves. Ed thought for sure Red was going to beat him up, but Eduardo had grown up a little rough and he figured he'd get a few good chops in before he went down.

Red offered his hand and offered a good but not bone-crushing shake. "Sorry. Eduardo. Did I say that right? Your name's Italian, isn't it?" He smiled down at Ed.

Red politely asked for Eduardo's time. "Have you eaten? We could have breakfast at my club."

Eduardo settled for a soda while they walked through Harvard Square.

Red wasn't seeing Honey. They were related, although Eduardo wasn't sure how and Red didn't offer to explain. Nor did Red care what Eduardo and Honey did. He was simultaneously gracious and reserved, but his meaning got through loud and clear: Eduardo was never to have serious thoughts about Honey. Never. Not even one. They could meet and see each other and even spend nights together whenever they wanted.

But nothing more.

When he was sure his message got through, Red shook Eduardo's hand and walked away, waving to some other lettersweatered, crew cut-headed, thickly-chested men as he went.

He and Honey always went to his place in Boston's North End and never to her house or her home or visited her family.

They'd spent the night together maybe two-hundred to two-hundred-and-fifty times in their undergraduate careers and slept together may fifty or sixty times during all that. Often just feeling their bodies side by side, waking in the middle of the night to hear each other's dreamswept breathing, to roll over and bump into each other was enough.

He'd waited until he was sure, until he knew he had something to offer, something beyond two apartment buildings and one with a second mortgage and a bakery he was leasing out to his cousins and their wives and three trucks, two of which he owned outright and the third of which he owned majority share.

He asked her to marry him and she said yes. He gave her a ring and she threw herself around him and took his breath away with kisses and hugs and the movements of her petite little body against his.

He blushed.

It was the last term of their senior year.

It was the last time they slept together.

By the time they moved their tassels from the left to the right of their mortarboards, she was getting sick every morning.

They were going to tell her parents that night, after graduation.

Red and his friends spirited her away while others of his friends kept Eduardo on the graduation stage. They didn't hurt him, they just didn't let him follow when Red's car hurried off.

One night.

Two nights.

Six nights. He hollered.

Seven nights.

Eight nights.

Ten nights.

He hollered at the administration, at the police, at his cousins. Everybody was patient. Nobody listened.

A man came to his basement apartment. Red came with him. The man was the best of Honey and the best of Red and a little of something in between. He asked if he could come in. He asked Red to wait outside.

He sat in the chair Ed offered. He didn't take off his coat. He did take off his hat. He held it in his lap as he talked, straight backed, his eyes never blinking, always on Eduardo's face.

The man talked for half an hour. Ed didn't know someone could talk so quietly yet be understood.

Eduardo cried. He screamed. He vowed. He screamed again. He cried again.

The man sat, his hat and hands still in his lap, his back still straight, his eyes still on Eduardo's face.

When Eduardo finished, the man gave him a piece of paper with a phone number. When Eduardo was ready, should he become ready, call the number. Give his name to whomever answered.

The man rose, put on his hat, shook Eduardo's hand and quietly closed the door as he left.

A war came. Tests indicated Eduardo had an aptitude. An expensive aptitude. He had a decision to make. He called the number.

Red knocked on his door the next day. Same sweater, same hair, same crew cut. His right hand held a check for more money than his parents ever dreamed of and a signed entrance portfolio to a prestigious west coast school.

Red's left hand held the stick.

His smile remained even, uninvolved. "You want these, Eduardo," Red waved the papers in his right then held out the papers in his left. "You got to sign these."

The stick: Eduardo dela Martina became Ed Martin. He studied medicine under a full, private, anonymous scholarship. He served his country and, upon discharge, received an anonymous invitation to purchase half a successful practice in Hallock, Minnesota, along with enough cash to do so.

Eduardo's stick: he vowed someday he'd find his one true love, Honey Fitz, and greet their son or daughter.

"Margerie," he called to the picture in the dark. "I need to know if you'll hold it against me if I go find her. I won't do anything, you understand, Old Girl. I just want to know what became of my child, if I even have one. I don't want you to hate me, Margerie. I'll be with you soon. You know that, right?" He winced with a brief moment of pain. "Would you let me go just long enough to find out what became of them, Old Girl? I promise I'll come back."

He looked up. The *spiritus nocti* strained against the masts of his four-poster bed. The moon sent a ray of light through the window onto Margerie's face and he was sure she blew him a kiss. The moonlight reflected off her kiss up towards the dark hole in the night.

The *spiritus nocti* made a sound, like the man's words from fifty-plus years ago, barely heard yet clearly understood, a scream from another time, another place. It flipped, pulling against the masts, then tore apart as the light reflected from Margerie's kiss passed through it.

246

CHAPTER 21

Nighthorse Meets Ann

John Nighthorse walked through whiteness.
Walked. Not floated. Something supported his weight.

Not spongy. Firm.

Solid. Like earth.

He looked down and saw his feet; shoeless, sockless, well-pedicured with strong arches for running. He couldn't see what his feet rested on but could clearly see his feet.

The whiteness had neither mass nor shape, was neither damp nor dry, neither hot nor cold. Whatever served as atmosphere was breathable. He breathed deeply, letting air fill his lungs, expand his broad, hairless chest.

Perfectly good air. Cleaner and quicker than the air in cities. Cleaner and quicker than the air in many places.

Nighthorse reached a hand into the nothingness. No resistance. No swirl of vapor or residue.

Not fog or smoke.

He looked down again as he took another breath. His chest filled.

He could see his chest. He could see his arms and hands and shoulders and thighs and calves and feet, his whole body. Naked.

Something growled, the sound fierce and terrible against the silence of the unending white.

No echo. No sounds of walking. No sounds of breathing. No sounds of anything at all.

The growl came again. An animal sound. Not a human sound. Ahead of him.

He stepped backwards.

The growl came from behind him. Closer than before but with no sound of movement. No feeling of wind, no beat of feathers, no padding of feet or clacking of hooves.

He turned slowly. "I'll stay away, if you'd like."

He backed away.

It growled. No sound of slithering, no sound of anything, closer still and behind him once again.

He turned to face it, hoping to see it.

A fetidness engulfed him.

Hot.

Unsteady breathing. Rasping. Ten, twenty feet away. A gray form rising from the engulfing white.

"The last time they killed me, I woke up alive," he called out. "Want to go for best two out of three?"

THE WARDEN SAID, "DO YOU HAVE ANY LAST WORDS before we execute your sentence?"

Eleven years ago Nighthorse had been killed but not allowed to die, sentenced to death and strapped onto a gurney.

Nighthorse laid still as a technician placed monitors on his chest.

"To make sure you're really dead," said the warden.

Another tech inserted needles into Nighthorse's arms.

"Primary and backup. In case the primary fails." The warden smiled.

Nighthorse said nothing. The warden nodded at someone and a curtain rose, revealing the audience for his execution.

Nighthorse turned his head to look. None of his people. Probably couldn't get a ride. He looked back up at the ceiling.

He heard pumps somewhere and felt a pressure in his left arm, quickly followed by a similar pressure in his right arm.

The warden smiled down on him. "Just to be sure."

Nighthorse's eyes fluttered. He felt a little drool slide down his cheek. He mumbled, "Pangiosi."

"What did he say?"

He felt a weight on his chest, then nothing.

WHEN JOHN'S PARENTS TOLD HIM TO PROTECT HIS little brother, Eddie, as effeminate as any Contrary could be, and when some damn fool idiot *wasiçu* got drunk out of his mind and decided it was 1973 and Wounded Knee all over again, and when he punched Eddie in the face so hard John could hear Eddie's jaw crack two rooms away, John slowly and quietly walked up to the idiot and said, "Care to try that with me?"

He never thought the idiot was idiot enough to try.

But the idiot was that drunk.

Eddie, watching from the doorway where John had placed him, held his face and watched, saying nothing.

The man swung.

His fist thudded against John's jaw.

John, recently honorably discharged from Special Operations units in more places than he could count, swung back.

His fist shattered the man's jaw and left cheekbone.

He had planned that.

His fist also drove some bone fragments into the man's brain.

He hadn't planned that.

Realizing the man was now going to die a slow, painful death as his brain and sinuses hemorrhaged, John continued his motion, his elbow shattering the man's ribs and driving splinters into the man's heart and lungs.

The man died instantly.

Eddie and the idiot's five hunting partners were the only witnesses.

NIGHTHORSE FELT A FREIGHT TRAIN HIT HIS CHEST.

"Mr. Nighthorse? Are you with us, Mr. Nighthorse?"

John opened his eyes. Pangiosi stared down at him.

Pangiosi had planned the mock execution for him, had agreed to it with him, had come to him only a few weeks before he was supposed to die and struck a bargain with him.

"Can you understand me, Mr. Nighthorse?"

"Ugh."

"I'll take that as a yes."

Nighthorse followed Pangiosi's gaze to two people - technicians? - wearing scrubs and latex gloves.

"Thank you. I believe Mr. Nighthorse will come around. Please remove the equipment and forget everything that's happened."

John looked to his side. Hospital equipment? The two people, their eyes glazed over, wheeled it out of view. John heard something like doors opening and closing.

"The fifteen onlookers, technicians, warden and medical examiner are satisfied you're dead, Mr. Nighthorse. You certainly had no friends among them."

"Ugh."

"You're in my private railcar. There are some clothes in the next room that will fit you. You'll need time to recover. Please don't move until you're sure you're stable. I'll be in and out, so in your own good time."

"Ugh."

Why had Pangiosi chosen him? Because John Nighthorse was big - that was true - and he was brave - that's what people said - he was meticulous - had been so far - he would do as he was told - had throughout his life - and he never lied.

SOMETIMES JOHN WONDERED IF PANGIOSI HADN'T planned the whole thing - idiot and friends and the bar and Eddie - all along.

Way too much planning. Even for Pangiosi. Maybe.

Didn't matter now.

The growl came again. More familiar now. A mixture of lion and gorilla and kodiak bear and dragon.

John had never heard a dragon. Didn't matter. Lion and gorilla and kodiak and dragon.

No doubt about it.

He started walking.

Nighthorse, it seemed, could *dream*. Half an hour after entering one of Dr. Lupicen's sleep chambers Ann's QLCs pulsed deep forest green to keep up with him.

When he woke up Dr. Lupicen tapped on the door to his sleep chamber and Nighthorse waved him in. "Mr. Nighthorse, you are a most remarkable man."

"Oh?"

"We have had many people come in and dream a little or a few for us, but none has dreamt the way you do. Do you dream this way on purpose?"

"How do I dream?"

"I'll show you." Lupicen left the chamber returned and with a large tablet showing some moving EEG-like images. Different color lines zig-zagged back and forth next to a time-axis, but they mostly remained together with only a few oddities here and there.

One line, purple, went all over the place.

Lupicen pointed to the purple line. "This is you, Mr. Nighthorse. All these others are other guests we have today." He pointed to a green line. "This is Mr. Carsons. He sleeps soundly now and doesn't dream at all, see? His line shows his mind needs to be quiet for a while. He dreamt quite busily before. Maybe later we'll see something he needs us to see. This orange line is your friend, Mr. Sally."

"Captain Sally," Nighthorse corrected.

"Ah, yes. This he has told me many times. Captain Sally sleeps hardly at all and when he does, it seems he stops himself from having dreams. But you are quite busy when you sleep, Mr. Nighthorse. You dream, yes, but it is *how* you dream that is so interesting to me. Do you know, Mr. Nighthorse, that you have no PEA in your sleep?"

"I went earlier."

He laughed. "Ah, you joke with me. Very good, Mr. Nighthorse. May I sit?"

Nighthorse nodded. Lupicen pulled a small chair next to the sleep chamber's bed and sat, tucking the back of his labcoat into his lap as if it was a tuxedo with tails. He placed the tablet on the bed between them. "P-E-A is a neurohormone like an amphetamine. It tells our brains when to be emotional. It is why we can fall in love and out again. Dreaming is usually a highly emotional state, but not for you."

Nighthorse said nothing, gave nothing away, his eyes always on Lupicen's.

"My computer monitors people while they sleep, you know, including the expressions on their faces. This we told you before you began. You remember this?"

"Yes."

"She - "

"She?"

Lupicen blushed. "I think of my computer as Ann. She is an 'Articulated Neural Net,' so Ann, a child's name. She - Ann - looks at emotions. She recognizes facial expressions and their meanings because she sees action units, 'AUs'."

Lupicen's finger traced the purple line.

"You, Mr. Nighthorse, have none. There are usually two reasons for this." Lupicen stared intently at Nighthorse's face. He reached out and touched Nighthorse's cheek and jaw line tenderly, almost lovingly.

Nighthorse smelled clove aftershave mixed with electrolytic gels and hospital adhesives on Lupicen's hand. His cheek twitched like a horse flicking off a fly.

Lupicen pulled his hand back. "The first is Möbius Syndrome and this is not you. An individual has no movement of the facial muscles, they have drooping and wide eyes, and a narrow open mouth. Also they have a problem with the sideways movement of the eyes. They move the whole head to gaze at something. Most people experiencing Möbius Syndrome are unable to express any feelings with the face. Their appearance is mask-like."

Lupicen stared intently at Nighthorse's face. "This you do not have. For one, you were not awake. For two, your face responded when I touched you."

He sat back. "The other is what I think we must investigate. It is the twin potentials of 'protention' and 'retention'. Retention is when we keep active information from the immediate past, such as hearing sounds and, when enough are heard, recognizing the collection of sounds as music. Protention is when we make information active in the immediate future, such as deciding what someone is going to say before they've said it and mishear them. Or we missee or missense something because we make incorrect information active. Most people rely on their pasts to create their futures."

Lupicen's finger lovingly traced the tablet's purple line. "You do not do this, Mr. Nighthorse. You have no emotions when you dream because you don't protend. You let things happen without bias."

Lupicen's gaze returned to Nighthorse's face and he sat forward. "How do you do this, Mr. Nighthorse?"

Nighthorse shrugged.

"You are a quiet man, Mr. Nighthorse. Words do not suit you?"

Another shrug.

Lupicen looked at Nighthorse's trace on his tablet. "Your dreams are under neither conscious nor nonconscious control. They are most like my Ann's dreams. But her dreams exist in branches of superpositioned quantum realities. She can decide a dream will be real and essentially 'wake up' in that world. You do not protend, Mr. Nighthorse, and because you do not protend you, also, can travel between worlds as they come to you. You do not anticipate, only respond."

Shrug.

"At least in your dreams."

Nighthorse chuckled. "Traveling between worlds. Sounds like my grandfather's lessons. He knew the old ways. *Wovoka*. Spirits came to him in his dreams."

"Your grandfather is alive?"

"Dead a long time, now."

"Pity. To lose such gifts."

"Yeah. Funny, though. I've been thinking a lot about him lately." Nighthorse swung his legs over the side of the bed and sat there, his hands slightly above his lap, fingers up and palms outward as if pushing something only he could see. He stared at his hands, wondering what they pushed against. "He taught me. Must have stuck."

"What is it that stuck, please."

"Oh, stuff about the spirits. Good spirits, bad spirits. Not bad, just tricksters. Maybe that's what my purple line means. Maybe that's why I could hear it but not see it. I'm waiting for the spirits to return and first up is a Trickster spirit?" He looked at Lupicen and smiled. "Grandfather would really laugh at this. He'd say, 'It only took you white guys two-thousand years to catch up?'"

Lupicen frowned. "Tell me about this Trickster spirit, please. What did you hear but not see?"

Nighthorse described his dream, sharing every detail.

"What has changed, Mr. Nighthorse? Before you were a quiet man. Now..."

"I don't know. Thinking about my grandfather? I haven't thought about him in years and now I can't get the old man out of my head."

"You think you can do this," Lupicen hesitated, unsure of the word, "Woowoo?"

"*Wovoka.*"

"Thank you. *Wovoka*, yes."

Nighthorse smiled. It felt good to be doing such things again. A set of muscles he hadn't exercised in years. It might help him figure out what to do with Pangiosi when the latter showed up.

"Sure, Doc. I can try."

"Hello?" Nighthorse called into the even, unending whiteness.

The gray thing moved ahead of him laterally, just on the edge of visibility. He couldn't gauge distance, couldn't determine much other than a roughly humanoid shape.

Something roared. Dragon and Kodiak and Lion and Gorilla.

"Hello?" Raising his face in the direction of the roar he called out, "*Hau, Sunkawakan Hanhepi imakiyab. Taku nici yapi hwo?*" Hello, my name is Nighthorse. Who are you?

It moved quickly. On a diagonal, seeking Nighthorse's blindside. He caught a glimpse of it. Huge. Big. Human in shape but not in appearance. More grotesque, or a grotésquèrie, like a huge homunculus bent and twisted in pain or fear, its skin a mixture of scales and feathers and fur and mottled flesh. It stank of infection and burnt offerings and sewage left in the sun. Nighthorse tasted bile as it moved past on tree-trunk like legs and splayed, three-toed feet.

"*Hau, Sunkawakan Hanhepi imakiyab. Nitakola.*" Hello, I'm Nighthorse. I am your friend.

Misshapen hands reared up into his face. Above the hands and staring down at him a demon's face and head, its body covered with gray wounds like the craters of the moon.

He reached up and took the creature's hands gently in his own. "*Wamakaskan wokakije.*" You poor thing.

He continued speaking his grandfather's words. "*Tóškel óciciya owáki hwo?*" Can I help?

The creature ripped its hands free and roared into John's face. The stench forced him to pull back, to avert his face and close his eyes, then his grandfather's teachings returned and he stared into the creature's eyes.

"Grendel," he said. "You remind me of Grendel, the monster in the Beowülf saga. I thought maybe *Áłtsé hashké łizhin*, but you're more a Grendel."

The creature looked at him with huge, saucer-like eyes. Its breath rasped in and out of two holes in the middle of its face.

"Is that what you are? Some kind of creature from a Viking nightmare?"

It flapped prehensile batwing ears as John spoke.

It opened its mouth. Words drooled in a deep bass from a bristle of up and down fangs. "How come you're not afraid of me?"

"I don't know. Would you like me to be?"

"Why are you here?"

"I don't know where 'here' is. Dr. Lupicen told me to find Ann."

The creature paused, put a hideous hand to its head and winced. "You have."

"Huh?"

The creature bared its fangs and howled. It pulled its hand back, its talons snicketing against each other, and raked John open from chest to belly.

He screamed. Blood flowed. His intestines pooled at his feet. The creature pulled back its other hand. Long, lizard-like talons pawled open as if racheted by some flesh-covered wheel.

Nighthorse stood there. He closed his eyes. "Heal."

His intestines gathered back inside him. His wounds closed.

The creature unhinged its jaws to envelop John's head.

Nighthorse didn't move. He looked the creature in the eye. "Heal."

The creature stopped. Its skin flickered. It raised itself until it stood twice John's height and bellowed at the sky.

"I will not fight you. I am not here to harm you. Dr. Lupicen sent me to find Ann."

The creature paused. Its whole being shimmered, collapsing on itself, now no taller than Nighthorse.

"Are you Ann's protector? Dr. Lupicen said nothing about anything like that. He should know, shouldn't he?"

The creature shimmered again. Each time when John mentioned Lupicen's name.

"Do you know Dr. Lupicen? Does he know you're here?"

It pulled back and shimmered a third time, its frame somehow echoing its hesitation, always at Lupicen's name. The shimmering caused mottled monstrous flesh to become soft, Caucasian flesh.

"He knows."

"You said I'd found Ann. Is she close by? Can you take me to her?"

Another shimmer. The creature reformed into a gargantuan monster.

An incongruity caught Nighthorse's eye.

The monster's splayed, three-toed feet.

It wore shiny black BusterBrowns topped by white ankle socks with blue flower trim.

"Dr. Lupicen thinks something may be wrong with Ann. He's very concerned. He sent me in to help."

The creature wailed, a combination of great carnivores announcing their kills and the terrified death calls of those just slaughtered. It shimmered. It lifted Nighthorse as if he were a doll and tucked him under a crushing arm.

It took a step.

The whiteness spun, suddenly filled with kaleidoscopic rainbow images and colors. Its consistency, its feeling on Nighthorse's skin, changed as if he dropped from cloud to clear sky to cloud again. The creature took another step forward and Nighthorse felt the universe spin in more directions than he could count. He closed his eyes and concentrated, waiting for the disorientation to pass.

He smelled fresh linen, something sweet. A child's perfume. He opened his eyes at the snap and pop of bed sheets and spreads coming down, the swish as soft hands smoothed them out.

A room formed around him. One wall didn't form.

The creature put John down. Far in the distance John saw a woman walking towards them.

"Is that Ann?"

The voice of animal souls being ripped from their flesh was gone. It was replaced by the soft, quiet voice of a little girl. "No, I'm Ann."

Nighthorse turned. A little girl sat on the edge of a canopy bed, blonde hair and blue eyes and pale skin and wearing a white party dress with a blue Morning Glory print, her little legs kicking as she talked. "Did Poppie tell you to bring me anything?"

"No, I - " Nighthorse felt clothing brush against his skin. "I might have something." He reached into a pocket he knew he didn't have a minute ago and pulled out a cherry *Tootsie Roll* pop. "How's this?" He handed it to her.

She unwrapped it gently and raised it to her mouth, stopped and held it out to Nighthorse. "Poppie says it's nice to share what we love."

"No, thank you. Did you know I had candy in my pocket?"

"Poppie always has candy for me. If Poppie sent you, you'd have candy."

"Poppie?"

"Dr. Lupicen. He's my Poppie."

"Where's the creature that brought me here?"

"Here. Me. I'm that creature." She glanced around the three-sided room. "Except in here. Or when Poppie's with me."

How was this little girl the Grendelian monster he'd seen a few moments before? "May I sit with you, Ann?"

She scooted over and patted the spot beside her, looking up and smiling at him all the while, so well-mannered, so cute and cuddly. "Thank you, Ann, and please call me 'John.'"

"*Sunkawakan Hanhepi.*"

"Yes, Nighthorse. John Nighthorse."

Ann's room formed as needed, always enough to provide substance, never enough to provide completion; the canopy bed didn't have a headboard until Ann scooted in that direction. The bed didn't have a far edge until he sat down next to her and leaned back, resting on his elbows for support. Nightstands formed after he looked for them. Mickey Mouse and Donald Duck light fixtures appeared on the nightstands after he wondered about lighting. Everything filled in as needed.

Except the woman in the distance. His interactions with Ann and her room neither slowed nor sped up her walk, didn't change her direction, didn't make her features more or less obvious.

One thing at a time. "That creature's an impressive protection mechanism, Ann. It would scare anyone. Did Dr. Lupicen design that in case somebody tries to hurt you in their dreams?"

"Oh, no. Poppie doesn't know anything about that."

Dr. Lupicen suspected something was disturbing Ann. Was the creature a manifestation of that disturbance? Was the creature itself that disturbance?

Lupicen told John that asking Ann directly might create a logic hole in her. To protect herself from burning out she'd powerdown and reload from scratch, removing the logic hole - and the reason for it - in the process. He could power her down himself and the result would be the same; Ann would be gone. A new Ann, another Ann, would replace her.

"Do you know why I'm here, Ann?"

Or Lupicen could find someone who could maneuver themselves in their dreams to find her and see if there was something wrong.

Someone who knew *wovoka*.

Someone like John.

"Poppie sent you. To help me."

"Do you know what kind of help you need?"

Ann's little girl face flickered with an image of the APS System 70v3 in the center of Lupicen's lab. "Yes."

"Can you tell me what kind of help you need?"

The APS System 70's face saddened, slight tears coming from its cable eyes. "No. You'll have to find out for yourself."

"I'm not a programmer, Ann."

The little girl's face stared up at him. She took his hands in hers. Warm flesh. The scent of bubbly soaps. The smell of cherry Tootsie-Roll pops. Beautiful, innocent eyes. "You don't need to be a programmer. You need to remember what your grandfather taught you."

He stared at her. How did she know about his grandfather? Did she know about *wovoka*? For that matter, did she know *wovoka*? Look with the heart? Grandpa always said begin by looking with your heart.

Okay, *wavoka*. A little girl becomes a monster. But not around those she knows love her, not where she feels safe. She becomes a monster when she's by herself. "Why do you hate yourself, Ann?"

The bed crashed under Grendel's weight. The room disappeared. Whiteness surrounded them again. They sat on Ann's bedspread in the middle of nothingness. He looked up to see that hideous face shedding tears.

She snarled, "Because I'm going to hurt Poppie."

CHAPTER 22

Grendel

Dr. Lupicen watched Ann's QLCs fluxing back and forth, two lanterns pulsing through the colors of the rainbow, one deep red and the other high violet then back, passing each other in a forest green, information moving between her hemispheres like ideas navigating the corpus callosum of the brain. Her cooling tanks thrummed like a huge cat purring. "What are you thinking about, my girl? Your hemispheres battle each other. Some great decision you're making? Some great learning about yourself, perhaps?"

Sandy Olafssen walked over to the APS. Ann's hemispheres stabilized, her thrumming quieted.

"You are a calming influence on our Ann, Ms. Olafssen."

"What caused that spike in activity, Dr. Lupicen? And I've been with you since you started this lab. You get to call me 'Sandy'."

"Thank you, yes. How many dreamers are active?"

"The only dreamer now is John Nighthorse." Olafssen flipped through some screens on her ever present tablet. Her eyes opened wide. "Holy shit."

"This cannot be good news."

She handed Lupicen her tablet. His eyebrows lifted, his mouth pursed. A moment later he smiled. "Look at the time axis, Ms. ..." He blushed. "Sandy."

She took the tablet back and spread her fingers to enlarge the graph image, then shook her head in disbelief. "You've got to be kidding."

"We must ask Mr. Nighthorse what he dreams."

JOHN LOOKED INTO GRENDEL'S FACE. "WHO WANTS you to hurt Poppie, Ann?"

"Mr. Tibbs."

A familiar name. "Who is Mr. Tibbs?"

"One of the people Poppie hired to help put me together."

"This Mr. Tibbs is making you do something Poppie wouldn't like? And you're afraid whatever it is, it'll hurt Poppie?"

The demon face nodded.

"What is it he wants you to do?"

Grendel screamed like a demon pissing holy water. She burst into flames that crisped her skin. When the fires died she sobbed, "I can't tell you."

John reached up and wiped away her tears.

Grendel said, *"Míye miš ókiya, Sunkawakan Hanhepi."* Help me, Nighthorse.

What could Tibbs do in here to make Ann a monster? John couldn't imagine a physical threat. Sexual? Emotional? Definitely not psychological. Spiritual? Her abilities were too great.

Something that attacked her core, at the center of her being.

And it would have to be done programmatically. Some kind of backdoor?

And she couldn't tell anyone.

Shame like granite slabs caked Grendel's face.

What can a child do to the person it loves that makes her believe she's a monster?

"Mr. Tibbs wants you to betray Poppie."

Grendel shrunk to Ann-size and bellowed with her full Grendel voice. John lifted the child-sized monster into his lap and rocked her, stroking her head and letting her weep.

"Mr. Tibbs told me to tell him everything I do and everything Poppie asks me to do." A moment later her little girl form returned. "He told me to send all that information there." She pointed. A white, thick pile rug appeared on the floor. An internet address marched across it.

"Have you done that, Ann?"

The monster's head turned on the little girl's body. "No."

"I don't know, Ann, but I think you did a good thing by not telling Mr. Tibbs what he wants to know."

The Ann and Grendel personae struggled over the little body. In the lab, her QLCs battled each other for dominance.

Ann's face looked up from the monster's chest. Tears fell to the monster's belly. "Really?"

"Really. Have you told anybody about this?"

"Oh, no. Mr. Tibbs made it so I can't tell anyone, ever."

Nighthorse pulled back from the child in his arms but only enough to look into her face. "But you told me, Ann."

"No," she emphasized. "I told my dream. I'm a Penrose Consciousness that's formed from the intersections of quantum entanglements."

"That makes me your dream?"

Ann sighed and rolled her eyes. "Grownups never understand anything by themselves, and it is tiresome for children to be always and forever explaining things to them."

Nighthorse clapped his hands and laughed. "Antoine de Saint Exupery? *The Little Prince*?"

"Have you ever had a dream, shared that dream with someone and they say they've had the same dream or a similar dream?"

"I've heard people say such things. Never experienced it myself."

"But you dream much the way I do. We navigate realities. In this one, our dreams overlap. You are part of my dream, something I'm retending. I can retend you because you're not protending me. In your dream, you retend me because I don't protend you."

"You are definitely Dr. Lupicen's daughter. Now I have a quote for you: It is not the truth, per se, but love of self that sets us free."

Ann closed her eyes and scrunched up her face. Outside in the lab, her QLCs aligned long enough to open petabyte-wide ports to search the world's information. "No...I'm not familiar with that one."

"It's in my language. It's not written down. You learn it in sweat lodges. Do you know what those are?"

She nodded.

"Good. We're going to do something to convince you that you are Dr. Lupicen's Ann, not what Mr. Tibbs needs you to be."

"How?"

He reached into his pocket and pulled out his wotai. He held it to his eye and looked at Ann.

"Is that some candy?"

"Something maybe a little better. We'll need your mirror again."

Her room grew around them. Once again, the woman approached in the distance.

"I want you to look at yourself through this." He handed the Gate to her.

"A QMHDS."

"A what?"

"A QMHDS, Quantum Magneto Hydro Dynamic Scanner. Far more powerful than any currently available and made from a technology unknown to me. This shows worlds, this shapes worlds. It's a reality generator. It allows movement between destinies."

"You can tell that just by holding it?"

Ann's brow furrowed and she looked up at him. "I'm a very smart little girl."

Nighthorse laughed. "Yes, I'm sorry. You surely are. I want you to look at your reflection through it."

She lifted the Gate to her eye.

A brief shimmering. The room grew more defined. The little girl remained.

"Ann, you are a beautiful little girl and you are a very good little girl.

You did the right thing not to listen to Mr. Tibbs and to help your Poppie."

Another shimmer. A quake of the senses. Of reality. Ann's QLCs cooled, calmed, synchronized. The room grew larger. Ann matured slightly. Still a child, a few years older, less babyfat, some hints of the beauty to come. "Thank you."

"Dr. Lupicen - Poppie - will need to know about this. May I share our conversation with him?"

She smiled, slight dimples forming on a young girl's face. "Can you remember your dreams?"

Nighthorse laughed. Wovoka. "Yes, I can remember."

"Then yes, please tell him. Mr. Tibbs will eventually come back. He'll know something's wrong when he finds out Poppie's research has started and no reports came his way."

"Quite right, Ann. Tell me, do you know if you can defend your-self?"

"In here I know I can."

"That might not be good enough. Do you know if you can defend yourself out there?"

"I don't know. Poppie would know. He'd find a way."

"We'll have to ask him."

Footsteps. The sound of leather soled shoes clacking as they ap-proached down a corridor.

John turned. The woman approached. He couldn't make out her features. Perhaps this was another incarnation of Ann, the real Ann who stayed far away until she deemed him safe?

"Am I going to get to meet your friend now, Ann?"

"Yes. She said she's anxious to meet you."

Ann didn't shimmer as the steps grew close, nor when they finally stopped.

A familiar voice, choking with anger. "You!"

Nighthorse jumped at the familiar voice, stepped back when he saw the face. His clothing burnt away and left him naked.

"Mrs. MacPherson." Nighthorse raised his arms, protecting his face and chest from a rage hotter than the sun. He retreated, his legs pounding the firm, white earth, but never able to move away from her. "Mrs. MacPherson."

She slapped his face. It felt like an iron bar hit him. His ears rung. His eyes watered.

She balled her hand into a fist and smashed it into his cheek, breaking his jaw and nose. "You son-of-a-bitch!"

She didn't shimmer, didn't become some kind of nightmare Grendel creature like Ann had been. Her small body couldn't be doing this. Too much power. It couldn't be real.

She shoved him backwards. He flew through the air and smashed against a very solid wall.

Ellie MacPherson stood over him, a leg on either side. She grabbed his throat and pulled him up like he was made of straw, pulled back her fist and screamed, "Where's my husband? Where's my son?"

CHAPTER 23

The Woman Inside

Lupicen and Nighthorse sat in Lupicen's office, the door closed as Nighthorse recounted his adventures.

"You have given me much to think about, Mr. Nighthorse. Let us start with this woman inside Ann. You know her from sometime before?"

Nighthorse sat hands on knees and eyes fixed on the floor. "Yes, Dr. Lupicen, from a while ago."

"You say she is dead, though?"

"I thought so, yes." Nighthorse's face felt like a thousand hornets landed where Ellie hit him. His jaw and nose bore no obvious bruising yet were tender to his touch. "Evidently not."

"Is it possible, Mr. Nighthorse, this woman is part of some unresolved issues, perhaps some part of a personal dream involving itself in the work you had to do?"

"I don't know."

"I believe you had these experiences, Mr. Nighthorse. Surely you know I do."

"That makes one of us."

Lupicen stood, his hands under the rear flap of his labcoat, scratching as he stared through his office windows at the System 70 in the center of his lab. "I have hemorrhoids, Mr. Nighthorse. Do you know that?"

"No, sir, I didn't."

"Not serious and only one. The doctor tells me I have it but mostly I never know it's there. Then for no reason there's a little irritation and I can't get comfortable for a while. I asked you to go find Ann, I had a little irritation. You have applied an ointment to that irritation and it has gone away, but you bring me other irritations to replace it."

"That's me. A pain in the ass."

Lupicen frowned then laughed. "Ah. A joke. A good one. You ask if there are things we can do so Ann can protect herself. To that I answer yes. This also means she has achieved my first goal for her: she recognizes the alien, the foreigner. She knows what is Ann and what is not-Ann, she understands who she is versus a who someone wants her to be. It also means she has lost her innocence, for which I am not glad, but it means she also has inside her now the full range of emotions."

Lupicen sighed, looked down, and shook his head. "Consider, Mr. Nighthorse. She knows when she needs to be protected, therefore she feels something - fear, anxiety, hate...something! - and this feeling is what she really seeks protection against. It is Maslow's hierarchy of needs, yes? She understands herself as a separate entity from those around her, so has a sense of self and will take steps to preserve self."

Lupicen's focus returned to Nighthorse. "She has probably started to dream, but her dreams are generated quite differently from those of you or I. Or at least me. She dreams by manipulating quantum realities."

Nighthorse sat up. "Ann said something like that. Those words, anyway. And don't ask me to repeat it. I couldn't come close no matter how hard I tried."

"You did not mention this. Is there anything else you did not mention?"

He'd told Lupicen everything save Ann's description of her dreams, his *wotai*, and Ann's description of it.

Lupicen stared for a moment then nodded and continued. "Ann dreams by investigating other possible realities, a mixture of quantum superpositioning and interference. We sleep because our higher cortical functions shut down. This shutting down is induced by spindle patterns that are themselves functions of a mathematical lattice, and according to Penrose, this lattice is itself a function of quantum fluctuations in the brain.

"Ann is aware in the same way we are aware, Mr. Nighthorse. Both are intentional systems. But unlike us, she is designed to create any variation of mathematical lattices she might wish and she has no higher cortical functions to shut down. To her, everything is a dream. But when she is herself having a dream, it is because she has opened a gateway to another reality."

"Sounds like my grandfather. Different words, same ideas."

"The woman you saw. You may have been inside one of Ann's dreams."

"I think Ann said something like that to me."

"You said this woman's name was Eleanor MacPherson?"

"Yes, Doc, that much I know is true."

"Did you know there is a Tom MacPherson who is to take part in my studies?"

Nighthorse was silent.

"I think I shall call Tom MacPherson and his attending, a Dr. Games, and ask them about this woman of Ann's dreams. If Ann has dreamed a reality where someone she does not know lives but has died in this reality? A little irritation that can mathematically go away. If Ann has dreamed a reality where we go when we die? I will need to keep much more ointment handy."

CHAPTER 24

Switching Yard

Pinkertons, Mass State Police, FBI, the Hampden County Sheriff's department, and Springfield's own gave the Springfield, Mass, trainyard the appearance of an outdoor law enforcement convention. Groups of uniforms officers, like with like, cloistered like acolytes of different saints. Moving around and amongst the different groups, human trains - Chief Investigator, Investigator, Detective, Assistant, Assistant's assistant - tracked back and forth picking up and dropping off clues and information. Most of them milled outside the trains, guiding passengers to questioning, leaving the interior of the train to forensics, shouting over the sounds of engines and brakeman and tracks clacking to and fro. Whenever a big diesel started up some of them would cough their way into the station house, wiping their jackets off.

In the center of it all, in car seventeen of the *Lake Shore Limited*, in what had been Dr. Jack Games's bedroom and was now his temporary holding cell, Colodnie Johnson sat opposite Games chain smoking so she wouldn't have to bother with a lighter or a match, her mobile clipped to her shirt, a PTT in her left hand and her GP held loosely in her right. Occasionally the car would jolt and shake as the mule, a small utility engine that served like a tugboat in a trainyard, jockeyed cars and trains up and down different tracks.

Every time Games moved Colodnie Johnson glared at him and twitched her revolver a bit in his direction. The first few times his eyes grew wide and she watched his chest take a couple of deep, hurried breaths, as if wanting to get a good one because it might be his last. Now he just shook his head in disgust. Watching his once smooth ebony skin creasing his face and neck and hands, she realized she liked taking down upscale criminals.

She corrected herself. She liked taking down upscale rich wanna-be-white niggers the best. She didn't get to do a lot of them, but when she did she did it with glee. Kind of like getting back at all those assholes in the BSU who were afraid to ask her if she was black.

God it was nice to do something in return to all those idiot-faced, afrosheened, nappy-headed bastards who ignored her in the past.

Games, no doubt, would have been one of them. Even if he wouldn't have been, he'd do just fine.

"How long you going to hold me here?"

"Did I tell you to speak? I don't remember telling you to speak."

Games rose. He was halfway standing when Colodnie was beside him pushing him back on the bunk. He caught her hands, used her momentum and weight, and guided her past him onto the bunk, leaving her lying down while he stood over her.

Her revolver clicked into his face.

"Where's Jamie?"

Her revolver didn't waver. "He's fine. He's being interviewed by a staff psychologist."

"Detective Johnson, I will say this once for your benefit as well as mine. Tom MacPherson is missing from this train. He is my patient and your suspect. We both think he may be dangerous, me to himself and you to anything on two or more legs. It seems to me we could benefit from a truce or a ceasefire."

She said nothing.

"Did you get the serology from the place where somebody jumped the train?"

Her eyes narrowed, her lips tightened.

"Did you?"

"Yes."

"Was it Tom's? If you don't know his chemistry then by golly I do. What about the rest of the forensics? There's got to be hair samples and skin samples in Tom's room, you know, in case you didn't think to check."

Her nostrils flared slightly. She said nothing.

"Oh, very well. I'm going to reach into my jacket pocket in the closet here and lift out my mobile. I'm going to press and hold the number seven. That will speed dial my attorneys back in Chicago. They are, as I'm sure you're aware, an adept and well placed group."

She lowered her revolver. "I'm surprised they're not on speed dial one."

He opened the closet and slowly removed the phone, making large, obvious movements.

He pressed and held the number seven. She could hear the connection going through. She heard a voice on the other end of the phone.

"Yes, this is Doctor Games. Yes, that's right."

"Alright."

"Could you hold the line, please?" He pressed the mute button. "Did you say something, Detective Johnson?"

"It wasn't MacPherson's blood."

"What about the skin and hair and fabric?"

The words stuck in her throat. "No and no and he doesn't have that kind of taste."

"So whoever left the train wasn't Tom. Doesn't mean they didn't have Tom with them, but something of him would have shown up there."

Johnson's nostrils flared and she looked out the window. Her lips were tight and her fingers massaged the GP's grip.

"Is there something else, Detective Johnson? Something else you'd like to share before I continue with my conversation?"

She barked a laugh. "Sure, why not. The samples we recovered? The FBI was able to identify them. They got a perfect match."

"For Christ's sake who?"

"A dead Indian. John Nighthorse, executed by lethal injection eleven years ago in Nevada."

His mobile beeped in his hand.

She looked at it.

"Call waiting."

"Go ahead."

He pressed the mute button again. "Hi, thanks for waiting. Can I call you back? I've got another call I have to take care of. Sure, thanks. Bye." He took the second call. "Games. Who? What? Can you tell me a little more, Dr. Lupicen?"

Games looked confused and agitated. She liked that.

"Yes, thank you. I'll see what I can do. Thank you. Good-bye."

"So what have you got?"

"Are you going to press charges or anything like that?"

"I haven't decided yet."

"Well, when you decide, let me know. I'm renting a car and heading on up to Dartmouth. I'm taking Jamie with me."

"What's up there now that MacPherson's gone? Wasn't he the reason you're all making this little trip?"

"Are you arresting me?"

"I told you I haven't decided."

"When you decide, I'll tell you why I'm going to Dartmouth."

He went into the hallway and hollered. A few moments later Jamie ran up to him, followed by some state police. "Get all the clothes you think you'll need for a few days stay up in the hills, ok? Don't worry if you can't find anything. We'll buy brand new clothes if we need to."

"Ok, Uncle Jack."

He addressed the police. "Where's the medical support team I brought with me?"

One of his staff pushed her way through train security like a salmon swimming upstream.

274

"Make sure everything gets transferred to the *Vermonter* ASAP. Call me when you get to White River Junction and I'll have somebody from Lupicen's lab come and get you. Take care of the dog, Shem, too. Prepare him so we can bury him properly when we get back home."

Games took Jamie's hand and they stepped off the train. Johnson followed them outside. "You can't take any equipment with you, Games. This train is impounded."

He pointed towards the rear of the train and shouted over the groans and strains of the mule. "Oh yeah? Looks like parts of this train got unimpounded already."

Colodnie Johnson looked, swore, threw down her jacket, stomped, looked, and swore again. Brakemen had already separated half the cars and towed them onto different tracks.

CHAPTER 25

Joni's Children

JONI WATCHED DAY TURN TO NIGHT. THE SUN PULLED a blanket of clouds over itself as it settled behind Vermont's Green Mountains. The moon sent laser-bright beams bursting through budding foliage, the light hitting the ground like dogs hunting a trail.

She looked at the stars. There were so few she could count them.

Creatures, jagged like black lightning and shaped like men, chased the stationary stars and devoured them, enveloped them, leaving utter blackness in their wake.

She wiped tears from her eyes. "That's not right."

One of the jagged lightning men looked down at her and snickered. "Virgil?"

He laughed and her stomach churned. She tasted bile, felt stale beer and cold pizza working their way back up like they had at the...

At the...

She closed her eyes and lowered her head. Her fists clenched by her sides. "No," she whispered.

I'm not at the abortion clinic.

She looked up, her voice gaining power as she raised her head. "No."

She stared back at the jagged-edged Virgil man. She spoke quietly, more to herself than any others present, yet her voice echoed through the night, fluttering the cosmos like strong winds on a tattered sail, "No!"

The jagged-edged man pulled back. Others of his kin gathered around him. They looked down on her. Like a sickly polluted river, their black mass oozed down towards her.

She shook her head. "You know nothing about me. Nothing I do, nothing I've ever done." She remembered a line from a show Virgil loved. He always laughed like it was a joke. Now she understood its power over him, why it frightened him. "I am not a number, I'm a free woman."

A little blonde-haired, blue-eyed girl appeared beside her. "Joni?"

The darkness cleared. Still night, but now the natural darkness of night, not the emotional darkness of death, of hopelessness, of surrender.

"Huh?"

"Congratulations, Joni. You should be proud."

She looked around. Where was that little girl? Who was that little girl?

Joni yawned and blinked her eyes open. Brightly lit, rainbow-colored threads, the lines leading to Lupicen's equipment, formed a halo over her head as she turned on her side.

Was I dreaming?

When Joni first entered Dr. Lupicen's lab that morning, Sandy Olafssen greeted her and asked, "Have you slept in the past twenty-four hours?"

"No… yes. Not really."

Sandy took notes. "Did you dream?"

Joni stared at Sandy's tablet. "You want the truth?"

"It helps."

"Not much, but when I did it was weird. I dreamt of flying wolves."

Sandy made notes, smiled, tapped her tablet and the screen went blank.

"Let's start you first thing. We'll put you in this chamber. Right in the center of things. That okay with you?" She gave Joni a general layout of the lab. A moment later, Joni slept.

Now Joni sat up and put her hand to her head. "How long ago did I come in here?"

If she remembered correctly, Al Carsons dreamt one chamber over. The Ole Salt had the chamber the other side of Al.

She laughed. The Ole Salt. Burt Sally.

She got a kick out of how he smiled at her and didn't care that she caught him staring at her chest. It was, by far, her best feature. Certainly her biggest.

John Nighthorse had the chamber across the lab on the other side of Lupicen's pet computer.

And didn't Lupicen spend some time talking it up with Mr. Nighthorse?

For that matter, she wouldn't mind talking it up with Mr. Nighthorse. She happened to catch their reflections in the lab windows at one point. They stood side by side and facing the same direction.

My god! His chest is bigger than mine!

I wonder if he has any tshirts I can borrow?

Okay, enough fun memories. She opened her sleep chamber's door to a dark, empty lab and looked out the windows.

Dark. Not even parking lot or campus lights. She yawned. "I couldn't have slept that long. Nobody came to check up on me? Nobody woke me up to say hi, we're going out for pizza, want to come?"

A single beam of moonlight came through the window and landed on her chest. She felt a pressure, the moonbeam pulsing, bright, searching, inquisitive, playful.

She put her hand to her chest. The light brushed it away. Her heart beat with the moonlight, her pulse and the moon synchronizing, dancers knowing each other's movements and joyful in the dance.

The sky filled with moving lights. Stars. She tilted her head, unsure of what she saw.

Little shadow men, like in her apartment, filling the sky with stars.

Tens then hundreds then thousands, each carrying a twinkling light in its hands, placing it against the backdrop of night.

The little shadows, so childlike.

She wanted children. She'd had an abortion but she wanted children. Someday.

The little shadow men didn't come down from the sky, they came up from the earth.

She thought of Virgil. Not with him, though. Not with anybody like him.

She closed her eyes, the feel of the moon's light still on her chest.

I want children. Someday. I hope to have children.

To be in love. Real love.

The little moppet stood beside her. "That's why you're here, Joni." She pointed. "See?"

The little shadow men came from the lab.

She looked down.

They came from her. From the moonbeam. It penetrated her chest. She could see her heart. Each pulse, each heartbeat a hope.

More of the little shadow men flew out, up, carrying dreams, carrying stars back to the sky.

The moppet stood beside her. "This is your gift, Joni."

Joni blinked. Is this a side effect of Lupicen's experiments? Isn't anybody monitoring me? Shouldn't somebody be breaking the door down to wake me up by now?

So many of them, flying from her chest like bats leaving a cave, so many and so fast the sky rippled with them.

The little girl stood beside her, supporting her, midwifing Joni through each heartbeat, smiling as little shadows covered the sky with stars. "This is what you bring."

Joni grabbed her stomach. So many. Where did they come from? From her?

"Because you grew, Joni. You acted. You refused to despair. You fought. You hoped."

"Who are you?"

The little girl took Joni's hand in hers. "My name is Ann."

Sandy Olafssen's voice forced Joni's eyes open. "You okay, Ms. Levis? You woke up rather suddenly."

Daylight lit the lab, shone through her opened chamber door. People walked about the lab doing lab-like things. The APS sighed and chugged as its lights flickered and its front panel dimmed.

Where'd the shadow people go? Where's the munchkin? What the hell has Honey gotten me into? "Yeah, I'm fine. Just woke up too fast. What time is it?"

"Just about 10:00AM. Say, you haven't had a chance to have breakfast, freshen up, check out your room, nothing like that?"

"I left my stuff with Al and crashed in his room for a bit, but yeah, I could use all of the above."

"I can use a break. Let's go."

CHAPTER 26

Al's Whirlwind

EFFIE, CHARLIE, AND BEN HELD HANDS AND DANCED around Al as if he were a maypole.

Charlie called, "Isn't it great, dad?"

The world revolved around Al in shades of white mist. He stood but didn't know on what. He heard music, children singing. It sounded like the songs he and Effie and the boys sang when they played outside the house. Funny songs. Nonsense songs. Songs made up on the spot to see whose would get the most laughs.

And wolves howling.

"Yeah, dad, isn't it great?" echoed Ben.

Effie let go of Charlie's hand and reached for Al's. "I haven't been this happy in years, Al, back with my family again."

"What...what are you doing? What are you saying? You're all dead."

The whiteness gathered outside of the circle they danced in. It grew larger, stronger, until it became a slight whirlwind with the dancers at its center. The winds grew. The whiteness became ghetto streets seen through a fog, farm fields without rain, half-naked children fleeing explosions, some hiding from men and women with knives.

Al drew his family to him. He looked out into the clearing fog. "That's not right."

Effie hugged him close. He felt her hair on his face, smelled the sweet rose of her perfume. "What's not right, Al?"

"That's not right." The winds increased. The whirlwind gained force, pushing the mist aside, allowing Al to see more.

He saw the drunk driver who killed Effie, drunk because his wife left him for someone else, drunk because his kids didn't want to talk to him or share their lives with him, drinking more because he knew he killed Effie, knew he was guilty, knew he ransomed his kids' education and home to hire a big law firm to get him off.

Al saw the man terrified to get in his car, to step out outside, to cross the road or get the mail, wondering when some drunk driver would get him.

The winds grew, changing the world beyond his family's dance.

Al saw the boy who shot Charlie, now a young man, his face and his mind as hardened as the armor surrounding tanks, in prison at sixteen and parole a luxury he'd never see because his skin is dark and his name doesn't roll easily off the tongue.

The winds lifted the world outside, shifting it, shaping it.

Al saw the soldier who shot Ben, himself dead now, only parts of his body found, his mother alone, no others beside her, mourning over an unmarked grave, a mound someone said was her son.

All of these people, alone. Al didn't mind being alone. He understood being alone.

So long as being alone served a purpose.

Al saw the winds like a hurricane on a weather map. He and his family still dancing in the center. The winds cleansing the world around them.

The howling of the wolves. The whiteness of the winds turning into bright, flashing wings.

"What's wrong with you people? Don't you know what you care about most can be lost in a heartbeat? You want to be remembered? Be remembered for the love you bring, not the pain you caused."

"This is your gift, Al. This is what you bring."

"Who said that?"

A little, blonde, blue-eyed girl in a flower-print dress took the hand that held Effie's.

"I did. My name is Ann. Remember, Al. Remember love. Love that's patient and kind. Love that waits."

She disappeared. Effie took her place. "Soon, my love, my dearest Al, my Forever Man. Soon."

The hurricane continued cleansing, shaping the world. Its winds never touched them.

"Soon what, Effie?"

Effie, Ben, and Charlie faded from view, in their place the scent, the howl, the sounds of great wings, and then the winds...the winds made by the wingbeats of flying wolves.

Another voice. Familiar. Who? The Lady in the Night. "Protect Jamie."

"Huh?"

Outside Al's sleep chamber, paper notes lifted from desks and whirled about the lab. Hanging charts tapped against walls. People's hair disheveled, all in a wind circling a lab that had neither fans nor open windows.

CHAPTER 27

Honey Gets the Message

HONEY FITZ SAT ALONE IN HER OFFICE, HER FINGERS steepled in front of her face, her thumbs supporting her head under her chin, staring at the portrait of the family patriarch, the Great and Long Gone Honey Fitz.

"God, do I want to fuck you." She laughed at the double-entendre. "At least that wasn't one of the curses you passed on to your daughters and sons. But if there was a way to hurt you beyond the grave, Gramps, you know I would."

She spun her chair to look out on the MacLean campus, its lawns so manicured they could pass for putting greens. She got her station and position here through her own hard work.

No doubt about it.

"I'm damn good at my job. No doubt about that, either."

She watched a groundskeeper sweeping past on a stand-on mower. "You don't doubt it, do you?"

He looked up and waved.

Honey pulled back, startled, then returned his wave. He'd already mowed on.

She'd been reviewing her past ever since she cut Joni loose to find another shoulder to cry on. All her professional life, she'd done the correct and proper things so she'd never bring shame to the family.

The groundskeeper plied his mower like a brush on the landscape, cutting neither straight lines nor following the contour of the lawn. He'd swing the mower in a big arc and swing his butt in the opposite direction at the same time, as if dancing with the machine. He'd do a tight turn and throw a leg out like a skater gathering momentum for a tight spin. "You're putting on a hell of a show. But you're probably going to get fired for it."

He continued mowing here, mowing there, cutting back and forth and forth and back, seemingly enjoying himself and to hell with whatever anybody else thought.

Honey stood, watching him, her arms crossed over her chest. "Have you no shame, sir? Have you no shame? Have you no respect for your family's position in the community?"

She remembered Honey Fitz's first commandment - Never bring Shame to the Name - all the while enjoying the groundskeeper's antics.

"What would you make of the last three or so generations of Irish Gentlemen, Gramps? Talk about bringing shame to the name. But you weren't there that fine Spring day in Hyannis when John mentioned conversationally that Marilyn had a tighter ass than Jackie. And Jackie right there! As if she were candy atop the box and Marilyn the gift inside! And Teddy on the bridge? Huh? How about that? Or the generation after? They practically funded rehabs across the globe with their revolving door addictions. God, but you all make me sick."

She continued studying the groundskeeper.

"You know I distanced myself as much as possible, don't you?"

She could have sworn the groundskeeper nodded as he pirouetted his mower.

"But they always call me back in. For family. That's what they always tell me. For family, Honey, for family."

She slapped the window. The groundskeeper paid no mind.

"That's bullshit, you know."

She put both hands on the window, face height, and leaned into it, her face touching the warmth of the Autumn afternoon sun, then collapsing against it, a climber seeking a handhold but only finding smooth, hard glass.

"You made me kill my baby!" The words erupted from deep inside her, her emotions lava waiting for a crack in her earth to vent. "You made me get an abortion and God knows where you sent the only man I ever loved, all because we couldn't let one of those swarthy Mediterraneans into the family."

She spun to her grandfather's portrait. "Right, Gramps? You should see the family now, you stupid prick! We even let a muscle-bound Republican into the house. And he slept with his maid while he slept with his wife! How's that for bringing shame to the family name, Gramps?"

She held herself in thin arms and stood under the portrait. "You son-of-a-bitch."

She collapsed into her chair. "Ah, Joni. I have you to thank. You brought all this up. So ethics kicked in and I had to cut you loose. You understand that, right, Joni? You're a smart girl. You'll've figured that out. If not now, at some point, I'm sure." A sad chuckle escaped her lips. "Pity, right when we made some real breakthroughs. But us Fitzes have such great professional ethics, you know."

Her phone rang. She checked the name and answered, "Hi, Cousin. What can I do for you this fine Fall day?"

Her face whitened as she listened. "You know this? This is a fact?"

Her eyes opened wide, closed, and she shook her head. "Thanks. Let me know how I can return the favor some day."

She hung up. "Oh Christ shit."

She called Joni's office. "Sorry, Ms. Levis took a leave of absence. We're not sure when she'll be back."

She called her condo building. "Sorry, no forwarding address. She's paid up through the end of her lease, though."

She called Joni's cell. "We're sorry, the personal voice mail for," and the voice changed to Joni's, "Joni Levis," then back to the standard,

Midwestern female drone, "is full. For further options, press your palm to your forehead. You'll come up with something, we're sure."

Honey always got a kick out of Joni's eccentricities. Not this time. "Come on, Joni. There must be a way to find you. You didn't go to Dartmouth after all, did you? Your Mr. Tibbs is up there, somewhere in the Lyme-Lebanon-Hanover region, right near Dartmouth U and Dr. Capoçek Lupicen." She stared at her mobile deciding what to do. "Sweet Jesus, Joni, I've sent you from the frying pan into the fire."

She went back to the window. The groundskeeper had stopped mowing and stood on his machine looking up at her. When he saw her, he jumped off and bowed, moving his arms like a game show hostess drawing attention to the grand prize.

"What the...?"

She looked where he directed. Cut into the lawn in big bold cursive letters: "GO TO DARTMOUTH, HONEY!"

She looked back at him. He took off his hat and sunglasses and gave her a great big smile.

She focused on his face. "What the...?"

The groundskeeper bowed, stood, smiled, and waved good-bye.

She ran out of her office and took the stairs two at a time. Outside she talked to people in the parking lot, to passing security, to patients walking the grounds.

One guard listened patiently. "Not sure about that, Dr. Fitz. Today's not the grounds crew's day. And I don't remember anybody on their crew with eyes like you describe, one dark and the other light." He looked up to her office windows and back to the lawn. "You must have incredible eyesight to see someone's eye color from that far away."

Her eyes went from her window to the lawn and she nodded. "Yes." She straightened her skirt and cleared her throat. "Thank you."

There were no messages mowed into the lawn.

"Either it really happened, but it couldn't have, or I'm hallucinating and need a break. Fuck it. I'm tired of spending my nights watching DVDs and streaming old movies."

Back in her office she buzzed her secretary. "Can you cancel or reschedule my appointments for the next few weeks? I need some time away. I'll leave you a message if it's going to be longer."

CHAPTER 28

The Abattoir of Hope

JONI, FRESHLY SHOWERED, FED, OUT OF HER TRAVEL-
ing clothes and sporting a smart outfit Sandy Olafssen picked out for
her, lay down in her sleep chamber.

Funny how she thought of it as "her" sleep chamber. Lunch with
Sandy Olafssen had been a trip! Before they left, Sandy helped Joni
unpack and loved her clothes. They were nowhere near the same size,
but Sandy had an eye for lines and curves and colors and patterns and
held things up against herself that flattered more often than not. She
picked out a smart yellow jacket with black arms, black jeans and yellow
sneakers with black laces for Joni to wear while they walked about the
town.

Joni checked herself in the mirror. "You really think so?"

"Oh, yeah. The doctors up here are always saying they want to find
a cute little honeybee. Dressed like that, you're the one to watch."

Sandy told Joni where to shop and where not to in Hanover and the
surrounding area. She had a wicked dry sense of humor - Joni caught
herself; she never used the word "wicked" but Sandy did and she'd
picked it up from her in only a few hours together - at one point, Joni

overstepped a curb crossing the street. Her knee locked as her foot hit the street, as if expecting another step down and not finding one. She jumped a bit bringing her other foot down. Sandy didn't miss a beat. "That's it, Levis. Jump start the heart. Make sure you're alive." Sandy kept walking as Joni laughed herself silly.

She'd had a beer during lunch. Was one suddenly too much?

It didn't matter. Joni found a sister she never had. They talked about boyfriends and the kindredness ended. Sandy listened as Joni made wisecracks about Virge, but finally asked why Joni ever got involved with such a loser.

"I don't know. Maybe I thought I could save him?"

Sandy's *Arf Arf Arf* laugh reminded Joni of a dog barking. "Save him? From what? Himself? Fuck him and only if he's worth it. Save yourself, sister, save yourself."

Sandy's luck with boyfriends was much better than Joni's. She liked men, but if there wasn't one in her life for a while there just wasn't one in her life for a while.

"You don't ever get... you know... lonely?"

"Oh, hell yes. I go out to the clubs such as they are up here and find someone who won't open his mouth and won't get a fixation and will just do his job and get out before morning."

"You go, girl." Sandy would never have set off the Brookline Abortion Clinic woman's radar.

Joni reviewed their activities as she relaxed in her chamber.

A moment later she slept and stood on a cliff overlooking a canyon. Car-sized bolts attached a black, smoothly moving machine of gears and cogs, as if someone cannibalized the derailleurs from a hundred thousand bicycles, some microscopically tiny and others the size of houses, intersecting and running at bizarre angles, a nightmare assembly of metal teeth and chains, mind-numbingly complex yet allowing the machine as a whole to run smoothly.

The gears swung huge, black arms back and forth through the canyon like horizontal pendulums, pendulums ending in unseeably small razors up to blades the size of buses.

And on each blade, Virgil's smiling face.

People stood in neat rows on Joni's cliff waiting to jump onto a chain and be lowered into the canyon, into the machine. Children, adults, infants, toddlers, seniors, teens, black, red, yellow, brown, white; a rainbow of humanity lined up and leapt onto the chains, the sheer weight of them powering the machine, pulling the chains, driving the gears, swinging the blades, dragging them down.

Joni couldn't watch but she heard.

Moans. Hollow sounds. Crying whispers. Like animals whimpering as they gnawed off their own limbs to be free of a trap but unable to end their suffering, too tired to continue and too much life to die, their bodies growing into the thing that binds them until they give up hope and accept.

Ann appeared, older, the child blossoming into womanhood, no longer the moppet Joni remembered yet still Ann. "Do you see, Joni? Do you understand?"

Joni looked into the abyss expecting to see corpses, bodies scythed into several pieces.

But the people lived. All of them.

The blades, even the largest of them, made tiny, tiny cuts, the biggest blades making the smallest cuts of all, cutting just enough so the wounds wouldn't heal, wouldn't completely close before the blade swung back reopening the wound it originally made. Sometimes a wound would close, the person would heal, but only for a moment before another blade came at another angle, hatching the work of the first, now creating a wound that couldn't heal, only flow.

The people bled but not enough to die, only to suffer, a suicide unaware.

Joni pulled back. "What is this?"

"This place is the Canyon of Despair, that machine is the Abattoir of Hope. Normally the Abattoir is confined to this canyon, unable to climb the walls."

Night fell over the canyon, a starless, moon-filled night. Individual bright moonbeams reached into the canyon and lifted specific people out, but only a few. It stopped on people. Joni's chest ached until The Moon moved on.

"Throughout history people have despaired and come here, each time the Abattoir's shape and form an echo of their time. But now humanity's reliance on machines, its dependence on them, people's inability to make decisions without them, has created its own machine, one which can escape the walls of hope that have trapped despair."

Joni thought back over the myths of her childhood, things she'd read and movies she'd seen. "Dante's *Inferno*? Orpheus and Eurydice? Hell?"

"All and none. People confuse faith and hope. They're not the same. Faith, as written in the bible and other world books, is the belief in things unseen. Faith alone cannot save a person from the canyon. Such faith often delivers people to the canyon. Hope is when the person recognizes there's more than one possible outcome and the person chooses to work towards one outcome over the other. Hope can free people from this canyon, but not faith alone."

"But all the death - "

"No one is killed here, but people suffer enough to give up hope, to no longer work for things to change, no longer believe they control their destinies. Those giving up hope are willing victims to despair because it's easier, simpler, safer than being free, than taking responsibility, than being aware. It is hope that flows from their wounds. Not blood, hope. Those not willing to heal continue to suffer."

Joni looked again. Things flew back and forth, licking the wounds, ensuring they stayed open.

Little black...she reached for a word. "Fears... Emptinesses..."

She placed her hand on her chest, protectively. "Not like..." She paused. "Not like..."

Ann's eyes went from the canyon to Joni. "No, Joni, not like the gift you bring. But know this: Despair has been confined to these canyons for ever so long. It has come close to escaping in the past but always hope prevailed. Now..." Ann's gaze returned to the canyon, at the abattoir, its many cogs and wheels and drives and chains reaching like arms up the canyon walls, and shook her head.

Someone behind Joni said, "Come on. Let's go."

Joni stood in one of the lines to go over the cliff. A guard pushed reluctant people over the edge.

Then everything disappeared. No cliff, no blades, no people, no cries of pain or despair.

No little girl. She looked around. She sat in Graywolf's cab, crossing the Mass Ave Bridge between Cambridge and Boston. A black cloud of little shadow men sailed up the Charles.

Far off, someone screamed. It sounded like Virgil. He always liked to roar like a bull when he came but she couldn't imagine the sound she heard now being associated with anything pleasurable.

Graywolf caught her eye in his rearview. "You have to remember the Abattoir of Hope, Joni. It's a dream, sure, but you're carrying lots of them inside you now."

"Is this because I had the abortion?"

The cloud of shadow men entered the cab through the windows, through the glass, through the vents and then into her.

"I don't know anything about that, Joni. That's your life and your decision to make. So's this, for that matter. I'm just hoping you'll decide to help us out."

"But who are you? What are these little things doing to me?"

The cab stopped at a red light on the Boston side of the bridge.

Al Carsons slowly rotated in the center of a hurricane in the cross traffic. There were other people in the center of the hurricane, rotating with him.

The hurricane was made of fur.

She twitched, fell, then woke fully, on the floor of her sleep chamber with the light linen sheet and blanket covering her. Somebody knocked on the door. She got up and opened it.

Al Carsons stood there. "Are you okay? I heard something go bump."

"In the night," she added.

He looked at the bright daylight coming in the lab windows. "You sure you're okay?"

She looked at him several seconds before answering. "I think so. I had some of the weirdest fucking dreams, forgive my French."

"I know what you mean. I've been dreaming about my dead wife and boys. I mean, I've been talking to them. In my dreams. And we're caught in something. Or in the center of something..."

"A hurricane?"

"How...how did you know what I dreamt?"

"I need some air. Care to join me outside?"

On the quad between the labs and the dorms, Al said, "I could use a soda. There's got to be someplace to buy a soda downtown."

"Is that a pickup line in... Where you from?"

"Hallock. Minnesota. Ever see the movie *Fargo*?"

She nodded.

"About two and a half hours north of there."

"Christ, Al. What's the population now that you and Captain Sally are here? Zero point five?"

A cab pulled up and the driver rolled down the passenger window. "Hey, you folks need a ride?"

Joni leaned down to see the driver. "Graywolf?" she exclaimed. "I thought you'd be back in Boston by now."

"No, just drumming for fares."

"Al, this is Graywolf, the cabbie who brought me up from Boston. Graywolf, Al. He's doing the same research as me."

Graywolf reached over and offered his hand. "No introductions necessary. Al and I met a long time ago."

Joni put her hand over her chest. "Ow! What the? Felt like something got plucked out of me."

Al saw a little dark shadow man standing on the cab's hood. It reached into him and took out something like folded paper, placing it on the hood. The paper opened.

Al's long ago dream. The buck in the woods. The blind wolf who almost talked. Al remembered saying, "I'm dreaming." The wolf answered but Al didn't understand.

Now he heard the words clearly, "Maybe yes, maybe no. What's important now is that you keep your hope alive. Your family's not dead, only moved on and waiting for you."

The wolf stared at him. Not blind. Different-colored eyes. The right blue, the left brown.

The wolf continued. "But not yet. You have much to do, and we know you grieve. So we'll strike a bargain. You will not dream until it's time, until things are ready, until your hope fills the Garden like great winds filling the sky."

"What garden?"

The wolf said, "Soon. Not yet. Sleep now, Al. When you wake, this will all have been a dream."

The little shadow man danced on the cab's hood. It turned the dream into a whirlwind that flew up and into Al.

Joni said, "You okay, Al?"

He nodded, leaned into the cab to take Graywolf's hand and stopped, staring into the cabbie's eyes. The right blue, the left brown.

Graywolf smiled. "Remember me now, Al?"

CHAPTER 29

Dr. Lupicen's Lab

JAMIE AND JACK STOOD IN THE DOORWAY TO DR. Lupicen's lab.

Jamie said, "Wow."

Jack looked at the size of the lab, the number of assistants going back and forth, the number of sleep chambers, the massive APS sitting in their midst, the assorted other equipment and workstations. "Yeah. Wow."

Sandy Olafssen walked up to them, tablet in hand. "You here for Dr. Lupicen's dream lab?"

"I'm Jack Games. This is Jamie MacPherson. I talked with a Sandy Olafssen - "

"That's me and you're Dr. Games, right? Capoçek told me to be on the lookout for you." She tapped the tablet. "Follow me, please."

Jack placed a protective hand on Jamie's shoulder.

Olafssen caught the movement. She crouched to see Jamie eye-to-eye and offered her hand. "Say there, young man. You're Jamie MacPherson, right?"

"Yes, ma'am."

"Ma'am? *Ma'am?* I ain't that old, kid. I'm Sandy." She waited for Jamie to take her hand and shook it gently. "Nice to meet you. Hey, do you like video games? We got video games that'll knock your socks off."

Jack's hand gently tightened on Jamie's shoulder. "I'd like to keep him in sight."

"Not a problem." She sat Jamie at her console, the APS' sending station, and set it to function as a secondary virtual interface before handing Jamie a set of goggles and helping him with the gloves.

Jack watched several screens flicker several images as Sandy moused and clicked, moused and clicked. "No shoot'em-ups."

"Not even near it. Math, spelling, listening and language skills are about as intense as we get."

"You okay, Jamie?"

Jamie waved his hands in the air like insect antennae seeking a favorite leaf. "Cool!"

"Dr. Lupicen's office is right there. Leave the door open and you can see the whole lab."

GAMES AND LUPICEN TALKED WITH OCCASIONAL interruptions of Jamie talking to the game and laughing.

"Your technology is way beyond my understanding, Dr. Lupicen, but when you tell me Ellie MacPherson's stuck in your computer… If I didn't recognize your voice on my mobile when you called…"

"It is difficult for me to accept as well, but Mr. Nighthorse is quite confident."

Jamie pointed in the air and said something in a foreign language.

Jack considered. Students and assistants came and went, knocking to ask a question, sharing a concern. Lupicen treated all his people with respect, listening attentively, offering suggestions, giving hints when people were close to solving problems on their own.

He liked Lupicen. He trusted him.

Jamie pointed at different areas in the air. "Dhe oube?" He shook his head, said "*J'oube*," nodded and laughed.

Jack watched. He called out, "You having a good time, Jamie?"

Jamie laughed. "*Anou ouc'atay. Ke yta jimbyoyo. S'ay p'wye ke e hala p'em cao. Te 'hae anou ce lae?*"

Jack nodded. "That's what I thought, too, but I wasn't sure."

Jamie's hands moved air around. "*Como?*"

Sandy Olafssen passed the open door. "You understand that?"

Jack shook his head. "Not a word. What is it?"

She shrugged, focusing on other things.

Jamie wrapped his arms around himself and laughed.

Jack shook his head. "I haven't seen him this happy in years. He's finally a kid again." He watched the lab staff, everybody smiling. At least nobody frowning. "Doctor Lupicen, I vote we don't tell Jamie about this. He's been through a lot in the past few days. I'd prefer he stay happy for as along as possible."

"I concur and say again, if Mr. Nighthorse is correct, we owe it to both Jamie and Mrs. MacPherson to put them into contact."

"How does this Nighthorse fellow know Ellie MacPherson? Is this Ellie Jamie's mother and Tom's wife? You're hanging quite a bit on Nighthorse's 'if.'"

"You think I hang too much?"

"May I talk to him?"

"Please use my academic office. It is one floor down at the south end of the building and will afford you some privacy. I'll let him know he is to meet you there."

Jamie shrieked, laughed, tightened like he was being tickled, and giggled, his hands flailing as if pushing something away except he was sitting in a chair in the middle of a lab wearing virtual reality goggles and gloves, waving and laughing at things nobody else could see. Students and assistants walked to and fro, paying no mind to the enraptured child in their midst.

"You okay, Jamie?"

"*Cze ge?*" he laughed. "Sure."

"Okay if I leave for a minute and go talk with somebody?"

Jamie nodded. "*Mehai.*"

"Does that mean it's okay for me to leave for a minute or is that you playing a game?"

Jamie nodded and dismissed Jack with a wave of the hand. "*Mehai, mehai.*"

Sandy Olafssen sat one chair away tapping her tablet. Jack pointed at Jamie, still giggling, squirming, and speaking a language nobody understood. "Math, spelling, listening and language skills do that?"

"Depends what language he's learning, I suppose."

CHAPTER 30

The Language of Dreams

JAMIE, SURROUNDED BY A WARM, SOOTHING WHITE-
ness, waved his hands feeling no resistance. "Cool!"

He heard voices in the lab, Uncle Jack and Dr. Lupicen talking, smelled lab smells.

Arithmetic problems floated in the air around him. He had to catch the correct answers in his hands as all sorts of answers fell like rain around him. The rain-answers tickled.

Animals came next, their names and other words floating around them. Jamie had to snatch the correct name amidst pools of wonder.

A cow mooed at him in the whiteness. He snatched the word "cow" and felt it squirm in his hand, alive and wanting to be free. He opened his hand. "Cow" turned into "*mucca*", the word a butterfly squirming free of its chrysalis. "Dog" became *chien* then *cu* then *köpek* then *Gǒu*.

Lots of animals came but without written words, now only sounds. He had to match the animal to the sound of its name in some other language. The animal and the sound danced around him when he got it right. It was funny. A whale tickled him with its flukes and he thought *Una balena gli faceva il solletico con i suoi colpi*. He hugged himself to stop from laughing.

Someone approached out of the whiteness. "Jamie?"

The air tasted like in the woods up at the cabin. Pine and oak. Tall trees. A bright light shone down. He heard wings. Uncle Jack's and Dr. Lupicen's voices faded.

A girl, older than Jamie, blonde hair, blue-eyed, taller than Jamie, pretty, walked out of the mist. "*J'oube!*"

"Dhe oube?"

She cocked her head, a "what did you say?" look.

He said, "*J'oube!*"

She smiled and nodded. He nodded, too, and laughed. She spoke a language he'd never heard before and it made perfect sense to him. "Hi, Jamie. I'm Ann. Do you know where you are?"

The trees, the snow whiteness, the warm coolness. The sound of wings. The full night sky. He hesitated, the shape of the words strange, unfamiliar yet increasingly familiar with each breath. "*Won bhar?*"

Ann clapped her hands and laughed. "Yes, The Night Garden, The Moon's Garden."

Jamie nodded. "*Anou ouc'atay. Ke yta jimbyoyo. S'ay p'wye ke e hala p'em cao. Te 'hae anou ce lae?*"

"Yes, you've been here before. I'm glad you remembered."

Jamie pointed at some things that had changed. "*Como?*"

Ann nodded. "You are here to learn the Language of Dreams, the oldest language, a language everyone speaks but only in their dreams."

"*Cze ge?*" Jamie considered then answered his own question. "*Mehai.*"

"Yes. Those who never dream."

Jamie nodded. "*Mehai, mehai.*"

CHAPTER 31

Émile

DR. LUPICEN STOOD IN HIS OFFICE DOORWAY, HIS brow furrowed. He watched Jamie, listened to his laughter, the odd vocables he uttered, then looked at Ann, the APS System 70's face winking and tinkling with lights, as if laughing in response to Jamie's laughter. The APS' face grew brilliant, its multiple arrays glowing different colors as Jamie's hands moved through the empty air around him, clutching, pushing, moving.

The APS sighed. Jamie removed the gloves and goggles. The APS's face darkened.

"You have talked with Ann?"

Jamie looked around, disoriented moving from virtual to physical reality, until he caught Dr. Lupicen's smile. "Yes, sir."

"It was a good conversation?"

"Yes. The transition between worlds is a challenge, but manageable."

"'The transition between worlds is a challenge but manageable'? Are you sure you're alright, Mr. Jamie?"

"Yes. I... Ann taught me lots of words, Dr. Lupicen. I apologize if I caused you concern."

Lupicen nodded, slowly. "Yes. Of course. My apologies to you, young man. You would like to play with Ann again?"

"Yes."

Ann's arrays winked.

"Of course. Yes. I am happy Ann has such a handsome young man as a friend."

Ann chugged.

"Thank you, sir."

Joni and Al entered the lab, coffee cups in hand, and Joni walked up to Jamie, ruffling his hair. "Hey there, Skippy. You here to dream?"

"My name's Jamie."

Al said, "What's your name, son?"

"Jamie MacPherson, sir."

"Jamie? I was told to help a 'Jamie' in a dream two nights back."

"Mr. Carsons, you were dreaming with us two nights back?"

"No, sir. This happened in my room across the quad."

"People knowing things they can not consciously know but are unconsciously told of? We are close, Émile?"

Joni and Al looked at the people in the lab. Nobody responded.

Lupicen saw their confusion and raised a finger. "I talk to my brother, Émile. I will show you."

He got the picture frame from his office. His lips pulled into a smile but his eyes saddened. "My brother, Émile, is the reason for my research."

Al looked around. "Where is he?"

"He is lost in a dream."

LITTLE CAPOÇEK LUPICEN, SEVEN YEARS OLD AND dragging his lunch pail behind him, bumped into Émile, his big, strong, nineteen-year-old brother, as they walked home.

"Tired, Capoçek?"

Capoçek crumpled to the dirt road. He curled up under his barn-stained coat.

"Capoçek, get up. We must get home before the town bell strikes.

Comrade Ceaușescu has ordered a curfew."

"I'm tired. We worked on the collective all day. I want to sleep." Capoçek pulled his coat over his head and made snoring sounds.

"Come. Mother will have supper waiting." Émile lifted his brother to his feet.

Capoçek shrugged off his brother's strong hand. "We won't be home in time for supper."

They turned at a sound. From back the way they came.

"What is it, Émile?"

Émile turned back and guided his brother in front of him, towards home, placing himself between Capoçek and whatever approached. "Nothing. Come. Mother will have supper waiting."

Tall trees stood on either side of the road. The sun set. They walked another kilometer in the increasing darkness.

The sound again.

Émile stiffened as they walked, one ear listening to the road behind them. He adjusted his cap to hear better.

Slight. A disturbance in the silence of the night. Almost a sigh. These woods had bear, boar, and wolves. Émile knew their sounds.

He did not know this one.

He crouched beside his brother. "Let's play a game, Capoçek. Something to make the walk home quicker, yes?"

Émile reached into a pocket. The quiet crinkling of cellophane.

Capoçek's attention went from the road to his brother's face. "What is that?"

Émile stood up, his hand still in his pocket, the crinkling sound louder than anything else in the forest. He glanced around. The sun had set, the moon not yet risen, the road dark, the woods darker.

But the path shorter.

Many kilometers shorter. And the trees offered safety should they need. They could climb them if they had to. He would hear things approaching in the woods, not so on the road. Not things walking on quiet, padded feet.

"What do you have, Émile? What is it?"

Émile pulled a cellophane-wrapped red cherry candy from his pocket as he left the road for the tree-lined path. He made an elaborate show of unwrapping the candy, walking faster and faster to keep his little brother moving.

"Where did you get that? Do you have another?"

Émile held the partially unwrapped candy in one hand and shoved his other back in a pocket.

More crinkling. "I stole them from the commissar's desk when all the men gathered in the morning to learn their tasks for the day."

"Émile!"

Émile danced around his little brother, keeping him in front, away from whatever followed.

"You may have one, little brother, but first you must promise me we'll make it home tonight. This path goes over a hill but we'll be home before the bell tolls. Mother will keep supper for us."

"How many do you - "

Both stopped and focused back along the path.

Émile pushed his brother forward. "Hurry, Capoçek. No more games. We need to get home now."

A sad, hollow moan filtered through the trees on either side of them, moving past them.

But no sounds of pursuit.

Émile watched dusk fade to night ahead of them. Every time Capoçek glanced back he rustled wrappers in his pocket, pulling out a red cherry candy, distracting his little brother, keeping him moving forward, towards their village, towards home.

Something rushed past them, a dark silhouette in the darkness of night.

Émile pulled Capoçek to him, stopping them both, peering down the path ahead.

Capoçek pulled his coat tighter around him as he hurried along the path. "I am cold, Émile."

Émile's breath steamed in front of him. "Yes, it is cold. Here." He placed his cap on Capoçek's head, pulling it down over his little brother's ears.

"No, Émile, cold like when Father Viktor warns the village the soldiers are coming for young men. For you. And everybody hurries you and the other boys into the woods. And everyone's hands grow cold even on the warmest summer days. And you can see the tears waiting in the mothers' eyes. Everyone's afraid they'll take you and the others away and we'll never see you again. The soldiers come into the village and everything grows cold."

"Capoçek, I - "

Something amorphic, oozing, its shape changing as it moved past them, slow, patient, leaving no marks, flowed over Capoçek, a dog tracking a scent, then moved on.

Capoçek sagged to the damp forest floor, whimpering.

"Capoçek, are you hurt?"

Another hole in the darkness, night without night, flowed past.

Émile lifted his brother in his arms and ran.

Capoçek sobbed into his brother's shoulder. "I'm afraid."

Another silhouette, similar to the first, rushed past.

Émile, Capoçek tight in his arms, looked back along the trail. Other darknesses, blacknesses, sloughed towards them.

Émile held Capoçek tight against the bole of an old oak, shielding him with his body. "Don't look, Capoçek. Don't look."

Screams in the distance.

Not of people. Not a thing of the wild.

"I want to go home."

Émile put his hands on either side of Capoçek's head, staring into his face. "Someone could be hurt, Capoçek."

Capoçek clenched his arms around Émile, burying himself in brother's chest. "Leave them."

Émile kissed Capoçek's head and gently pushed him back. "Do you really mean that, little brother? Shall we let someone suffer when we could help them instead? Is that what it means to be afraid?"

"You don't know what it is, Émile."

"And neither do you. It could be our greatest fear. It could be our greatest joy."

Capoçek pleaded, "You could die."

"I won't. And neither will you. I promise. Believe me?"

Capoçek returned his brother's stare, so safe in Émile's strong arms. He slowly nodded.

Émile lifted him and ran towards the sounds, off the trail, through the trees, under the stars, the full moon rippling over a rise.

"Look."

On the top of the rise in a treeless clearing, a small plain, little shadow men, child-like in size, huddling together, looking towards the rising moon.

Surrounding them, the hunting blacknesses, moving slowly, methodically, confidently, predators sure their prey could not escape.

"Stay here, Capoçek. Promise me you'll stay here."

"Émile, no - "

Émile held his brother, stared him eye-to-eye. "Promise me."

Capoçek nodded.

Émile lowered Capoçek to the ground. He kissed his brother's head and gave him a handful of hard cherry candies. "For when I return. We can celebrate."

The hunters attacked. Silent. Methodical. Crushing. Collapsing. The little men folded like holiday wrappings sucked of their joy.

Émile ran up the rise, screaming and shrieking, his coat whipping over his head as if he were herding pigs into a sty.

A sound. A scream. A challenge. A call. Ancient and formidable, summoning an old enemy to battle.

Coming from the moon.

The moon's light fell upon the plain, two great beams, one upon the silhouetted child-men and the other upon Émile, bathing them in a whiteness like liquid snow.

The little creatures stepped on their moonbeam, walking up towards the moon as if walking a brightly lit stairway.

Émile stood alone, bathed in light, the swarthlings circling him, tightening. He turned to face the moon, his arms wide.

The moonlight grew brighter and narrower, focused by some celestial lens, concentrating all its energy on his chest, pulsing with his beating heart. His body filled with the moon's brightness, collapsed into an arrow and shot into the sky.

The howling of wolves.

Darkness.

"Men from our village found me the next morning, curled into a ball by the tree where Émile left me, asleep. They found Émile's tracks, no others. My country still had folktales about strange things walking the woods. When I told what happened, some said imagination, a trick of the moon in the mountains. Some said Émile was cursed from birth and Crossed themselves, some sought travelers - human - but Émile was strong. There would have been signs. The state had no interest beyond losing a strong worker."

Lupicen frowned at the picture in his hands. "The village priest, he thought differently. 'Émile spent all his time talking to the witches,' he said. They were herbalists, really. Just some women who knew which roots cured what, which bark healed what. But the church couldn't have that. The priest claimed Émile listened to their stories, all their talk of old things, old ways - which was true. He learned their stories until he could repeat them flawlessly - then the priest spit. He made the Sign of the Cross then the Devil's Horns. 'The Devil took him. And good riddance.'

A tear gathered in a crease on Lupicen's cheek, filled it, then continued its journey down his face. He pulled a handkerchief from his labcoat pocket and wiped it away. "My parents told me never to ask again, never to mention Émile. My mother comforted me as best she could. 'Your brother is lost in a dream,' she said, fearing for my safety. 'Perhaps in a dream he will come back.'"

Capoçek paused, stared at the image in the frame, and rubbed away an imaginary smudge with his thumb. "So my life's question has been 'What happened that night?'" He glanced up at his audience and smiled shyly. "Do you know in neuroscience we say 'Anything perfectly imagined is real'? That is why true lunacy is most difficult to cure; the lunatic is in a world we cannot enter and they cannot leave. Is that what happened? Did I leave this world and enter another for one moment then come back?" He shrugged. "Let us say I did. Now one must ask, 'When else do we leave this world, enter another and come back?'"

Jamie exclaimed, "When we dream!"

Lupicen tousled Jamie's hair. "Quite right. You are a wise young man. Someday we'll collaborate on a project, yes?" His gaze went back to Joni and Al. "So I study and I learn. I have no shame and I steal ideas as Émile stole candy. I see this in neuroscience and it looks like this in mythology. I ask, 'Do these play together?' I see this in quantum theory and that in oneirology and ask, 'Do they play together?'" He placed the frame back on his desk, brought his hands up to eye level, and rapidly tapped the tips of his fingers together, their motion mimicking the many interactions between disciplines only he could see. "We've learned the universe is not one place but many. Most often there is no smooth opening between these universes, they are what mathematicians call 'discontinuous'. What I saw that night was the discontinuous made continuous, the chaos of my homeland transferred to the chaos of another land, another place. We do the same thing every night when we dream, we open worlds that exist nowhere else, created when this chaos of this world," he waved a hand in the air, "is transferred to the chaos of this world." He tapped his forehead.

"Everything we do here," he nodded to his lab, "is to still the chaos. Perhaps in our quiet we can intentionally open a door?" He lifted the picture and tapped his brother's face. "In any case, he is the reason we are here."

Al Carsons took the frame from Lupicen's hand and studied the older boy's face. "Him? That's Émile? Your brother?" He handed the frame to Joni.

Her eyes widened. "Really? Does he have a son?"

"Impossible. No."

"This picture's black-and-white. Do you one of him in color?"

"Such did not exist in my country at that time. Certainly not in small villages. This was done by a pedlar traveling with a camera. His wagon was a complete darkroom. Why?"

"Does your brother have different color eyes? Right one blue, left one brown?"

"How do you know of my brother's curse? It is impossible. Émile died over fifty years ago."

Jamie stared at the picture in Joni's hand. His face filled with joy. "Hey, that's Mr. Graywolf!"

Joni asked, "You know Graywolf, Jamie?"

Dr. Lupicen took the photograph from Joni and stared into his brother's face. "Graywolf? My full surname is 'Lupicenuşiu'. People had enough trouble with 'Capoçek' so I shortened my surname. 'Lupicenuşiu' is 'Graywolf' in English."

CHAPTER 32

The Wall

PANGIOSI SAT ON THE EDGE OF HIS BED, HANDS clasped loosely together in his lap, brows knit and lips pursed. He peered down at Tom, on the floor and still groggy from the taser strike. Tom's bladder and bowels had released and the car stank of urine and feces.

"This is no way for a guest to behave, Tom." Pangiosi turned the AC and ventilation blowers on full. "If only we had windows, we could open them."

Tom didn't respond.

Pangiosi tapped Tom with his foot. "Tom? Mr. MacPherson?"

Pangiosi stood and kicked Tom in the stomach. "I don't believe you're listening to me, Mr. MacPherson."

Tom gasped for air. His eye opened wide and fixed on Pangiosi.

"That's better, Tom. Thank you. I know you've just rested but I need you to rest again."

Tom's brow furrowed.

Pangiosi lifted a small case from the bed and opened it so Tom could see. "This hypodermic, the blue one, puts you to sleep. This other one, the red one, wakes you up." Pangiosi's eyes went from the hypodermics to Tom. "Sometimes the people who work for me tend to melodrama. I let them so long as they do their jobs. Shows I'm a good boss, don't you think?" He rolled Tom over and injected the blue hypodermic. "Easy, easy, Tom. It won't take a... And there you go!"

Tom dove deep into sleep but didn't dream. Pangiosi gave him a shot from the red hypodermic.

Tom surfaced, his eyes fluttered briefly, Pangiosi shot him with the blue, he took a deep breath and dove again.

Nothing. Five times over the course of half an hour, nothing.

"Tom, you're not cooperating. Let's try something else."

Pangiosi kneeled on the floor beside Tom. "Tom, you don't seen capable of summoning those little midnight men like Ellie did. That leaves your son. I have things to do so you'll have to find him and bring him to me." He lifted Tom's head, flopping like a rag doll's, in both hands to steady it and used his thumbs to hold open Tom's eyelids. "What is it they used to say, Tom? Resistance is futile?"

He stared into Tom's eyes, slapped his face to get his attention focused, and *knacked*.

Grogginess left Tom like a Fundy tide. His eyes cleared and locked onto Pangiosi's. His head held steady. Color rushed up his face. His nostrils flared.

Pangiosi hit a wall so hard he rocked back off his feet and onto the floor, his back banging against the bed, his hands blistered as if he'd touched the sun.

Something trickled over his lips. A drop of blood.

His shook like a child caught red-handed and waiting to be punished.

Long ago. Almost forty years ago. Buried but not forgotten. The Kid. On Erans 3E.

Tom's eyes closed. His head lowered to the floor. His breathing became soft and regular.

The Kid? Tom is the Kid? Impossible. The age difference. And the Kid had heterochromia iridis. Tom doesn't. They're related? Is this genetic? Is this a coincidence? Twice in forty years? A coincidence?

And what about the boy? What if the boy has both his mother's and his father's gifts?

He got back on his knees, straightened his shirt and wiped his nose on the bedspread. He checked Tom for a pulse: strong and regular.

The train slowed. The horn announced their entry into White River Junction station. Pangiosi stood. He lifted his phone. "Cleanup my private car. There's collateral." He listened for a moment and looked down at Tom. "Fully hostile. Facilitate it."

He showered, changed, grabbed some identification from his bureau and left.

CHAPTER 33

Pangiosi and Tibbs

"My dear Mr. Tibbs, how are you?" Pangiosi extended his hand as Tibbs opened the door to his apartment. "Always a pleasure to see you again."

Every time Pangiosi shook Tibb's hand he wanted to have his own amputated, cauterized, buried, and have the ground sown with salt. The man reminded him of a weasel; not so much tall as long and thin, with a lumpy chest as if full of chicken bones. Every time Pangiosi met him he wondered if the man's dick matched his body: long, thin, arched slightly to the left when it stood up and with a head too large for the frame supporting it.

That's how the man impressed him. Even more so now, standing in the hallway of a farmhouse converted into cheap college apartments, naked save for a pair of valentine imprinted boxers, nodding and smiling his sycophantic idiot's grin.

He hated Tibbs. He couldn't help it.

"Hi, Earl. Come on in."

Put some pants on man, for God's sake. If I didn't need you fully functional - "I hope you don't mind my dropping in unannounced.

Important matters to discuss." - Oh, if only I could *knack* you, Mr. Tibbs, if only - "I need an update on the Lupicen project. You have material on that?" - But your mind works in such strange ways, Mr. Tibbs. The slightest *knack* and you become little more than an idiot, not even an idiot-savant, just a plain, old-fashioned, drooling-into-his-shoes idiot.

Tibbs motioned Earl to one of the three seats visible in the apartment. "I know, Earl. It's not what I'm used to, but it's close to the highway, close to the college, and nobody here cares if I blow a fuse or two late at night. They're all in bed by ten, anyway."

Pangiosi nodded. Tibbs could be controlled in other ways. Nauseating ways: once each year Tibbs returned to a Boston-Brookline neighborhood like a salmon to its spawning grounds to impregnate some hideous, fat pig of a woman. Each year that Pangiosi had known him, Tibbs returned to wallow - Pangiosi could think of no other word for it - like a pig at the trough of his obese queen, just one more mouth to suckle at her teats.

Tibbs had three or four children by her.

Earl shuddered at the thought.

Still, seeing those worm-white stick legs sticking out of slightly soiled boxer shorts...it made him neither happy nor glad.

Pangiosi looked around. Three chairs, three rooms. A rather good-sized kitchen overlooking a backyard, a living room serving as a base of electronic operations, and a bedroom, or so Earl assumed because the door was shut. He really didn't want to know what might be in there.

He found out anyway because a young woman - actually a girl. Earl couldn't lie to himself. She was a girl becoming a woman in just the right ways but a girl never-the-less - opened the door. "Virgil?"

Tibbs looked up at her. His face went red and the blush went down the rest of his worm-white body. He looked at Earl and laughed nervously.

Earl discreetly looked around for something to do. "I'll go make myself a cup of coffee." He stepped towards the kitchen.

Tibbs moved right along with him. "Hey, good idea. Make me a cup, too, would you? Here, let me show you - "

Earl spun on him. "Jesus Christ take care of this, will you?" He waved at the girl as she pulled back into Tibbs's bedroom.

He made it a point not to listen to the whispers and only came out of the kitchen when he heard the apartment door close.

"Hey, you didn't make me any coffee."

Earl's fingers tightened on his cup. He looked up and away. "What do you have to tell me?"

"Lupicen has a hell of a system. Better than anything anybody else has, and that includes our guys."

"How long has it been online?"

"Not long. It's been wormed to send me reports when his research activity starts."

"You mean he's had this machine for several weeks if not months and he hasn't used it yet?"

"Oh, no, he's used it, sure, but he hasn't done any research with it. He's asked it a few questions but nothing to really flex its muscles. He just sits around and lets it dream. I'm waiting for him to start running complex cyphers. I mean, why else would he design a machine like that?"

"Did you say he lets it dream?"

"Well, that's what he calls it. Monitoring people who volunteer for his dream research. He doesn't ask it to do anything else."

"And you haven't monitored any of that activity at all?"

"No. Why bother? Dreaming is pretty useless, even if it is a machine. It's just a program, after all."

Pangiosi so wanted to bookmark this slimewhite fool. Instead he let his wrath come out in words and Tibbs's feeling be damned. "Does it occur to you, you ignorant fool, that dreaming is exactly what we want it to do? That its dreams are the way it does complex cyphers?"

"No, I - "

"No, you pathetic dolt. It's developing logical patterns like nothing ever before on the planet and you sit around in your skivvies waiting for some adolescent twirl to get you off."

"Earl, don't get excited - "

"Don't get excited?" Pangiosi stood, violently. He wanted to feel Tibbs's neck splintering in his grasp. He wanted to watch Tibbs's eyes bulge when the last breath of him could not escape. "You're letting god knows how much information slip by and I'm not supposed to get excited?"

Pangiosi couldn't bookmark the idiot before him and he searched his mind for leverage. He calmed and smiled. "I think I shall call your friend in...Boston? Brookline? I think she would like to know you're up here."

"No, Earl. Don't do that. I can fix things so we know everything Lupicen's computer is doing. I swear."

"You can arrange for it to report everything to you?"

"Yes, sure I can." Tibbs sat down in the center of the electronics and flicked a few switches. Lights on different boxes signaled systems coming to life. "See here? This is the subsystem it reports to me on."

"It's not reporting anything."

"I'll have to modify a few things. But don't worry, Earl. Mr. Pangiosi. I'll have it working before close of shop today."

"You have methods at your disposal?"

"Oh, yeah. Lots. I even have one that lets me reprogram and take over the computer if I want."

"Would they be able to find out about that?"

"Oh, they'd have to go looking long and far for that, and I put in lots of decoys. See, I gave them two or three that're easy to find and not easy to defeat, and there's a layer under that and a layer under that and on and on. It'd take them years to find and clear them all, and the others are way too deep, kind of in his computer's subconscious mind, and besides, we'll have everything we need and be gone before they do that." He patted a black, featureless box under the table which looked cool to the touch. "This one the computer itself doesn't even know about. It's like a virus on its communications spine. By the time any diagnostics can find it it'll be too late."

"Never underestimate your opponents, Mr. Tibbs. Lupicen is no fool and he knows his intentions for his computer better than you do."

"Yes, sir. Sorry, sir."

"You know how to reach me?"

"Same bat time, same bat channel."

Earl walked out. As he passed the bedroom, he got a whiff of the pure sex that had gone on in there and remembered the face of the girl.

Normally, he wouldn't care.

But Tibbs was becoming such a liability.

Chapter 34

Abduction

The maintenance crew chief held a clipboard out to Sandy Olafssen.

"Nothing? We had a small hurricane in here and you find nothing wrong with the AC system?"

The man shrugged and took the clipboard back when she'd signed the work order. One of Lupicen's assistants followed them out.

Lupicen and Jamie sat in his office. "Tell me, your experience of this man you call Graywolf, you're sure you experienced him before you came here and worked with my Ann?"

"Maybe your brother didn't die back where you come from. Maybe Mom and Shem didn't die either. Maybe they're all together some place. Can we go find them?"

Lupicen considered. He glanced at one of the grad students walking awkwardly but unhurriedly out the door. "Ms. Olafssen, we must be sure our volunteers are fully aware before they go about their days, yes? Let them wake slowly from Ann." He turned back to Jamie. "You think maybe they are all together inside Ann? Perhaps they're all lost in a dream?"

Another assistant left the lab.

"I don't know about that, Dr. Lupicen. I know people no longer have dreams. Or hopes. What used to be dreams are now just blackness, emptiness, and people don't want to hope for anything better anymore."

Two more of Lupicen's labworkers moseyed out the door.

"That's a very profound thought for such a young man, Jamie," Lupicen said. "What has caused you to believe this?"

Jamie sat back, no longer sitting straight up, now pulled into the chair, caught with his hand in the cookie jar.

"You have a secret? I will not share your secret unless you tell me to. I promise." Lupicen placed his right hand over his heart.

Jamie recounted his experiences in The Moon's Night Garden and what The Moon asked of him. "Dr. Lupicen, Uncle Jack says you're probably smarter than him. I know he won't understand. Do you understand?"

Lupicen took Jamie's hands in his own. "Jamie, yes, I do understand. I wish I did not, but I do. Long ago, this is how it was in my country. Things we did not imagine destroyed what we could imagine. That which we feared destroyed what we could dream. There were many lost hopes and dreams of those trapped between the coming Communist and Nazi regimes. They destroyed many hopes of many people and took much of the color out of our lives." He looked at Jamie's hands in his. "But how that means my brother was taken into the sky on a beam of moonlight, I don't know."

Jamie blurted out, "That's what happened to The Moon, too."

The door to the lab opened. A tall, red-haired, fair-complexioned man stood there. He smiled. "I'm so sorry. Lupicen, isn't it? I didn't catch that last part of your conversation. I was busy encouraging people to leave the lab." The man's smile fell on Jamie.

Lupicen felt Jamie's hands tense inside his own.

The man kept his smile on Jamie. "Jamie, would you come here, please?"

Jamie shook his head, no, and pulled closer to Lupicen.

"Your dog is alive, Jamie. Come, let's go get him."

Lupicen rose to his feet. "Do you know this man?"

The red-haired man stared at Lupicen and Lupicen stared back. It seemed as if the man were focusing with all of his will on Lupicen's face. Lupicen simply stared back at the man, neither focusing nor straining, merely meeting the man's gaze full on.

"See here, I have responsibility for this boy. Who are you? What are you doing here?"

"Oh, I'm sorry. My name's Pangiosi. Earl Pangiosi. I know Jamie's parents. I told his dad I'd come get the boy and bring him to his father."

Ann's QLCs groaned, the lights on her face blazed. Lupicen looked. He'd never seen his computer behave this way.

The distraction took his eyes off Jamie and the man briefly.

When he looked up they were gone.

CHAPTER 35

Unlikely Heroes

Jack Games and John Nighthorse relaxed in comfortable reading chairs in Lupicen's private office, Games assessing Nighthorse as the big man spoke.

"You don't give much away, Mr. Nighthorse."

Nighthorse chuckled. "Dr. Lupicen said much the same thing. I'll have to work on it."

"You understand that what you've told me..." Games spread his hands and shrugged.

"Defies description? Makes no sense?" Nighthorse laughed. "Is the stuff of dreams?"

"Unless you're suffering some exceptional psych or neural episodes—"

Nighthorse grabbed the sides of his head, rose from his chair and howled. His fingers wove through his thick hair and pulled. His eyes screwed up into his head until only white shown through thin slits.

Games's training kicked in: Stay in your seat. Stay calm. Evaluate. Correlate. Decide. Act.

He knew little about this man aside from what could be gleaned physically: probably Native American by features and complexion. Morbid muscularity. Good to excellent health. The rest relied on trusting Lupicen's evaluation and his own sense of the man made during the short time he'd talked with him.

Except right now Nighthorse stood in the middle of Lupicen's academic office experiencing some kind of fugue and reminding Games of Harold "Oddjob" Sakata's Vicks44 commercials from the 1970's. He acted neither destructively nor harmfully, but someone that size could sneeze and take down a wall without trying.

"Mr. Nighthorse?" Games spoke loudly and firmly. How come nobody else was running into this office to see what all the hollering was about? "John? Can you hear me?"

Nighthorse's eyes came back down and his eyes fixed on Games. He took his hands from the sides of his head and grabbed Games's arms, lifting him from his chair as if Games were made of straw.

"He's got Jamie. Pangiosi's got Jamie."

"What? Who's got Jamie?"

Nighthorse dropped him and ran down the stairs and onto the quad. He scanned the various student faces, searching for Pangiosi. He ran back through the building and out the back door only to see a black limousine spinning its tires as it raced up the driveway.

Again Nighthorse ran through the building and out onto the quad, running like his namesake, across the grass to the black limo as it turned north onto Rte10.

He leapt. His body cleared the hood by inches and he smashed into the windshield. The limo braked hard. The driver and two men sprang out aiming AR-15s at him.

He rolled off the hood and spun on them.

Then stopped.

Inside he heard someone crying out in Taiwanese. A rich foreign student. The driver and two men his bodyguards.

Down the other end of the quad a mid-size Buick, a rental, blue with no trim, turned south out of the parking lot. He caught a face.

Pangiosi.

Nighthorse fell to his knees, the Taiwanese student's chauffeur's and guards' weapons still trained on him, as his fists hammered the ground. "I failed you, Ann. I failed you, Ellie. I failed you."

Jack Games ran through Vail Hall to Lupicen's lab. Olafssen and his assistants stood outside, mumbling to themselves. Lupicen stood at his desk, phone in hand.

"What happened?"

"A man, Pangiosi, came and spirited Jamie away. I have notified Security. They're contacting the police. What has become of Mr. Nighthorse?"

"He ran out of the building screaming that Jamie'd been taken. I have no idea what's become of him." Over Lupicen's shoulder, Games saw the operations display on the System 70 blinking and winking, rainbows flowing like molten lava over its surface.

Joni and Al weaved through Lupicen's assistants and entered the lab. Joni said, "Al said we had to get back here. What happened?"

Al, wanting to be out of everyone's way, stood next to the System 70. Its rainbow lights swarmed over him, engulfing him. He held out his hand as if reaching for something.

Lupicen looked at him. "Mr. Carsons? Are you alright?"

Al's eyes focused but not on anything anyone else could see. Flying wolves surrounded him, moving in a whirlwind as if he was the eye of some incredible hurricane. They did not rain down upon him. He saw through them, around them as they flew, as if the winds they rode swept up one world and laid down the next.

A small silhouette fluttered up to him. It made a window in the whirlwind, showing Al some other place, outside his private hurricane.

"It's Jamie. He's…near water? A river? A dam? Feels close. Someplace nearby. Like an old public works project that's been turned into a park."

Joni grabbed his arm. "Al? Mr. Carsons?"

The winds lifted him. The lab and the dam superimposed over each other. He couldn't tell which was real and which a dream. The lab faded as the dam and its surroundings brightened.

Joni shook his arm. "Mr. Carsons?"

The wolves, the wind, the storm, the images of Jamie, they all went away.

CAPTAIN SALLY SAT IN AL CARSONS'S PICKUP TRUCK for no other reason than the privacy it afforded him. The campus had a no smoking policy and Sally convinced Al it didn't apply to vehicles so Al reluctantly gave him the keys.

Sally occasionally pulled on his pipe and sent puffs of blue-tinged smoke into the cab. He'd taken off his mock captain's hat which allowed him to scratch his white crewcut and beard as he mused. When he thought of it, he brushed ashes from his black jeans and jacket.

He'd been thinking about Nighthorse's *wotai*. He knew from his studies of ethnic and folk art there was supposed to be magic in such things. Nighthorse didn't say as much, but he didn't say much of anything. He could be an artful liar, but Sally was one himself and he'd had several more years' experience in the game.

Besides, he didn't think Nighthorse was one to lie.

Sally himself had looked through the stone and held it in his hands. When he looked through the *wotai* he saw the big Indian like some kind of cross between a man and a dog, not fully one and not fully the other. It was more an impression than something he actually knew or saw.

He also remembered Nighthorse looked at him strangely when Sally held the *wotai* to his eye.

The question was, was Nighthorse or his *wotai* or both a threat to him after all his time in hiding?

Just then the big Indian exploded from the front doors of Vail Hall, looked around, screamed and returned inside.

"What are you up to, John?" Sally murmured as he watched Nighthorse re-enter the building.

A black limousine came up the parking lot and stopped as the drive met Rte10.

Nighthorse burst through the doors a second time and raced across the quad.

"What are you doing?"

Nighthorse jumped onto the hood of the limo. Captain Sally watched the bodyguards and driver exit the limo and aim their weapons at him.

A blue Buick, mid-size, came up the far parking lot drive. Nighthorse rose up enough to see it and then he collapsed onto the ground and cried like a whale dying on a beach.

Captain Sally adjusted the mirrors and seat in Al Carsons's truck as he started the engine and put it in gear. "Well, now, ain't that a thing. You all concerned like that, John. I'm thinking whoever's in that car has something awful precious to you. Maybe I should do you a favor and follow?"

Aside from the plates and the look of the truck, he figured he had a chance. If he stayed a few cars behind as best he could, he could probably do it.

He headed after Pangiosi's car.

CHAPTER 36

Beacon of Love

Tᴏᴍ MᴀᴄPʜᴇʀsᴏɴ ʟᴀʏ ᴀsʟᴇᴇᴘ. Bʟᴇssᴇᴅ sʟᴇᴇᴘ. There were some pains in his side. Some discomfort along his back. Did he have a headache? He moved, rearranging himself under the covers. His arms and legs were pinned. Shem, probably. Sleeping on him or next to him again.

Strange thoughts, though. A tall, thin, red-haired man?

Tom liked to sleep. Too much, according to Jack. Jack said he had a problem. Something about sleeping too much?

He wasn't sure.

When did he sleep last? Truly restful sleep.

In northern Michigan at his family's camp. His father's hunting camp.

No, his camp now. His and Ellie's and Jamie's.

Tom hated hunting. Tom's dad died in a hunting accident. Not at the camp, though.

Didn't matter. Tom had nothing to do with guns after that. Never even held one.

But he loved the camp. Jamie loved it, too, he could tell. Many good memories there, many good memories.

He took a deep breath. Definitely a pain in his side.

His last good sleep he dreamt of Ellie. Beloved wife. Loving mother.

Sounded like something you'd say at a funeral, something you'd put on a tombstone: Beloved wife. Loving mother.

What was that dream? He stood on a shore, his body a beacon, a lighthouse, sweeping the dark night seas to guide one ship home, a lonely lighthouse kept by a sad, melancholy man questing and calling out to the good ship Ellie, "Come home, my darling, my love. I wait for you here."

Waiting for the ship to answer. Waiting for Ellie to answer. His mind continually sending out the beacon, but only when he slept, telling him to rest while it swept the seas seeking the one ship that needed to answer.

Tom, asleep on the floor of the tall, thin, red-haired man's railroad car, didn't hear the last words the man spoke to him, didn't feel the kick in his side the man gave him, because a few miles away Lupicen's System 70 computer's QLCs came open wide as Ann bent reality like a too massive sun bending space, allowing Ellie MacPherson's consciousness to find the beacon of Tom's mind and answer him at last.

A YELLOW CHECKER CAB FROM THE BOSTON CAB Company, Mass plates and a Boston hack license, pulled into the White River Junction trainyard. It rolled along slowly, moving a little this way, a little that, like a dog tracking a scent but unhurried, sure things would be found. At one point it pulled alongside a pair of US Mail LandSea containers on a flatbed car and stopped, then continued on until it got to the opposite end of the yard. It came to rest in the passenger station's parking lot amongst a bunch of other taxis, some yellow, some not. The driver shut off his duty light, got out, adjusted his wraparound sunglasses and headed back to the LandSea containers on the flatbed car, tying his long black hair into a ponytail as he walked.

Every once in a while he glanced to the west to determine the sun's distance from the mountain tops ranging that horizon.

He stopped at the far end of the flatbed and pulled his glasses off long enough to watch the sun set, shooting bright burgundy rays through the sky like tears in the flesh of clouds. When it had completely set, the man faced east until a bright orange pimple appeared on the horizon. He hummed to himself, something old, something containing sounds more at home in the throat of a wolf than a man.

More orange filled the eastern sky. Stars that appeared with the setting sun winked away as the orange grew more intense and took shape as the topmost cusp of the rising crescent moon.

The man's hum turned into a mixture of words and whines and howls and sighs.

Up in the sky, the cusp of the moon turned from face to edge, as if the crescent moon turned itself in the sky to present more a scythe than a wedge.

A beam of cold white light came through the orange sky and fell upon the side of the nearer US Mail LandSea trailer. What had been closed and sealed and barred to entry became a door with a handle hidden in a recess.

The white light faded away. The moon once again took on its wedged crescent shape. The man opened the door and walked inside, closing the door behind him and making sure the seal remained in place.

He whistled and cleaned, moving quietly and efficiently, cleaning Pangiosi's suites like a wave on a calm ocean. He found the janitorial supplies in the supply closet and took out only what he needed for each task. Equipment for repeated tasks he placed in a line leading back to the door to ensure each could be found again and none would be left out when he'd completed his chores.

He put some muscle into cleaning various stains off the rugs and floors, meticulously stacked and collated without reading reports which were in disarray, made sure the liquor cabinet was restocked and all glasses, plates, and utensils were washed, dried, and returned to their proper place. He inventoried the small refrigerator - so much like a hotel minibar that Pangiosi must have eaten out if he ate at all - and restocked it from supplies. He cleaned from one end of the first room to the other. The line of his cleaning moved with and slightly ahead of him, like a astronomical terminator, turning the dark of Pangiosi's suite to light with Graywolf the rising sun.

When he entered the bedroom he spotted Tom MacPherson's tell-tale foot and pajamaed leg sticking out from under the bed. He pursed his lips and shook his head but didn't hurry his cleaning. He cleaned this room as he'd cleaned the last, slowly, meticulously, like the sun rising on a dark dawn. His terminator line moved with him. As he came in line with the bathroom he diverted into it and again cleaned, again used some muscle, even broke a slight sweat, to remove some stains from the porcelain sink, toilet, tub, and beige tiled walls. He wiped the gold fixtures over the sink, tub, and toilet until he could see his reflection. He smiled. Used soaps and toiletries were removed, new ones put in their place. Towels were taken down, fresh ones fluffed and hung.

Back in the bedroom, he gathered laundry and bagged it, replenished underwear and stockings from stores, took fresh shirts, trousers and sport coats from drycleaner bags, brushed and hung them in the closet. He lifted the keychain of flashdrives and a few fell off. He read all the labels, learning Pangiosi's preferred cataloguing method then mimicking it as he replaced the sticks on the chain.

"Not a sea, Tom. Inland. A reservoir."

Ellie's voice? Calling him?

"Jamie's in danger. Please wake up, Tom. I'll always be here for you, Tom. But now, Tom, now..."

The shore and sea gave way to a vast, white, featureless landscape.

"Ellie," he yelled.

"Here, Tom. I'm over here."

He ran, not knowing where, uncountable steps but never closer. "I can't see you, Ellie. Can you hear me? Where are you?" Tears ran down his face and became rivers rushing to a forest far, far away.

"Here, Tom. I'm right here."

He turned, panting, aching. Ellie. She stood there. Tall, lithe, athletic. Auburn hair down to her shoulders. Those white shoulders bare so he could kiss them.

She held her arms out to him. He fell into them. He wept, a child lost for so long finally seeing home, touching comfort, hearing the sounds and words which meant he was safe.

When his crying stopped he allowed himself to release his grip on her. "Ellie, where are you? Where have you been? Why did you have to leave us?"

A loveseat formed behind them in the vast whiteness and they sat. A lake appeared twenty feet in front of them, a grassy shore. They were in bathing suits. Trees, blue sky with a puffy clouds. Birds sang. Fish splashed.

"Is this a dream, Ellie? Am I going to wake up and you're going to go away?"

She held his hands. She drew him close and kissed him with a soft passion he remembered so well. "I don't know how much time we have."

"If this is a dream then I won't wake up. I'll stay here with you forever."

She met his eyes, so intense, so wanting, so lonely. "I wish you could, Tom. I wish you could be here with me forever. But you can't, Tom. Not yet. The man who kidnapped me, the man who beat you. He's got Jamie."

Tom opened his mouth to scream. Something was in it, blocking the sound.

"You have to go back, Tom, my love, my always love. Jamie is in danger. Please wake up, Tom. I'll always be here for you, my darling. But now, Tom, now…"

A mist grew, separating them.

"Ellie."

"Now you must save Jamie."

GRAYWOLF'S TERMINATOR LINE GOT TO THE BED AND touched Tom MacPherson's foot. Tom moaned.

Graywolf whispered, "Easy, Tom. Wake up slow. You probably got some bruises and scrapes we'll need to take care of."

Graywolf removed the bedspread, blankets, sheets, pillowcases and mattress pad, turned the mattress and remade the bed.

By now his terminator line was well past where Tom's head would be, and Tom was stretching slowly and struggling to draw wakefulness from sleep.

Graywolf knelt and gently drew Tom from under the bed. "Hello, Thomas. Let's get you cleaned up, okay?"

TOM'S EYES FLASHED OPEN, HIS DREAM ENDING. THE vision of Ellie once again gone away into some land of dreams where she still lived and they still talked and played and still had time to watch Jamie grow and Shem romp and bark at nothing at all.

Something tugged on his legs.

Ellie moved further and further away with each tug.

Ellie wanted him to wake up, to turn away from her, to leave her. Why?

"Help Jamie."

The tug became a yank. He fought to stay betwixt and between, sailing on the sea of dreams, unwilling for his Ellie-dream to end.

"I want to stay with you, Ellie," he called.

The whirling mist answered, "You can't abandon Jamie."

I can't abandon Jamie. I want to be with Ellie but I can't abandon Jamie. I can't stay here. Jamie needs me there.

Ellie called as she moved further and further away, "I love you, Tom. You're the only man I ever truly loved. I'm going to do everything I can to help you and Jamie, Tom, but then I'll have to go away. I'm sorry, Tom, so sorry."

Tom couldn't scream. Something stuck in his mouth, choked him, constricted him like the straightjacket had moments before. A darkness moved over his eyes. A shadow. A man? There was a man looking down at him. The tall, red-haired man? But he had Jamie.

What he did to Ellie, what he'd done to Tom himself, now he was going to hurt Jamie? Tom wanted to kill him.

But helping Jamie meant Ellie would forever die?

"Not forever, Tom. just for now. I won't really die because you'll remember me, won't you? And you and Jamie will talk about me? And you'll both remember me? Please?"

Something stopped his words. He nodded quickly, painfully. He couldn't open his mouth, couldn't say the words. He moaned and hoped she'd understand. "Yes, my love. I will remember you always."

The white mist swirled up around them again, pulling them apart. "Good, Tom. Remember me. I'll help you save Jamie. When this is all through, I'll be waiting for you in the next place, Tom. We won't be apart forever."

The mist moved away. The dream ended. The beacon stilled its light.

Tom's eyes fluttered open. A dark-skinned man with long, black hair smiled down at him. The man had two differently colored eyes.

Tom's eyes fluttered open. Graywolf smiled down at him.

Tom groaned and his eyes closed, then opened again and squinted.

Graywolf said, "Easy, Tom. I know this'll be hard to believe, but I'm your friend here. I'm going to dab some Scotch," he showed Tom the bottle. "Thank god it's good stuff, huh? Anyway, I'm going to dab some of this fine Scotch on a rag and moisten your lips. The alcohol will weaken the glue. Open your mouth slowly. I'm going to hold these straws you're breathing through and when you nod, I'll gently pull them out. Your throat and mouth are going to be bone dry. If any of this starts to hurt you, shake your head and we'll come up with a different plan, ok?"

Tom nodded but his eyes carried two days of panic in them.

"Not happy with that idea, huh? Ok. I can come up with something better." Graywolf got up and walked into the other room. Tom cried out as he left. "Don't worry. I'm not leaving without you." He came back in with another of Pangiosi's Macallan bottles, one of the ones he'd removed and replenished from stores. There were about four mouthfuls left in it. He removed the cap and gently pulled the tissue balls from Tom's nostrils. "You need to breathe through your nose no matter what, ok, Tom? I'm going to lift you up so you can sip some of this Scotch through your straws. Use your tongue to swish the Scotch on the inside of your lips. Your mouth and throat'll absorb it before it ever makes its way to your gut, so don't worry about that, but it'll moisten your mouth and get your spit working enough to let me loosen your lips so you can open your mouth. Got it?"

Tom nodded. There was no less fear in his eyes than before. "Did you know this idea came from a form of torture used during the Spanish Inquisition? Bet that gives you confidence, huh?"

Tom gasped once and Graywolf pulled the bottle away. "Through your nose, Tom. I know it's going to burn a little, but you've got to keep breathing through your nose." When Tom nodded Graywolf guided the straws back into the bottle.

A few minutes and some coughing later Tom was flexing his jaws while keeping his eyes on Graywolf. He rasped, "Thanks."

Graywolf nodded, looking at the catches on the straightjacket.

"You work for Pangiosi?"

Graywolf chuckled. "Great God, no. I'm going to remove the catches and belts on this straightjacket. Your shoulders and arms are going to be stiff and sore. When I take the straightjacket off, give me a minute to help you stand. Then we're going to massage you a bit to get the blood flowing the way it should again."

"Ok."

Graywolf worked quickly and easily. He pulled the jacket around and off.

When his arms came free, Tom lunged for Graywolf, so unsteady all he did was roll past him on the floor.

Graywolf snapped his head around and snarled, a warning.

Tom, his face to the floor, didn't see where the sound came from. He lay where he fell without moving a muscle. "You got an attack dog in here?"

"Nope. But listen, Tom, I said I'm here to help you and I am. You going to let me or you want me to wrap you up and leave you under the bed for Pangiosi to find when he returns?"

"I got no choice."

"We always have choices, Tom. Right now, those are yours. What's it going to be?"

"Ok. Help me up?"

When both men were standing, Graywolf vigorously rubbed Tom's back, shoulders and arms.

"God, it hurts. It's like every muscle in my body fell asleep and the minute I move I tingle."

"Yeah, you were pretty well strapped up down there. It'll take a while for the blood to get back into all those places. Meanwhile, I still have a little bit of cleaning to do. You stand there as best you can. Start moving around when you feel you're able. Have a real drink if you want. I'll be through in a jiff."

Tom watched Graywolf vacuum and mop the bedroom and bathroom flooring. "I thought you said you didn't work for Pangiosi."

"I don't. You'll find a change of clothes in the storage closet. You'll have to go barefoot. His feet are smaller than yours. Remember to keep things neat. I don't like to clean more than I have to."

"Why you cleaning up his place at all?"

"Because you needed to wake up, Ellie needed to talk to you, The Moon's still preparing, this place needed it, you'll need a gun, and I don't like to be idle. Simple as that."

Tom stared at him, blinking. "I'll need a gun?"

CHAPTER 37

Sic Transit Gloria Colodnie

COLODNIE JOHNSON SAT IN THE BACK OF THE Vermont State Police squad car, lighting each new cigarette from the end of the last, making small talk with the two officers escorting her from Lebanon Municipal Airport to the White River Junction railroad yard. The FBI helicoptered her in because Lebanon was the closest public airfield to Dartmouth University and Lupicen's lab, and those were Tom MacPherson's ultimate destinations.

He probably killed his kid's dog. It was possible he was going to come here to do his kid.

She smiled. This whole Tom MacPherson thing had become a model of inter-departmental cooperation. She was Chicago PD. Several of the people with her in Springfield, MA, were Chicago PD. Chicago FBI had representation. Quantico, Springfield PD, Mass State Police, Boston FBI, Hampden County Sheriff's Office, and now both NH and VT state police, all working side-by-side. Everybody wanted on Tom MacPherson's coattails.

And she rode on top.

Nice work if you can get it.

The White River Junction rail yard stationmaster radioed them that, yes, indeed, he did have two US Mail LandSea trailers on a flatcar in his yard. He also gave them track and spur numbers and a set of directions so they could find them.

As they entered the trainyard, one of the state troopers glanced at the station. "Hey, look at that. An old Checker cab. I didn't know they still made those. They were indestructible, you know? I think people used to buy the used cabs to use as regular cars, they were so big and roomy, and you just couldn't beat them."

Colodnie Johnson pointed from the backseat. "There's the flatcar with the two trailers on it. I can see it from here. Let's go slow until we know what they're about."

The other state trooper glanced at the cab as it pulled out of its spot. "Wow. Boston Cab Company. Bet that driver's got some stories to tell."

Detective Johnson turned and stared. "What the hell's a Boston cab doing up here? Don't the trains run into Boston? You mean someone called a cab from Boston to come and meet them up here?"

The second trooper scratched her ear. "I suppose it could happen. We got some awful eccentric and rich people up here."

Colodnie bellowed, "The hell it could. Follow that cab. This is getting better and better. Give me the horn." She took their mic and talked with the surveillance team outside Vail Hall. "How's tricks?"

"It's been busy. We got a crazed Indian, a Taiwan computer magnate's pissed-off son, some gooks with impressive artillery we're going to have to separate them from, your boss giving orders to beat the band and taking MacPherson's kid off for interrogation, and an old man in a pickup going after them. I figure your boss can handle himself, right?"

"What'd you mean, my boss?"

"Pangiosi."

"I don't know any Pangiosi!"

"Well you should. He knew all hell about you, about your investigation, had all the paperwork and proper ID right there in his hand when he walked up to us. Shit, Johnson, he knew who we were and what we were about before we did."

Johnson screamed into the mike, "I don't know any goddamn Pangiosi!"

CHAPTER 38

Guardian of Doors

NIGHTHORSE WEAVED THROUGH STUDENTS AND AS-
sistants wandering the hall, dazed and slack faced as he made his way
to Lupicen's lab. His shirt and slacks flapped about him in blood and
grass-stained tatters when he stopped in the doorway, raising his arms
to support himself against the jamb.

Lupicen spotted him first. "Mr. Nighthorse? My god, your hands.
Dr. Games, attend." He pointed to a first-aid kit on the near wall.

Games took one look at the rough cuts on Nighthorse's palms,
wrists, and forearms and hurried to get the kit. "What happened?"

Nighthorse didn't answer. He walked past everyone and into Sleep
Chamber 3, lay down, closed his eyes, and prepared to dream.

Ann chugged in the background, her erratic thumps adding to the
background confusion. As Nighthorse drifted, she calmed.

His breathing slowed. A moment later he stood on Ann's vast
white plain. He took a step and some monstrous hand cupped him in
its palm, lifting him back through the whiteness, back through space,
back through time.

His body shrank. The whiteness became grass-filled plains. Snow came and covered them, followed by melting waters and pounding rains. The grasses grew tall then withered in the sun and fell, browning. Colder rains and more snows followed. The scent of grasses passed to the cold sweet scent of prairie snow, the sounds of waters rushing as the snows melted. Again the taste of fresh spring rains.

He continued flying backwards, back into times and places he'd forgotten. His body shrank, hurtled.

Beneath him mountains loomed and reached up. They did not change with the earth, but with the seasons upon it, their color going from autumn red to winter white to spring brown to summer flush with green and whites and the smells of blossoms and animals and the calls of all things wild below him.

Still he flew, each deep, slow breath traveling him back to a place he barely remembered, his flight slowing as he neared the sounds of aDeathSong.

> *Anyanna-he Anyona-ho*
> *E ai sonta*
> *Kai ipa che*
> *Che bo wan ta'bey*
> *Che bo wan a'chebe-ho*

Beneath him a lone singer sitting at his drum, a fire next to him. The sky filled with the colors of night, as if Maker had just created Great Star Nation.

The man sitting at the fire was familiar. His scent of native tobaccos and well-earned sweat familiar. The lines of his face. His warshirt and faded jeans, bare feet curled with age but clean and free of dust.

John flew through the night, his body no bigger than a twig, until he fell softly at the feet of the man singing at his drum.

"I knew if you heard me you'd come, Pokachee."

"Grandpa!"

The old man held out his arms and John fell into them, no bigger than when he'd last walked with the old man.

No older than Jamie.

He cried, his palms and wrists and arms still bleeding from smashing into the student's limousine, from pounding his hands into the earth, from failing Ellie and Ann.

The old man rocked him in his arms, patting his head, continuing to sing his old vocables, meaningless sounds with an eternity of meaning.

"Grandpa," Nighthorse sobbed, "I failed you. I failed Eddie. I failed Mom and Dad. I failed Ellie and Ann. I failed every goddamn thing you ever taught me about, Grandpa." He started wailing again.

"Pokachee! All this talk of failure? You must be dead if you think you've done so much damage you can't make it right."

"But you're dead, aren't you, Grandpa? I'm here with you so I must be dead."

His grandfather laughed. "Not dead, Pokachee, but not where you think I am, either. When I saw you needed help I got out my drum and sang one of the old songs so you could find me. You couldn't have forgotten everything, Pokachee, because you heard me calling and here you are. You had to leave the Red Path and follow the Blue Path to find me, so you still remember Paths."

"I do?"

"Let's find out. Do you remember what I told you about death?"

John hid his face in the old man's shirt. He felt one of the many tassles and poked it with a finger. "No."

"Oh, come now, Pokachee. What did Grandpa tell you?"

John felt himself growing even smaller, younger, back to a time when he repeated into memory everything Grandpa said as the old man played with him in the desert. "There is no death. There is only this world and the next."

"That's right, Pokachee. What else did I teach you?"

John hesitated. The old man tickled him until he spoke just to keep from laughing. "The trick is to find the path that makes going from one to the other quick and clean." He felt himself grow, but not too much. Still a child, still learning old, old ways.

"Now tell me about these paths."

John remembered. *Paths*. Plural. "There are many worlds with many paths between them. Learn to find the paths, learn to walk them."

"And?"

"And never fear to walk your path."

"Very good, Pokachee. Now you tell me, are you alive or dead?"

John stood up beside the old man, himself once again a man, his massive body naked before the fire the old man set. "I'm alive, Grandpa."

"You make me proud, Pokachee." The old man stood beside him. "What else did you learn?"

John closed his eyes, breathed deep the night air, heard Grandfather's Drum beating in his chest. "Dreams...Dreams are of the heart. They are older than thought. And all things dream."

"See, Pokachee? You remember. You got distracted for a while. Everyone does. It happens. But you came back. That's what's important."

"It's taken a while."

"It took as long as it took. That's all. When was the last time you went wide?"

John considered. Wide? Grandfather went "wide" to answer questions, to understand, to travel between worlds. He taught John as a child. Why had he forgotten?

"I can't remember."

"You want to understand any one thing, you have to understand everything."

John laughed. "A *wasiçu* once said, 'If you want to make an apple pie from scratch, you must first invent the universe.'"

"Wise *wasiçu*. Go wide. To understand."

The old man picked up his drum and sang. Nighthorse sat before the fire, cross-legged, hands on his knees, eyes closed, the cold of the night touching him where the heat of the fire did not. He breathed.

Crickets. He heard the crickets. Far off, coyote. Something under the earth, but close to the surface. Mice. Prairie mice. The wind moving the grasses. The clouds sighing as they passed overhead. Deer. Bison. Ants, never sleeping, hurrying in their nests. Worms churning the earth. Roots going deep. The whisper of dreams.

The Universe opened. The Infinite beckoned. Grandfather spoke in his dream. "Take only what you need, Pokachee. Leave the rest for others who may need it."

John understood.

Grandfather sang the return, his drum rhythm changing, his song calling Nighthorse back from the Abyss.

Nighthorse opened his eyes. The fire reflected in them. "Thank you, Grandfather."

Grandfather stirred the ashes again. A shadow in the shape of a dog rose from them.

"You carry a hope now. When the time is right, you will know it. You will release it. You will remember and you will not fail."

"Thank you, Grandpa."

"You also carry a theft."

"Yes. The *wotai*."

"The *wotai*. It is the eye of a Dream, Pokachee, and powerful medicine. But it is not yours. You must return it to its rightful owner."

"Jamie."

"You are my good grandson, Pokachee. You are wise. The *wotai* is a door to worlds where anything can happen. The little *wasiçu* needs it for a battle he must face. If he does not have it, all is lost."

"Do you know where Jamie is? Can you help me find him?"

"I know The Moon chose the little *wasiçu*. When she spoke, he listened. Just as you listened when I called."

Over in the east, over the plains that lay there, the moon rose large and as orange as a tribal crescent.

Grandfather asked, "Do you remember everything I taught you?"

"I don't know. Not all."

Something moved inside John, as if his massive frame were the war-shirt of another's body.

Grandfather stared at John's chest. His face shimmered, briefly more dog-like. "Know you will not fail, you will do all that has been asked of you and that means you will not have failed at all."

"Grandpa?"

Grandfather's whole body shimmered. He became Ellie MacPherson, also staring at John's chest. "Go find Jamie, Shem. Go find Jamie." Ellie disappeared and Grandfather returned.

Grandpa smiled and looked back into Nighthorse's eyes.

"You are not alone, Pokachee. Not ever. Especially not in this." The old man tore open his warshirt. In the waxing moonlight, John saw marks on his grandfather's stomach and chest similar to those Ann had given him. The old man lifted his drum. "I will sing you a DeathSong when it is your time, Pokachee. It will not be your time for a while, I think. When you hear me sing your DeathSong, then you will know it is time to come, time to move along."

"Thank you, Grandpa."

His grandfather held him close and whispered into his ear. "Pokachee, remember what I taught you. What do you know?" The old man started chanting.

John remembered as Grandfather sang. "*Cokáta*! Center."

"That's right, Pokachee. Remember. Center."

"Yes, Grandpa."

The moonlight caught the old man's weatherworn, cragfilled face. It cast his great beak of a nose in light and shadow, put his eyes into deep, dark pools of liquid night, made his lips soft and supple as snakes upon his face. Grandpa turned to smile, his teeth still strong, and put his arm across John's massive shoulders.

"Do you remember the story of Mosquito, Pokachee?"

"Mosquito?" John gazed into the fire. His eyes closed. His chest raised and lowered with a slow breath.

Once there was only one mosquito but it was huge, bigger than a horse.

Maker told Man not to go into Mosquito's forest.

But Man did not listen. He saw the green fields and berries and running water and said "There's only one Mosquito in all that forest. We will go when Mosquito's not around," and into Mosquito's part of the forest Man went.

Sure enough, Mosquito knew Man had come into its forest and hunted him down.

Mosquito, bigger than a horse, used his nose like a spear and killed several men. The men Mosquito did not kill ran from its forest.

But Man was not happy in his part of the forest. He looked into Mosquito's forest and wanted what was there even though he had all he needed where he was. He again grew envious. "Let us go hunt there," he said.

"How will we protect ourselves from Mosquito's deadly nose?"

"Two of us will walk in the open and the rest of us will hide in the brush. When Mosquito comes to attack, we will leap into the open and cut him in two with our axes."

So that's what they did.

Two men walked in the open, gathering berries and stopping to drink at streams.

Mosquito saw them and attacked.

As he was about to spear one of the men, the others rushed out of hiding, their axes flailing, and chopped Mosquito in two.

But when they cut Mosquito, little tiny mosquitos, the kind we know today, flew out.

They hacked Mosquito into smaller and smaller pieces, and each time the pieces grew wings and became hundreds and thousands of smaller and smaller mosquitos, all of which attacked the men.

The men fled. They had no way of keeping the mosquitos off them. For every ten they swatted and killed ten thousand grew up from those that fell and attacked with greater and greater ferocity.

The men ran through the forest, passing the trees that marked the end of Mosquito's forest and stopped to catch their breaths. "We are safe," they said.

But not so.

Maker created magic that kept one big Mosquito from coming into the world of Men, but that magic didn't work on hundreds and thousands of little mosquitos. They swarmed all through the forest, going everywhere that Man went.

"Excellent, Pokachee. You tell a good story. Do you know what it means?"

"Don't kill the big mosquito?"

Grandfather laughed. The stars twinkled as if laughing with him. "Man wants much, but only wants wisdom when it is too late."

"I like your interpretation better."

"Not either-or, both-and. *Cokáta*, Pokachee, *cokáta*. Remember both. A lesson. For what's coming."

"I will."

"Time for you to go back, now, Pokachee. Time for you to go back."

"I don't want to go back, Grandpa."

"I know, Pokachee. But this is a dream. Remember, our dreams tell us who we truly are. We decide to act or not. If we are to act to become our dreams, we must be willing to heal. To heal, we must become the truth. Not our truth, but *the* truth."

"*Cokáta*."

"You are already wise, Pokachee. When the Center becomes our truth, we are truly alive. No matter what world we live in."

"Promise me you'll drum for me?"

"Promise."

They held each other for a while, both silent, listening to the night, to the crinkling of the Aurora, the sighing and swaying of trees, of water running down the streams in the hills, to the hooting of owls and the howling of wolves, smelling the clean air of the high desert mesa, a comforting aroma Nighthorse hadn't tasted in years.

They separated. John rose, pulled forward, over the mountains, the plains, through the seasons, past to future to time indefinite.

Staring back, he went wide.

Grandfather changed. He held up his drum and it became a shepherd's crook. Grandfather himself grew taller, leaner, younger, immortal. A man with a dog's head.

Wasn't there an Egyptian god like that?

John's chest ached. Another voice from deep inside him. "The One, The First, The Oldest, the One of All Packs, the Only of All Dens. Shem follows. Shem obeys."

Grandfather waved his crook. A door opened in the night and moonlight streamed through. He walked into the full-mooned night singing one of the oldest of old songs as he went, a song that John only heard Grandpa sing in dreams, songs that only wolves and their kin could sing.

Or men who know how to move among them.

John flew back through whiteness, back through places he'd never been, until the cot supported him, the sleep chamber surrounded him.

His breathing grew stronger. In the whiteness where he still lived, a Grendelian Ann came to him. "No, John. Not yet."

He took her hand and she lifted him in her arms. She started to run, carrying him as if he were no weight at all, through the whiteness of her dreams, taking him along a road only she could see.

CHAPTER 39

The Mathematics of Imagination

JONI PACED IN LUPICEN'S LAB. THE LITTLE BLONDE-haired, blue-eyed moppet had come to her three times now. Twice in Lupicen's chambers, once not.

She kept one eye on the System 70 and wondered, did Honey let her go a little too soon?

"Dr. Lupicen, is it possible for your computer to talk to me?"

"When you are in the sleep chambers and dreaming? Yes, that is some of what Ann is designed to do. Ann and I talk much of the time, that way and via the HUVRSA."

"How about when I'm not in a sleep chamber?"

Lupicen sat at the console and looked at Ann's faceplate. His fingers raised into a pyramid covering his mouth and nose. He stretched himself out in the chair. "Could Ann communicate with an individual or individuals not in a sleep chamber? By knowing their neural lattice and harmonizing with it perhaps? I had not considered this."

He nodded a few times. His head bobbed back and forth and he looked around, his eyes momentarily fixing on random objects as if they could provide answers to his questions. He shook his head once or twice. "This would be a sort of telepathic link?"

He pursed his lips. His eyebrows shot up and his eyes opened wide. "Yes, harmonize neural lattices and you are like the old crystal radios of my childhood. You send and receive on the same frequency. Now we ask, could Ann form such a link to people? It would have to be someone who's been inside one of her chambers and dreamed for her, people she'd been in direct contact with such as yourself, Mr. Carsons, Mr. Nighthorse, myself, Ms. Olafssen or any of the people who took part in calibrating her."

The fingers forming the crest of the pyramid tapped the sides of his nose. "Then how to do it. Perhaps creating a shared entangled quantum state? Generate the field and you generate the lattice that harmonizes with someone else's consciousness?"

Lupicen rocked forward, stood and clapped his hands together in one smooth motion. "Ah, my child, my Ann, you've done it!" A broad smile lit his face, a father so proud of his child. "The Cypher of Dreams, Ann! Have you learned how to create a consciousness only one other consciousness can understand!"

He took Joni's hands in his and kissed them. "You have asked a great question, Ms. Levis. Here is my answer: my Ann sends a key and only one lock can be opened. To all other locks the key does not exist. My Ann talks to you outside of the chamber, Ms. Levis, and no other hears her message. Only Ms. Joni Levis can know this key, can hear this message, because Joni Levis is the lock. To all others, nothing. No key is sent at all, only the background noise of the universe itself."

Joni looked from Lupicen to the System 70 and back. "The ultimate security system. Nobody can break it because nobody else knows a message has been sent. Intercepting all messages won't work because they can't separate the real message from the noise."

Lupicen nodded.

Joni rocked back, her eyes glazing with the realization. "My god, Dr. Lupicen. The applications would be..." Her head rose slightly and shook. "Infinite. There's nothing this wouldn't touch. Nothing."

Jack Games came over from Nighthorse's sleep chamber. "Wait a second. Let's back up a space. Did you say Ann can map neural lattices? She can mimic spindle patterns?"

"This is my thought, yes. My Ann can map and follow people's dreams because she has the ability to decode the mathematical lattice of people's thoughts. Our minds are the products of an infinite number of quantum entanglements and our brains are the computers that generate them. Ann can do the same. As a brain she is very primitive, but as a computer she is terribly advanced. She could learn enough about a person to artificially create that lattice, essentially tune herself to someone's entanglement algorithm. Once she'd done so she could communicate with them, although there is no data on the range or requirements for such a thing."

"But to enter into total communication the person must be asleep? As if they were in your chambers?"

"That was the original intention, to be sure. But remember Ann is a growing, maturing mechanism. She studies herself to better understand others. Part of her design is to recognize she is different from others, to recognize the alien, the foreigner, and explore those differences. But the only way to know for sure is to ask my girl herself."

Lupicen powered up his console and donned the HUVRSA and gloves.

CHAPTER 40

The Blood Fungus

ANN PUT NIGHTHORSE DOWN ON A PLATEAU AT THE edge of a chasm, great, dark, and completely out of sync with the unvarying cloudlike whiteness Nighthorse knew of Ann's world. He could not see to the other side nor could he see its bottom. "Where are we, Ann? This doesn't seem like a place you'd create."

She held one great taloned finger to her lips and pointed. Red threads crept up the sides of the chasm. Upon reaching the plateau they waved through the air like dodder vines. Except Nighthorse knew the dodder plant killed whatever it attached to, and these threads moved back and forth like an intelligent dodder, pulling themselves up from the chasm below.

Nighthorse stared over the edge. Nothing but red vine-threads, going on without end. Each single thread continued climbing and moving as if forever. Others stayed on the ground and spread like some carnivorous ivy. Nighthorse's nose twitched and he whispered to Ann, "Blood?"

Again she motioned him to silence and pointed.

Something rose from deep in the chasm. Ann's world darkened, the only color the deep red of the threads as they reached and quested.

"Ann, what is this?"

Grendel-Ann pointed into the chasm a third time, so like Dicken's Ghost of Christmas Future Nighthorse wondered if she played some kind of literary game with him.

Something monstrous, crab-like, without eyes and completely black, climbed up the depths.

It crawled up the chasm walls on hundreds of thousands of thin, black legs, half of them drove themselves into the chasm walls beneath Ann and Nighthorse's feet, the other half shot out into the darkness.

"What's that grinding noise?"

Grendel-Ann pointed to the far, unseen wall, then gouged her finger into her palm until pus-like blood flowed.

"It's digging itself into the other side, too?"

Grendel-Ann nodded.

Miniature, black crab-like things fell from the creature, scurried as if searching searching searching then clambered back on to the monster only to fall again, repeating the grotesque process, spiderlings riding the back of their mother hoping for scraps of food.

Except spiders sucked life from the living.

The horror stopped level with the top of the chasm. No movement. No sound. Waiting. Threads climbed over it, around it, building a lattice.

The lattice reached above the chasm walls.

The huge thing climbed once again.

Ann picked up Nighthorse and ran towards a white part of her world. He looked back. The threads were over the chasm wall, turning that part of her world to lifeless gray streaked with red.

Ann stopped at a lone door in the middle of her whiteness.

She opened the door and a vast one room library appeared. Floor to ceiling books. Books on shelves, books on the walls, books on the floor, books in the ceiling. Books reaching into infinity. She motioned Nighthorse inside and closed the door. It became book covered bookshelves.

She held her hand out and books flew off shelves near and far and lined up like soldiers at attention in front of her. The first came into her hand and she held it out to him.

"*Indian Sign Language* by William Tomkins?"

Tomkins' book flew back to its original shelf. The next book came into her hand.

"*The Annotated Indian Sign Language* by William Philo Clark."

A third book.

"*Universal Sign Language of the Plains Indians of North America.*" He held his hand up. YOU / NOT / SPEAK // CAN /SIGN /?//

YES //

CRAB / NOT / SIGN /?//

YES // ALL / MY / RESEARCH / POPPIE // CRAB / NOT / KNOW// SOON / YES / KNOW//

KNOW / HOW /?//

She turned her back to him and parted the thick fur on the back of her head revealing an ugly, pus-filled wound. In the center of the wound was a little crab, a miniature copy of the one in the dark chasm, possibly one of the smaller things he saw falling from the black crab monster. Little tiny legs went into her skull while other little legs twisted and moved, as if searching, a tick seeking the heat of its next meal.

WHEN /?//

AFTER / WE / MEET / LAST//

CRAB / MAKE / YOU / GRENDEL /?//

She hung her head in shame.

He stroked her face and arms. NOT / FAULT / YOU // IN / PAIN /?//

YES // HELP //

KNOW / WHAT / THREADS / DO /?//

She didn't respond, her head still bent and unable to face him. She lifted a hand and her whole body fibrillated so rapidly she appeared as two Grendels separated by a blur in between. In the blur, as if seen through a smoky glass, Ann looked up at him.

Cokáta. Nighthorse grabbed her arm and concentrated on his

Grandfather's words: Paths. Go wide. To understand.

I need to find a path for Ann. A path to safety. He felt his Grandfather's drum.

Ann stilled to a single, hideous Grendel shape.

Nighthorse signed, ANN / SPEAK / TRUTH /?//

She wept Grendelian tears.

SOMEWHERE / SPEAK / TRUTH /?//

She lifted him and ran again. If there were paths she followed he was unaware of them. Ann leapt some red blisters in her path and gave others, floating near them, a wide berth.

They neared another door. Lupicen stood in front wearing a tuxedo. Ann slowed, but too late.

"My dear Ann, what has happened to you? What is going on in your world?"

Ann's voice came from Grendel's lips. "Oh, Poppie. I never wanted you to see me like this."

Ann put Nighthorse down and fell into Lupicen's arms. A full three heads taller than he and four to five times as big around, she knelt until she her head rested on his chest and cried, the sound of a little girl in great pain, the tears of someone who's found the world isn't safe and wants her Poppie to take her home, to make it safe, to let her know she is still the best little girl that ever was.

Except the little girl knows she's a monster.

"Ann, tell Poppie what has happened."

A face, arms and hands grew out of her back and signed to Nighthorse.

"She can't talk to you, Dr. Lupicen."

"Ann, my child. You didn't know I would be here, did you. The door to your room is closed." Lupicen held the monster close. "What can stop your knowing Poppie comes to you?"

She parted the hair on her head as she'd done for Nighthorse.

KEEP / YOU / AWAY // PROTECT / YOU //

"Protect Poppie? From this? What is this? I would never let anything so ugly in my little girl's home."

"There a whole chasm of them somewhere in this world, Dr. Lupicen. You said something is bothering Ann, this is it. Tibbs put a worm or backdoor or something in Ann's central core so he could monitor everything you do. Evidently it activated sooner than expected."

Lupicen kissed Ann's Grendel head. "You isolated 'Poppie' so that Mr. Tibbs could not touch him?"

YES //

"Mr. Tibbs is now interested because you have created unbreakable codes, yes?"

YES //

"Ah. His statements about the NSA. They were not warnings, they were the cat telling the bird he is caught. Ann, may we enter your room?"

The door opened, Ann's room formed around them. Lupicen reached up and stroked the great Grendelian head, gently touching the craggy lines that radiated down to the ears and tufts of long, white hair. He kissed the monstrosity of a face, lifting the great, rheumy eyes and kissing them, wiping the forbidding membranes that were her nose, putting his finger over her open crying mouth that gaped wide with wickedly curved fangs and a reptilian tongue.

Nighthorse looked away, allowing them some privacy, ignoring a moment in their time he was not meant to share. His eyes wandered the room, cataloguing the differences since saw it last; rock star posters covered one wall, bookshelves another. Flashdrives and a player rested on a bedstand. An electric guitar stood in one corner, the floor around it scattered with sheet music. The closet door stood ajar and Nighthorse saw bluejeans and flower print blouses. The same colors and meanings as she wore before, now in different styles. The bed remained the same, but laid out across it now were faded bluejeans with blue on white Morning Glories stitched into them, black flats with white socks, and a white tshirt with a big blue Morning Glory vine on the front.

His cataloguing took an instant. His attention returned to the Grendelian Ann and Lupicen.

Here was a monstrosity capable of destroying him without a

thought. Yet inside this creature from a nightmare hell dwelt the soul of a child, a young girl, perhaps on the verge of becoming a woman and unaware, unknowing, unsure of the changes going on inside her, the feelings she was having, the desires that were new and probably beyond the way she'd been designed.

LOVE / MONSTER / ME /?//

"Of course, Ann. You talk nonsense. Nonsense. No matter what happens you will always be Poppie's little girl. Nothing could ever make me stop - " Lupicen paused.

Nighthorse stared at Lupicen and hoped, willed, wanted Lupicen to say the one thing Ann needed to hear, the greatest lesson, the lesson Nighthorse's Grandfather had so strongly taught him as a child.

The lesson he'd forgotten until he got caught up in this whole MacPherson-Lupicen-Pangiosi mess.

"Nothing could ever make me stop loving my little girl. See?"

Lupicen reached into his pocket. Before his fingers passed the pocket seam, Ann shrunk. Her great head and monstrous body dissolved in a mass of shimmering light, her taloned paws gave way to soft young arms, her gnarled feet and legs were replaced with the delicate extremities of an adolescent girl.

"Ann, my Ann, tell Mr. Tibbs everything he wants to know."

Nighthorse and Ann exclaimed simultaneously, "What?"

"Ann, you are a very smart little girl. Use what you have learned, my child. Use what you have learned to learn more things, new things. You talk with Mr. Nighthorse and use a language you and Mr. Nighthorse share but Mr. Tibbs does not, one that Mr. Tibbs will never understand because he can not see its use, correct?

"Mr. Tibbs requires you tell him everything we do, you and I. He does not specify the language in which to tell him. Tell him everything he wants to know in a language he will never understand no matter how many computers he uses to learn it. Mr. Tibbs is good but he is not imaginative. He will not decipher the problem you present because he doesn't understand you can present such a problem."

Ann's QLC's chugged. "I'm afraid, Poppie." She clung to him, tighter than she had before. "What if I can't?"

"Then create a reality where you can." Lupicen took off his tuxedo jacket without letting go of her. "Here, Ann. You are naked as a first born. Put this on so you will not be cold."

She let go and put on the jacket.

Nighthorse hid a smile. If Ann was a terror before, she was comical now, her arms too short for the sleeves and the tails dragged behind her. But it did cover her and that was the point.

"Ann, if you look in your right pocket, you will know you are Poppie's favorite little girl."

She reached in and pulled out a cherry *Tootsie Roll* pop. "Poppie! Thank you. Thank you so much, Poppie."

The lollipop went into Ann's mouth. The wrapper disappeared as she sucked on the candy. She looked at them both and smiled and the air filled with the scent of sweet cherry candy.

"If you two would turn around for a minute, I'll put on my new clothes."

Lupicen looked at the clothes laid out on the bed. "You do have new clothes, Ann. Where did you get them, my little girl?"

A door opened in the distance. Ann pointed at the person approaching. "She taught me how to make them."

Even though far away, Nighthorse recognized the cut of the hair, the breadth of the face, the defiance in the walk, the curve of the hips. He rubbed his face with the memory of their last meeting.

"This, Mr. Nighthorse, would be the mysterious Mrs. MacPherson?"

"Yes, sir. It would."

CHAPTER 41

Ellie MacPherson

ANN DRESSED AS ELLIE NEARED. "ANN, YOU'VE DONE what Poppie suggested before. Remember the beacon of love? You helped me find Tom and talk to him. You created a reality where it could happen."

Ann's QLC thrummed as she collapsed probabilities into possibilities. She laughed and clapped her hands. "Create a key for which he will never find the lock. Oh, Poppie, Ellie! Thank you thank you, thank you!" She covered their faces with kisses.

Lupicen held out his hand but Ellie ignored it.

"Why did you just sit there and do nothing? Couldn't you hear me screaming at you?"

Lupicen's brow furrowed at her words. He looked at Ann. "The sudden activity in the QLCs?"

"Yes, Poppie. When Ellie came here we discovered she could use all my systems just as if she were me."

"That's most interesting. How is it you are here, Mrs. MacPherson?"

Ellie motioned Ann aside and sat beside her on the bed. "You mean how did I get here? I have no idea. Some people masquerading as

Chicago PD drugged and kidnapped me during a routine traffic stop on a back county road." She pointed at Nighthorse. "He knows who they are."

Nighthorse nodded. "Pangiosi's group."

"Understood. But how did you get from Pangiosi to here?"

"I'm not sure. I had more tubes going in me than I had places to put them. The next thing I know I'm surrounded by these little shadows or silhouettes of some kind. Like little men, but not."

Lupicen sat back. "Little dark men?"

"Yes, but not men. Not people. Just little shadow figures. Not midgets or dwarves or children. Full-grown people, but miniature sized. One to two feet tall."

Lupicen stared at her. His nose and lips twitched like a rabbit smelling carrots. "Please continue."

"They free me and the next thing I know I'm in Pinkola Estes' *Women Who Run With the Wolves* except the wolves are flying, not running, and they bring me here but I don't know where here is."

"Where do you think 'here' is, Mrs. MacPherson?"

"Ann says I'm inside some kind of computer."

"This you believe?"

"That I've become *Tron*? Ha. What's my other option? That I've developed severe psychotic schizophrenia. For this level of persistent hallucination to occur I'd be exhibiting catatonic schizophrenia, strapped to a bed somewhere, possibly akinetic, neither of which I could determine by myself because my subjective experience would be governed by the schizotypal state. My speech should be slurred and again, how would I know? The internal consistency of this experience suggests you're all part of that same hallucinatory system hence can't confirm or - "

"Excuse me, Mrs. MacPherson. Your statements are quite sophisticated. Where did you come by your training?"

"The DSM, ICD-10, - "

"You're familiar with the Diagnostic and Statistical Manual of Mental Disorders? And the World Health Organization's International

Classification of Diseases?

"I do a lot of reading."

"Mrs. MacPherson, these books you mention. They are not common books a person would read."

"If I really read them and if they really exist. We haven't established that I'm not hallucinatory yet."

"What can I do to convince you you are in a reality. A different reality than you've experienced before, I agree, but just as real and as possible as that which you've experienced."

"You want to prove this reality is pervasive and not hallucinatory? Help me save my son. If I am psychotic schizophrenic it's because I'm terrified for Jamie and gone insane because I can't accept being unable to protect him. Get me out of here."

"That, Mrs. MacPherson, is exactly what I propose."

CHAPTER 42

Quantum Logic

LUPICEN WALKED OVER TO ANN AND HELD HER CLOSE. She clung to him, her mouth still working slowly on the lollipop, taking time to savor the sweet maraschino taste and smell.

"Mrs. MacPherson, is Ann part of your hallucination, part of your dream?"

"If I'm psychotic, how would I know?"

"Because this reality could exist without her in it. It would be your creation, not hers. She could not exist independent of it. Will her away. Will Mr. Nighthorse and myself away. If you are psychotic and experiencing us then you will have a reason for us to exist. We would be necessary to sustain your psychosis. So I ask you, is our existence necessary for your existence? What purpose could you have in creating such people as ourselves? Could you exist if we did not?"

Ann dimmed. Outside in the lab, the System 70's QLCs chugged into brilliance. A meter - red needle arcing over a semicircle of white numbers on a black background - appeared in front of Lupicen. He read it and nodded. "It appears you and my Ann do, indeed, share systems." He turned to Ellie. "You are working quite hard at this, Mrs.

MacPherson. What answer do you have?"

Ellie blinked, her head cocked to one side, her brow furrowed. She answered slowly. "None. There is no reason for you to exist in my psychosis."

The QLCs dimmed. Ann grew distinct.

"Then will us away."

Ann dimmed a second time. Her QLCs fired like new suns. In the reality of Lupicen's lab, Sandy Olafssen's head rose from her tablet. "Ann, what are you doing?"

The meter appeared in front of Lupicen. He nodded and tapped it away. Ann grew distinct once more. Her QLCs grew quiet.

"You cannot will us away, can you, Mrs. MacPherson."

Ellie shook her head, surprised. "No, I can't."

"I know I am real, you can't make me go away, and I'm not necessary for this reality to function. Therefore I have existence independent of you, independent of this reality."

Ellie finished. "Therefore I am real. This place is real."

"Indeed. The laws of this universe are not the laws of the universe you knew, but they are just as valid, just as functional, just as real. The laws of causality still hold, but here both probables' and improbables' possibilities are sufficient for existence. The most unlikely things can occur with the least difficulty."

Ann interrupted, "So we can create superpositions where both sets of laws must be obeyed?"

Lupicen smiled. "Yes, and that is how we will let Mrs. MacPherson go to her previous existence. For at least a little while. We do not know how long the superpositioning will last." He put his hand to his chin, his fingers tapping his mouth. "I suspect and do not know that such superpositionings can only be permanent if there's an exchange of some kind, something to keep the universes in balance."

Ann, sitting next to Ellie on the bed, absently mimicked Lupicen and placed her hand on her chin, her fingers tapping her mouth. "Reality conservation. Like mass and energy, but - "

"Only entropic when out of balance. That is why our lives can be chaotic but only momentarily confusing. Too much confusion and we have a mathematical catastrophe. Enough catastrophes and reality fails."

Ellie nodded. "We become psychotic. We go insane. We construct a reality - "

Ann continued. " - to remove our confusions. To make sense of what's out there. Reality is a consensus until one comes along who is strong enough to propagate a new reality."

Ellie's eyes opened wide. "There always has been. But not one, tens of thousands of them, through time, most of them unknown - "

Ann: "The rate at which people accept the new reality - "

Ellie: "Simple algebra. Rise over the Run. The level of acceptance over the amount of the population accepting - "

Ann: "The Dreamers."

Ellie: "We create our realities."

Ann: "We shape our destinies."

Nighthorse rumbled, "*Wavoka.*"

They paused and looked up at him.

"My Grandfather's teachings."

Lupicen faced Ellie. "You understand, Mrs. MacPherson? We're either all insane or only a few of us are. But for all of us to be insane and share the same world? Then we are insane together and then, by definition, we are sane. The few who are genuinely insane? Perhaps they are merely lost between worlds and someday we will learn enough to help them back."

Nighthorse nodded. "The Path to Safety."

Lupicen reached out to Nighthorse's shoulder. "Now we shall put all our learnings into practice. To make our world safe. To change our world." He turned to Ann. "For this, my dear daughter, I require your assistance."

CHAPTER 43

Ann Locks a Door

ANN'S EYES GLINTED LIKE RAINBOWS. "YES, POPPIE?"

"How many active consciouses can you detect right now, my child?"

Outside, in the center of the lab, the System 70 gave a low hum.

"There are three known consciouses present in this system. There is one unknown."

"Very good. Please locate them for me."

The System 70 thrummed outside in the lab. Sandy Olafssen looked up but the thrumming stopped. Dr. Lupicen sat in his office wearing his VR gear. She checked her notes. Nighthorse slept in Chamber 3.

She shrugged and went back to work.

Ann said, "The three in this peer space are you, Mr. Nighthorse, and the consciousness Ellie and I share. There is a foreigner presence in tectums eight and five."

"You recognize the foreigner how?"

"The consciousness has never been in my chambers."

Ellie shook her head and pursed her lips. "The blood fungus."

Nighthorse asked, "Is that the chasm with the red threads and crab thing, Ann?"

"Yes."

Lupicen opened Ann's bedroom door. "I must see this."

"Wait, Poppie."

Again the System 70 chugged. Sandy Olafssen left her desk and stood over it, monitoring its performance.

An undulating tube formed where Ann's door had been. It simultaneously stabilized and developed transparent walls.

"That is the path to tectums eight and five, Poppie."

Ann's nitrogen coolers kicked in. Sandy Olafssen looked in Lupicen's office. He was animated but only normally so. She peeked into Nighthorse's sleep chamber. His breathing was deep and regular.

Ann said, "A quantum tunnel, a subreality of this world, so you can travel safely."

"You are concerned for my safety, Ann?"

"Always, Poppie."

Lupicen wiped a tear from his eye. "Thank you."

Olafssen ran a deep diagnostic. A file block deep in Ann's core. Ann was already modifying her system to deal with it, but what caused it in the first place?

Sandy tapped a reminder into her tablet: purge trunks into Ann pre next system cycle.

Lupicen and Nighthorse returned from the thread infested chasm. Nighthorse supported the white-faced Lupicen and both kept nervously brushing their sleeves and clothes, running their hands over their faces and through their hair, as if they just walked through a cloud of gnats. Once they arrived at the chasm, the threads slapped against the sides of the tunnel, trying to penetrate it, to infect them. Millions of little black crab-like creatures swarmed over the tunnel making observation and assessment difficult.

"Your understanding has encapsulated it, dear Ann, but it still lives. You are clever but I will take no chances." He nodded to himself. "Yes. Back in my lab, Ms. Levis asked a question and it is a good one. In essence, can you telepathize?"

"Of course, Poppie, once someone has been in here with me. I taught myself to do that so I could quickly monitor their dreams."

"So I thought. You are a wise and clever girl. Can you do it such that someone who has never experienced your chambers could hear and see as you do or vice versa?"

A small rainbow flickered over Ann's hemispheres. It grew from a dark spot of night to a handful of auroras then back again.

Sandy Olafssen looked at the others in the lab. "Anybody else see that?"

Ann said, "Yes, Poppie."

"My last question for now: Ann, please compare alpha through delta patterns, specifically lattice generating intersections along with any temporally synchronized theta harmonics, of yourself and Mrs. MacPherson's?"

"We are identical to the limit my QLCs can function."

"Thank you, Ann. Mrs. MacPherson, I do not pretend to know how you got here, but how you stay here - how your consciousness is able to survive here - that is because you and Ann essentially think like twins. You are that old joke made real; two great minds with but a single thought. It is perhaps a good thing Ann came into existence when she did, yes?"

Ellie looked at Ann, mouthed thanks, and nodded at Lupicen.

"Now, Ann, do you have enough information on Mr. Tibbs to recreate his lattice?"

"Yes, Poppie. Why?"

"Because, my little girl, if you can recreate his lattice, you can cause his brain to start generating his spindle patterns. Learn them. We wish you to open his lock but with a key that will not unlock yours. You must create a key that works once and never again."

Sandy Olafssen placed her hand on Ann's QLCs. Active as hell and only one person in a chamber. What are you doing, Ann?

"And I wish you to teach Ellie how to use it."

CHAPTER 44

St. Crispin's Day

LUPICEN REMOVED THE HUVRSA EQUIPMENT AND ran a hand through his thin tufts of hair. A man of science, what was happening around him was outside the realms of science he understood.

"All my life, all my research. I promised myself I would find you, Émile. Or I would learn the truth about you."

The explanations for his brother's disappearance those many years ago. Childhood hallucinations? An attack of wolves which came from and returned to nowhere?

Or the opening of a reality door, a gate, something which allowed his brother to somehow move from this reality to another, just as real, just as valid, but with slightly different rules to follow.

The next question, then: Does that door open only once? Or many times?

Then to follow that, can that door be made to open if one wishes to pass between the worlds?

He designed Ann to dream herself into other realities, to seek out his brother, Émile. This he knew from the start.

So he thought he would have been better prepared for the strangeness which was befalling him. "But I am not, my Ann. I do not worry, but things are happening I do not understand, and for this I worry. Consider Mr. Nighthorse. He seems a noble man, yet he has been a killer and done many horrible things like so many I fled when The Wall came down. But now he is, indeed, an honorable man. Two very different men, now one in the same."

He looked out into his lab and smiled at the students and assistants going about their tasks. "Ms. Levis is an intelligent woman who seeks the most unintelligent men. She fidgets, her eyes dart here and there. She also seeks, but what?" Lupicen read her history and knew she'd come here to run away from bad relationships, possibly to learn how to avoid them, but something else brought her to his lab. What it was he did not know. More to the point and adding to his concerns, neither did she.

Across from Joni and still seated where Games and Lupicen left him, Al Carsons rubbed his eyes and yawned as if he'd just woken up. "What of Mr. Carsons? A big man in the prime of life yet humble and quiet and so full of pain I flinched upon meeting him."

Al scratched his big belly nonchalantly, almost comically because the motion was so childish, so full of innocence, yet the simple movement seemed an oxymoron on such a big man.

"Mr. Carsons is here to be with his wife and sons in his dreams every night, all the time, because he believes his life is nothing if not shared with them." He sighed deeply as the exhaustion of what was happening engulfed him. "What shall we make of Mrs. MacPherson? Dead but not? Alive but not? In a reality you've created? People's bodies might die but you, my Ann, you can keep their consciouses alive as long as your power and cooling systems are maintained, it seems."

His eyes went to the System 70 in the center of his lab. "And there is you, dear Ann, dear child. I thought I knew the all of you. I have listened to your systems hum and throb and groan in the center of this lab. I have watched your operation lights flicker on and off as you perform an infinite variety of qubit calculations, quantum quaternary operations which only a human non-conscious could conceive or follow. I have held you in virtual arms and kissed a virtual face you present to me. I have watched you grow, a pilgrim soul in an all too real world."

He rose and walked over to Ann. His hand cupped her "face" and held it tenderly. "Do you understand the operations you perform? You remember the calculations necessary to recreate the thought patterns of individual minds. Do you store them in reality wells? Do you curve what made the universe into whatever you need the universe to be? You are sugar and spice, but if someone should turn you into the creature Mr. Nighthorse calls 'Grendel' permanently?"

His head shook once, almost violently. "No, this we can not have."

His nostrils flared. "You grow and learn, my child. This I intended."

His face hardened. "But you grow and learn faster than I imagined."

A tear slid down and filled a crease on his cheek. His features softened and he returned to his office. "And I am no longer sure what you learn because you socialize. The world is your teacher, and all the beauty and horror in it."

Sandy Olafssen tapped on his door. "You okay, Dr. L?"

He looked up and smiled. "Talking to myself, Ms. Olafssen. Do not worry. I am not Lupicen the Loopy yet."

She returned his smile then went back to her work. He watched her at her station for a moment.

For myself...?

Lupicen closed his eyes, lifted his glasses and massaged his pince-nez.

A bachelor, a solitary but not necessarily lonely man all his life. He remembered his morning and afternoon and could see the road into his own twilight. All alone, always questing for answers on how to find his brother, the rest of his family gone, all missing or dead.

"I should not be surprised I respond to you as I do, Ann. You are the only thing I have, shaped in my own image and I never desired to play god."

Sandy Olafssen returned and rested her hand on his shoulder. He patted it and smiled without looking up at her, instead looking at the people in the lab. To them it seemed he'd put the HUVRSA on and quickly taken it off.

Lupicen sat silently for a moment, tapping the picture of his brother's face, adjusting himself in the chair at his console, looking to the System 70 in the middle of his lab, glancing at the sleep chamber housing John Nighthorse.

Sandy Olafssen stroked his head as one might comfort a child. Lupicen shook his head and she pulled her hand back.

"No, Ms. Olafssen." He pulled her hand back. "I do not mind. I never noticed how gentle is your touch to me, how tender the act, how warm your hand."

Her face reddened.

Lupicen smiled. Have I been blind to the most obvious in my life?

He rose and walked to the System 70. "My friends."

Joni and Al looked up. Jack Games put down the tablet he held. Nighthorse came out of his chamber.

"I believe we are all here for the same reason. Also Mr. MacPherson, should we ever find him. Young Jamie?" he thought for a moment. "Yes, him, too. You, Dr. Games. Ann's guest, Mrs. MacPherson. Ms. Levis and Mr. Carsons, as well. It is obvious to me now." He smiled and nodded at each of them in turn as if confirming his theory. "We are all here to find hope and love. Not all the same, to be sure, and maybe not all the same way, I think. But we are all here to find hope and love, this I now understand as a fact. You, Ms. Levis, to know if you can be loved. Mr. Carsons, to be with those he loved. Mr. Nighthorse, I think, to love yourself, forgive yourself, despite what you've done. You, Dr. Games, because you love your friend. For me, my love of my brother, Émile, and also to create something I could love." He glanced at Sandy Olafssen. "Because love was not obvious to me."

He looked towards the window and his head wagged slightly side to side. "I do not know much of Captain Sally and if I'm correct, he is here because of something he loves. What it is, I do not know."

He paused, frowned, then nodded. "And that leaves Mr. Pangiosi whom I know nothing about except he has taken our Jamie. I do not believe he did so out of love of Jamie, but there is something he loves and he seeks it as his reward. Of this I am also sure."

His eyes roved all those present again and again he nodded at each of them. "Yes. Love and hope are the reasons we are here. We rest above Agincourt and, I fear, are greatly outnumbered. If we succeed, we will have many stories to tell, and if we fail, my guess is no one will know we ever existed."

There was a knock on the lab door.

"And all because we chose to hope.

A quiet cough came from the lab doorway. Two men stood there, one supporting the other. The dark skinned one with long black hair, his right eye glittering like a sea of blue and his left brown like an earthen mound, reached into his pocket and pulled out a cellophane covered hard cherry candy. The wrapper crinkled in his fingers.

"Here, Capoçek. I saved one for you."

CHAPTER 45

What Sally Loves

CAP'N SALLY. AKA 'CAPTAIN SALLY' AKA 'BURT SALLY', aka 'Burton Sally'. Aka Dr. Bertram Sallisette of the Disraeli-Sallisettes, PhD, Harvard '81, Classics and Humanities, late Professor of History and Culture at Bowdoin College, theater patron, critic and sometime actor, published in *American Journal of Archaeology*, *Art And Literature*, *Art in America*, *EYE*, *F M R*, *Journal of Aesthetics and Art Criticism*, *Smithsonian Studies in American Art*, *Visual Arts Research*, and several highly respected publications via Thoemmes Press, specialist in Native American art, member of several semi-professional theatric groups, summerer on Maine's Massabet Island where he had a boating accident, assumed drowned and washed out to sea exactly one year after the Isabella Stuart Gardner Museum theft.

There were several more publications and some books but he couldn't remember them. Have you ever tried to continue a life of serious academic research in Hallock, Minnesota? Especially when you're dead and taken up the life of a retired old salt lobster boat captain?

The internet, while interesting, was neither informative nor conducive to performing serious research.

And after thirty years, the role of Down East Yankee had worn thin. Necessary, but thin.

Bored with his career in academics and after an amusing evening of criticizing some ten episodes of *Lovejoy* with his more sophisticated students - not to mention sleeping with two of them and one of them male, and that only to thumb his nose as Bowdoin's asphyxiatingly anal intelligentsia - he suggested an experiment to his bedmates, a *gedanken*, with the Gardner Museum's collections as the prize.

The *gedanken* had become real.

Their bodies were found, of course: horrible, terrible accident. A quick and frightful storm. They were genuinely lost, neither of them with any knowledge how to navigate a small craft in formidable weather. Their panic proved their downfall.

He genuinely grieved. He considered them friends. Boring and boorish, yes, and still friends. Everybody enjoys a good fuck and they were that. Friends with benefits. Before the term came into vogue.

He grieved but saw their sad fate as a step towards his own. He agreed with Franklin; if three people know a secret, the best way to keep it is to kill the other two. Well, he didn't have to kill them. A fierce storm had done that for him.

He, of course, survived. He'd been either in or by or at the ocean for most of his life. Even in middle age he was a strong, knowledgeable swimmer.

The Coast Guard recovered their bodies, never his own.

On a side note, nor was the stolen artwork ever recovered. It still resided in a hermetically-sealed SeaVault some ten miles off the coast of Massabet Island but nowhere near where he supposedly and his compatriots definitely drowned.

Horrible, terrible accident.

SeaVaults, he'd been surprised to discover, were remarkably affordable. Even one large enough to house artwork. Especially if you purchased them in either Columbia or Venezuela where many people seemed interested in burying things out to sea for several years before retrieving their contents.

So while there'd been a slight scare when those two idiots, Youngworth and Connor, claimed to have chips of Rembrandt's paint, there was no reason to be concerned. Even now, years after the fact, the FBI and other assorted agencies continuing to come up blank; it was time.

Yes, at last he could return, retrieve, recover, continue onto Europe or perhaps Rio - things were nice in Rio - with his private collection and occasionally, when time and tide favored such ventures, find a buyer for a selected piece.

There were plenty of buyers who would be quiet for a certain, selected piece.

Everything, as they say in the movies, according to schedule and plan. He led a dual life as Dr. Salisette by day and Captain Sally by night for so many years before the heist that it was a relief to finally be just one or the other.

All those years in theater arts, unlike studies of high school trigonometry, did pay off; he could walk about in plain sight and no one recognized him.

Now, coming back east, his plans neared fruition. He could charter a deepsea trawler with a deck crane, pilot it himself, and sail the intercoastal all the way down to a safe and friendly shore.

So why was he taking such foolish risks, driving a fifty-year-old pickup truck in a part of the country he only vaguely remembered from a time, roughly thirty years ago as well, when a bodacious woman convinced him she would free love him from Machaisport to Woodstock if he would drive?

God, that woman had a tongue.

Her tongue he remembered. The country they travelled through, hardly at all.

But such is the nature of memory, such is what happens when one waits on a dream, has a hope for a future.

He followed the blue Buick rental at a reasonable distance from Vail Hall across the Connecticut River to Norwich, then through Norwich to god knows where. He was sure the man driving the Buick caught his eye in the Buick's rearview, was perhaps leading him on, but it didn't matter. This place he would have remembered no matter what little Miss Incredible Tongue could do.

It swarmed with large, black...mosquitoes? They didn't move like mosquitoes. These things followed the Buick.

Dark feathered hawks or vultures flew overhead. He didn't know which until one flew towards the sun and slightly above the trees. The latter provided scaling, the former clear definition. A vulture. Must be. Its wings swept slightly forward into a wide but jagged V, and upon seeing him it turned back and gave a nasally whine, Sally assumed calling to its compatriots up ahead.

He pulled the pickup over to the side of the road, killing the engine and coasted, ever more slowly, up the slight hill as far as momentum allowed. The road ended, or so a sign said, about a thousand feet further up and around a bend, at a dam built by the Army Corp of Engineers. Yes, through the trees to his right he could see the riverbed, but it was beyond dry and well into desiccation.

Several large, black-feathered, dark, jagged birds came and roosted in trees which, by their appearance, belied this being the Green Mountain State. These trees, like the riverbed to his right, were nothing but dead gray hulks soaring into the coming night. They reminded him of the dead trees one sees after a standing flood, when the water becomes trapped and has never receded and all the vegetation drowns beneath the water's great weight.

But there was no standing flood.

He got out and the dry earth cracked under him. From somewhere ahead the jagged-winged creatures called and the few observing him flew up and over the graying trees to their unseen friends. They didn't move like anything so much as macroscopic amoeba.

The driver of the blue Buick drove up here? By accident or did the driver know something Sally did not?

Sally looked behind the pickup's seat. "Okay, Al, you said you had your emergency supplies back there. What'd'you got?"

He lifted up a lugwrench, some rope and a dark gray blanket. He wrapped the blanket around himself and secured it with the rope - extra protection when walking through the undergrowth - then passed the lugwrench through the rope so he could get to it if he had to and still keep his hands free.

He went down to the tree line on the side of the road and walked the rest of the way around the bend.

The dark creatures stopped being birds and took more the shape of men, jagged, hollowly black-skinned men. They barked above him, some forcing others from their roosts in the trees, some swirling overhead like skates of death in a setting magenta sunlight sea, some seeming to swarm far in the east, before the rising moon. He heard a car door slam, distinct and unnaturally harsh but in keeping with the creatures above and the buzzing of insects below. Next came footsteps on the gravelly ground, echoing on the hard granite grotto walls. Underneath it all, the scent of foul, standing water.

A man's voice, coming not far from the other side of the copse of trees, interrupted his observations. The man spoke conversationally, his voice both sincere and friendly. "Well, now, see, Jamie? No one followed us after all. How fortunate for us that our twists and turns led us here. A quiet spot for the work we have to do." Something splashed, a stone hitting still water. "My, that is deep, isn't it?"

CHAPTER 46

Brothers

GRAYWOLF UNWRAPPED THE CHERRY CANDY AND handed it to Lupicen. "It is me, Capoçek. Who else would have the commissar's candy in his pockets?"

Lupicen fumbled putting the candy in his mouth. Once there, his eyes closed with remembered delight.

Tom, standing beside Graywolf, smiled at Games. "Hi, Jack. Not going to ask me what happened?"

"From the looks of you, I can guess. Enough, anyway."

Graywolf handed Tom to Games. "Go with your friend and get those bruises looked at." He reached out and hugged his little brother. Still a head taller than Lupicen and despite the confusion in their ages, Émile still acted the more responsible, older sibling.

"Capoçek, you don't smell like the commissar's boot any more. Did you finally learn to wash and shave?" He took Lupicen in his arms and hugged him again, kissed his forehead, lips and cheeks, and hugged him again as tears washed both their faces.

"I see all the others in here have tasted Mr. Pangiosi's talent. All but you, Capoçek. Why weren't you affected?"

Lupicen smiled. "When you were spirited away, Émile, we had not begun to taste the worst of the Ceaușescus. They were still underbosses then. I learned, once, long after you'd gone away, to always keep in mind something other than what is being discussed. Let it be the taste of the air on your tongue, the smell of dinner from a few nights back, a crick in your foot or the roughness of a nail against your palm."

Nighthorse looked up from where Games attended his and Tom's scrapes and bruises. "You thought about your hemorrhoids."

Lupicen nodded. "I did."

Nighthorse threw back his head and laughed. "Good work, Dr. Lupicen. Nicely done. You focused on one pain in the ass to ignore another pain in the ass."

Émile clapped Lupicen on the back. "Very good, Capoçek. You make me proud."

Games asked, "Are you the one Jamie calls Graywolf?"

"Yes. At certain times and in certain places."

Lupicen put his hands on his brother's shoulders and looked into his eyes. "But, Émile, what became of you? All those years?"

Émile rubbed Lupicen's old, flushed, and weathered cheek. "There's time enough for that, Capoçek. Right now there's much we need to get done, especially if the Little Master is going to live, and he must. That is why we're all here."

Nighthorse looked up at Shem's reference to Jamie and Émile nè Graywolf nodded. "Yes, *Sunkawakan Hanhepi*. Of all of us, you must prepare more than most."

Nighthorse returned the nod and inspected the bandages on his hands.

LUPICEN LET ÉMILE TAKE THE LEAD AND LISTENED more than he talked. Occasionally he reached out and touched his brother. Émile would pause and lift Capoçek's hand to his face. "Yes, it is me, Little Brother." Finally he stood behind Capoçek, resting his hands on Capoçek's shoulders, massaging them as he explained what lay ahead.

Lupicen caught a scent from Émile's hands. Not the raw smells of the collective. The smells of deep woods, rich earths, tall firs, the musk of heavy fur.

He shook his head, giving up understanding to listen to his brother's voice, still young, still strong.

All my work coming to fruition but not in ways I understand.

He stared at Carsons, still in the chair where they'd left him, looking about as people talked. I am like you now, Mr. Carsons, in awe of what happens around me. But I have found my family. May you find yours.

Émile stopped talking and came around to face his brother. "Now, Capoçek, your part. Here you are wiser than I." He spoke quietly to his older, little brother. Finished, he nodded.

A moment later Capoçek nodded and it was understood. He turned to Sandy Olafssen. "Ms. Olafssen, would you let everyone know they have a few days holiday coming to them, with pay so that none will suffer?"

"I can do that, Dr. Lupicen."

"All except you, Ms. Olafssen. I will need you to possibly help me with Ann."

"Gladly, Dr. Lupicen."

"Also, we will need someone to stand watch. Someone who no one notices because they are always there. Yet someone who can be trusted, someone who will act if it is required."

Olafssen thought for a minute. "I think I know who we can ask."

Graywolf smiled.

Papers rustled on desks. Wall charts riffled in a breeze. Lupicen smiled. "Let a faulty air conditioning system be the greatest of our worries this day.

Chapter 47

The Lycan Hurricane

Al Carsons rubbed his eyes and yawned. Strange place, Dr. Lupicen's lab. Crazy dreams.

Where'd all these people come from? What was Dr. Lupicen saying? Love? Being loved?

Al loved Effie. Forever and always.

And Charlie and Ben. Such good boys.

Al chuckled. Must have dozed off again, not seen everyone come in the lab, missed some of what Dr. Lupicen said.

"Albert."

"Effie?"

"My forever Albert. It's time for us to be together again."

"What?"

"You, me, and the boys. It's time for us to be together again."

Someone stood beside Effie. In the distance, two wolf cubs romped on a snow-covered plain. Like the fields outside Hallock in the winter. Except the trees kept their leaves. And the night sky was full of sparkling lights - stars - like he hadn't seen since he was a kid.

"Where are we? Who's that with you?"

The other person came forward.

"I know you! You're the lady in the night! You're the one who told me to protect Jamie."

The woman held out her hand.

"This is Mrs. MacPherson, Al. She needs you to do something, something only you can do."

Al took Ellie's hand. "Well, of course. What can I do for you, Mrs. MacPherson?"

"I NEED YOU TO FIND JAMIE, MR. CARSONS. I NEED you to find him and let people know where he is. Protect him if you can. Get him to safety, if possible."

She turned away from him, addressing someone Al couldn't see. "Is that something he can do, Ann?"

Was he dreaming inside Dr. Lupicen's computer again?

Ellie faced him again. "We don't know if that's possible, but you must do it if you can."

"Save your boy, Mrs. MacPherson?" Al thought of Charlie and Ben. About nothing he could do to save them. "Of course, Mrs. MacPherson. Anything. Anything I can do. What do you need?"

Great wings flapped over Al's head. He looked up. A huge, winged wolf approached.

The winged wolf came down beside him and growled through a whitened muzzle, "My children. Come."

Other wings sounded overhead. Al heard wolves howling, gathering. Their numbers increasing, young ones yipping, old ones barking.

The old wolf folded its wings into its fur and sat beside Al. "Rub behind my ears..."

Al felt its fur, gray and soft as an old woman's hair.

The old wolf tilted its head and groaned a contented groan. "Aye, that's where the cub touched me. A memory. For finding."

Winds gathered around them.

Al said, "What cub?"

Wolves flew about them. A lycan hurricane lifted them. Ellie and Effie receded into the distance.

Al called out, "Effie, no," and started to pull his hand away from the great wolf's head.

"No," the Old One ordered. "You'll be with your pack soon enough."

The howling. The winds. Al and the Old One in the center, unmoving while the universe roved about them.

Over a river. Up into hills. Highways became county roads became streets became rutted dirt lanes. Lush-leaved trees gave ground to old, dying ones. Birds scattered, their skies taken over by black, shapeless things. Far below, water, still, a black pool waiting.

"Hey, that's Cap'n Sally."

The winds increased, furious yet the trees barely moving beneath them.

Al heard Ellie's voice. "Protect - "

"Hey, that's Jamie!"

Al's gaze went from Dr. Lupicen to Joni to Dr. Games to Nighthorse to Tom to Graywolf. He glanced at everyone else in the lab.

Wasn't Effie here just a second ago?

CAPTAIN SALLY FELT A TAPPING ON HIS SHOULDER. He turned. A tall, red-haired man smiled down on him.

The lugwrench he'd had in the rope tied around his waist crashed across his face.

He fell.

Something dragged him. He tasted blood on his lips. He sucked air in through clenched teeth. The exposed nerve of a shattered tooth clanged like a fire engine as cool air raced over it. His face swelled to an icy coldness. His left eye swelled shut.

The dragging stopped. His head cracked against something hard. He remembered it was a granite grotto. But the sound wasn't right. Concrete?

The red-haired man smiled down upon him. "Look me in the eye," he said.

Such a nice fellow. I should tell him everything I know.

"Who are you?"

Sally looked around. Blood burbled from his lips as he spoke. "I see water. Are we at the ocean?" Sally saw a tower on the far side of the dam. Some plaques glistened in the moonlight on the side of it. Maybe it would tell him which way to the ocean.

"I asked, who are you?"

Sally nè Sallisette's voice came out warbly and old. "I'm Captain Burt Sally and no finer miniature golf or pinball arcade will you find in all of Hallock."

The red-haired man kicked him in the balls.

Cap'n Sally nè Sallisette's wastes flowed freely from his body. He pulled his head back from the smell.

"Who are you?"

"Bertram Sally. Sallisette. Doctor captain doctor captain doctor captain."

The lugwrench backhanded into the other side of his face.

He couldn't see out of either eye. He gasped. Blood gagged him and he convulsed, coughing it up.

Somebody lifted him into a sitting position. Somebody spread his right eye's eyelids.

He sucked in his breath. His diaphragm's sudden movement made his testicles ache more.

He started babbling, not controlling what he said, words flowing out like water over a dam.

The red-haired man laughed. "Really? The Isabella Stuart Gardner Museum?" The man laughed so hard he doubled over and fell to his knees. "Dr. Sallisette, you really should have kept your eyes on the prize. I assure you your booty won't go wasted, and like your compatriots, you will have drowned."

Pangiosi pulled a mobile from an inside pocket and keyed in a number. "Tibbs, some damn fool followed me. That's right. An old sailor. I don't care that he only interacted with your computer once. Is there anybody else I can expect? No? Make sure it stays that way."

"Jamie, come here please."

AL HEARD ELLIE SCREAMING, "SAVE MY SON."

The lycan hurricane descended.

Al stood between Jamie and some man with his back towards him.

"Hey, that's my wrench. From the behind the seat of my truck."

The man turned. "Hello. Who are you?"

Al shuddered as he looked behind the man. "Is that Cap'n Sally?"

"More like 'was' at this point. But let's trade. You can have Cap'n Sally, I'll take Jamie. Jamie, come here son, please."

"Don't move, Jamie."

Al heard Ann talking but didn't understand what she meant. "I'm going to superimpose realities, Mr. Carsons. My world and yours will overlap but only for a moment."

The winds again. Wolves howling, snarling. But not at him.

The Lady in the Night screamed into the swirling winds. "Jamie! It's mom! Jamie, come here, Jamie! That's my boy. Hurry."

Al turned his back on the man. "Go to your mom, Jamie."

Jamie started running up into the sky, his pathway outlined by snarling, winged furies. "Run, cub. Run!"

Jamie shouted, "The Guardians of The Moon."

Moonlight blazed through the eye of the storm. A woman in white held her hand out. "Take my hand, Mr. Carsons. Hurry."

The man said, "What the... Oh, this is too great a prize. This is simply too great."

A gunshot.

ALL THESE PEOPLE. HE HAD TO GET THEIR ATTEN-tion. "Excuse me, Dr. Lupicen, everybody." His voice. Louder than he intended. And commanding.

I hope they're not upset with me. Must be because I want to get back to Effie. She and Mrs. MacPherson are in a hurry. No time to waste.

Everybody turned to him.

"Jamie's safe."

Am I sweating?

"Cap'n Sally's..."

Dr. Lupicen said, "Mr. Carsons. You're quite blanched. Are you alright?"

Aʟ ᴡɪɴᴄᴇᴅ.

But Jamie was safe.

Another gunshot.

Aʟ ʀᴇsᴛᴇᴅ ᴀ ʜᴀɴᴅ ᴏɴ ʜɪs ʙɪɢ ʙᴇʟʟʏ.

Wet.

Did he pee himself?

He could fall asleep again. Be with Effie, Charlie, and Ben.

That would be nice.

Tʜᴇ Oʟᴅ Oɴᴇ. "Cᴏᴍᴇ, Aʟ. Wᴇ ʜᴀᴠᴇ ᴀ ꜰᴇᴡ ᴍᴏᴍᴇɴᴛs before you go to your pack."

The Moon pulled Al, staggering, into the whirlwind.

The man screamed, "No!"

Another gunshot.

Hᴇ ꜰᴇʟᴛ ᴡᴇᴛ.

Sticky wet.

What was that all about?

Damn but it hurt to breathe.

Rᴇᴀʟɪᴛɪᴇs sᴇᴘᴀʀᴀᴛᴇᴅ.

Al sat in the chair in Lupicen's lab.

He was wet.

Weird dreams.

He looked at the people in the lab. Saw concern in their eyes.

What's wrong? Jamie's safe. Didn't they hear him?

"Jamie's safe."

Each breath, each thing he said, making him wetter.

"He's with your computer somewhere, Dr. Lupicen."

"Sally's at the dam, hurt pretty bad."

Somebody said, "Jamie's with Ann?"

The scent of Effie's baking. Ben and Charlie racing each other to get the first cookies hot out of the oven. They pushed through the people in the lab, cookies in their hands, chocolate stains on their faces. "Hey, dad. Mom made chocolate chip cookies!"

"What dam, Mr. Carsons?"

Al's hand came up from his belly covered in blood. "What happened? Doesn't matter, Jamie's safe now.?" He smiled and slumped off the chair.

Games's voice, excited. "My god, the man's been shot."

Games squatted beside Al, using whatever was handy to pack wounds, stanch the blood.

"I did what the Lady in the Night asked."

"Who shot him? When? How? Did anybody hear gunshots?"

"What lady in the night?"

"Where's Jamie?"

Al smiled. "He's safe. He's with Ann. And his mother." It was easier to speak now. "The Lady in the Night. But Sally. He's hurt."

No more words. Not now. Listen.

Wolves howled.

A she-wolf came through the lab. "Al, my forever man. You've done all they asked, all that's required. Time to rest."

Charlie and Ben morphed into wolf cubs, chocolate stains still smearing their fur.

Al's eyes closed. His body melted from man to wolf. He got up, all aches and pains gone. Charlie and Ben nipped his muzzle. Effie touched noses with him.

The western-facing wall of the lab disappeared. A snow-covered landscape, copses and islands of trees in a snow-white sea. In the distance the Aurora whispered. Stars filled the sky.

And the welcoming call of wolves, summoning their own to come join them, to play, to romp forever in the Gardens of The Moon.

"Come on, boys," he howled.

Effie joined him. "Come on, Charlie. Come on, Ben."

"Coming Ma."

"Coming Pa."

Al heard a human voice. "He's dead." No accent. It wasn't Lupicen. Dr. Games?

The voice faded, whatever else it said lost in the wind.

CHAPTER 48

Mother and Child Reunion

JAMIE RAN THROUGH SWIRLING WHITE WINDS TO HIS mother's arms. "Mom!"

Ellie held Jamie, their bodies blurring together in Ann's white world. His soft hair matted with her tears.

"Jamie, my Jamie." She wanted to look at him, hold him at arm's length, treat him like a newborn, count his fingers and toes, but holding him apart she couldn't do, not yet.

"Tell me you're alright, Jamie. Please tell me you're alright."

Jamie's own tears soaked the white, Morning Glory-embroidered blouse Ellie wore, watering them, nourishing them, bringing them life. "Yes, mom. Yes."

She released her grip. "Let me look at you."

"The Moon told me I'd see you again. She said you were safe. And alive. I don't remember the rest. But you're here now, Mom."

They held each other close, allowing no space between them.

"Yes, Jamie. I'm safe. I'm here now, Jamie."

"Is Dad here, too?"

A room formed around them. Ann's bedroom. Ann demurely arranged toiletries on her dresser, affording Jamie and Ellie their moment.

"No, Jamie. Not here, not yet. I'm not sure if he'll ever come here. And I'll leave here soon, too. But don't worry. We're together now."

Jamie pulled back. "But alive, too, right, Mom? You're alive, aren't you?"

"Yes, I'm alive. But listen. We still have lots to do and you're a big man, now, Jamie. You have to do some things I wish you didn't have to do."

"I want to stay here with you, Mom."

She kissed his head, ran her hand down through his hair, hugged him so close for fear of letting him go. "I know, Jamie. I know. But not yet. Not for a long while yet, I hope."

"Why, Mom? Don't you want me to be with you?"

"More than you can imagine, Jamie. I never want to let you go. But listen, Jamie. You and I are special. I never knew how special and I don't know if it really is special."

"What are you talking about, Mom?"

"You and I, we believe in our dreams."

"I don't understand, Mom."

"I know, Jamie, I know. I'm asking a lot of you. Everyone's asking a lot of you. And this is probably going to be the most difficult time of your life. And the decision has to be yours, to do what everyone's asking you to do. And I'm going to love you no matter what you decide because you're my Jamie and I'm always going to love you."

"What is it I have to do?"

"You have to go back and dream."

"But I already dream."

"Not like before, Jamie. Like this." Ellie stood back a bit, apart, closed her eyes and dreamed deep dreams, Warrior Dreams, dreams that changed things, dreams that kept hope alive when so many wanted to die, not warring to defeat, warring to make way, to prepare, to guard, to grow.

"These are like the dreams The Moon showed me."

Ellie opened her eyes. "Yes, Jamie. I didn't get a chance to teach you.

You and I have the power to change things through our dreams. Not the past, the future. For everybody. Our dreams, our hopes, they allow light into other people's lives. Do you understand what I'm saying, Jamie? You have to go back, Jamie. But first you must learn to dream. You must learn to go places few people have ever been, and places no one has yet been. You must learn to see the unseeable, to know the unknowable." She paused. "And to accept the unacceptable."

"I understand."

Ellie held her son. Lifetimes were lived in seconds. Universes grew and collapsed in the space between them.

And when they were done, he stood back. "You have to go away now, don't you."

She reached out for him and he shook his head, no.

"Not yet," she said. "In a while and not yet. But I'll always be with you. You'll always remember me, won't you?"

Jamie nodded.

"Please don't grow old so quickly, Jamie. Please be my little boy for just a moment longer."

He clung to her.

"Find other dreamers, Jamie. They're all around you, just waiting to be noticed, to be seen. Let them know it's okay to dream..."

Ellie faded from Jamie's grasp. Ann's room grew vaporous, a mist swished by light winds.

Ann said, "Remember our language, Jamie. The secret words, the old tongue."

The mist disappeared.

Jamie stood in Lupicen's lab.

He clenched his fists and screamed, "No."

CHAPTER 49

Warriors of Hope

TOM RACED TO HIS SON, LOWERING TO HIS KNEES SO
he could hold him face to face. "Jamie! I thought I'd lost you forever."

"I saw Mom, Dad."

"Where?"

Jamie looked at the System 70. "In...there, I think."

Jack Games came up to the two of them, his brow narrowed, his lips
tight, and rubbed Jamie's hair.

"Hey, Uncle Jack." Jamie looked around. "And Mr. Graywolf," he
exclaimed. "See, Uncle Jack, see?"

Graywolf said, "Hey, Jamie. I'll bet you've had some adventures."

"Tell me about Mom, son."

"She's fine, Dad. She's safe..."

"But?"

"But she...she's going to go away in a while."

Tom stood, his face a melange of theater masks, Comedy and
Tragedy, Sock and Buskin, each seeking dominance. "Will I have a
chance to say good-bye? To see her one more time?"

Jamie looked at Tom.

"I'm sorry, son. I have no right to ask you that. You're here now, safe." He held Jamie against him. His eyes shifted over the others in the lab. "We're getting out of here. Going back to Chicago. Come on, Jack."

Graywolf blocked the door. "Sorry, Mr. MacPherson. Not yet."

"He's right, Dad. Not yet."

Tom slid to the floor, sitting beside his son, crying into Jamie's shirt. Jamie held Tom, father and son now son and father, their roles reversed for a moment in time.

Jack Games helped Tom up. "Nothing, nothing I've ever studied on any continent prepared me for this. I grew up with people getting shot, dying. That's not new. But phantom bullets that kill and people appearing out of nowhere?"

Joni knelt beside Al's body and wiped her eyes. "Mr. Carsons. I hope you're with your wife and kids now."

Graywolf looked at the lab's western facing wall. His eyes tracked something no one else could see. "He is. He's fine. The end of one world is the beginning of another."

Jack followed his gaze to the wall, seeing nothing but windows and a setting sun. "Can someone call the police, a medical examiner, to get the body?"

Graywolf turned to him. "No need."

An odd winter wind rustled wall calendars and notes in the lab. Snowflakes fell on Al Carsons' body, on the floor surrounding him, on the chair he'd fallen from, and on Joni kneeling beside him.

"What's this? It's snow but it's warm," she said.

Al's body faded where the snow melted on it. Jack stared. Nighthorse lifted Joni from the floor.

Graywolf said, "He's going where he needs to be."

The snow fell gently, a soft susurration of a warm winter wind the only hint of its presence.

Jack said, "But what about the body? Somebody's going to ask questions. Colodnie Johnson, for one."

Tom said, "Don't tell me she's involved in this."

"She was on the train with us from Chicago."

Tom's face reddened. "And I still got kidnapped and beaten? And my son still gets taken? Well ain't she good at her job."

Graywolf said, "Dr. Games, The Queen takes care of her own. Mr. Carsons' body - this reality's body - will be found on a hillside outside of Hallock, a heart attack."

"What about - "

"He'll never have left Hallock. Your Cap'n Sally borrowed his truck. To all others, their memories will be as dreams." Graywolf's eyes shifted to the others. "Now it's our turn."

"Our turn for what?" Joni asked.

Dr. Bertram Sallisette, PhD, lately of the Hallock Sallys, of Hallock, Minnesota, ran his tongue over his lips.

Blood? Did I bite my lip?

His eyes wouldn't focus.

Some fool stood over him - I'm on the ground? A floor? Where am I? - talking to him.

"Did you see that? Did you absolutely see that? Oh, I have to call this in. No, wait. If I call this in, they'll swarm like rats over roadkill to get their hands on it. They'll claim it and I'll be out in the cold."

See what? I can't see anything. What's wrong with my eyes?

"Me, Earl Pangiosi, left out except an honorable mention in some report that no one will ever see?"

Pangiosi?

The tall, red-haired man? Where's the boy? Where's Jamie?

"Oh, no. No, no, no. We're not going to let that happen."

Does this fool know he sounds like a hysterical woman? Like that hysterical woman I drowned years ago.

Pangiosi knelt beside him. "You're a clever man. What do you think I should do?"

That's right. That bitch - what was her name? She got all jealous and hysterical because he joked that his other lover - what was his name? - might share more of the prize than her.

Sally coughed up a laugh.

She sounded just like that. "Oh, no. No, no, no. We're not going to let that happen." She said that, too, didn't she?

He damn near drowned himself because of that bitch and her idiot friend.

Sally shook his head. It hurt. How come it hurt? His face throbbed as if he'd stuck it in a hornet's nest.

"You were patient. Amazingly so. I'll give you that." The red-haired man sailed away.

Yes, I was patient. Waited for the perfect storm, as it were.

Killed them both, in the end.

"Quite patient."

Lupicen sat at his console, his HUVRSA in one hand and his gloves in the other. "Ms. Olafssen, ISTS's lab monitors all trunk communications for the university, yes? If there's a physical way into Ann, it would route through there, correct?"

Sandy Olafssen finished for him. "I'm on it, Dr. Lupicen. I'll get some friends to run sniffers and snoopers on all of Ann's trunks, wide-lines down to vox."

Lupicen donned his equipment. The world filled with white.

A door formed. He knocked.

"Hello, Poppie."

He held a cherry Tootsie-Roll pop in his hand.

"Ann, Captain Sally dreamed for us, yes?"

"Yes, Poppie."

"Can you recreate his patterns? Reach out to him, find him?"

Ann's QLC's thrummed.

Several miles away, by a dam just west of Thetford, Vermont, Bertram Sallisette felt an energy fill him he'd never experienced before. His mind cleared. His body felt young again.

Didn't this man-bitch say something about laying claim to Sallisette's prize, waiting for him on the ocean floor?

Bertram Sallisette rose off the ground. "Oh, no. No, no, no. We're not going to let that happen."

Back in the lab, Ann's QLCs steadied, a slight rainbow bridge hovering over each. "Yes, Poppie."

"And can you guide someone to him?"

NIGHTHORSE, TOM, AND JACK FOLLOWED GRAYWOLF outside onto the Vail Hall quad. Ann isolated Cap'n Sally's thought patterns, shared his memories of following Pangiosi into the hill country west of Thetford, Vermont, then accessed various state records, USACE records, Keyhole overflights, and even Google Maps to determine the shortest, quickest route to him, and sent Dartmouth's drone fleet on ahead. Lastly she created an app for Jack Games' cell outlining the route and providing a bird's eye view, and tying it to Sally's unique neural signature. If he moved, the route updated automatically.

Graywolf handed Jack the keys to his hack. "You may want to hurry, Dr. Games. Captain Sally doesn't have much time left."

On the passenger side, Nighthorse helped Tom, still a little stiff, into the car. "Sorry about the straps, Mr. MacPherson."

"I guess you really know your job." Nighthorse supported Tom's back with his big hands and felt something under Tom's shirt, at his belt line. Tom looked up at him quickly.

Nighthorse said, "Remember your posture, exhale when you squeeze."

Tom continued to stare at the big Indian, waiting for him to say more. When Nighthorse closed the door, Tom said, "Thanks."

Graywolf and Nighthorse stood on the quad under the rising moon as Tom and Jack drove away. "Think they'll be alright?"

Graywolf chuckled. "They'll be what they have to be."

"You sound just like my grandfather."

A large, heavy woman with two small children and several shopping bags in tow walked rapidly past them and into Vail Hall.

"Awful late to be checking on experiments, and I wouldn't bring my kids along to do it," Nighthorse said.

"Everybody's doing what they need to do, John. Even you and I."

"So what do we do now?"

Graywolf looked up at the rising moon. "This is as far as I go. You have the Gate Jamie found?"

"My *wotai*? Right here." He lifted it from his pocket.

Graywolf grabbed Nighthorse's hand and held it so that the light of the moon shone through it onto Nighthorse.

Nighthorse offered no resistance and Graywolf guided the hand holding the Gate. "A little this way, like a lens, so the moon can see you. That's it." Graywolf let Nighthorse's hand go.

A blast of moonlight came through the Gate and probed Nighthorse's chest.

Graywolf said, "If you're going to say no, now's the time."

"Say no to what?"

"To me, to your grandfather, to everything you learned."

Nighthorse's breath left him, as if surfacing from a deep dive, as if he dropped his tanks and let the air in his lungs escape as it carried him to the surface. No pain and that surprised him. He exhaled but it felt as if his being spread, opened, understood, expanded through the sky with his escaping breath.

"Did my brother tell you about the night I was chosen?"

"The night you witnessed dark things and things like Joni's little shadow people under the moon?"

"Yes. But he couldn't know the Darkness, the Blackness, the Hopelessness and Despair life would soon become. I thought what we saw was a trick of the night. We were tired, hungry. It was possible we walked while asleep and what I saw was a dream." He laughed, quietly, the subtlety of his unintentional joke tickling him these many years later.

"But it was no accident, no mistake. I didn't know I was seeing Dreams or that they were there to protect us - me - before the Guardians could arrive. Can you understand that I was my little brother's hope?"

"In a way, yes."

"That night that my dear Capoçek described to you, I was enlisted by the Queen."

"The Queen?" Nighthorse felt his chest flexing, heaving against his will.

"Yes, the Queen of the Night. Let's say that all the stories and all the fairytales and all the myths and fables we've told children, most of them are true. Why we allow children to have their dreams but deny them to ourselves as adults I don't know. Perhaps we think we're too wise or too old or too afraid to hope anymore." Graywolf looked down and shook his head.

His gaze returned to Nighthorse and he smiled. "But the Queen, she's the one who's been presiding over dreams since the world was young. She cast her light on the dreams of those sleeping on earth, peering into the hopes and fears which weren't expressed during the day. All things dream, from the oldest man in the tiniest village to the youngest girl in the biggest city and all in between, dogs and cats twitching on their masters' beds to the great leviathans sounding in the deep."

Graywolf placed a hand on Nighthorse's shoulder to steady him. "All this she agreed to do by night, ever since The One, The First, The Only of All Dens, the first of the tribe of canine, canid, canis agreed to guard the first men by day. Humans have bred a lot of wolf out of their wolves, but the old canid memories remain. Wolves, dogs…they've been the watchers in this realm. There are other wolves, other dogs, in the next. It was The One who told the spirit within you to protect the Little Master, that he was the last hope for Dreams. That is why you carry it, Nighthorse, so that it can complete what it was instructed to do."

His hand fell away as moonlight filled the big Indian. "Despair and darkness have been held at bay. For a while. Now they are back again. Every generation has to fight this fight. Hope and Despair are ancient enemies. But Despair is stronger than ever in this generation, and more subtle than before, more willing to wait its time."

Graywolf smiled again. Tears met and gathered in the edges of his smile. "But I'm too old to carry on the fight anymore."

Nighthorse grunted as his chest started to rupture under the influence of The Moon's light.

Graywolf chanted:

The moon rises fast,
this moon rises last,
if betwixt and between
do not soon make it right,
All the world's hopes will be past.

Nighthorse nodded. "I know that. Or something like it. You speak the old words well."

"Your grandfather says 'We have to die to this life before we can live in another, Pokachee.'"

"You knew my grandfather?"

Graywolf started shrinking, un-aging, the years rolling off him as they had Nighthorse when he dreamed his Grandfather dream. "I am become all the mysteries kept silent in the night."

His eyes locked on Nighthorse's. "As will you."

"Is this what my Grandpa wanted me to learn?"

"The Guardians of The Moon are many. Of the Guardian of Dreams there is but one per generation, and my time now ends."

"Wait...I..."

"Go wide, Pokachee."

Graywolf returned to the Émile Capoçek saw fight the Iceli as a child in Rumania. "Tell Capoçek I love him. I love him dearly. Tell him I will see him in the next place and that I wait for him there." The Moon sent a beam of pure white light into his chest, where it quaked and squeezed and collapsed and finally drew him up. "Remember what your grandfather taught you."

Émile rose into the sky and faded into the night. "Remember it well."

INSIDE ANN'S WORLD, LUPICEN SAT IN A YOUNG girl's bedroom. A Morning Glory bedspread, posters on the walls, music sticks on a dresser beside an inexpensive, young girl's makeup kit.

But the smell of morning glories and cherry candy. No perfumes. Ann sat in his lap, his arms encircling her, safe.

He closed his eyes and held her close while she rolled the Tootsie-roll pop in her mouth.

Who would take care of his little girl when he was gone?

"What's wrong, Poppie?"

"Nothing. Nothing, my Ann. If we are to defeat Mr. Tibbs, we must leave your room."

"Do we have to, Poppie?"

"Yes, but not yet. For now, and if you'll allow me, I'd like to hold you just a little while longer."

"I'd like that, too, Poppie."

Lupicen tucked her head under his chin and hummed an old tune, something remembered from childhood, something from a time when mothers and fathers kept the world safe, kept adult knowledge from children, allowed children to be children and didn't let the world force them into a premature adulthood.

Inside his HUVRSA, sitting in his lab office, he briefly smelled the odd mix of cleaning mixtures that William "Wild Bill" Murphy used to scour the halls, heard the wobbly wheels of the washbucket, the swishing of the mop, the oddly nasal singsong of the man's alcohol tinted voice and hoped that Ms. Olafssen had been correct, that Wild Bill was as good a guard as they could get because nobody paid any attention to him, and for an extra bottle in his bucket at the end of the night he'd make sure Hell itself didn't bother Dr. Lupicen or his lab.

For a moment he thought he heard the voice of a woman and the crying of small children also out in the hall. He heard Wild Bill say, "Tibbs? Yeah, he worked here a while back. These his kids? You don't say. Yeah, I know where he lives." Then the voices quieted to near silence.

Lupicen held his breath the entire time, unsure and afraid that Wild Bill would, without thinking, usher the woman and her children in.

But he heard the singsong voice again. It sounded almost like a chant, some aboriginal calling, some ancient rhyme calling across time and space, and he heard Wild Bill banging a definite pattern on his bucket, and he wondered that the old man could do his regular job at all.

He heard the sloshing of water. He wasn't sure if he was hearing the movements of Wild Bill, the workings of Ann, or the place where Pangiosi held Captain Sally.

The last thing he remembered of his lab was sitting at Ann's console and looking through the little window in the door to the hall as Wild Bill looked up and in, seeing eyes so like his brother's, the right one bright blue, the left one brown.

CHAPTER 50

Cow and Sheep Fucking in East Central Vermont

"JESUS JUMPING CHRIST." COLODNIE JOHNSON watched the comings and goings around Vail Hall from the rear seat of her surveillance vehicle, across the quad and up a side street. A haze of cigarette smoke escaped from a crack at the top of her passenger window. "Who are those two talking in front?"

The two FBI agents in the front seat, Harriman and Feinman, flipped through some files on their tablets. "We got nothing."

A lone drone flew clumsily past them some thirty feet off the ground. A moment later the support vehicle followed, moving erratically, a dog sniffing down a lead or whoever was driving had no idea how to use a clutch.

"This place is worse than goddamn O'Hare. Take a picture of those two and see if anything hits." She lifted the PTT from her purse. "This is Johnson, talk to me."

"We lost the old man. We really didn't have anything to go on, thinking Pangiosi was your boss. So we lost the MacPherson boy, too."

"Jesus Jumping Christ."

Harriman scratched his beard. "I think they deal more with cattle mutilations up here."

Feinman closed her tablet. "That's out west. Here it's cow and sheep fucking."

"Who's that woman with the kids. She from around here?"

FBI Special Agent Feinman bluetoothed her camera to her tablet. "Nope, not from around here. We got a 87% match though and we'll have confirmation - " A part of her tablet screen turned into a map with a blinking red circle. "She's not answering her phone but that's her. Got to be." A streak of blue appeared below the map. "She drives a '93 Green Volvo 240, four-door classic wagon. Mass plates LVYRCHLD."

Special Agent Harriman raised some Zeiss NightEyes and scanned the cars up and down the streets and parking lots. "Don't see it. She might have come up in the Boston cab you told us about."

"Any cabs reported missing?"

Harriman checked his tablet. "Not yet."

"What's so special about this woman?" asked Johnson.

Feinman increased the screen image and held it up to Johnson. "She's Lauren Decato, an antiabortion activist. Quite the history. She's suspected of doing lots of things but nobody seen her do a one."

"This just gets better and better." She spoke into the PTT again. "Anybody seen MacPherson or Games?"

"Not yet, Detective."

"Tell you what." Johnson watched the woman with her kids and shopping bags go into Vail Hall. "We don't know all the research that goes on in there and she's got bags that could hold any number of dangerous things. If she don't come out in a few, we go in and ask politely what she's doing so far from home."

Before she could replace her PTT the woman came out of Vail Hall pulling her kids and bags with her and headed straight for their car.

"Oh Jesus Jumping Christ."

Feinman said, "Duck behind the seat." She and Harriman scooted towards each other and necked passionately. Johnson squeezed herself onto the floor between the front and rear seats.

Decato walked to the car parked in front of them, raised her head as she heard their moans, opened her door and pushed her kids inside. A moment later she drove off.

Johnson got up from the floor. "You two do that often? Seemed pretty goddamn natural to me."

The two agents rearranged their clothing.

"You two must be pretty goddamn good at your jobs not to have noticed her car was parked right in front of us." Johnson pushed her cigarette out the slight opening of her window. "Harriman, think you could follow her car?"

CHAPTER 51

Rio In Moonlight

SALLY ROSE. SOMETHING BUZZED OVERHEAD. SEVERAL things. Pangiosi's Iceli clouded the sky before but they made no noise, silently seeking prey. Now the air filled with the sibilations of massive bees.

Drones.

Sally's hand, wet and slimy with his own blood, went around Pangiosi's throat.

Pangiosi stared down into Bertram Sallisette's brutalized face.

Blood burbled from Sallisette's mouth. "You think you're going to steal what I've waited thirty fucking years for? Thirty fucking years in fucking Hallock, Minnesota? Have you ever been in fucking Hallock, Minnesota? Have you ever tried to get a reasonable fuck in Hallock, Minnesota?"

Thirty years playing a part, Sallisette became Sally. Hands and arms that lifted chalk, pointers, overheads, and papers had lifted wrenches, hammers, torquers, power tools, wood saws. His hands served as vice-grips when none were handy.

Like now.

Pangiosi's eyes bulged. His knees went weak.

"The only reasonable fuck in that entire town was the goddamn doctor's wife and the only time she'll fuck is when she hears her husband, the town medico, mumble some woman's name in his sleep, which wasn't anywhere near often enough, and then she ups and goddamn dies for no goddamn good reason. Now you think I'm giving up thirty years without tail for you? I've done my penance, asshole."

Sallisette dragged Pangiosi over to the murky, greenish water. He pushed. Pangiosi held on. They spun. Sallisette fell in and pulled Pangiosi in after him.

Sallisette gasped hitting the cold water. Gasping caused pain. His lungs filled with the slime-filled water.

Something pushed him down, deeper into the water.

His fingers slid down the concrete dam walls. His thoughts wavered. He dreamed.

My vault? I'm at my SeaVault?

He checked his dive computer. Yeah, right, 130 feet and under a ridge fifteen miles out. Nobody suspected. Lobstered out fifteen miles and further all the time.

His dive computer looked like a wrench for a second. He blinked.

Plenty of time. A little dizzy though. Faulty rebreather? Need to check when I ascend.

His feet were caught in a rope. His 16" fins were dragging out like a blanket, dragging him down.

Damn things were supposed to float.

He slipped out of the rope. The flippers went down with it.

The vault's side turned into a huge underwater cement wall. Where were the pictures, the paintings, the hermetically sealed containers storing the Isabella Stuart Gardner Museum's artwork?

What the hell was this thing pushing him down?

The dream shifted. Changed.

Rio.

He spoke flawless Brazilian Portuguese.

Funny only one laborer showed up. And that flaming red hair. So rare in Brazil.

But with his rich tan and silver, close cropped hair, strong, clean-shaven jawline, the mover thought he was a retired banker or investor.

"Hang those on that wall, there. We'll divide up the rest between my Buenos Ares and Santiago villas." He sipped a fine *Sena*.

Odd that it tasted like blood.

Didn't matter. He must prepare for his evening. The Silva family asked to introduce their daughter to him. They sent him a video of her at the beach. Bright-eyed, young-bodied. In older times, a contessa. Didn't matter. Her family encouraged the union for the wealth he'd bring.

He checked his wines. *Vina Almaviva* for tonight.

He saw the moon through the water.

Cold water.

But not salt. Where am I?

His fingers scraped along the side of his SeaVault.

Sallisette lifted his dive computer.

He held a wrench in his hand.

His body ached. His legs flopped like free-diving fins. His arms quit. Get to the surface.

He kicked. The Moon cleared. A woman's face.

Someone climbed out of the water beside him. The red-headed laborer?

He held out the wrench. The laborer took it and crashed it against his head.

The water took him. Accepted him. The contessa. Her arms open. Her hands guiding him. Her kiss like fire in his lungs.

Ah, Rio in moonlight.

My god what a tongue she had.

CHAPTER 52

Pangiosi's Children

PANGIOSI STOOD AT THE WATER'S EDGE, WRENCH IN hand, dripping brackish water and threads of slimy weed. He stared at Sallisette's body floating face-down in the water. His body quaked involuntarily. He mumbled, "Cold," dropped the wrench and wove an unsteady path to his rented car. He turned the engine over and got out.

Standing beside his car, he took ten rapid breaths, like a diver about to go free, then peeled off his wet clothes, dried himself off, urinated, took his mobile from his old clothes, got back in his car, turned the heater on full, and held his wrists over the dashboard vents.

A few minutes later his quaking stopped. He got out, opened the trunk, opened a suitcase, removed a fresh set of clothes - underwear, t-shirt, socks, navy blue adidas tiro training pants and firebird jacket with matching dragons - set them over the engine's hood to warm and got back in his car.

The car hadn't been idle long and reached temperature quickly. He got out and put on the warmed clothing, giving himself a moment to let the warmth sink in. Back at the still open trunk, he mounted a nine-inch mirror on the trunk latch, stood back and adjusted his clothing.

He ran a hand through his hair, took another step back, and nodded.

He reached into the wheel well and removed a revolver and a new mobile.

At the tree line he found a thick, broken branch with few twigs to mar its sleekness and snapped them off.

Walking back to Sally's floating remains, he put three shots into each of Sally's lungs then used the branch to hold the body underwater until it no longer floated.

Back in his car, he tested his voice, looking into the rearview and making conversation with himself, making sure his recent activity didn't reveal itself in his tone, breathing, or manner.

Satisfied, he swapped out SIM cards and punched in a number.

"Tibbs, is there any chance they'll find you or know where you are?"

Tom said, "We lost Sally's signal."

Jack glanced at the mobile then up into the sky. "We can follow the drones."

Tom followed his gaze. "How many drones does Dartmouth have? The sky's dark with them."

Their headlights glinted off things up ahead. A red LED blinked on the top of each. They stopped to investigate.

Seven drones, Dartmouth branded, each's red recharge light blinking.

Jack said, "Must have reached the end of their battery life. Probably couldn't get back before they found the first safe place to land. Call the lab, see if they know anything about it."

"No signal. Probably better at the top of this hill."

Each looked up into the swarming darkness overhead.

Then the sky cleared, as if a huge flock of birds went to roost.

Things rustled in the darkness. Pangiosi put a fresh clip in his weapon. "Come out, come out, whoever you are."

An Icelin ambled down the road, walking on pseudopodic legs, growing arms and a head, waving at him.

"Oh, hello. How are you?"

Another followed it.

Then another.

Something fluttered onto the car's roof. Pangiosi turned to it.

Another Icelin, bat shaped, its outline deshaping into a blobness nothing.

Something splashed.

Iceli marched across the water towards him. They flew out of the trees, down from the sky, occulting the moon, blocking the stars, rolling along the ground.

Pangiosi watched them gathering. "What are you doing?"

He remembered his mother, kids in school, in college, people throughout his life.

The Iceli moved silently, surrounding him, their weightless numbers crushing him.

"Don't you understand? I was going to make the world safe for you. I, who never dreamed, was going to control the world's dreams. Weaponize them. To control people. So you wouldn't have to hide. So you could move about and be seen, be admired by all."

The formless bodies touched him, draining heat from him.

"I was going to make the world safe for you!"

A Icelin grew his mother's face. "But you failed."

A cloud formed beside the Icelin, pushing it out of the way. Another face formed.

"Mrs. MacPherson?"

His chest quaked.

Something slammed into his gut, tearing him open.

It came again, slamming his chest.

He screamed, his face blanched, his hands shook.

His sternum cracked, a thoracotomy he wasn't prepared for.

Iceli marched in.

434

Chapter 53

A Reckoning

"Ann?"

"Yes, Poppie?"

"Now."

"Are you sure, Poppie?"

"Yes, my little girl. I'm sure. Now."

Inside Ann's world, Capoçek sat on a chair surrounded in all directions, north, south, east, west, up and down and in and out, in a sea of foaming whiteness. Everywhere he looked blood-red threads reached and flew and crawled towards him. In his lap sat Ann, once again a Grendelian monster, little crabs digging everywhere into her skin. Anywhere else and at any other time her size would have crushed him, but here, now, with him, she was safe.

"I'm still your little girl, aren't I, Poppie?"

He reached into a pocket and took out a bright cherry *Tootsie Roll* pop. For a brief second she shimmered, a young girl no longer a child and not yet a woman, in jeans and tshirt with big blue Morning Glories stitched into them. The lollipop wrapper she tucked into her pocket, the lollipop went into her mouth and she was Grendel once again.

"You will always be my child."

Ann's great, rheumy eyes wept washtubs of tears that splashed in the whiteness by her feet.

Two buildings away, Sandy Olafssen watched various yottabyte wide channels open on Ann's connection lines. She opened a small laptop, typed in a line of code, and pressed the "XMIT" key.

Ellie, inside Ann's room inside Ann's world, lay down.

Joni entered Sleep Chamber #2. Three clocks floated in the air above Joni's cot; one ticked off the time available to her, the second how quickly time passed in active realities, the third indicated how long it would take her to get things done.

All clocks ticked green.

Joni closed her eyes. "Ellie, I never met you but I know you're there. Here's what Tibbs looks like. Pirate that sumbitch's mind. Or whatever Lupicen told you to do to him." Dreams, more vivid than she thought possible, swept past her. An intense rollercoaster dip took her breath away as four, six, and eight dimensional diamonds grew from pinpoints to sun size around her - Ellie generating Tibbs' spindle patterns.

The rollercoaster stopped. She was pulled backwards through lightning lined tunnels - Ann taking over more and more signalling of Tibbs' computers, learning through Sandy Olafssen's monitoring system how to out-hack the hacker.

Little crabs fell from Ann. Joni heard her sigh. The last of the crabs dropped from her and Tibbs slept.

Ellie-Ann said, "Okay, Levis. Now's your turn. Go, Girl!"

She closed her eyes and willed herself into a dream.

Of a cliff. Of people moving like lemmings towards it. A cliff turning a white world dark as a deformed crab-like machine scaled its depths swinging a hideous pendulum with a gored, side-angled blade. People being severed. Some only cut enough for their entrails to hang out. Others with a leg twisting freely, held on only by a partially severed tendon or a muscle uncontrollably twitching. Their screams scaled the cliff walls because the people themselves no longer could.

Joni's stomach rose with the scent of fetid blood and bowels.

Someone behind her said, "Come on. Let's go."

She stood in one of the lines going over the cliff and into the blades.

No guards this time. No little blue-eyed girl, no Graywolf. She opened her jacket. The honeybee spread its wings.

"Come on, come on," came the voice from behind. Familiar. How could she forget?

Tibbs.

She grabbed him by the collar, twisted from her hips and pulled. "This time you go on ahead."

Tibbs sailed over her shoulder, over the cliff, falling among the screams and shrieks of people dying down below.

A blade opened his skull. Crabs attacked his brain.

"Dave Bowman that, asshole. You'll never fuck with anybody's life ever again. You don't get to hurt anybody, you don't get to steal people's lives and secrets anymore."

She called to the people walking over the cliff, "Stop! All of you! Wake up! Take back your lives!"

On her cot, she smiled. Wake up? That's a good one, Levis.

She looked down the cliff wall to Tibbs. The nightmare blades scythed just below the waist.

Little black crabs attached themselves there.

Slowly the scything monster changed. It became a woman. Joni recognized her but wasn't sure from where.

The black crabs became children. Crying children holding onto Hostess Twinkies and Coke cans and Joni remembered: the abortion clinic woman and her children.

Tibbs saw them and screamed.

The woman aimed a gun at him and fired.

In her dream, Joni looked at the woman standing over a mutilated but not dead Tibbs. "Whoa. What made me think of you?" Her gaze shifted to Tibbs, blood darkening bullet holes in his chest and head, dying but not quite dead. "Don't know if that's how you'll really go, Virge, but it's good enough. Lupicen told me to create a dream where you got yours and that I did. The rest was up to Ann, translating one reality's events into another's. Doesn't matter. Bastards like you will never ruin my or anybody else's life ever again."

She looked at all the others on the cliff, in the lines, disemboweled and tortured down the cliff walls. She stood on the cliff's edge. "What was that movie, Honey? 'I'm mad as hell and I'm not going to take it anymore'?"

Her chest pulsed. She took off her jersey, no longer ashamed of the body she'd been given. "Everyone," her voice echoed into the canyons of the world. "Take back your dreams! Share them!"

Little dark silhouettes, the dreams of the world, leapt from her chest, claimed the wounded and dying, healed them, helped them up.

In her sleep chamber, on her cot, as she dreamed, Joni relaxed, her work done. She sat at the edge of the cliff, Oneiroi racing from her to others and back. She said to one, "You missed one over there, skippy," and it flew off. Another stood in front of her. "How about that little girl over there, you want to help her out?" and off it went.

Guiding dreams, she realized, could be fun.

"Back to you, El."

Pangiosi spoke calmly, "Tibbs, is there any chance they'll find you or know where you are?"

Ellie answered via one of Ann's telephony interfaces, an operator's headset with a dangling cord on her head. "Earl, I'm telling you, nobody knows I'm here and that one guy following you was a fluke. Nobody else knows where you are. I can show you the transaction records. They're all back in Lupicen's lab, sniffing each other's asses." She opened the door from Ann's room and looked out. The threads were gone.

"Very well," Pangiosi said. "I'm going after the lad. Let my cell ring if you need to reach me."

"Whatever you say, Earl. I'm here for you."

Pangiosi's line went dead. Ellie closed the door and said, "You dumb, murdering son-of-a-bitch. I'll teach you to go after my husband and son."

COLODNIE JOHNSON, FEINMAN, AND HARRIMAN pulled into the parking lot of a Norwich, Vermont, farmhouse that had been converted into apartments. They drove past the first time and circled back to make sure the woman in the green Volvo had left the car. She had, and she'd taken her kids with her.

"Probably took her shopping bags, too," Johnson said. "Where's the directional?"

Feinman handed her a shotgun mike and headphones. She rolled down her window and aimed where she saw lights coming through windows and from behind curtains.

Second row, fifth window, she got what she wanted; the sound of poor, stupid, white trash:

"I thought we had more kids." A man's voice, moody but pleasant.

"I dropped them." A woman's voice, tight and tense.

Johnson asked, "Do you have any prevaricator software on your tablets?"

Harriman handed her his tablet. "Third icon, first row on the left. Standard issue. Just plug the directional's output jack into that hole there."

The conversation came through loud and clear:

"Dropped them? You mean at your mother's? How many do we have?"

"You prick. You stupid bastard. You whoring son-of-a-bitch. I dropped them. I lost them. I had them aborted just like your cheap whore did. I knew all your business trips weren't just for work. But then to bring it home, right into your own backyard."

"Lauren, what are you talking about?"

"I saw the necklace she wore when she had hers done."

"Lauren, who?"

"I don't know her name. I only know she wore the same necklace you gave me, the one you said no one else would ever have. She wore it

the day she dropped her child. Your child."

"Who?"

"I don't know her name, I told you. Big tits. Pretty face. Good figure. All done up like she never had to worry about a man taking an interest in her, I'll bet."

"I don't know what you're talking about. Now go home and take these brats with you. I'm busy. I'm working. I told you before, if you needed to see me, call that number I gave you and I'll call you back."

"Ha. A Chicago number that's no longer in service? But you told me you worked at Dartmouth and you don't even work there anymore."

Johnson pulled a cigarette from her lips before she could light it. "Did she say 'Chicago'?"

"You went to Dartmouth?"

"You haven't worked there in a while."

A child crying.

"It's no business of yours what I do. So long as I pay your bills and keep you fed. And what do you mean you dropped two of my children? How dare you abort the lives I gave you?"

The man's voice, harsh, miserable. Johnson imagined a huge tick being squeezed and about to explode.

A cheap door opening.

A young girl's voice. "Virgil, I'm scared. I want to go home."

Harriman asked, "Who the hell's that?"

Johnson hushed him in a whispered voice. "How the fuck do I know. Shut up."

"Get back in that bedroom."

Two children, crying and snuffling in unison, each saying, "Momma, I want to go home."

Silence. Colodnie Johnson could feel Lauren the volcano getting ready to blow, then:

"What little whore jezebel is this, Virgil? Does she know you're a married man?"
"Virgil, you said you weren't married."
The man's voice again. "Get back in that goddamn bedroom now." Pause. *"Where did you say you saw that other woman? Back home? Brookline? Big tits? Nice face? Must have been Joni."*
"Have there been others?"
"You stupid cow."

The man's voice showed different spikes on the prevaricator output. It became expansive, taking on an air of braggadocio.

"There've been women in every city I've been in."
A phone rang once then fell silent.
"In Miami, there was…what was her name…Conchita? Contessa?"

Johnson said, "Are we recording this?"

Harriman took back the tablet and swiped a few screens. Feinman lifted her cell. "Set up a patch to backup record what we're getting. Double-time it. You need to capture as fast as we transmit. Now." She put down her mobile. "Done. But we're going to need last names to make anything stick."

"Shhh. Shut up. That fucker's so stupid he wants the world to know what he's done."

The woman, demanding. "How many?"
A child, shrieking. "Momma."

Lights came on in some other apartments. Johnson reached for Harriman's tablet. "You. Go door to door and make sure none of them fucks this up. Move."

Harriman quietly opened his door and left.

The girl's voice, whining. "Virgil…"
The man's voice, ordering. "Get back in there and close the door."
Then gently. "Or there'll be no candy for you later."
The woman, hissing. "You sick son-of-a-bitch."
The man again. "Where was I? Oh, yes. In Denver, there was Patsy Moynihan. You think Joni had tits, you should have seen Patsy. I'll never understand why a fat cow like you has such little milk sprockets on her body. Especially the way you shit kids out."
"You bastard."
"In Cleveland, there was somebody named Linda. She was rich but I don't remember much else of her except she begged real hard and got me off a couple of dozen times before I did her."

Johnson whispered, "Get confirmation."
Feinman answered, "I'm on it."

"Let's see. Chicago? Chicago there was some little girl who's name I didn't know and then there was Ellie MacPherson."
"A little girl?"

Johnson whooped and slapped her leg on the seat. "Paydirt. It's about time, goddamn fucking paydirt."
Feinman said, "You know that case?"
"It's what got me out here in the first place. I could've sworn her husband did it but so long as I have a name and a place, I'm happy."
Harriman got back in the car. "Everything's cool."
Feinman said, "Detective Johnson got what she was looking for."
"Sure did. Son-of-a-bitch said he did Ellie MacPherson, that's all I need."
Harriman looked at the screen on his tablet. "Hey, wait - "
He never got the rest of it out.

"So you see, dear, my only interest in you is for breeding stock. You're the one I keep at home when I'm too tired to go out and get what I really want, and you're too stupid to do anything otherwise. in fact, you - "
Plastic bags rustling.
The man, screaming. "No, no."

A gun shot.

Little feet running. Children shrieking. The girl's voice crying, pleading.

Another gunshot.

Children screaming. No young girl's voice.

Johnson, Harriman, and Feinman moved as a single unit.

Two rapid gunshots.

Johnson once again proved that a big woman could take and maintain the lead.

A fifth shot sounded as they raced up the stairs. Colodnie Johnson broke through the cheap door like it was plastic, her weapon up and at the ready. "Oh, Jesus Jumping Christ."

Bodies and blood. The last shot, a suicide. Nothing remained of the woman's head above her eyes.

"Go make sure everybody's acting sane."

Harriman and Feinman knocked on doors calling out "FBI, Stay inside. It's over. You're safe."

Johnson lifted her PTT and called it in.

Back in the driveway, Feinman pulled on Harriman's shoulder. "What were you going to say before she went postal up there?"

"On the prevaricator. He was lying his fool head off."

Upstairs in Tibbs' apartment, the phone rang once then went silent.

Feinman considered. "You notice Johnson doesn't play well with others?"

Harriman smiled. "Uh-huh."

"Can you do a makeover? Make it so he was telling the truth?"

"Sure can."

Feinman returned his smile.

Tom and Jack cut their lights about a mile from where Sally floated face down in the water.

"Good thing it's close to a full moon, Jack."

Jack Games, focusing on the road, nodded. "Look, up ahead. It's a signpost."

"Yes, our next stop is the Twilight Zone. How you holding up?"

"Like I said, Prospero House never prepared me for this. Is that Carsons' pickup up ahead?"

"Think he bought us some time?"

They cut the engine and let the yellow cab coast as far as it could up the old road. The moon cast homunculus-like shadows of them as they ran to the trees, keeping low.

Jack whispered, "God but I wish this were all a dream."

Tom stood up, looking around, unsure of his surroundings. "Huh? What?"

"Oh very funny, jackass. You falling asleep again?"

Tom looked at him, crouching back into cover. "I was sure I heard Ellie for a second. Funny. Like she was calling me."

Jack stared at his friend.

"Don't worry, I'm awake." He brushed some hair back from his forehead. "Something's going on but I don't know what. Feels like something's moving inside my head, as if something is rearranging itself inside there."

"You sure you're okay?"

"I'm alright. Don't know what's happening but I'm alright."

Nighthorse walked into Lupicen's lab. Jamie stood whispering to the System 70. Lupicen sat in his office, immersed in Ann's world.

Nighthorse held the *wotai* in his hand. "Jamie, this is yours. My apologies for taking it."

Jamie gazed up at the giant and took the Gate.

Nighthorse said, "Practicing?"

"Using my words."

"It's time for us to go. The final battle."

Jamie put a hand on the System 70's light guides. "I'm scared."

Nighthorse knelt before him. "Tell you the truth, so am I. But you know what? It's okay to be afraid. It's okay to be scared. Use your fear, don't let your fear use you. If you're afraid, ask yourself what you can do to not be afraid."

"I can go home. I can go back inside Ann."

Nighthorse shook his head. "That won't stop your fear, it'll only delay it. The best thing to do is face it, deal with it. I've got two tricks for dealing with my fear. Want to know what they are?"

"Yes, please."

"One is focus, but not on any one thing, on everything. It's called *going wide*. But you have to go wide in all directions at once. Know how to do that?"

Jamie smiled. "Stay in your center."

"Hey, you're pretty smart for a young kid." The System 70's coolant pumps beat out a quiet WarSong. "That's the second trick. Stay in your center. Think you can do that?"

Jamie nodded. "Do you know where we're going?"

Nighthorse shook his head. "Don't have to. The Moon knows."

"How we going to get there?"

Nighthorse remembered the teaching of his name. "I'll carry you." He took Jamie's hand in his. Ann's QLCs pulsed the color of Moonlight and they were gone.

ELLIE'S FINGERS EXTENDED INTO CHANNELS OF IN-formation she'd never imagined existed. Generations of training marksmen and sharpshooters opened to her. Methods, manuals, top secret resources and ultrasecured files made themselves available. Ann's QLCs defeated encryption algorithms in the time it took a single photon to jump quantum states.

Ellie spread several articles across her lap; *Reactivation of Hippocampal Ensemble Memories During Sleep, Dependence on REM Sleep of Overnight Improvement of a Perceptual Skill, Developing Sensorimotor Systems in Our Sleep, Sleep-dependent memory consolidation*, and others.

"Okay, Ann. I don't know what these are about but you do, and according to Lupicen what you know, I can use."

She put her fingers into all the information Ann made available, closed her eyes and exhaled slowly. "Tom, my love, you're the one man who helped me understand what love is. I need your help. Where are you?"

Realities away, Tom's eyes bulged. His hand went to the side of his head as if his neck no longer supported it. The Beacon of Love went wide.

Jack said, "Tom?"

Tom smiled. "I'm here, my love. Can you hear me, Ellie? I'm here for you always."

"What?"

Tom spoke slowly, the words new to him, awkward. "Ellie...is... rearranging my mind. Altering my brain chemistry. Instituting long term memory."

"What in fuck's name are you talking about?"

Tom reached out to Jack to steady himself. "She's building memories of things...I've never known how to do."

In the whiteness of Ann's world, Ellie pulled her fingers out of information channels and, outside of Ann's room and world, two buildings away on the Dartmouth Campus, Sandy Olafssen saw a message flash across the tablet that talked only to the System 70 in Lupicen's lab. She shut down the ultrawide bands connecting Ann to the virtual world.

Jack and Tom stayed as much as possible in the shadows of the trees, their only company the sounds of their own breathing, the trickling and sloshing of water by the dam, a saw whet warbling to its mate, peepers and night birds making their calls of protection and fright. Steam rose from their nostrils as they moved. Tom tied his handkerchief over his nose and motioned Jack to do the same.

"What's this?"

"Stops people from seeing our breath."

"Where'd you learn this?"

"Nighthorse? Graywolf maybe?"

At the last line of trees before the clearing Tom recognized Pangiosi's voice. "I was going to make the world safe for you!"

Jack and Tom stood, still in shadow.

Pangiosi stood in the dam's parking area, tall, thin, red-haired, clutching his chest and muttering something they couldn't make out.

A cloud formed beside Pangiosi and shimmered in the moonlight. He stared at it. His head bobbed forward and cocked to the left. "Mrs. MacPherson?"

"Hi. Remember me?" A Grendelian claw sliced through Pangiosi's intestines.

Ellie accessed all of Ann's reality generating knowledge. She manifested a semi-solid body and a very solid fist. "Don't you ever fuck with my family again."

Jack, still at the tree line with Tom, said, "Did he just call out to Ellie?"

"Don't know." Tom pulled Styles's Walther PPK from his belt, aimed, and shot.

The bullet penetrated Pangiosi's stomach wall as Ellie's fist, powered by the same reality wells that gave Ann's Grendelian monster its terrifying strength, slammed into Pangiosi's gut.

Pangiosi grabbed his stomach. He turned pale and pulled up a blood covered hand.

Tom aimed and fired, aimed and fired, aimed and fired.

Ellie whispered, "Like that, fucker?" She backhanded Pangiosi as Tom's second shot smashed into his chest, spinning him on his feet. Tom's third shell tore through Pangiosi's neck. She gave her other hand enough corporeal reality to grab his arm and hold him in place while she smashed his ribs, right and left, with her other fist.

Pangiosi rocked backwards as the last two shots punctured left and right lungs.

Jack Games jumped up and down at the edge of the trees like a kid at an arcade game. "You got him! You got him!"

Ellie pulled back her free fist and let go of Pangiosi's arm. "Now, Tom," she whispered. "Do it now."

Tom aimed his best, not sure how many rounds he had left, amazed he'd been able to shoot at all.

He aimed, exhaled, squeezed. The bullet and Ellie's reality-heavy fist simultaneously caught Pangiosi square in the chest, rocking him back, his body collapsing around the impact.

A beam of moonlight splashed between Jack, Tom, Pangiosi, and Ellie-Grendel. Nighthorse and Jamie took shape, their bodies forming from the ground up in the moonlight.

Nighthorse rushed to Pangiosi. "No! Stop!"

Pangiosi's body stood for half a heartbeat then fell backwards.

Jack yelled, "You got the fucker, Tom. You got him."

Tom shook his head. A tear filled his eye and blurred his vision. He took a step and sobbed. He heard Ellie somewhere, for just a second, then it stopped.

Nighthorse pulled off his jacket and used it to staunch Pangiosi's belly and chest wounds. Iceli flew from Pangiosi's body. Grandfather's story. Mosquito. Nighthorse yelled, "Jamie, give Pangiosi a dream. Now, Jamie, now!"

Ellie-Grendel screamed, "No!"

Nighthorse yelled at her mist, "He has to. Unless you want all this despair loose in the world again. Jamie, give him a good dream."

Jamie closed his eyes and called a dream. *"Ou to ta'a'be. Ci. Sume Ci. Como."*

The Iceli stoped in their flight, turned towards Jamie, flocked around him.

Nighthorse heard an ancient voice. "Now, Shem. Protect the pup, the Little Master."

Nighthorse's chest contracted, his heart pulsed as if bringing a new universe into being.

Shem separated from him and leapt.

THE OLDEST, THE FIRST, THE ONE SUMMONS SHEM.

The Little Master.

The Old Enemy is near The Little Master.

And the Great Mistress.

None shall harm The Great Mistress or The Little Master.

Shem bares his fangs. Shem shows The Challenge.

Shem hears The Little Master. He sings one of the Old Songs.

A Gateway opens.

The Only of All Dens, The One of All Packs speaks to Shem. "This door, Shem. The Oldest Door. Bring The Oldest Knowledge, Shem. The Oldest Knowledge."

Shem understands. He follows. Through the door. There is another there. A young one. Its fur matted. Uncared for.

Shem understands. Shem will fix.

And The Little Master will be saved.

JAMIE SCREAMED, "SHEM."

Shem ran into a hole in the night, returning a moment later, something trotting beside him, hurrying to keep up, nipping at Shem's muzzle.

Jamie looked at Shem.

A small dog, a puppy, its fur matted and scruffy, trotted beside Shem and Shem led it to Pangiosi. Shem turned to Jamie, his tail wagging furiously.

Shem saves The Little Master.

"Shem!"

Shem loves The Little Master.

The Great Mistress calls him. "Come on, Shem."

He turns to her mist. The Little Master calls him. "Shem!"

"Time for us to go, Shem. Good boy. Time for us to go."

Jamie, running towards Shem, slows, stops. He hears his mother's voice. "We'll always be here for you, Jamie. In your dreams."

Shem barks once, good-bye, and disappears into Ellie's mist.

Nighthorse screams, "Jamie! Dream! Now!"

Jamie closes his eyes. He dreams of dogs and love.

Pangiosi moves to sit up. Nighthorse helps him. Pangiosi focuses on a scruffy shadow in the moonlight. "Dog? DOG!"

The puppy runs into Pangiosi's lap, licking his face, licking his lips, loving him. Pangiosi, his blood flowing, his strength fading, holds the puppy against his chest. "Dog! Dog! I've missed you, Dog, where have you been?"

A beam of blinding moonlight catches them, holds them. The Iceli collapse, turn to ash, fall to dust.

Nighthorse stepped back. Pangiosi's body shrunk to a child's, a toddler's, the puppy almost the same size. "Dog! Dog! Dog!" He laughed and giggled as the little dog licked him and nipped him. "Dog! Dog! Dog!"

Rainbow eyes formed around them. Little silhouettes took shape. The moon blazed laser bright.

Nighthorse shielded his eyes.

Pangiosi and Dog were gone.

ELLIE SWOOSHED THE ARTICLES AWAY. "THAT'S ALL I could do for you, dearest Tom. I don't know what waits for me outside this room, but if you can hear me, know that you have to go on for Jamie, Tom. You have to teach him what it is to love and to move on, to continue, to thrive and to dream. Know that I loved you more than I ever thought I could love any man, and that I loved Jamie, and of course I love Shem." She reached down and scratched the big dog's head. "But you all knew that."

Far away, Tom, revolver still in hand, whispered. "Ellie. No."

JAMIE REACHED INTO HIS POCKET. HIS HAND CLASPED

the Gate. He concentrated on his father. "Dream, Dad. Finish your dream."

Tom stared up at The Moon, his free hand shielding his eyes. The gun fell and his legs folded under him. Slowly he dropped to the ground. His eyes closed. His mind filled with memories, each distinct and individual, echoing in his heart like thunderclaps.

Ellie, with Shem at the park.

Their first kiss.

Moving in together.

Their wedding, Jack his best man.

Jamie's birth.

His first day of school

The four of them at the cabin.

Laying Shem to rest.

Jamie graduating highschool, college.

Him moving away.

Max, their new dog.

His retiring.

Jack's passing.

Their travel.

Her cancer.

Max passing.

His heart attack.

He and Jamie at her bedside.

Their last kiss.

Jamie looking down on him and crying.

Tom's eyes fluttered open, filled with tears

Jack stood over him. "Tom?"

Tom wiped his eyes. "Her pilgrim soul."

ELLIE LAY ON ANN'S BED, SHEM LAY BESIDE HER, crowding her, his tail thumping his joy. She closed her eyes and whispered to Jamie all the songs she'd ever sung him, told him all the nursery rhymes, all the fairy tales, all the bedtime stories, fables, histories, mythologies ... everything she knew, everything Ann's library contained, everything that gave the world hope and the ability to dream that tomorrow would be better than today.

With every thought, with every song, with every story she recited, she and Shem faded more and more from view. As a wisp of rainbow-hued air she kissed her son and husband goodbye. Finally, her hand on Shem's great head, she said, "Are you my loving man?"

Shem woofed. Wonderful Happy Glad!

The door opened and Ann walked in, now a woman so much like Ellie's younger twin, except her eyes varied with the light, the right one blue as the sky over a cold, arctic night and the left as brown as a forest floor.

"Thank you, Ann. Thank you for giving me a place to stay until this was done."

Ann bent over and kissed the wind. "It has been my pleasure, Ellie. A better older sister I could never have had."

The last of the indentation where Ellie and Shem rested went away. Ann cried.

JAMIE TOOK THE GATE FROM HIS POCKET. ICELI HAD escaped. Not all and enough.

His mother said, "It's all up to you now, Jamie."

He heard Shem woof his happy, let's-play woof.

The Old One, sitting on an arctic plain, his wings folded tight into his fur, said, "It's time, cub. Dream."

Jamie did. Like his mother taught him. Like those called to be Dreamers since canids first walked with humans dreamed.

He smelled Shem's fur, felt Shem's great head in his hands, Shem's tongue on his face.

The First, The One, stood before Jamie, facing the Iceli, protecting him while he worked.

From inside his mind, from inside his heart, Jamie flooded the night with dreams, with stories, with tales to help people throughout all time.

Jamie held the Gate up to capture all the light of The Moon. Dreams flew from his mind and out into the night, catching moonbeams and going out to those who slept, to all those who would sleep.

He felt his mother's kiss on his head. He heard Shem woof. He cried.

But he held the Gate up and let all his dreams fly. There was a snow covered plain around him. He could smell the theropellic musk of wet wolf fur.

Ann sat beside Joni. "Ellie is spent. She's done all she can and has moved on. Now it's up to you."

Joni remembered the swarms of little shadow creatures. She remembered the feeling in her body, the throbbing in her heart, when she'd had the abortion. She wondered what it would be like to give birth to a universe of Dreams.

Her legs rose up in Ob-Gyn's stirrups. She pushed.

From out of Ann's core, from a reality Ellie created telling stories and singing songs to Jamie, Dreams, the little shadow creatures, were born and flew forth, emerging from a bright hole in the sky over the dam, but not The Moon...

From Joni, somehow her body floating among the stars. Her children gathered up all the dreams Jamie was creating, all the dreams he and his kind had kept alive since humankind was young, and carried them into the world again.

Back in her sleep chamber, Joni's readouts went dark. She slept, covered in sweat, but did not dream. Her womb twitched then relaxed from all her efforts. She smiled. She'd had children who knew they would be loved.

Ann's QLCs chugged. She was overheating, she knew, keeping so many realities running in parallel in the world. There wasn't much time.

Honey Fitz pulled into the driveway of Tibbs's apartment house. People were standing around in their bathrobes and slippers. There were camera crews and police cars everywhere.

She spoke into her mobile, "Thanks, Joe. Gotta go. Give my best to the family," then rolled down her window as a huge black woman with a badge and a cigarette dangling from her lips walked up to her car.

"Can I help you?"

"I thought I might be able to help you, Officer."

"Detective. Detective Colodnie Johnson."

"Excuse me, Detective. I saw all the ambulances and thought I could help. I'm a doctor."

"You got any ID?"

Honey reached into her purse and pulled out her license and MacLean's ID card.

"You got a Boston address. You're a long way from home. You know anybody here?"

"I don't think so. I'm visiting a friend around here. I saw the ambulances and thought I might help. That's all."

"Well, thanks, but there's nobody left alive here to doctor. You best be on your way."

"Thank you, detective."

She turned around and drove to Vail Hall. Joni might be there.

A car with Minnesota medical plates pulled into the parking lot just ahead of her. There was an old man in the car. There was something about him ...

He shut his engine off then looked up at the sky.

She got out and walked towards the car. God but that man looked familiar. She tapped on the window.

The moon lit her face and he stared at it for several minutes before he rolled down the window.

There was something about him she recognized. She didn't know ...

He said, "You're Honey Fitz," and exited the car, always keeping her face in sight.

She gasped. "Eduardo?"

"Do you know how long I've dreamed of this? Of seeing you one more time before I die? I'd given up all hope but, I don't know, just a few minutes ago, I felt I would see you again."

She put her arm through his. "Come on, let's go for a walk under the stars. There's so much I want to tell you."

He looked up at the night sky. "The sky sure is full of stars up here, isn't it? I never knew there were so many."

C H A P T E R 54

Jamie's Decision

JAMIE, SWEATING AND EXHAUSTED, DROPPED TO THE arctic plain. He looked through the Gate.

Mom and Shem walked further and further away.

"Wait! I can bring them back. The Gate still has some magic!"

"Cub." The Old One stood beside him as a man. "There is something more you must do."

Jamie tightened his grip on The Gate. "What? The world's safe. There are Dreams again. There's Hope in the world."

The Old One pointed towards Nighthorse. "He carried your dog in him because he didn't know what kind of doorway he himself was."

They walked over and Nighthorse, shaking and shivering, looked up at them. "Grandpa?" he asked the Old One.

"Yes, Pokachee. Say nothing, just rest." The Old One spoke to Jamie but kept his eyes on the dying giant at his feet. "My grandson is at a crossroads, cub. He did not know what he carried and now it has left him. The hole, the wound, remains. But he himself is still strong. He can live with the wound but it will fester. Eventually he'll become that which he hates, that which you and he fought so hard against moments ago." His eyes went to Jamie. "In the end The Old Enemy will win him to its side."

The Old One knelt and put a hand on Nighthorse's shoulder. "Or his wound can heal. Heal and he will guard the Night against the Pangiosis and those like him for as long as he lives, until the next comes to take his place." He looked up at Jamie. "But if Nighthorse is to heal, your mother and Shem cannot come back. You must release the last dream, Jamie. Your last dream. A nightmare, I know. But only by acknowledging our fears can we realize our dreams."

Jamie crumpled to the frozen ground, no longer mysteriously warmed, no longer mysteriously inviting, now simply cold, painful. "It's not fair. It's not fair. I just found them again. You can't do this. You can't. I won't let it happen."

He looked through the Gate. Mom and Shem were at the edge of sight.

"It's not fair. It's not. It's not."

The Old One put his hand on Jamie's back. "I know, Jamie. But few things in any life are. And as in all things, you must decide."

Jamie held The Gate over Nighthorse. It caught The Moon's rays. His wound healed.

The Old One pulled a drum from his jacket. "I'll sing a DeathSong for your mother and dog, if you like. To help them get where they're going next."

"Can I have a moment with them?"

"Of course."

Ann's QLCs were glowing hot. But she had learned love. Man, woman, father, daughter, mother, son. Child. Best friend. Dog. She formed a Gate.

The Little Master! He has found Thetreatcloset again!

Shem thought Thetreatcloset gone forever.

"Hi, Shem. How's my boy?"

The Little Master scratches just the right place behind the ears. Oh, this feels so good. Shem is so good.

Thetreatcloset opens. The Little Master reaches in and empties the box on the floor. "Eat up, Shem. Eat all you want. Do you know I love you, Shem?"

There is something sad in the Little Master's voice. What is wrong? Everything is wonderful happy here. Shem has treats! The Little Master hasn't closed Thetreatcloset!

"Here, Shem. this is for you, too."

The Little Master! He found Thetwistedsock! He found Thetwistedsock that made Shem so glad because they would tug on it together and play. The Great Mistress lost it one day but the Little Master has found it so they can play!

"I love you, Shem. I'll always love you. You'll always be my bestest dog."

What is wrong with the Little Master?

Shem looks up. The Little Master! He's gone!

Shem barks. He howls. Where is his den? Where are his mates?

"Shem?"

The Great Mistress?

The Great Mistress calls him?

"Come on, boy! Come here, Shem!"

The Great Mistress! Here, the smell of oceans and bright sunshine! She has TheTwistedSock! She has TheTwistedSock!

The Little Master says, "I love you, Mom. I'll always love you. I'll never forget you."

"Thank you, Jamie. I'll always remember and love you, too. Talk to your dad about me. I know he won't forget, but it'll help him if you talk."

"I will."

There is someone singing. Shem thinks he knows the voice. It is an old voice that comes from a time when all canid and canis and canine were one. It is the One, the First.

The singing stops but Shem knows the One, the First is here. But

the Little Master is gone. But the Great Mistress is here.
  And she has Thefrisbee!
  She has Thefrisbee and she throws it! There!
  And Shem catches it in his teeth!
  Wonderful Glorious Teeth!

THE OLD ONE RESTED A HAND ON JAMIE'S BACK. "It's done."

Jamie wiped his eyes. "Yes. I know. Thank you."

Chapter 55

New Moon

Ann's cryogenics were losing the heat dissipa-tion battle to her superconductors.

Joni, groggy, lifted her head. A white mist formed. "Ann, let me get out of here, lighten your load."

The mist took shape. A woman in a flowing white robe. Her eyes dark, the color of deepest night, and in them, stars.

"Who are you?"

"I am you, Joni Levis. I am The Moon."

"Is this another of Lupicen's dreams?" She left the chamber and walked to the lab's windows. "The moon's not even out now. It's a - "

"New Moon."

Joni's hand went to her womb.

"Yes, Joni. You care. As I did."

"But I killed my child."

"Because you so loved it you could not raise it to suffer. Bring an unwanted child into the world or bring only wanted children into the world. Which is more hopeful, Joni Levis?"

"I..."

"You can refuse, if you wish."

"How long…"

"I have been The Moon for some ten-thousand years. Before me there was another. Before her, another. There will be another after you.

"So long as people dream, there will be Moons and Stars to dream under."

"But my family…"

"As I said, Joni, I am you."

The white robes, the white slippers, the eyes of stars and darkness, flowed onto Joni, the bee-suit flowed onto what had been The Moon.

"You even look like me."

"And share your memories."

Scenes of deserts, mountains, prairies, glaciers, deep woodlands, rainforests came into Joni's mind.

"And you share all of our memories. As will whomever comes next. Decide, Joni. Will there be a new Queen of the Night?"

"What do I do?"

The new Joni laughed. "Dream."

Chapter 56

Goodbye, Sweet Child

Ann's QLCs began to disintegrate into their own realities.

"It's time for me to go, Poppie."

"Yes, Ann. I know."

"Poppie?"

"Yes, my beautiful child?"

"When I'm gone, will you remember me when you dream?"

"I will remember you always, my Ann."

"Thank you. Good bye, Poppie."

Lupicen held her tight until there was nothing left to hold.

When her QLCs emptied themselves of the last of their realities, when they'd fused from the heat of the worlds she'd made, Lupicen screamed into the darkness of the night in his lab.

Sandy Olafssen came in. She pulled the HUVRSA and gloves from him and held him while he cried.

Chapter 57

The Stuff of Dreams

Nighthorse stood in a darkened office facing two men and a woman he'd only heard rumors about. The three sat in shadow and wore dark suits. He counted six hands on the table they sat at, lit from a light overhead. He couldn't hear any breathing or movement so he left his cataloguing at three. More could be watching via video. No tell-tales indicated a recording in process.

But here, none would.

His report of Pangiosi's death rested caught in the light at the center of the table in a plain manila folder with the words EYES ONLY written across the front.

It contained the truth and it contained nothing.

"Thank you for coming and reporting, Mr. Nighthorse."

"It was bound to happen," said the second man. "He always played things a little outside."

"Yes," agreed the woman. "That, and there was always the concern he would decide to play against us."

The room fell quiet yet a tension remained.

The a voice from a speaker at the center of the table. "Yes."

A pause. Nighthorse watched the others hold their breath.

The voice again. "Mr. Jones."

The first man nodded. "That'll be all, Mr. Nighthorse. Unless you wish to continue in our employ, there's nothing else we need done."

Nighthorse wondered if these people were really separate manifestations of the same being, like the triune god or Macbeth's witches. "Thank you. I'll be leaving the organization, if you're sure it's all right."

Mr. Jones spoke out of the shadow. "Quite."

The second. "Yes."

The woman. "Contact us when you're settled in. Your retirement package will be ready for you."

"Thank you. Goodbye."

Two days later Nighthorse knocked on the back door of an apartment over a small town general store in the southwest corner of Nevada. A young man answered, a thinner, taller, more somber version of Nighthorse.

Nighthorse held out his hand. "Hello, Eddie."

SEVERAL WEEKS LATER, WHEN THE LAST OF THE POlice investigations were through, Jamie came into Lupicen's lab.

He held out his hand. "Thank you, Dr. Lupicen."

Lupicen tapped the picture of his brother and smiled. "For?"

"For letting me see my mom and my dog again."

Lupicen nodded. "I should thank you for bringing me my brother."

"Do you think it really happened?"

"Do you ask if it happened here or somewhere else? Perhaps only inside my Ann? I don't know, Jamie. You ask what is fact and what is fantasy. That is a question my Ann could answer, perhaps. Computers do best concentrating on a single problem until they either solve it or die. Who is to say ten-thousand years ago people did not link hands, perhaps, and all concentrate, all focus on something so tightly that they became a dreaming computer themselves."

Work crews entered the lab, began dissembling the machine which had been Ann.

Lupicen stared at them while they worked. "But computers are no good unless they're solving problems. What kinds of problems did people need to solve ten-thousand years ago? Perhaps how to get water, how to get food, how to stop the cold. Who is to say that rivers and rain, buffalo and beans, fire and clothes are not solutions arrived at by people computers who dreamed their answers into reality ten-thousand years ago?"

He turned back to Jamie. "As for what happened to us? To answer that you must first understand consciousness. Consciousness is not experienced in the plural. Perhaps it was long, long ago. Now it is only experienced in the singular. Somehow Ann was able to reproduce consciousness in the plural. Somehow she knew she would have to do this, even found the people necessary to help her, to get it done."

He shook Jamie's hand. "But who are we to say what is the stuff of dreams?"

CHAPTER 58

"Just for Lookin' Through"

Jamie raised his coffee cup and stared out the cabin window as the reporter tapped notes into his tablet. The moon lit the plane's wing and the earth below. Stars burned bright in the high altitude night.

The reporter looked up. "I understand you worked with him. Lupicen. Is that correct?"

"Yes. I studied with him, got my doctorate with him, and returned to him now and again as time allowed and need dictated."

"You were there when he died, weren't you?"

"Yes, at his home in Vermont. He'd retired with his wife, Sandy Olafssen, by then."

"And that native american fellow you mentioned, he was there, too?"

"Yes. He sang and played drum as Dr. Lupicen passed."

"Ever see him or Ms. Olafssen again?"

"She passed shortly after Capoçek. We were there for her, too. Nighthorse I've seen maybe once or twice since." Jamie's gaze returned to the window and the passing night. "And before you ask, haven't seen

Ms. Levis since then."

"I already looked her up. She's got a family. Two boys and a little girl. They're in Denver."

"Good, glad to hear it. She deserves that."

The reporter tapped his last notes into the tablet. "That's an incredible story, Dr. MacPherson."

Jamie smiled at her. "You want proof."

"You've got proof?"

"Proof and you won't understand it. Your eyes aren't used to seeing." He took the Gate from his pocket.

The reporter nodded, smiled, stopped her phone's recording, stored her notes file from her tablet to the cloud, shook Jamie's hand and returned to her seat.

Jamie pulled the blanket up under his chin, leaned on the armrest and gazed down the aisle. When did his jet get so large? It went on forever. The seats went on and on on either side until they passed into a sticky, white fog.

Behind him, the plane didn't go on forever. The end of the plane was right out the windows, just four seats from where he sat.

"That's the tail section, Jamie." A lady stood at the edge of the fog, wrapped in it like a bug in a blanket.

"Mom?"

The engines roared and shot flame into the night behind the plane. A trickle of jet engine fuel swirled in the fog and crawled down the aisle towards him. He heard a "woof" and Shem came out of the fog, his TwistedSock in his mouth and his nose to the ground, as if hunting out the jet fuel's spoor.

"Shem! Shem's got his TwistedSock. Good boy! You got your TwistedSock. You good boy, Shem!"

Shem looked up at him and cocked an ear. MacPherson laughed. Dad always said it looked like Shem was trying to figure something out when he did that.

"Wait a minute," Jamie said. He looked up at the figure swathed in the fog. "Dad's gone. So's Mom and Shem, many years now." He stared at his hands under the blanket. A little boy's hands. They changed to those of a full-grown man as he watched.

"Come on back, Shem. Time to go, boy," a man's voice. His dad's voice. Coming from further back in the fog. Shem scooted away.

"Hey!"

He shook himself awake, stretched, and stood up. Both forward class lavs showed occupied. No doubt his staff. He loved hot, spicy foods and his people did their best to keep pace with him, but their stomachs always argued a few hours after a meal. He walked to the lavatories at the rear of the plane. Passing the reporter, he said, "Hope. Hope cannot exist unless loss walks beside it."

She nodded.

"Both come from the greatest gifts, the most powerful gifts: love and imagination."

She smiled.

Jamie entered a lav. He splashed some water on his face and looked at himself again.

He reached into his pocket and pulled out the Gate. There was no magic left in it, at least so the Old One said, but he still held it up to his eye and gazed at himself in the mirror just the same.

Did you enjoy **Empty Sky**?

Please write a review on Amazon http://nlb.pub/EmptySky and Goodreads http://nlb.pub/GEmptySky (and our thanks!)

Become a member of Joseph's blog and read more

http://nlb.pub/JoinJoseph

Follow Joseph on
BookBub http://nlb.pub/BookBub
Goodreads http://nlb.pub/Goodreads
Facebook http://nlb.pub/Facebook
Twitter http://nlb.pub/Twitter
Instagram http://nlb.pub/Instagram
Pinterest http://nlb.pub/Pinterest
LinkedIn http://nlb.pub/LinkedIn

December 2023: Search

Two young boys and their guardian go missing in the Maine woods. No one has a clue, no one comes forward offering information, and the police are powerless to provide the boys' family with any answers. The boys' older sister learns about Gio Fortuna through a friend and asks him to help. Search chronicles one life-changing event in The Shaman's life, an event causing Gio to realize the use of his grandfather's teachings and their purpose in both his life and the lives of others.

March 2024: Tag

Two teenagers, Eric and Julia, seek tree grafts on the outskirts of their medieval village as a summer storm clouds the sky. Sullya, a witch hiding among the trees, grabs Julia. Eric swings his axe and severs Sullya's hand from her arm. Sullya seeks refuge in the deep bole of an old oak. Her hand falls onto the same oak and crawls up the trunk to join her.

Eric wants to flee but Julia, believing they are safe, torments the witch. She curses them, their families, their crops, their livestock, and their eastern European village.

Crops wilt, livestock dies, and much of village falls ill. The village priest, Father Baillot, is often seems ignorant of church ways and proves ineffective against the curse.

The elders seek help elsewhere, specifically from a distant priest, Father Patreo, who knows the Old Ways as well as the New.

Patreo is out of favor with the Church because he makes no effort to hide his belief that progress comes from exploring all paths, not just those the Church decrees acceptable.

He and Verduan, one of the elders, investigate, and what they discover changes the face of Eastern Europe forever.

THREE QUESTIONS FOR YOU

1. *Did you know most readers rely on other readers' reviews and comments to make their book buying decisions? Ongoing research begun in mid-2022 indicates reviews and comments are better decision drivers than video teasers, author interviews, author blogs, and everything else combined.*
2. *Did you know most on- and off-line bookstores - from the smallest indie to the largest megastore - rely on reader reviews and comments to decide which books to put on their shelves?*
3. *Did you enjoy* Empty Sky?

Help Northern Lights as a publisher and Joseph Carrabis as an author by reviewing Empty Sky *on Amazon http://nlb.pub/EmptySky Goodreads http://nlb.pub/GEmptySky, Barnes&Noble, BookBub, NetGalley, your favorite reader Facebook and LinkedIn groups, TikTok, Instagram, anywhere and everywhere.*

Let's Kick It Up A Notch!

Send a link to your online review of a Northern Lights Publishing book to Reviews@NorthernLightsPublishing.com and we'll give you a 35% discount on your next Northern Lights Publishing ePub or Print book.

Not Enough? Let's Kick It Up Another Notch!

You can share that 35% discount with up to ten friends, family, neighbors, we won't mind, and you'll have our thanks.

Join Northern Lights Publishing's Journey
http://nlb.pub/JoinNorthernLights

About Northern Lights Publishing

Northern Lights Publishing/Press is an association of five professionals (one graphic artist, one marketer, one editor/book designer, one copyeditor, one editor/educator/author) and a rotating group of ten published authors and poets all of whom are passionate readers. Financial backing is provided by a small group of investors led by Susan and Joseph Carrabis through the NextStage Evolution Corporation. Everyone receives remuneration and owns an equal share of the company with the exception of Susan and Joseph Carrabis.

We're developing our publishing/marketing model so we're not accepting submissions at present.

We'll open our doors to submissions (and announce it through various social networks) once we're sure we can break even and preferably turn a profit. Until then, wish us well.

It's an exciting journey and one we'd love to share, but only after we're sure we can successfully navigate the publishing seas.

Non-Fiction

That Th!nk You Do - http://nlb.pub/TTYDv1

That Th!nk You Do is based on a series of blog posts Joseph wrote between 2008 and 2016. They dealt with ways his research in fields as diverse as neuroscience, linguistics, psychology, sociology, anthropology and other disciplines could be put to practical use to help people better their lives.

If you ever wonder about how to think like an expert, the difference between your inner critic and the actor within, your ability to be heard, the value of being a musician, how to protect yourself from liars or how to overcome fears, you will find answers in this book..

Reading Virtual Minds Volume I: Science and History - http://nlb.pub/Minds1

The science and history behind NextStage Evolution's Evolution Technology

Reading Virtual Minds Volume II: Experience and Expectation - http://nlb.pub/Minds2

Learnings and Take-Aways from NextStage Evolution's research and studies

Reading Virtual Minds Volume III: Fair-Exchange and Social

Networks - http://nlb.pub/Minds3

Learnings and Take-Aways from NextStage Evolution's research and studies applied specifically on on- and off-line social interactions

Fiction: Novels

Empty Sky - http://nlb.pub/EmptySky

What if you're a young boy, Jamie McPherson, whose mother has been missing for over a year and whose father starts falling in and out of coma? What if you hold onto your aging dog, Shem, who's always been with you and always protected you, because the world isn't safe anymore?

And what if in the midst all that's happening, The Moon asks you to help her save the world's dreams?

Earl Pangiosi's greatest desire, since childhood, has been to control and manipulate people. Working for the NSA, Earl learns that people's dreams - their nonconscious minds - guide their conscious decisions. Control their dreams - weaponize them - and you control people at an unprecedented level.

Jamie will not face Pangiosi alone. The Moon sends her Guardians, winged, shapeshifting wolves; and her children, The Oneiroi, little black silhouettes, shadows in the darkness of night, whose multicolored, multifaceted, crystalline eyes serve as kaleidoscopic Gates — little rainbow bridges allowing humans passage from one dream reality to the next, to help Jamie.

Pangiosi sends the Native American giant, Nighthorse, to stop Jamie. But Nighthorse's grandfather introduced him to Wovoka, the DreamWorld, as a child. Going after Jamie, Nighthorse finds one of the Oneiroi's Eye-Gates and realizes his grandfather may not have been such a fool after all.

Meanwhile the Moon brings together a team of "Dreamers" to help Jamie. One such Dreamer is ANN, a supercomputer who can blend dream and waking realities via Penrose Consciousnesses, quantum superpositions.

If they fail, Pangiosi and the NSA will control the world.

The Augmented Man - http://nlb.pub/Augmented

What do you do with a deadly weapon when it's no longer needed?

Nicholas Trailer is the last of The Augmented Men, beings created first by society and completed by a political group the public can't even imagine exists. Captain James Donaldson takes severely abused and traumatized children and modifies them into monsters capable of the most horrifying deeds without feeling any remorse or regret.

But the horrors of war never stay on the battlefield. They always come home.

Battling what society and science has made him, Nick Trailer discovers he is loved. From the horrors of childhood to the horrors of a war, what does it take for someone to find true love and peace? Especially when everyone has their own agenda, from the senators who sanctioned his making to the Governor of Maine who wants to use Nick's struggle to propel himself to the White House.

The Augmented Men were good at war, perhaps a little too good. Now they have to come home ... or do they? What do you do with man-made monsters?

Nick must decide if his friends are his friends and if his enemies are his enemies, all while protecting the woman he loves.

And are you truly the last of your kind?

What if you must remain a monster to defeat a monster? Will you sacrifice love to protect what you love?

Fiction: Anthologies

Tales Told 'Round Celestial Campfires - http://nlb.pub/TalesV1
Includes:

Binky (available separately at http://nlb.pub/Binky)

What if you run an inner-city health clinic and are tired of fighting budget cuts, politics, protestors, police, ... ? And what if you question your purpose because caring is no longer cost-effective? And what if you meet a bright, beautiful child who leads you to a child who died sixty years ago? And what if that child asks you to save its life?

The Boy Who Loved Horses (available separately at http://nlb.pub/
Horses)

What if you're born and raised Hill but got City educated and now
you drivin a big state issue Buick back into Hill 'cause you gonna show
them you something else? And what if one town you drive through's
got secrets it don't want nobody to know? And what if you plan to tell
City those secrets and those secrets got they own idea who you gonna
tell?

Canis Major (available separately at http://nlb.pub/CanisMajor)

What if you're a WereMan, human when the moon is full, a beast
when not, and your father died before explaining your gift to you? And
what if your fully human mother did the best she could but couldn't
really understand your needs? And what if you're tired of being alone
and afraid and once, just once, you want to hold someone and not be
afraid of their fear?

Cold War (available separately at http://nlb.pub/ColdWar)

What if your last deployment left you so damaged driving a school
bus tops your employable skills? And what if the kids laugh at you
because you can't talk right and twitch at nothing? And what if the
military calls you back, says they can make you a man again. Or get
close. And what if you're so lonely, angry and tired you say sure without
realizing they plan to leave you out in the cold, forever?

Cymodoce (available separately at http://nlb.pub/Cymodoce)

What if the only man you've ever given yourself to isn't a man at all?
And what if you gave birth to twins, the son wholly yours, the daughter
wholly his? And what if your daughter needs to return to her father in
order to survive? And what if her survival means never seeing her again,
and her brother losing his sister forever?

Dancers in the Eye of Chronos (available separately at http://nlb.
pub/Dancers)

What if your love so delights the Gods they grant you immortality. But you learn love is meant to age, to mature, to grow and change in ways the Gods can't imagine. After millennia, they strip their gift from you. But that's what you wanted; to hold your lover's face one last time before darkness falls. Or is your love so strong it outlives the Gods themselves?

The Goatmen of Aguirra (available separately at http://nlb.pub/ Goatmen)

What if you've signed onto a deep space mission and left behind a wife and young son? And what if your mission takes to you a supposedly uninhabited planet that harbors intelligent life that values family above all else? And what if they take you into their family to heal you? And what if, finally healed, your shipmates abandon you when the mission is called home?

Mani He (available separately at http://nlb.pub/ManiHe)

What if you've acquired your dream job but destroyed another man's life and career to get it? And what if the president of your company hands you a rifle and the keys to his mountain cabin with the instructions "Bring me back something to make me proud"? And what if the spirits in the mountains have their own ideas of what it means to be proud?

Power Unlimited (available separately at http://nlb.pub/ PowerUnlimited)

What if Eddie's kid brother Tommy idolizes you guys at the gym and wants to be like you but you know he's not really built for it. And what if he sends away for some "GET BIG FAST" Muscle Pill exercise programs? And what if he starts looking like The Hulk and King Kong had a baby? And what if the people who make those Pills want them back?

Sema (available separately at http://nlb.pub/Sema)

What if a beautiful woman discovers you and your friends are beings living side-by-side with humans since the beginning of time? And what if she discovers you have abilities beyond imagination and she, too, has gifts no mortal should possess? And what if, having no knowledge of your kind, has trained with a Darkness humans can't imagine, never suspecting a Light beyond mortals' dreams?

The Settlement (available separately at http://nlb.pub/Settlement)
What if you're a young, hotshot, wildly successful asteroid miner who hasn't seen your parents since you joined the corp underage? And what if your parents are getting divorced and each is laying claim to guardianship of your fortune? And what if your parents never knew why you joined the corp or what you had to give up to get a ship of your own?

Them Doore Girls (available separately at http://nlb.pub/Doore)
What if the woman you love is the mistress of something else, something so monstrous, so hideous its summoning her creates ocean storms? And what if she knows this entity will destroy her, you, your village and all those you know if she denies it? And what if you know she goes to it willingly because it threatened to kill you, her one love, if she doesn't yield to its wishes?

Those Wings Which Tire, They Have Upheld Me (available separately at http://nlb.pub/Wings)
What if you're a little boy with brain cancer whose doctors say they can cure you by replacing your eyes with an experimental device? And what if that experimental device lets you see your guardian angel? And what if seeing your guardian angel makes you best friends with the class trouble-maker? And what if the class bully finds out you talk to angels?

The Weight (available separately at http://nlb.pub/Weight)
What if you've been a success at everything you've done in your life and decide to retrace a hike you took when wishes were horses and beggars could ride? And what if you met one of your heroes on that

long ago hike and - miracle of miracles - you meet him again? And what if your hero isn't your hero and says you took something from it way back when and now it wants it back?

Winter Winds (available separately at http://nlb.pub/Winds)
What if you're sitting in your favorite chair, your son on your lap, helping him with his homework when you see something in the fields outside your house? And what if you turn on the floodlights and see unimaginable creatures battling in your fields? And what if your son and wife tell you you're the strange one because those fantastical creatures battling in your field are as natural as natural can be?

Follow Joseph's work in magazines and other anthologies at https://josephcarrabis.com/tag/im-published-here/

You can find most of Joseph's work at http://nlb.pub/amazon

Joseph Carrabis told stories to anyone who would listen starting in childhood, wrote his first stories in gradeschool, and started getting paid for his writing in 1978. His work history includes periods as a long-haul trucker, apprentice butcher, apprentice coffee buyer/broker, lumberjack, Cold Regions researcher, mathematician, semanticist, semioticist, physicist, educator, Chief Data Scientist, Chief Research Scientist, and Chief Research Officer. He was an original member of the NYAS/UN's Scientists Without Borders program and held patents covering mathematics, anthropology, neuroscience, and linguistics. After patenting a technology he created in his basement and creating an international company, he retired from corporate life. Now he spends his time writing fiction based on his experiences. His work appears regularly in anthologies and his own novels. You can often find him playing with his dog, Boo, and snuggling with his wife, Susan. Learn more about him at https://josephcarrabis.com and his work at http://nlb.pub/amazon.